CW01597071

*Teaching the New English*

Published in association with the I
Director: **Ben Knights**

*Teaching the New English* is an innovative series concerned with the teaching of the English degree in universities in the UK and elsewhere. The series addresses new and developing areas of the curriculum as well as more traditional areas that are reforming in new contexts. Although the series is grounded in intellectual and theoretical concepts of the curriculum, it is concerned with the practicalities of classroom teaching. The volumes will be invaluable for new and more experienced teachers alike.

*Titles include*:

Charles Butler (*editor*)
TEACHING CHILDREN'S FICTION

Michael Hanrahan and Deborah L. Madsen (*editors*)
TEACHING, TECHNOLOGY, TEXTUALITY
Approaches to New Media

Anna Powell and Andrew Smith (*editors*)
TEACHING THE GOTHIC

*Forthcoming titles*:

Gail Ashton and Louise Sylvester (*editors*)
TEACHING CHAUCER IN THE CLASSROOM

Lisa Hopkins and Andrew Hiscock (*editors*)
TEACHING SHAKESPEARE AND EARLY MODERN DRAMATISTS

Gina Wisker (*editor*)
TEACHING AFRICAN-AMERICAN WOMEN'S WRITING

---

**Teaching the New English**
**Series Standing Order ISBN 1-4039-4441-5 Hardback 1-4039-4442-3 Paperback**
(*outside North America only*)

You can receive future titles in this series as they are published by placing a standing order. Please contact your bookseller or, in case of difficulty, write to us at the address below with your name and address, the title of the series and the ISBN quoted above.

Customer Services Department, Macmillan Distribution Ltd, Houndmills, Basingstoke, Hampshire RG21 6XS, England

---

*Also by Anna Powell*

DELEUZE AND HORROR FILM

PSYCHOANALYSIS AND SOVEREIGNTY IN POPULAR VAMPIRE FICTIONS

*Also by Andrew Smith*

VICTORIAN DEMONS: Medicine, Masculinity and the Gothic at the *fin de siècle*

GOTHIC RADICALISM: Literature, Philosophy and Psychoanalysis in the Nineteenth Century

EMPIRE AND THE GOTHIC (*edited with William Hughes*)

GOTHIC MODERNISMS (*edited with Jeff Wallace*)

BRAM STOKER: History, Psychoanalysis and the Gothic (*edited with William Hughes*)

FICTIONS OF UNEASE: the Gothic from Otranto to the X-Files (*edited with William Hughes and Diane Mason*)

DRACULA AND THE CRITICS

# Teaching the Gothic

Edited by

Anna Powell
*Senior Lecturer in Film Studies, Manchester Metropolitan University*

and

Andrew Smith
*Professor of English Studies, University of Glamorgan*



palgrave
macmillan

First published in 2006 by
PALGRAVE MACMILLAN
Houndmills, Basingstoke, Hampshire RG21 6XS and
175 Fifth Avenue, New York, N.Y. 10010
Companies and representatives throughout the world.

PALGRAVE MACMILLAN is the global academic imprint of the Palgrave Macmillan division of St. Martin's Press, LLC and of Palgrave Macmillan Ltd. Macmillan® is a registered trademark in the United States, United Kingdom and other countries. Palgrave is a registered trademark in the European Union and other countries.

ISBN-13: 978–1–4039–4929–5 hardback
ISBN-10: 1–4039–4929–8 hardback
ISBN-13: 978–1–4039–4930–1 paperback
ISBN-10: 1–4039–4930–1 paperback

This book is printed on paper suitable for recycling and made from fully managed and sustained forest sources.

A catalogue record for this book is available from the British Library.

A catalog record for this book is available from the Library of Congress.

10 9 8 7 6 5 4 3 2 1
15 14 13 12 11 10 09 08 07 06

Printed and bound in Great Britain by
Antony Rowe Ltd, Chippenham and Eastbourne

*To scholars, teachers, and lovers of Gothic everywhere*

# Contents

# Acknowledgements

We would like to thank Professor Ben Knights and Jane Gawthrope at the English Subject Centre for their support of this project, which takes its place within the "Teaching the New English" series of teaching guides developed by the English Subject Centre. We would also like to thank Paula Kennedy at Palgrave Macmillan for her enthusiasm for this project. A number of people responded to a questionnaire relating to postgraduate developments, and we would like to thank Marshall Brown, Stephen Behrendt, Ranita Chatterjee, Jeffrey Cox, Eugenia DeLamotte, Michael Eberle-Sinatra, Ben Fisher, Michael Gamer, Kathy Gentile, Teresa Goddu, Faye Hammill, Tamar Heller, Lisa Hopkins, Kate Lawson, Terry Phillips, David Punter, Marjean Purinton, Jean-Paul Riquelme, Angela Wright, and all the contributors to the volume for their responses. We would also like to thank the respondents who wished their anonymity to be preserved. Thanks also to Professor Judy Simons for making some relevant reports on postgraduate recruitment available to the editors. Finally, we would also like to thank Joanne Benson and Ranald Warburton for their love, support, and tolerance throughout the editing process.

# Series Preface

One of many exciting achievements of the early years of the English Subject Centre was the agreement with Palgrave Macmillan to initiate the series "Teaching the New English." The intention of the then Director, Professor Philip Martin, was to create a series of short and accessible books which would take widely-taught curriculum fields (or, as in the case of learning technologies, approaches to the whole curriculum) and articulate the connections between scholarly knowledge and the demands of teaching.

Since its inception, "English" has been committed to what we now know by the portmanteau phrase "learning and teaching." Yet, by and large, university teachers of English—in Britain at all events—find it hard to make their tacit pedagogic knowledge conscious, or to raise it to a level where it might be critiqued, shared, or developed. In the experience of the English Subject Centre, colleagues find it relatively easy to talk about curriculum and resources, but far harder to talk about the success or failure of seminars, how to vary forms of assessment, or to make imaginative use of Virtual Learning Environments. Too often this reticence means falling back on received assumptions about student learning, about teaching, or about forms of assessment. At the same time, colleagues are often suspicious of the insights and methods arising from generic educational research. The challenge for the English group of disciplines is therefore to articulate ways in which our own subject knowledge and ways of talking might themselves refresh debates about pedagogy. The implicit invitation of this series is to take fields of knowledge and survey them through a pedagogic lens. Research and scholarship, and teaching and learning are part of the same process, not two separate domains.

"Teachers," people used to say, "are born not made." There may, after all, be some tenuous truth in this: there may be generosities of spirit (or, alternatively, drives for didactic control) laid down in earliest childhood. But why should we assume that even "born" teachers (or novelists, or nurses, or veterinary surgeons) do not need to learn the skills of their trade? Amateurishness about teaching has far more to do with university claims to status, than with evidence about how people learn. There is a craft to shaping and promoting learning. This series of books is dedicated to the development of the craft of teaching within English Studies.

*Ben Knights*<br>
**Teaching the New English** *Series Editor*<br>
*Director, English Subject Centre*<br>
*Higher Education Academy*

## The English Subject Centre

Founded in 2000, the English Subject Centre (which is based at Royal Holloway, University of London) is part of the subject network of the Higher Education Academy. Its purpose is to develop learning and teaching across the English disciplines in UK Higher Education. To this end it engages in research and publication (web and print), hosts events and conferences, sponsors projects, and engages in day-to-day dialogue with its subject communities.

http://www.english.heacademy.ac.uk

# Notes on the Contributors

**Lucie Armitt** is Senior Lecturer and Head of English at the University of Wales, Bangor. Her principal publications include *Fantasy Fiction* (2005); *Contemporary Women's Fiction and the Fantastic* (2000); *Readers' Guide to George Eliot* (2000), and *Theorising the Fantastic* (1996). She has also edited *Where No Man Has Gone Before: Women and Science Fiction* (1991). She is currently working on a monograph called *Gothic Literary Studies: the Twentieth Century*, for the University of Wales Press.

**Patrick Brantlinger** is Rudy Professor Emeritus of English at Indiana University. He has edited *Victorian Studies* (1980–90), and is the author of, among other books, *Rule of Darkness: British Literature and Imperialism 1830–1914* (1990); *Crusoe's Footprints: Cultural Studies in Britain and America* (1990), and *Dark Vanishings: Discourse on the Extinction of Primitive Races 1800–1930* (2003). He is also coeditor of the Blackwell *Companion to the Victorian Novel* (2005).

**Steven Bruhm** is Professor of English at Mount St. Vincent University, Halifax. Receiving his Ph.D. from McGill University in 1992, he is the author of *Gothic Bodies: the Politics of Pain in Romantic Fiction* (1994) and *Reflecting Narcissus: a Queer Aesthetic* (2000), as well as authoring numerous articles on gothicism and queerness. He is coeditor with Natasha Hurley of *Curiouser: On the Queerness of Children* (2004). and is currently at work on a project entitled "Only the Dead Can Dance: Choreographies of Mortality."

**Lauren Fitzgerald** is Associate Professor of English at Yeshiva University, where she teaches courses in British Romanticism and the Gothic as well as directing the Yeshiva College Composition Program and Writing Center. She received her Ph.D. from New York University. Her articles on Romantic period Gothic have appeared in *Gothic Studies, Romanticism on the Net, The Wordsworth Circle*, and other publications. She also publishes in composition studies and is currently working on a study of Gothic authorship and plagiarism.

**Jerrold E. Hogle**, whose Ph.D. is from Harvard, is Professor of English, University Distinguished Professor, and Vice-Provost for Instruction at the University of Arizona. He has won Guggenheim and Mellon Fellowships for research along with numerous teaching awards. In addition to his work on Romantic poetry, most notably *Shelley's Process* (1989), he has published widely on the Gothic, most recently in his books *The Undergrounds of The Phantom of the Opera* (2002) and *The Cambridge Companion to Gothic Fiction* (2002). He is currently working on a study of the Gothic subtexts in numerous works of English Romanticism.

**Avril Horner** is Professor of English at Kingston University, London. Her Ph.D. research, on the poetry of Geoffrey Hill, was undertaken at the University of Manchester but her publications focus mainly on women's writing and Gothic fiction. Recent major publications, co-authored with Sue Zlosnik, include *Daphne du Maurier: Writing, Identity and the Gothic Imagination* (1998) and *Gothic and the Comic Turn* (2005). She is currently working with Janet Beer on *Edith Wharton: Sex, Satire and the Older Woman*, to be published by Palgrave Macmillan in 2007.

**William Hughes** is Professor of Gothic Studies at Bath Spa University College, where he leads undergraduate modules in nineteenth-century and contemporary Gothic. A graduate of the University of East Anglia, Norwich (where he researched a Ph.D. on the writings of Bram Stoker), he is the author of *Beyond Dracula* (2000); coeditor with Andrew Smith of *Empire and the Gothic* (2003); *Fictions of Unease* (2001, also with Diane Mason); and *Bram Stoker: History, Psychoanalysis and the Gothic* (1998). He is currently writing a monograph on Victorian hypnotism for Manchester University Press.

**Allan Lloyd-Smith** is Senior Lecturer at the University of East Anglia, Norwich, UK. His books include *American Gothic Fiction: an Introduction* (2004); *Uncanny American Fiction* (1987); *Eve Tempted* (1984); *The Crucible* CD-ROM (Penguin); and he has edited with Victor Sage, the collections *Modern Gothic: a Reader* (1996), and *Gothick: Origins and Innovations* (1994). He is a graduate of the University of Sussex (BA and MA) and Indiana University (Ph.D.) and the founder of the International Gothic Association. He has published many articles on American literature and culture.

**Anna Powell** is Senior Lecturer in Film Studies at Manchester Metropolitan University. She is the author of *Deleuze and the Horror Film* (2005) and *Psychoanalysis and Sovereignty in Popular Vampire Fictions* (2003). She has published chapters on women's vampire literature; occult themes in the films of Kenneth Anger; occultism in the films of John Carpenter; and articles on *Near Dark* (*Screen* 1995) and *The Blair Witch Project* (*Spectator* 2002). A chapter on religion in UK Goth culture is forthcoming (2006). She is currently writing a monograph, *Deleuze: Altered States and Film*.

**Andrew Smith** is Professor of English Studies at the University of Glamorgan, where he is Head of Humanities. He is the author of *Victorian Demons: Medicine, Masculinity and the Gothic at the fin de siècle* (2004) and *Gothic Radicalism: Literature, Philosophy and Psychoanalysis in the Nineteenth Century* (2000). He has coedited several collections of essays including *Empire and the Gothic: the Politics of Genre* with William Hughes (2003); and *Gothic Modernisms* with Jeff Wallace (2001). He is currently writing a monograph on the ghost story for Manchester University Press. He edits, with Professor Ben Fisher, the series *Gothic Literary Studies*, published by the University of Wales Press.

**Professor Gina Wisker** is Head of the Centre for Learning and Teaching, University of Brighton. She gained her BA, MA, and Ph.D. from Nottingham University. Her most recent books include *Postcolonial and African-American Women's Writing* (2000), beginners guides to Angela Carter, Sylvia Plath, Virginia Woolf, and Toni Morrison (2000–2003), *The Postgraduate Research Handbook* (2001), and *The Good Supervisor* (2005).

**Julian Wolfreys** (D.Phil. Sussex) is Professor of English at the University of Florida. He has written, edited and coedited numerous books and articles. Among his most recent publications are *Occasional Deconstructions* (2004), *Thinking Difference: Critics in Conversation* (2004), and an edition of Richard Marsh's novel, *The Beetle* (2004). A monograph on *The Pickwick Papers* is currently in press and is due for publication in March 2006.

**Sue Zlosnik** is Professor of English and Head of Department at Manchester Metropolitan University. She works on nineteenth- and twentieth-century narrative, with a particular interest in Gothic. Her books include *Daphne du Maurier: Writing, Identity and the Gothic Imagination* (1998) and *Gothic and the Comic Turn* (2005), both co-authored with Avril Horner and published by Palgrave Macmillan. Other recent publications include essays on Robert Louis Stevenson and J. R. R. Tolkien.

# A Chronology of Significant Works

| | |
|---|---|
| 1757 | Edmund Burke, *A Philosophical Enquiry into the Origin of Our Ideas of the Sublime and the Beautiful* |
| 1764 | Horace Walpole, *The Castle of Otranto* |
| 1768 | Horace Walpole, *The Mysterious Mother* (drama) |
| 1773 | John Aikin and Anna Laetitia Barbauld "On the Pleasure derived from Objects of Terror, with Sir Bertrand, A Fragment" |
| **1776** | **The American Declaration of Independence** |
| 1777 | Sarah Reeve, *The Champion of Virtue; a Gothic Story* (reissued in 1778 as *The Old English Baron*) |
| 1783–1785 | Sophia Lee, *The Recess* |
| 1786 | William Beckford, *Vathek* |
| 1781 | Henri Fuseli, "The Nightmare" (painting) |
| **1789–94** | **The French Revolution** |
| 1789 | Ann Radcliffe, *The Castles of Athlin and Dunbayne* |
| 1791 | Ann Radcliffe, *A Sicilian Romance* |
| 1791 | Ann Radcliffe, *The Romance of the Forest*, Horace Walpole, *The Mysterious Mother*, The Marquis de Sade, *Justine; or, Good Conduct Well Chastised* |
| 1792 | Mary Wollstonecraft, *A Vindication of the Rights of Woman* |
| 1794 | William Godwin, *Things as They Are; or, The Adventures of Caleb Williams*, Ann Radcliffe, *The Mysteries of Udolpho* |
| 1796 | Matthew Lewis, *The Monk* |
| 1797 | Ann Radcliffe, *The Italian*, Samuel Taylor Coleridge, *Osario*, William Wordsworth, *The Borderers*, Samuel Taylor Coleridge, "Christabel," Matthew Lewis, *The Castle Spectre* (drama) |
| 1798 | Charles Brockden Brown, *Weiland; or The Transformation*, Wordsworth and Coleridge, *Lyrical Ballads*, including Coleridge's "The Rime of the |

| | |
|---|---|
| | Ancient Mariner," Francisco Goya, "The Sleep of Reason Produces Monsters" (etching) |
| 1799 | Charles Brockden Brown, *Edgar Huntley; or the Memoirs of a Sleepwalker* Wordsworth and Coleridge, second edition of *Lyrical Ballads* with Wordsworth's Preface |
| **1803–15** | **Napoleonic Wars** |
| | Charlotte Dacre, *Zofloya, or The Moor*, Walter Scott, *The Lay of the Last Minstrel*, Charles Robert Maturin, *The Fatal Revenge*, Wordsworth, "Elegiac Stanzas, Suggested by a Picture of Peele Castle in a Storm, Painted by Sir George Beaumont," Percy Bysshe Shelley, *Zastrozzi* and *St. Irvine* |
| 1813 | Lord Byron, *The Giaour* |
| 1816 | E. T. A. Hoffmann, "The Sandman," Coleridge, *Christabel* |
| 1817 | Lord Byron, *Manfred* |
| 1818 | Jane Austen, *Northanger Abbey*, Thomas Love Peacock, *Nightmare Abbey*, Mary Wollstonecraft Shelley, *Frankenstein* |
| 1819 | Walter Scott, *The Bride of Lammermoor*, John Polidori, *The Vampyre*, John Keats, "La Belle Dame Sans Merci" and "The Eve of St Agnes," Percy Bysshe Shelley, *The Cenci*, Lord Byron "Fragment of a Story" |
| 1820 | Charles Robert Maturin, *Melmoth the Wanderer* |
| | James Hogg, *The Private Memoirs and Confessions of a Justified Sinner* |
| | Thomas Holcroft, *Tale of Mystery* (drama), John Keats, *Lamia*, J. R. Planché, *The Vampyre* (drama) |
| 1826 | Anne Radcliffe, "On the Supernatural in Poetry" and *Gaston de Blondeville* |
| 1830 | Walter Scott, *Letters on Demonology and Witchcraft* |
| 1831 | Mary Wollstonecraft Shelley, revised edition of *Frankenstein* |
| **1833** | **The Abolition of Slavery (GB)** |
| 1838 | Charles Dickens, *Oliver Twist* |
| 1838 | Edgar Allen Poe, "Ligeia" |
| 1839 | Edgar Allen Poe, "The Fall of the House of Usher" |
| 1843 | Edgar Allen Poe, "The Black Cat" and "The Pit and the Pendulum" |

| | |
|---|---|
| 1844–8 | G. W. M. Reynolds, *The Mysteries of London* |
| 1847 | Charlotte Brontë, *Jane Eyre*, Emily Brontë, *Wuthering Heights*, James Malcolm Rymer, *Varney the Vampire; or, The Feast of Blood* |
| **1848** | **"The Year of Revolutions" in Europe**<br>Karl Marx, *The Communist Manifesto* |
| 1849 | William Harrison Ainsworth, *The Lancashire Witches* |
| 1851–3 | John Ruskin, *Stones of Venice*, Nathaniel Hawthorne, *The House of the Seven Gables* |
| 1852 | Arthur Hughes, "Ophelia" (painting) |
| 1853 | Charles Dickens, *Bleak House* |
| 1856 | Wilkie Collins, *After Dark* |
| 1859 | Edward George Bulwer-Lytton, "The Haunted and the Haunters," Charles Darwin, *The Origin of Species* |
| 1860 | Wilkie Collins, *The Woman in White* |
| 1862 | Mary Elizabeth Braddon, *Lady Audley's Secret*, Christina Rossetti, "Goblin Market" |
| 1864 | Sheridan le Fanu, *Uncle Silas* |
| 1868 | Wilkie Collins, *The Moonstone* |
| 1870 | Charles Dickens, *The Mystery of Edwin Drood* |
| 1871 | Sheridan Le Fanu, *Carmilla* |
| 1872 | Sheridan Le Fanu, *In a Glass Darkly* |
| 1873 | Amelia B. Edwards, *Monsieur Maurice* |
| 1875 | J. H. Riddell, *The Uninhabited House* |
| 1876 | Cesare Lombroso, *The Criminal Man* |
| 1885 | Henry Rider Haggard, *King Solomon's Mines* |
| 1886 | Robert Louis Stevenson, *The Strange Case of Dr Jekyll and Mr Hyde*, Vernon Lee, *A Phantom Lover* |
| 1887 | Henry Rider Haggard, *She* |
| 1888 | Rudyard Kipling, *The Phantom Rickshaw and Other Tales* |
| 1891 | Oscar Wilde, *The Picture of Dorian Gray* |
| 1892 | Charlotte Perkins Gillman, "The Yellow Wallpaper," Max Nordau, *Degeneration* |
| 1893 | Ambrose Bierce, *Can Such Things Be*? John William Waterhouse, "La Belle Dame Sans Merci" (painting) |
| 1894 | Arthur Machen, *The Great God Pan* and *The Inner Light* |
| 1895 | Robert W. Chambers, *The King in Yellow*, George Macdonald, *Lilith* |

| | |
|---|---|
| 1896 | H. G. Wells, *The Island of Dr Moreau* |
| **1897** | **Queen Victoria's Diamond Jubilee** |
| 1897 | Bram Stoker, *Dracula*, Richard Marsh, *The Beetle* |
| 1898 | Henry James, *The Turn of the Screw* |
| **1899–1902** | **Boer War** |
| **1901** | **The death of Queen Victoria** |
| 1902 | Arthur Conan Doyle, *The Hound of the Baskervilles* |
| 1903 | Bram Stoker, *The Jewel of Seven Stars* (revised 1912), Arthur Benson, *The Hill of Trouble* |
| 1904 | M. R. James, *Ghost Stories of an Antiquary*, Arthur Benson, *Isles of Sunset* |
| 1911 | Gaston Leroux, *The Phantom of the Opera*, Bram Stoker, *The Lair of the White Worm* |
| 1912 | Edmund Gill Swain, *The Stoneground Ghost Tales* |
| **1914–18** | **First World War** |
| 1919 | Sigmund Freud, "The Uncanny" |
| 1919 | Robert Wiene, dir. *The Cabinet of Dr Caligari* |
| 1922 | F. W. Murnau, dir. *Nosferatu: Eine Symphonie des Grauens* |
| 1925 | Rupert Julian, dir. *The Phantom of the Opera* |
| 1927 | H. P. Lovecraft, *The Case of Charles Dexter Ward: a Novel of Terror*, Fritz Lang, dir. *Metropolis* |
| 1929 | Ernest Jones, *On the Nightmare* |
| 1931 | M. R. James, *Collected Ghost Stories*, Todd Browning, dir. *Dracula*; Rouben Mamoulian, dir. *Dr Jekyll and Mr Hyde*, James Whale, dir. *Frankenstein* |
| 1932 | Carl Theodor Dreyer, dir. *Vampyr* |
| 1934 | Dennis Wheatley, *The Devil Rides Out* |
| 1937 | Edith Wharton, *Ghosts*, Charles Addams, *The Addams Family* (cartoon book) |
| **1939–45** | **Second World War** |
| 1938 | Daphne du Maurier, *Rebecca* |
| 1939 | Alfred Hitchcock, dir. *Rebecca* |
| 1942 | Jacques Tourneur, dir. *Cat People* |
| 1943 | Jacques Tourneur, dir. *I Walked with a Zombie*, Truman Capote, *Other Voices, Other Rooms* |
| 1944 | Lewis Allen, dir. *The Uninvited* |
| 1945 | Elizabeth Bowen, *The Demon Lover, and Other Stories* |

| | |
|---|---|
| 1946 | Mervyn Peake, *Titus Groan* |
| 1949 | Simone de Beauvoir, *The Second Sex*, A. N. L. Munby, *The Alabaster Hand* |
| **1950–53** | **Korean War** |
| 1950 | Mervyn Peake, *Gormenghast* |
| 1951 | John Wyndham, *The Day of the Triffids* |
| 1954 | Isak Dinesen, *Seven Gothic Tales*, Richard Matheson, *I Am Legend* |
| 1957 | Terence Fisher, dir. *Dracula*, John Wyndham, *The Midwich Cuckoos* |
| 1959 | Robert Bloch, *Psycho*, Shirley Jackson, *The Haunting of Hill House*, Mervyn Peake, *Titus Alone* |
| 1960 | Roger Corman, dir. *The House of Usher*, Alfred Hitchcock, dir. *Psycho* |
| 1961 | Roger Corman, dir. *The Pit and the Pendulum* |
| 1962 | Ray Bradbury, *Something Wicked this Way Comes* |
| 1963 | Robert Wise, dir. *The Haunting*, Edward Gorey, *The Gashly Crumb Tinies; or, After the Outing* |
| 1964 | Robert Aldrich, dir. *Hush, Hush, Sweet Charlotte* |
| **1965–73** | **Vietnam War** |
| 1965 | Roman Polanski, dir. *Repulsion* |
| 1966 | Jean Rhys, *Wide Sargasso Sea* |
| **1967** | **"The Summer of Love"** |
| 1968 | George A. Romero, dir. *The Night of the Living Dead*, Roman Polanski, dir. *Rosemary's Baby* |
| 1970 | Roy Ward Baker, dir. *The Vampire Lovers* |
| 1973 | William Freidkin, dir. *The Exorcist* |
| 1974 | Stephen King, *Carrie*, Tobe Hooper, dir. *The Texas Chainsaw Massacre*, David Pirie, *A Heritage of Horror: the English Gothic Cinema*, Juliet Mitchell, *Psychoanalysis and Feminism* |
| 1975 | James Herbert, *The Fog* |
| 1976 | Anne Rice, *Interview with the Vampire*, Brian de Palma, dir. *Carrie*, George Romero, dir. *Martin* |
| 1977 | Dario Argento, *Suspiria*, Stephen King, *The Shining*, Jim Sharman, dir. *The Rocky Horror Picture Show* |
| 1978 | John Carpenter, dir. *Halloween* |
| 1978 | Edward Said, *Orientalism* |

| | |
|---|---|
| 1979 | Angela Carter, *The Bloody Chamber* |
| 1979 | Werner Herzog, dir. *Nosferatu; Phantom der Nacht,* Ridley Scott, dir. *Alien* |
| 1980 | Suzy McKee Charnas, *The Vampire Tapestry,* Stanley Kubrick, *The Shining* |
| 1981 | Whitley Streiber, *The Hunger,* John Landis, dir. *An American Werewolf in London* |
| 1983 | Tony Scott, dir. *The Hunger* |
| 1984 | Iain Banks, *The Wasp Factory,* William Gibson, *Neuromancer,* Jody Scott, *I, Vampire,* S. P. Somtow, *Vampire Junction,* Wes Craven, dir. *A Nightmare on Elm Street,* Neil Jordan, *The Company of Wolves* |
| **1985** | **Glasnost** |
| 1985 | Anne Rice, *The Vampire Lestat,* Donna Haraway, *The Cyborg Manifesto* |
| 1986 | David Lynch, *Blue Velvet* |
| 1987 | Toni Morrison, *Beloved,* Alan Moore and Dave Gibbons, *Watchmen,* Alan Parker, dir. *Angel Heart,* Joel Schumacher, dir. *The Lost Boys,* Kathryn Bigelow, dir. *Near Dark* |
| 1988 | Clive Barker, *The Books of Blood,* Neil Gaiman, *The Sandman No. 1,* Amitav Ghosh, *The Shadow Lines,* Thomas Harris, *The Silence of the Lambs* |
| 1989 | Nancy Collins, *Sunglasses After Dark* |
| 1990 | Tim Burton, dir. *Edward Scissorhands,* David Lynch, *Twin Peaks* (TV series begins) |
| 1991 | Brett Easton Ellis, *American Psycho,* Jewelle Gomez, *The Gilda Stories,* Patrick McGrath, *Spider,* Jonathan Demme, dir. *The Silence of the Lambs* |
| 1992 | Poppy Z. Brite, *Lost Souls,* Francis Ford Coppola, dir. *Bram Stoker's Dracula,* Bernard Rose, dir. *Candyman,* Tim Burton, *Batman Returns* |
| **1993** | **The World Wide Web** |
| 1993 | Barry Sonnenfield, dir. *Addams Family Values* |
| 1994 | Alex Proyas, dir. *The Crow* |
| 1995 | Joyce Carol Oates, *Zombie,* David Fincher, dir. *Seven,* Kenneth Branagh, dir. *Frankenstein* |

| | |
|---|---|
| 1996 | Neil Gaiman, *Neverwhere*, Robert Rodriguez, dir. *From Dusk till Dawn*, Andrew Fleming, *The Craft*, Michael Cohn, *Snow White: a Tale of Terror* |
| 1997 | *Buffy, the Vampire Slayer* (TV series begins), Paul Anderson, *Event Horizon*, Jean-Pierre Jeunet, dir. *Alien Resurrection* |
| 1998 | Alex Proyas, dir. *Dark City*, Hideo Nakata, dir. *The Ring* |
| 1999 | Sarah Waters, *Affinity*, Tim Burton, dir. *Sleepy Hollow*, Thomas Harris, *Hannibal* |
| 2000 | Mary Harron, dir. *American Psycho* |
| **2001** | **"9/11"** |
| 2001 | Iain Sinclair, *Landor's Tower*, Alejandro Amenábar, dir. *The Others*, The Hughes Brothers, dir. *From Hell* |
| 2003 | A. S. Byatt, *Little Black Book of Stories*, Barbara Vine (Ruth Rendell), *The Blood Doctor* |
| 2004 | Dan Brown, *The Da Vinci Code*, Iain Sinclair, *Dining on Stones*, Joel Schumacher, dir. *The Phantom of the Opera*, Stephen Sommers. dir. *Van Helsing* |
| 2005 | Hideo Nakata, dir. *The Ring 2* |

# Introduction: Gothic Pedagogies

*Anna Powell and Andrew Smith*

From the Oxford of medieval scholasticism to the "university in ruins" of postmodern globalization, Gothic and pedagogy intersect. As the nineteenth-century academy favoured mock-Gothic architecture, so the contemporary experience of teaching and learning is itself Gothicized in important ways. Like the Gothic mode itself, contemporary English Studies combines high art and popular culture. It has embraced a post-modern Gothic, in the fiction of Angela Carter, Iain Banks, and others. It has widened its subject-base to include previously marginalized forms like the horror film. Such self-reflexive texts attest to the continued vitality of the Gothic tradition they pastiche.

The ghosts of long-dead poets and novelists are welcome to haunt our lecture-theatres, reanimated by our pedagogic passion to reveal the secrets of literary history. Teachers and their students themselves produce new hybrids as we rework and cross-fertilize texts in our seminar-laboratories. At times, the imaginative reach of the seminar itself opens up to those liminal spaces where insight lurks. At this juncture, there is an urgent need for a pedagogic intervention that reflects, and reflects upon, our theory and practice as teachers of Gothic in Higher Education, and to open up the considerable pleasures it offers to those lecturers and students who work in it.

There are significant reasons why we teach and study Gothic and why the field should attract increasing numbers of enthusiastic converts among lecturers and students. From its former marginality to the literary canon as prescribed by English Studies, Gothic has become a fully-fledged and popular topic with its own undergraduate units and postgraduate degree courses, scholarly associations and journals. Gothic is a vibrant, flexible mode, mutating to fit changing cultural and ideological dynamics. Neither Gothic literature and film, nor studies of them, operate in a monolithic generic paradigm. Both creative and critical work expand the ideological and stylistic parameters of the form to produce, rather, a multiplicity of Gothics, including postcolonial, postmodern, and Queer versions.

Gothic stimulates ambivalent kinds of pleasure as desire and dread work on us in tandem. As well as the immediate appeal of this sensational affect, the pedagogic possibilities of the field are considerable. These include close analysis of specific textual operations, intellectual engagement in, and debate of, major critical theories and the study of historical and cultural contexts. As well as being marked by historical antecedents, the genre/mode embraces contemporary cultural forms and concerns. It is, unsurprisingly, a popular subject with students, who welcome the opportunity to study in college a popular cultural form they might already enjoy outside. Recruitment figures reveal a steady increase as more courses and units are developed. Students who enjoy literature and film with extreme content, stylistic excess, ritualized narrative, suspense, and uncanny atmosphere can learn to use theoretical concepts and terminology that enable deeper understanding of these pleasures. They can be offered tools to explore intriguing and complex issues and encouraged to make evaluative judgements that pertain both to textual work and its historical and cultural resonance.

In the "dark ages" of Leavisite "New Criticism" Gothic was rarely visible per se on the English curriculum.[1] Before the 1980s the Gothic frequently made a brief appearance on our "typical" undergraduate degree syllabus as a necessary adjunct to Jane Austen's *Northanger Abbey* (1818) although canonical novelists such as Dickens and the Brontës, and Romantic poets like Coleridge and Keats had clearly deployed it as a thematic trope and expressive technique. The neglected status of the mode in Higher Education was undermined by a "Gothic renaissance," both literary and critical, which has been gaining momentum over the last twenty-five years.

In the late 1970s, Gothic tropes reappeared in critically acclaimed fiction, most notably in the self-reflexive feminist appropriations of Angela Carter (*The Bloody Chamber,* 1979). Gothic "pulp" gained critical attention as well as mainstream best-seller circulation with the flamboyantly purple, yet generically self-reflexive novels of Anne

Rice (beginning with *Interview with the Vampire*, 1976). Her page-turning "airport Gothics" reflected increasingly visible and vocal gay cultures in the USA in an erotic climate that produced Jim Sharman's film version of the successful Broadway musical, *The Rocky Horror Picture Show* (also 1976). In the same year, new forms of contemporary Gothic were screened in "troubled teen" films with a supernatural edge: Brian de Palma's *Carrie* and George Romero's *Martin*. John Carpenter's *Halloween* presented Michael Myers, a masked monster with an uncanny presence who attacks sexually transgressive teens until defeated by a chaste "final girl" in 1978.[2] Ridley Scott's 1979 blockbuster *Alien* blended Sci-Fi and Gothic in its motifs, themes, and the machinic eroticism of H. R Geiger's sets and attracted unprecedented critical attention to its tough "feminist" hero Ripley (Sigourney Weaver).

Contemporaneously, developments in continental critical theory and their application to literature and film offered new critical tools for the analysis of Gothic texts. There was, however, a slight time-lag between film theory and literary theory, manifest in the 1973 publication of an early keynote study of Gothic film, informed by auteur theory: David Pirie's *A Heritage of Horror: the English Gothic Cinema*.[3] Freudian psychoanalysis and its reworking by Melanie Klein and Jacques Lacan were a rich resource for Gothic theory via their pivotal critical concepts of the uncanny: the mother's body as haunted house; the "return of the repressed"; oral sadism and ambivalence. Psychoanalytic theory in tandem with ideological critique was applied to Gothic by David Punter's ground-breaking study, *The Literature of Terror: a History of Gothic Fictions from 1765 to the Present* (1980).

The term "Female Gothic" was defined by Ellen Moers in *Literary Women* (1976).[4] Feminist critical interest in Gothic fantasy constructions of gender was fuelled by Julia Kristeva's concept of abjection in her book *Powers of Horror* (1980).[5] It was also motivated by the project to validate Gothic novels as hitherto neglected "women's fictions." Cultural studies and Marxist historicism enabled studies of the sociohistorical contexts of Gothic fiction as well as their fictional representation by the texts themselves. Structuralist work on narrativity, such as Tzvetan Todorov's *The Fantastic: a Structural Approach to a Literary Genre* (1975) facilitated new formal perspectives on the mode.[6] These pioneering critical approaches initially used by scholars to identify generic parameters and open them up to ideological critique, have been widely applied, developed, and debated and are still very much alive. They function as a basis for current Gothic syllabi as well as stimulating fresh generations of scholars.

The wider currency of Gothic for youth culture was also attested to by the burgeoning Goth music and fashion generated by the early 1980s marriage of punk and New Romantic.[7] This led to an upsurge of nostalgic interest in historical Gothic literature, art, and architecture, as well as a market for new Gothic films. Doom-laden riffs accompanied melancholy lyrics gleaned from Gothic literature and film of vampires, decadent eroticism, and nocturnal, angst-ridden outsiders dabbling in the occult. The Goth band Bauhaus opened Tony Scott's vampire film *The Hunger* performing "Bela Lugosi's Dead" in 1981. By the 1990s Goth had produced its own authors and "auteurs" such as Poppy Z. Brite in the novel and short story and Tim Burton in film. The mutations of Goth and its absorption into mainstream culture via recent TV series like *Buffy the Vampire Slayer* and *Angel* and controversial rock icons like Marilyn Manson are still instrumental in forming the cultural tastes of the undergraduate intake on our Gothic courses.

As Gothic Studies gained momentum, Gothic literature and cinema attained increasing critical credibility. Novels and films were validated as works of thematic and stylistic complexity as well as providing considerable insight into the social and historical contexts of their production, distribution, and consumption. Gothic gradually gained academic credibility to become a significant element in the English degree curriculum at both undergraduate and postgraduate level. It is currently undergoing rapid expansion both in the UK and North America as increasing numbers of staff and students opt to work with it as a distinct strand in the curriculum. Gothic Studies combines a celebration of popular film and literature with cutting-edge theoretical approaches to texts and contexts. The international expansion of scholarly research is attested to by journals such as *Gothic Studies* and the biennial conference of the International Gothic Association.

The present volume is structured with a dual focus in being written by a group of published Gothic scholars who also have considerable expertise in teaching and course development. The collection foregrounds a sense of Gothic pedagogy's own intellectual history as the constraints and opportunities of teaching are viewed through the prism of extensive classroom experience. It also offers us valuable insights into teaching resources and evaluations of critical and theoretical trends. Distinct, sometimes conflicting, perspectives and their relative merits are considered and debated. The authors offer critical surveys and evaluations of existing scholarly work, and exciting possibilities for future development. They offer insights into pedagogic activities: curriculum development and classroom delivery; the establishment of Gothic MAs; the supervision of postgraduate students on research projects; as well as its mainstay in most colleges, the teaching of large classes of undergraduate students. The writers map the specificity of Gothic as a historical genre as well as signalling its hybridity as a mode that is open to, and fruitfully cross-pollinates with other modes and genres. The collection aims to stimulate further input into the development of the subject area. We hope it will open up a pedagogic forum for the Gothic curriculum and encourage an interchange of ideas between those involved in teaching it.

The book addresses a range of issues that have influenced the teaching of the Gothic over the past twenty-five years, and provides a chronology to aid contextualization. It includes an appraisal of how theories such as Marxism, Psychoanalysis, and Feminism have altered our conception of what constitutes a Gothic tradition, and a reassessment of how these changes have impacted on pedagogic practice. Indeed there has been recent interest in addressing scholarship on pedagogy and the Gothic, as evidenced by special panels at international conferences and by the publication of the excellent MLA's *Gothic Fiction: the British and American Traditions* (2003) edited by Diane Long Hoeveler and Tamar Heller in the well-established "Approaches to Teaching" series.[8] This current volume takes a different approach: some of the contributors examine how changes in intellectual history have impacted on curriculum design and so influenced what (and how) we teach. The early chapters address how developments in criticism and theory have shaped our approach to teaching the Gothic.

William Hughes in "Gothic Criticism: a Survey, 1764–2004" examines the relationship between three different traditions of Gothic scholarship. The belletrist tradition which began in the eighteenth and nineteenth centuries has a vestigial presence in some of today's criticism. The generic survey, which emerged in the early twentieth century reads the genre historically or theoretically; and a tradition which emerged towards the end of the twentieth century is more associated with the specialized study of an individual author or issue within the field. This chapter provides an important reconsideration of how scholarship on the Gothic has developed over the past two hundred and forty years and thus invites reflection on how we might convey this in our teaching.

In "Theorizing the Gothic" Jerrold Hogle explores how a range of critical theories including historicist, materialist, and psychoanalytical readings, have changed the way that we read and teach particular Gothic texts. Hogle discusses how a diverse selection of different theoretical approaches to *Dracula* (1897) have influenced the way that the novel is taught, and how such approaches map a history of the changing critical values in the academy. The chapter therefore provides a sophisticated evaluation and contextualization of how the "Gothic" has been reshaped by critical theory.

Lauren Fitzgerald in "Romantic Gothic" examines how changes in scholarship on romanticism have impacted on how we understand the romantic Gothic. Fitzgerald also explores how our understanding of the romantic Gothic has shaped the critical reception of romanticism on which our teaching is based. Contemporary theory has also played a role in how we see the romantic Gothic, and after exploring these critical debates and how they have influenced notions of canonicity, Fitzgerald addresses how the teaching of the 1818 edition of *Frankenstein* brings together ideas about gender, the Gothic "canon," identity, and romanticism.

In "Victorian Gothic" Julian Wolfreys explores how our conceptualization of the Victorians relates to our understanding of the Gothic. Many critics have claimed that after the Gothic heyday of 1780–1820 the Gothic comes to infiltrate seemingly "realist" modes of writing. To that end Wolfreys examines how the Gothic destablizes the notion of "realism" and consequently deconstructs preconceived ideas about Victorian literature. Wolfreys discusses a range of Gothic writings from the period which reflect on the idea of haunting, and which illustrates how the Gothic comes to haunt certain realist tropes. These offer considerable potential for classroom use.

Lucie Armitt in "Postmodern Gothic" explores how formations of Gothic reveal a genre in radical transformation. New, hybrid forms emerge as the Gothic meets other generic strands like magical realism. The stylistic and thematic scope, and the affective potential of each form are expanded in the process. This chapter documents some of the ways in which the postmodern Gothic novel *The Crow Road* (1992) by Iain Banks, which mixes traditional Gothic motifs with the disruptive and playful elements of magical realism, can help us teach our students to "see" and "hear" through literature. Postmodern Gothic hybrid texts can also be used to encourage students to construct "writerly" readings.

In "Gothic Sexualities" Steven Bruhm examines how developments in Queer theory have enabled critics to readdress representations of pleasure and pain in the Gothic. Bruhm discusses how the Gothic's fascination with states of pleasure and pain make it especially available to Queer readings. As an example, he explores how an approach to Anne Rice's *Interview with the Vampire* (1976), which employs a post-Freudian notion of identity formation as part of a Queer theory perspective, both opens up the novel to a new reading and illustrates how such theory can be taught in the classroom.

Avril Horner and Sue Zlosnik in "Female Gothic" discuss how changes in criticism on the Female Gothic have affected Gothic canon-formation and stimulated debate over the relationship between textual production and gender (both masculine and feminine). They also explore the reasons for developments in curriculum design on courses on the Female Gothic and situate this debate not only within scholastic developments on the form, but also to the implications raised by a new postfeminist phase of critical writings. They thus contribute a sense of how teaching the Gothic has developed across two decades.

In "Adapting Gothic from Print to Screen" Anna Powell explores the relationship between text and film and accounts for how this has been influenced by our understanding of the critical relationship between the two mediums in Gothic scholarship. Powell also pays attention to the genesis of the "horror" film and criticism of it. In addition she explores the similarities and differences in reading texts and reading films, after which she discusses how examining the relationship between Stoker's *Dracula* (1897) and film versions of the novel, provides a clear sense of how the two can be taught in conjunction.

Allan Lloyd-Smith in "American Gothic" discusses the types of national and intellectual complexities which students often find challenging. He also examines how issues such as race enable a reconsideration of the American Gothic tradition, one which creates relationships between writers of the early Gothic and twentieth-century authors. Lloyd-Smith provides a considered exploration of how to approach the teaching of particular texts and authors.

In "Imperial Gothic" Patrick Brantlinger explores how the form developed as a response to British Imperialism. The Imperial Gothic has some of its roots in Victorian adventure stories written for children and Brantlinger explores how the tradition mutated throughout the nineteenth and early twentieth centuries. Our understanding of Imperialism has shaped, and in turn been shaped by, the literature which it produced, and Brantlinger discusses this in the context of a range of writings by R. L. Stevenson, Rider Haggard, Bram Stoker, H. G. Wells and Joseph Conrad, amongst others. Scholarship on Imperialism has therefore shaped the types of curricula that teachers of the Gothic have developed.

Gina Wisker in "Postcolonial Gothic" explores the theoretical complexities which have informed how we read, and teach, Postcolonial Gothic. After contextualizing such theories and commentating on their strengths, Wisker discusses some of the difficulties typically encountered by tutors attempting to introduce such theoretically complex ideas to students. Wisker examines a variety of strategies for involving students in postcolonial debates and outlines a particular approach to teaching Toni Morrison's *Beloved* (1987), which brings together a range of issues (about race, hybridity, and gender) which are central to our understanding of postcolonialism.

In "Postgraduate Developments" Andrew Smith discusses how the respective UK and North American contexts have played a part in shaping postgraduate study on the Gothic. Smith accounts for the development of subject specific Masters awards on the Gothic in the UK as a consequence of the UK sector's emphasis on named awards. This contrasts with the North American context which appears to favour more general awards, with specific Gothic courses within them. Smith also examines data on the upward trend in postgraduate research on the Gothic in both the UK and North America. Finally, he outlines the course contents of a series of subject specific Masters awards on the Gothic, and discusses the types of issues concerning curriculum design and course delivery and recruitment that were considered during the planning of such awards.

Each of these essays has been especially commissioned for this volume. We hope that scholars and students will find here a helpful resource to enhance their knowledge of Gothic Studies and how it comes to be taught to them in the ways that it is. Above all, we would like to contribute to the quality and scope of Gothic pedagogy and to invite teachers to reflect on their own classroom practice in this important and stimulating field.

## Notes

1. For a challenging perspective on the history of Gothic criticism, see William Hughes, "Gothic Criticism" in this volume.
2. The concept of the "final girl" is used in Carol J. Clover, *Men, Women and Chainsaws: Gender in the Modern Horror Film* (London: BFI, 1993).
3. David Pirie, *A Heritage of Horror: the English Gothic Cinema: 1940–1972* (London: Gordon Fraser, 1973).
4. Ellen Moers, *Literary Women: the Great Writers* (London: The Women's Press, [1976] 1978), 90–110.
5. Julia Kristeva, *Powers of Horror: an Essay on Abjection* (New York: Columbia University Press, 1980).
6. Tsvetan Todorov, *The Fantastic: a Structural Approach to a Literary Genre* (Ithaca: Columbia University Press, 1975).
7. The Batcave, the prototype Goth club, opened in London in 1982.
8. Diane Long Hoeveler and Tamar Heller, eds., *Approaches to Teaching: Gothic Fiction: the British and American Traditions* (New York: MLA, 2003).

# 1
# Gothic Criticism: a Survey, 1764–2004

*William Hughes*

To chart the development of Gothic criticism, it might be argued, is to follow the progress of a genre from literary curiosity to distinctive and systematic cultural movement. A genre that forms the subject of a discrete and expanding body of criticism must surely, the argument runs, have gained acceptance within the Academy, and the right in consequence to police a canon or canons as well as affirm a body of generic conventions. To have attained such a worthy position, inevitably, implicates the genre in a mythical past-time when such a body of criticism could not have been contemplated, a less-enlightened age where Gothic was, if not precultural, then at least subcultural. This is a wonderful myth, and it is one which no doubt does much to reassure the critic at the dawn of the twenty-first century that he or she has escaped the strictures of a still-discernible Leavisite heritage. By accepting the Gothic, in teaching as well as in research, the modern Academy distances itself from an intolerant and elitist past, variously eighteenth-century, Victorian, or Leavisite. It proclaims a liberation of texts from obscurity and censorship, and in so doing sustains an edifice of the enlightened present. The Gothic, reassuringly, has been rescued from prejudice, has become something that the critics and authors commonly regarded as great, authoritative, or canonical, may now talk about openly with no embarrassment, save that of having to admit that their forebears were less enlightened.

Yet any such construction of a cultural journey from the fringe to something near the centre of literariness runs the risk of blurring over the essential paradox of the Gothic genre. Though academic criticism has historically proclaimed its subcultural origins, Gothic as a genre has never been beneath the notice of the most elitist of critics—as, indeed, it has never been outside of the creative achievement of the most canonical of authors. As a genre it is far from subcultural, being rather a balance of ephemeral textuality and canonical authorship, of allegedly transient fashion and persistent stylistics, and of a legitimacy historically and ironically applied through the attention afforded by the very institutional bodies whose criticism proclaims its irrelevance. Gothic criticism, an institution that has been in existence effectively from the very earliest days of the novelistic aspect of the genre, testifies not to a gradual acceptance but to an enduring interest from the outset, an interest where an apparently elite culture has always been engaged not merely in the explication of a popular (or populist) form, but in its production and dissemination also.

This much is evidenced by what must be regarded as the earliest experiment in the criticism of the Gothic novel, the preface to the First Edition of Horace Walpole's *The Castle of Otranto* (1764). Walpole's preface, which is effectively the evocation of taste and antiquity through an act of alleged editorship, must be read as a fiction integral to the work it precedes—as, indeed, must the preface to the Second Edition which revisits both the cultural context, and the literary conceit, of its predecessor. The two prefaces are, though, nevertheless, succinct manifestos both for the fledgling genre's stylistic content and for its wider cultural aspirations. Through the First Edition, the Gothic commonplaces of history and revenge, of a Roman Catholic past and a perceiving Protestant present, and of a closure derived from Christian morality are established, though the author's claims that his work contains "no bombast, no similes, flowers, digressions, or unnecessary descriptions" is as delusory here as it might be for many of the works that followed *The Castle of Otranto*.[1] It is the revelation, though, that this work was not a translation from "the black letter" of 1529 but rather a considerably more recent "attempt to blend the two kinds of romance, the ancient and the modern," that energizes what was to become a persistent debate around the genre.[2] Criticism reacted in a hostile manner to this hybrid, dismissing the improbabilities of the "ancient" Romance, whether supernatural or hyperbolic, as inimical to Enlightenment values. The revelations of the second preface, though, forced a revizitation of the already read, and the realization that the essence of the Romance had persisted to the present day—and that this popular example of the form was the product of no ignorant or uncultured author.

As Emma Clery notes, this revelation turned the amused tolerance of the critical establishment, represented by the *Monthly Review*, into an indignant statement of disbelief that "an Author, of refined and polished genius, should be an advocate for re-establishing the barbarous superstitions of Gothic devilism" in the present day.[3] In the belletrist tradition, out of which these reviews arise, a degree of scholarly antiquarianism, of the revival of a curiosity, is acceptable. Its fraudulent presentation, however, as was the case with Ossian as much as with *The Castle of Otranto*, was a betrayal—though the skill of that betrayal, and the craft that produced it, were invariably acknowledged rather than dismissed. Even where history, rather than superstition, is the issue, the same effective criteria are applied by the hostile reviewing establishment. The belletrist is, in effect, charmed by craft, but uneasy where liberties are taken with either fact or likelihood. Reading the historical Gothic of Sophia Lee's *The Recess* (1786), the *Gentleman's Magazine* praises that novel's "animated" and historically "correct" language, though the reviewer confides that "we cannot entirely approve the custom of interweaving fictitious incident with historic truth." Nevertheless, ambiguity remains a characteristic of these earlier responses to the genre: the review concludes that "These volumes . . . are calculated to supply not only amusement but instruction; and we recommend them with pleasure to the attention of the publick."[4]

The eighteenth-century belletrist tradition is, equally, the arena for the progressive explication of Gothic stylistics as much as it is the occasional mouthpiece for those uneasy with the appearance of such things in the Enlightened present. The formal essay, which in the belletrist tradition frequently emphasized aesthetic sensibility over directness of content, was as important an instrument as the literary review in the debate over the implications of Gothic. The framing prologue of Ann Radcliffe's *Gaston de Blondeville* (published posthumously in 1826) was first published in the *New Monthly Magazine* in the same year, its dialogic form embodying among another things an acknowledgement of the importance of the Burkean Sublime in first-phase Gothic aesthetics.[5] One might also note Nathan Drake's commentaries on the broad tendency of the genre in "On Gothic Superstition" and "On Objects of Terror," two essays published in a larger collection of *Sketches, Critical and Narrative*.[6] Characteristically, such works do not confine their compass to the eighteenth-century authors now canonically regarded as Gothic but, rather, range more widely, acknowledging in particular the antecedent of Shakespeare, and in the case of Drake, relevant issues in the work of more recent authors also.[7] They are, further, for the most part discursive pieces which move from the singularity of one text towards a generalization on the practice of writing both within and at times beyond the genre.

In this latter respect, the eighteenth-century belletrist tradition underpins one of the three main strands of Gothic criticism, this being the earliest of the discrete modes by which the Gothic has been explicated between the mid-eighteenth century and the present. With the decline in the first two decades of the nineteenth century of both the popularity and production of the first-phase Gothic came a corresponding reduction in the specific critical attention addressed to the genre.[8] The theoretical and aesthetic writings from this period of such erudite figures as Walter Scott, Charles Lamb, and Mary Shelley maintain the connection between practice and criticism, though a decline in the volume of essays and reviews produced from beyond the genre is perceptible across the whole century.[9] In many respects, criticism of the genre turns to burlesque at this historical juncture, with the timely publication of both Austen's posthumous *Northanger Abbey* and Peacock's *Nightmare Abbey* in 1818. In these works, as in many earlier critical writings on the genre, a familiarity with both literary convention and the idiosyncrasies of stylistic practitioners is assumed on the part of the reader, though the effect is not so much to demonize as to satirize, the lampoon seemingly generating no significant protest on the part of any "lachrymose and morbid gentleman, of . . . note in the literary world."[10]

Such gentlemen, aficionados of the genre, did not however expire with the first flush of its writings in the second decade of the nineteenth century. Driven not so much underground as out of the public eye by the rise of a materialistic age increasingly concerned with the fetishising of new technology, the exposure of perceived social wrongs, and the aggrandisement or embarrassment of imperial enterprise, Gothic criticism became the preserve of more minor monthly magazines, where revivals of folkloric themes, couched in a semblance of the language of the emerging discipline of sociology, might be juxtaposed with an original ghost story from the pen of J. S. Le Fanu, Charles Dickens, or Wilkie Collins. There is no single study of the genre, though, of equal topical weight to, say, Margaret

Oliphant's or H. L. Mansel's response to the Sensation Novel, or Elizabeth Lynn Linton's study of "Candour in English Fiction."[11] The Woman Question was but one of the issues that dominated the literary debate of the mid- to late century, its implications being debated variously through rational dress, comparative manners, the Sensation Novel, New Woman fiction, and the so-called Problem Novel. Arguably, no Gothic novel generated a level of social fascination equivalent to the products of these topical issues of the day, and so the genre remained a mode of fiction first and foremost rather than an arena in which to mobilize stridently the discords and fear of culture. Quite simply, Gothic, with its residual associations of history and the supernatural, did not readily lend itself to the contemporary, at least until the end of the century reintroduced a popular conception of barbarism into the context of a society readily perceived as too "refined and polished."

Issues, rather than generic form, are thus the enduring focus of the post-Gothic interregnum which spanned the breadth of the nineteenth century, until the *fin de siècle* and stylish decadence made the genre variously a manifesto for, and a symptom of, decadence. Outside of this revival, Gothic fails to inform or be exemplified in even broad studies of the present and future of fiction, such as Henry James's "The Art of Fiction" (1884).[12] The ghost story and the Gothic novel appear little, if at all, in the article-length criticism of the nineteenth century, though their publication as both fictions and as reviews associated with specific works, continues throughout the period. In major acts of criticism, though, one might perceive this as the dismissal of irrelevance, of nontopicality: Gothic may still be both written and read, but it is seemingly no longer at the cutting edge of the debate upon style or culture. It has, in a sense, become subcultural, beneath the critical notice of a literary intelligentsia who, paradoxically, continue to exploit the genre's conventions in works that may be as much experimental in style as they are profitable financially.[13]

This Victorian interregnum, though, has been superseded not merely by the other two major divisions of Gothic criticism—the generic survey and the narrower, specialist study—but also, in the late twentieth century, by a revival of the belletrist tradition itself. This revival, though, takes criticism of the genre out of the essentially public, nonacademic domain in which it had existed in the eighteenth and nineteenth centuries, and relocates it primarily (though not exclusively) within the publication systems of Western academia. Gothic, though still a highly popular and public form of fiction, has increasingly become criticized through literary theory, stylistic history, and psychological thought, even in the more accessible arena of the review. Though volume-length, single author works have been highly influential in the development of the criticism of the genre, it is important to acknowledge the presence of a substantial body of shorter works, effectively the inheritors of the brevity that characterized much of the early belletrist criticism. Gothic, though often criticized in the scholarly monograph, has returned to the journal—or to volume format publications whose customary eclecticism recalls earlier, serial publications.

In part this is a consequence of the rise of the formal academic conference, and the institution of published conference proceedings—the constituent articles of which are conventionally rendered at shorter length than the chapters commissioned for edited volumes of criticism. Though the genre has often been a component of academic conferences (particularly in the area of Romanticism) from their rise in popularity in postwar America and Europe, the existence of specifically Gothic symposia is a relatively recent phenomena: notable landmarks in the definition of the Gothic as a discrete field include the International Conferences on the Fantastic in the Arts, instituted in the 1980s, and the biannual conferences of the International Gothic Association, founded in 1991. Both have underwritten the publication of volume format proceedings, and the success of these has been echoed in the books produced by nonserial Gothic conferences organized by other bodies.[14] Strictly speaking, conference papers, whether published or delivered orally, are not belletrist. They characteristically lack the anecdotal ambience of the eighteenth-century tradition, and favour instead, for the most part, detailed exemplification and analysis. Definitive or provocative statements upon the nature of the genre, its prospects and limitations would tend, inevitably, to be delivered at greater length, though such matters as are raised in plenary lectures do find themselves in such works, where they may serve a similar keynote function. Belletrism, though, survives in the frequently eclectic and diverse composition of such collections, their appeal in many cases embracing not merely the breadth of historical production but also the literary genre's diversification into art, film, and theatre.

Journal publication, though, remains central to the dissemination of Gothic criticism. The relevance of Gothic form, as well as the detail of specific Gothic texts, has ensured that studies of the genre have frequently been embodied in academic journals whose main focus remains in theoretical areas such as gender studies or psychoanalysis, or is determined by historical or generic considerations. There have been few attempts, though, to maintain a single-focus Gothic journal. Though a scholarly periodical entitled *Gothic* was published in Baton Rouge from 1986, and a broader journal entitled *Udolpho* (which featured poetry and original artwork alongside critical articles) was produced in the 1990s by the Gothic Society, neither survived into the twenty-first century. *Gothic Studies*, the refereed journal of the International Gothic Association began publication in 1999, and continues to publish articles and reviews, alternating between general issues which examine a variety of Gothic topics and more focused guest-edited special issues on specific topics, authors, or periods.[15]

The literary preface, which essentially initiated the belletrist response to Gothic through Walpole's teasing forgery, also retains a currency in contemporary Gothic criticism. Though the anthology of Gothic stories, a popular medium for the dissemination of shorter works in the genre since the time of Montague Summers in the 1930s, did not immediately initiate a tradition of critical prefaces, such a feature does distinguish the more scholarly productions distributed from the late twentieth century.[16] Noteworthy contributions to this area of the field include Chris Baldick's Introduction to the 1992 *Oxford Book of Gothic Tales*, with its succinct tabulation of Gothic preoccupations and concentration upon the role of history in the reception of the genre, as well as Alan Bissett's exploration of the connections between the genre and Scottish culture in his preface to the 2001 anthology, *Damage Land: New Scottish Gothic Fiction*.[17] Such prefaces are short but indicative, Impressionist rather than analytical, and in a sense render the generic implications of the fictional work to follow in much the same way as Walpole's fictional translator, William Marshall. They are in the best tradition of the early Gothic: seemingly outside of the work, they create a fiction of context, a convention of interpretation—a precondition for the reader, even where that reader has, unlike Walpole's contemporaries, prior expectations of the genre.

The belletrist tradition, in its historical manifestation at least, forms part of what Robert Mighall and Chris Baldick consider to be the "shamefaced antiquarianism" that preceded the more belligerent and assertive "modern phase of Gothic studies."[18] It can be argued, though, based upon the evidence of who, exactly, was writing both Gothic fiction and Gothic criticism, that this mode of stylized antiquarianism was anything but "shamefaced." Baldick and Mighall's (2000) essay-length survey of Gothic criticism, though a significant landmark in the genre's introspection, is as prejudiced as the "modern" phase of criticism which they themselves disparage as being implicated in a left-leaning and allegedly libertarian critique of Victorian repression. In a sense, they too have Gothicized the past, not with repression necessarily, but certainly with a dismissal based upon perceived primitivism and dilettante irrelevance.[19] Gazing upon their division of two phases of Gothic criticism, the culturally naïve and the politically implicated, they find nothing to please them—at least until the act of criticism turns inward upon itself to critique the critical text and its theoretical basis over and above its alleged focus upon specific textual or generic issues.

This critique, though, does not apparently form part of the mission of earlier twentieth-century criticism, whether or not one adopts the rather artificial demarcations imposed within Baldick and Mighall's provocative essay. Moreover, the frequently observed contention that much criticism is committed to a view that Gothic is subversive to, or in revolt against, bourgeois hegemony, is not always borne out in the earliest twentieth-century surveys of the genre. These works are, inevitably, influenced by the belletrist and antiquarian traditions in which their authors were well versed. They are, essentially, generic surveys, in which political presence is muted beneath the need to clarify the detail, if not the existence, of an unfashionable though remarkably extensive body of writing. The first manifestation of Gothic criticism in the twentieth century, though often internally divided on thematic lines, took the form of extensive generic surveys rather than studies of single authors. Gothic, as it were, becomes interesting and worthy of study because of its overall persistence rather than through any authorial singularity. At this early stage, Gothic is a complex of issues and components: it is later criticism that divides these into the more discrete themes that inform both doctoral research and eventual monograph publication today

As Mighall and Baldick note, academic Gothic criticism arguably begins in the twentieth century with a complex of writings published between 1921 and 1938.[20] It is worth acknowledging, though, that Dorothy Scarborough had published a monograph on the representation of the supernatural in fiction as early as 1917, and that this work, not mentioned by Baldick and Mighall, directed attention to many of the recurrent landscapes, as well as characters, of Gothic fiction.[21] Edith Birkhead's *The Tale of Terror* (1921), with which Baldick and Mighall begin their critical chronology, is primarily an historical, author- and theme-based survey rather than an explanation for the development of the genre. Conservative as this may be, Birkhead's volume does bravely acknowledge the existence of an American Gothic discernible beyond customary British eighteenth- and nineteenth-century practice.[22] Eino Railo's influential *The Haunted Castle*, published six years later, owes a great deal to Birkhead's pioneering work, though his division of the survey into chapters based upon recurrent components such as "The Criminal Monk" allows a more discursive argument to develop. This latter, though, is at times compromised by what could be considered a reductive drive to anchor the thematics of Gothic upon the precedent of Shakespearean drama.[23] Railo's structural paradigm, and, indeed his attempts to legitimize the Gothic through the authority of an author and a genre already given credibility in the modern academy, almost certainly influenced in turn Mario Praz's *The Romantic Agony* (1933), which, in proclaiming Romanticism "an approximate term" revitalized again the potential dismissal of Gothic as merely a crude phase of Romantic sensibility.[24] The tendency to compromise Gothic with Romanticism is persistent, its influence extending beyond the 1930s to later works such as Robert Kiely's formalist survey, *The Romantic Novel in England* (1972),[25] though it might be said to have been inverted in later works which read the Romantic as being effectively Gothicized through its own internalization of the genre.[26]

Though the influence of other early twentieth-century critics such as Montague Summers cannot be discounted, nor indeed the synthesis of earlier works provided within Devendra Varma's *The Gothic Flame* (1957) be discounted, it is nevertheless important to establish a point at which the generic survey becomes a thoroughly modern and systematic critical medium.[27] David Punter's *The Literature of Terror* (1980) is not the first survey of the Gothic from its origins, and via Romanticism and America, to a perceived present, but it is possibly the most influential. It is the text which introduced many of the published Gothic critics of the 1990s to the genre when they were undergraduates. Discernibly a product of the liberal preoccupations and rising theories of the 1960s and 1970s, *The Literature of Terror* combines psychoanalytic thought with social consciousness in order to establish the genre as a serious attempt "to come to grips with and to probe matters of concern" to contemporary society.[28] Its rejection of the assumption that Gothic is nothing more than escapism is subtle, and the book's theoretical context is less intrusive than, for example, Rosemary Jackson's psychoanalytical adaptation of Todorov's theories in her *Fantasy*, published twelve months later.[29] *The Literature of Terror* is, also, the text which extended Gothic from its customary end-point in the nineteenth-century *fin de siècle* to more recent publications, many of which might not have otherwise been classified as generically Gothic. This extension includes possibly the first serious considerations of Walter de la Mare and Algernon Blackwood; a significant reading of the horror film; and the acknowledgement of a vibrant and *contemporary* Gothic tradition in the works of, among others, Oates, Pynchon, Ballard, Coover, and Carter through what Punter terms "Modern perceptions of the barbaric."[30] This latter definition, together with his original coda in pursuit of a feasible theory of the Gothic, underlines the systematic approach which distinguishes this survey from those of twenty-three, if not forty to fifty years earlier. Revised and reissued in a two-volume Second Edition by the same publisher in 1996, *The Literature of Terror* remains one of the two most influential survey texts of the late twentieth century, and is an essential reference—or departure—point for work at all levels.

Though other critics have subsequently published commendable surveys of the Gothic—Richard Davenport-Hines on the breadth of the genre, or the shorter temporal focuses of Emma Clery or Robert Miles, for example[31]—or have facilitated volumes of essays which aspire to similar coverage—the editorship of Jerrold E. Hogle, Marie Mulvey-Roberts, and, again, David Punter, is noteworthy here[32]—the main rival to the supremacy of *The Literature of Terror* comes from a relatively short single-authored work. Fred Botting's paperback *Gothic*, published as part of the established New Critical Idiom series in 1996, has attained a particular level of influence among undergraduate readers in particular, in part on account of its relative brevity, accessibility of argument and, inevitably, low cost. It is far from a simple reiteration of earlier theories of the Gothic, though, even though its coverage from the origins of the genre to recent developments in postmodernism and science fiction revisit territory already explored, for example, by Punter and others. The influence of *Gothic* is perhaps best indicated in the critical cliché that has arisen from the very first sentence of the work: "Gothic signifies a writing of excess."[33] It is not merely this, of course—Botting's introduction betrays a commitment also to generic "Transgression" and "Diffusion" before summarizing the response of "Criticism"—but that opening gambit has come to function as a definition of the genre far more generalized, and thus much more easily applied to disparate material, than any convention of character construction or plot locale. This now widely accepted definition is, in a sense, Botting's great achievement—far more than that attributed to him by Robert Miles, namely the reconstitution of Gothic as "Modernity's great tradition" rather than its subcultural or subversive antithesis.[34]

The succinct definition of the Gothic is, indeed, a preoccupation of the generic survey tradition, and the overall message of Botting's *Gothic* as defined by Miles echoes the tendency of recent criticism to formulate textual participation in the genre by attributes other than character, recurrent plot scenario, or physical location. Though there are as many potential definitions of the Gothic as there are critics to assert them, one recent contribution, from the pen of Robert Mighall, this time writing as a Victorianist rather than as a historian of critical discourse, stands out as a worthy counterpart to Botting's atemporal "excess." Mighall's contention that Gothic may be defined independently of any supernatural trappings is hardly novel—Punter's 1980 reading of Dickens's *Oliver Twist* (1837–9) defines that novel's Gothic context through violence rather than the occult, for example—but his assertion that Gothic is "a 'mode' rather than a genre, the principal defining structure of which is its attitude to the past and its unwelcome legacies," surely is.[35] Though critics have noted before that the past, particularly the repressed or dispossessed past, whether political or psychological, is inclined to return in Gothic fictions, none has ever placed this preoccupation in a position of defining centrality. Here and elsewhere, Mighall is perceptibly hostile to what he sees as the domination of Gothic criticism by psychoanalysis and its consequences: arguably, though, the rise of a historicist school of Gothic criticism may potentially deflect the critical debate away from textuality, this time not towards the psychology of the author but the intricacies of generic definition on both a syntagmatic and a paradigmatic plane.[36]

That process of definition and refinement is underpinned not merely by the tradition of generic surveys but also by way of the focused monograph, the most recent development in Gothic criticism. The antecedents of this area of the critical field, where for the most part a single author considers a specific topic, text, or writer within Gothic, taking for granted the pre-existence and accepted definition of both the genre and its canon, inevitably lie in the generic survey.[37] The scholarly monograph, and its fragmented counterpart, the critical article or book chapter, are in effect synecdoches of the broader drive of Gothic criticism, namely the construction of lineage and antecedent, temporal or otherwise, as an aid to generic identity, expansion, or definition.

Output in this quarter of the critical field is, inevitably, substantial, and any significant texts identified here can be representative only of one view of the myriad possibilities presented as the Gothic is placed under even more intense and directed scrutiny. Certain preoccupations will inevitably stand out at the centre of this complex pattern of definition and accretion, their often obscured origins being tacitly accepted and built upon by scholars working independently towards a larger, though not necessarily formal or systematic project. Possibly the most significant of these recurrent preoccupations is the Female Gothic, defined first by Ellen Moers in chapter 5 of *Literary Women* (1976).[38] This concept, which embraces both female authorship and the characteristic plots of a fictional tradition influenced by female psychological and political issues, is central to both generic definitions of the Gothic, to the wider problems of canon formation and resistance to the restraints of canon, as well as to broader women's issues beyond literary criticism. Most recently, it has informed a lively dialectic in a special issue of *Gothic Studies*, edited by Andrew Smith and Diana Wallace, with a critical gaze that englobes writing from the 1780s to contemporary lesbian fiction and builds significantly upon the range of works identified in *Literary Women*.[39] Even where the debate is not specifically enjoined to a revisitation of Moers's subdivision of the genre, the influence of Female Gothic, both as a specific style of writing and as a mode of criticizing that and other writings, cannot be ignored. This is certainly the case where the continuation of the Gothic into modernity is being considered, or where narratives of female danger are under scrutiny.[40] The Female Gothic, and its critical revisions and revisitations, remain arguably the silent context of broader projects in gender studies and the Gothic, and to a certain extent of Queer Studies also.[41] Notably, Baldick and Mighall, though appreciative of the positive outcome of the interaction of feminism with Gothic criticism, explicitly condemn the application of the Female Gothic as a restriction upon what might be said in criticism.[42]

Gothic criticism has resisted, to a certain extent, narrowly theological readings of the genre, though the cultural anti-Catholicism of much (and, particularly, earlier) novels in the tradition has been acknowledged. Victor Sage's important and liberal *Horror Fiction in the Protestant Tradition* (1998), which covers Gothic from its earliest days to postwar fiction, has its forbears in the rather more sectarian writings of Mary Muriel Tarr (*Catholicism in Gothic Fiction*, 1946) and Montague Summers (*The Gothic Quest*, 1938), the latter study (as Baldick and Mighall observe) struggling to square Protestant polemic in the fictional texts with its author's own Romantic and nostalgic view of the Faith.[43] As an adjunct to cultural anti-Catholicism, though, one might note also the demonization of other racial and religious identities, most notably Judaism, in the Gothic fiction of the nineteenth century in particular. Curiously, there is seemingly no consensus between these two forms of cultural Othering or racism: Roman Catholicism is attacked largely through its institutions (the convent, the Inquisition) its distinctive practices and ceremonies (the Confessional, in particular) and its representatives (sexually rapacious priests and vindictive nuns), where for the most part the Jew is reviled as a money-lender with an alien physiognomy. Carol Margaret Davison's *Anti-Semitism in British Gothic Literature* (2004) is an excellent introduction to this aspect of Gothic Othering, though the work of Jules Zanger (and its parallels in the meticulous physiognomical criticism of Ernest Fontana and Daniel Pick) cannot be ignored.[44]

These, of course, are among the cultural implications of—or encoded into—the Gothic. Such works chart the prejudices expressed in a tradition of writing, or make its texts available for appropriation by critical institutions mindful of the burden of proof, the need to illustrate a contention with examples derived from canonical as well as neglected texts. This is not to say that focused criticism of the Gothic has ignored those componential stylistic features within the text whose presence has historically permitted the application of a generic label. Critical appreciation continues to address those aesthetic issues which associated the early Gothic with the Burkean Sublime, whether these be implicated within the city, within more abstract conceptions of ocular or psychological darkness, or indeed with the enduring lure of exotic locations in the crafting of contemporary fiction.[45] Equally persistent as the construction of appropriately Gothic milieu is the attention paid to other textual features customarily regarded as componential to the genre, such as the Double or doppelganger, the ghost- and short-story traditions, and the Gothic Hero.[46] There has been a similar proliferation in the writing of books dedicated to discrete national schools of Gothic writing,[47] to the cinematic manifestation of the genre,[48] and, finally, to the explication of the works of those perceived as the major fictional authors in the field.[49] One final resource must be acknowledged: the critical breadth associated with the bibliographies and masterlists published with distinction by highly focused scholars such as Benjamin F. Fisher, Frederick Frank, and Ann B. Tracy.[50]

Gothic criticism is now, effectively, around 240 years old. In that period, it has changed greatly, and has moved from being an offshoot of dilettante reviewing to a highly professional scholastic activity, solidly located within the modern academy. At both of these extremes, Gothic criticism has endowed certain fictional texts with the imprimatur of genre, and marginalized others through their effective association with subgroups or liminal areas of specialism. Methodologically, it has moved from a text-centred antiquarianism, through a surveyor's commitment to historical antecedent, homogeneity, and continuity, towards a specialist's psychobiography and social psychology, to materialism, discourse, and gender studies and, perversely, back again to the novel as the focus of the critical reading. Yet, it has not undertaken these modifications in a linear fashion, maintaining instead a coexistence of methodologies and interests alongside a fairly stable body of "classic" texts, and an expanding heritage of newcomers. Gothic, far from being subcultural, is seemingly canonical in an age without canon, and criticism of the apparently ephemeral texts of the genre is concretized in expensive hard-backed volumes, written or edited by international scholars reputable within and beyond the Gothic field. Gothic criticism is a success, as saleable as the texts it purports to criticize or to understand.

However, the success of Gothic criticism might well constitute a danger to the future vitality, both of this branch of critical practice and to the body of fictional texts to which it is so intimately linked. The risk does not arise from any threat of marginalization, but rather from the canonical status which Gothic has accreted to itself in its teaching as much as in its criticism and textuality. As academic teaching in the Gothic becomes more widespread, so the pressure to direct formal publishing to areas of mass appeal becomes more acute. The Gothic is too rapidly becoming, for example, Ann Radcliffe, Bram Stoker, and Anne Rice, rather than Clara Reeve, Algernon Blackwood, and Poppy Z. Brite. This is not say that these other writers are excluded—scholarly revivals of the unreprinted works of Horace Walpole, Charlotte Dacre, and L. T. C. Rolt, for example, have been welcome—but it is becoming perceptibly more difficult to publish outside of the familiar (and already critically well supported) Gothic paths beloved of undergraduate students.[51] This is true of both critical writing, and of scholarly reissues of fictional texts. The success of Gothic teaching may well lead to the atrophying of Gothic criticism, and to the releasing of even more scholarly editions of *Frankenstein* and *Dracula* at a time when Roche's *The Children of the Abbey* and M. G. Lewis's *Tales of Terror and Wonder* remain difficult to obtain for the bulk of scholars. This shaping and possible restriction of the discipline, for the benefit of an expanded knowledge as much as to obtain a healthy quota of student participants, is the challenge that must be taken up in the critical practice of Gothic in the twenty-first century.

## Notes

1. Horace Walpole, "Preface to the First Edition," *The Castle of Otranto* (Oxford: Oxford University Press [1764] 1982) 3–6, at 3, 5, 4.
2. Walpole, "Preface to the Second Edition," *The Castle of Otranto*, 7–12 at 7.
3. *Monthly Review* (May 1765), 394, quoted in Emma Clery, "Against Gothic," in Victor Sage and Allan Lloyd Smith, eds, *Gothick: Origins and Innovations* (Amsterdam: Rodopi, 1994) 34–43 at 34.
4. *Gentleman's Magazine*, 56 (1786), 327, reprinted in E. J. Clery and Robert Miles, eds, *Gothic Documents: a Sourcebook, 1700–1820* (Manchester: Manchester University Press, 2000) 181. *Gothic Documents* provides an excellent condensation of much of the lively debate associated with the early Gothic, from its origins in translations of Classical thought and the

eighteenth-century Graveyard School to nineteenth-century retrospectives. For a well-informed overview of the interaction between British and Continental practitioners, often expressed through prefaces as well as in journals, see Terry Hale, "Translation in distress: cultural misappropriation and the construction of the Gothic," in Avril Horner, ed., *European Gothic: a Spirited Exchange, 1760–1960* (Manchester: Manchester University Press, 2002) 17–38.

5. Ann Radcliffe, "On the supernatural in poetry," *New Monthly Magazine*, 16/1 (1826), 145–52, reprinted in Clery and Miles, eds, *Gothic Documents*, 163–72.
6. Nathan Drake, "On Gothic superstition" and "On objects of terror," from *Literary Hours: Sketches, Critical and Narrative* (1798), reproduced in Clery and Miles, eds, *Gothic Documents*, 155–63.
7. Drake discusses Walpole's unequivocally Gothic drama *The Mysterious Mother* (1768), but finds scenes of terror also in Smollet, Collins, and the ballad tradition. See "On objects of terror," 162.
8. This decline was experienced most emphatically at the metropolitan centre of British culture. It is important to note, though, that the Gothic maintained a significant presence in the provinces well into the nineteenth century, as testified by the often substantial Gothic holdings of the circulating libraries and their popularity with readers of all social and educational levels. An excellent account of provincial library culture in its specific relation to Gothic is to be found in Franz Potter, *Twilight of a Genre: Art and Trade in Gothic Fiction, 1814–1834* (unpublished Ph.D. dissertation, University of East Anglia, Norwich, 2003).
9. Curiously, in *Night Visitors*, her pioneering study of the ghost story, Julia Briggs makes no mention of Shelley's "On ghosts" (1824), though she does comment on the importance of Scott's "On the supernatural in fictitious composition" (1827) and Lamb's "Witches and other night fears" (1821). See Julia Briggs, *Night Visitors: the Rise and Fall of the English Ghost Story* (London: Faber, 1977) 34–7. The three essays are reproduced in Clery and Miles, eds, *Gothic Documents*, 277–86.
10. The description is that applied to the superbly gloomy Kantian visionary Mr Flosky in *Nightmare Abbey*. See Thomas Love Peacock, *Nightmare Abbey*, bound with *Crotchet Castle* (Harmondsworth: Penguin, 1981) 37–124 at 44.
11. Margaret Oliphant, "Sensation novels," *Blackwood's* 91 (1862), 564–84; H. L. Mansel, "Sensation novels," *Quarterly Review* 113 (1863), 481–514; E. L. Linton, "Candour in English Fiction," *New Review* 2 (1890), 10–14.
12. James's article, published in *Longman's Magazine* in September 1884 is a response to Walter Besant's lecture of the same title, delivered in the same year at the Royal Institution. Both works are extracted in Stephen Regan, ed., *The Nineteenth-Century Novel: a Critical Reader* (London: Routledge, 2001) 69–78 and 62–8 respectively.
13. Consider, for example, James himself, who published *The Turn of the Screw* in 1898.
14. See, for example, Michelle Langford, ed., *Contours of the Fantastic: Selected Essays from the Eighth International Conference on the Fantastic in the Arts* (New York: Greenwood Press, 1994); Victor Sage and Allan Lloyd Smith, eds,

*Gothick: Origins and Innovations* (Amsterdam: Rodopi, 1994), which consists of papers from the First International Gothic Association Conference, held in Norwich in 1991; Karen Sayer and Rosemary Mitchell, eds, *Victorian Gothic* (Leeds: Leeds Centre for Victorian Studies, 2003), containing selected papers from the Victorian Gothic Colloquium organized by the Centre in 2003.

15. These include, for example, "Romanticism and the 'New Gothic'," *Gothic Studies* 3/1 (2001), edited by Jerrold E. Hogle, and "Italy and the Gothic," *Gothic Studies* 7/2 (2005), guest edited by Massimiliano Demata. *Gothic Studies* has also published selected papers from the International Gothic Association Conferences at Halifax, Nova Scotia (Vol. 2/1, 2000), Vancouver (Vols 4/2 and 5/1, 2002–3) and Liverpool (Vol. 7/1, 2005).
16. Montague Summers' *The Supernatural Omnibus* (London: Victor Gollancz, 1931), a substantial hard-backed volume with a heavy Victorian bias and a pretence of educated respectability, is probably the first example of a convention in edited Gothic publishing which survives to the present day.
17. Chris Baldick, ed., *The Oxford Book of Gothic Tales* (1992, reprinted Oxford: University Press, 2001), xi–xxiii; Alan Bissett, ed., " 'The dead can sing': an introduction," in *Damage Land: New Scottish Gothic Fiction* (Edinburgh: Polygon, 2001) 1–8.
18. Chris Baldick and Robert Mighall, "Gothic criticism" in David Punter, ed., *A Companion to the Gothic* (Oxford: Blackwell, 2000) 209–28 at 209.
19. Ibid., 210. Baldick and Mighall's argument owes much, it may be argued, to Foucault's "We 'Other Victorians'," the opening chapter of the first volume of *The History of Sexuality*. See Michel Foucault, *The History of Sexuality: An Introduction* (London: Penguin, 1984) 1–13.
20. Baldick and Mighall, "Gothic criticism," 211–21.
21. Dorothy Scarborough, *The Supernatural in Modern English Fiction* (New York: Putnam, 1917).
22. Edith Birkhead, *The Tale of Terror: a Study of the Gothic Romance* (New York: Russell and Russell, [1921] 1963).
23. Eino Railo, *The Haunted Castle: a Study of the Elements of English Romanticism* (New York: Humanities Press, [1927] 1964).
24. Mario Praz, *The Romantic Agony*, trans. Angus Davidson (Oxford: Oxford University Press, [1933] 1970) 1.
25. Robert Kiely, *The Romantic Novel in England* (Cambridge, MA: Harvard University Press, 1972).
26. See, for example, Michael Gamer, *Romanticism and the Gothic: Genre, Reception, and Canon Formation* (Cambridge: Cambridge University Press, 2000).
27. Montague Summers, *The Gothic Quest: a History of the Gothic Novel* (New York: Russell and Russell, [1938] 1964); Devendra P. Varma, *The Gothic Flame: Being a History of the Gothic Novel in England: Its Origins, Efflorescence, Disintegration, and Residuary Influence* (1957; New York: Russell and Russell, 1966).

28. David Punter, *The Literature of Terror: a History of Gothic Fictions from 1765 to the Present Day* (London: Longman, 1980) 402; cf. Second Edition, 2 vols (London: Addison Wesley Longman, 1996) Vol. 2, 181.
29. Punter, *The Literature of Terror*, First Edition, 402; Rosemary Jackson, *Fantasy: the Literature of Subversion* (London: Methuen, 1981).
30. Punter, *The Literature of Terror*, First Edition, 373–401. Volume Two of the Second Edition extends this premise yet further through two concluding chapters, "Contemporary Gothic transformations" and "Mutations of terror: theory and the Gothic."
31. Richard Davenport-Hines, *Gothic: Four Hundred Years of Excess, Horror, Evil and Ruin* (London: Fourth Estate, 1998); E. J. Clery, *The Rise of Supernatural Fiction, 1762–1800* (Cambridge: Cambridge University Press, 1995); Robert Miles, *Gothic Writing, 1750–1820: a Genealogy* (London: Routledge, 1993).
32. Jerrold E. Hogle, ed., *The Cambridge Companion to Gothic Fiction* (Cambridge: Cambridge University Press, 2002); Marie Mulvey-Roberts, ed., *The Handbook to Gothic Literature* (Basingstoke: Macmillan—now Palgrave Macmillan, 1998); David Punter, ed., *A Companion to the Gothic* (Oxford: Blackwell, 2000).
33. Fred Botting, *Gothic* (1996; London: Routledge, 2002) 1.
34. Robert Miles, "*Gothic* (The New Critical Idiom) by Fred Botting," *Gothic Studies* 1/1 (August 1999) 119–20 at 120.
35. Punter, *The Literature of Terror*, First Edition, 217–23; Robert Mighall, *A Geography of Victorian Gothic: Mapping History's Nightmares* (Oxford: Oxford University Press, 1999) xix.
36. See Mighall, *A Geography of Victorian Gothic*, xi–xiv; Baldick and Mighall, "Gothic criticism," 216, 225–6.
37. Mighall's own work, perversely, bridges the two traditions, in that it both accepts the existence of Gothic and then imposes further coordinates upon the current understanding of the genre's limits. These coordinates effectively bring other texts inside both the genre and its critical apparatus, forcing a redefinition. For all this, the focus of the book is avowedly not the Gothic as a conception but a complex of related cultural issues: the sexological and degenerate history of the nineteenth century.
38. Ellen Moers, *Literary Women: the Great Writers* (London: The Women's Press, [1976] 1978) 90–110.
39. Andrew Smith and Diana Wallace, eds, "Female Gothic," *Gothic Studies* 6/1 (May 2004) 1–130, *passim*.
40. See, for example, Susanne Becker, *Gothic Forms of Feminine Fictions* (Manchester: Manchester University Press, 1999) 8–10; Michelle Massé, *In the Name of Love: Women, Masochism and the Gothic* (Ithaca: Cornell University Press, 1992).
41. See, for example, Kelly Hurley, *The Gothic Body: Sexuality, Materialism and Degeneration at the Fin de Siècle* (Cambridge: Cambridge University Press, 1996).
42. Baldick and Mighall, "Gothic criticism," 227.

43. Mary Muriel Tarr, *Catholicism in Gothic Fiction: a Study of the Nature and Function of Catholic Materials in Gothic Fiction in England, 1762–1820* (Washington: Catholic University of America Press, 1946); Baldick and Mighall, "Gothic criticism," 216–17.
44. Carol Margaret Davison, *Anti-Semitism and British Gothic Literature* (Basingstoke: Palgrave Macmillan, 2004); Jules Zanger, "A sympathetic vibration: Dracula and the Jews," *ELT* 34 (1991), 33–43; Ernest Fontana, "Lombroso's criminal man and Stoker's *Dracula*," *Victorian Newsletter* 66 (1984), 25–7; Daniel Pick, *Faces of Degeneration: a European Disorder, c. 1848–c.1918* (Cambridge: Cambridge University Press, 1989).
45. See, for example, Richard J. Walker, "Blooming corpses: burying the literary corpus in the modern city," *Gothic Studies* 4/1 (May 2002) 1–13; Maggie Kilgour, *The Rise of the Gothic Novel* (London: Routledge, 1995); Joseph Grixti, *Terrors of Uncertainty: the Cultural Contexts of Horror Fiction* (London: Routledge, 1989); David Punter, "Arundhati Roy and the House of History," in Andrew Smith and William Hughes, eds, *Empire and the Gothic: the Politics of Genre* (Basingstoke: Palgrave Macmillan, 2003) 192–207.
46. Linda Dryden, *The Modern Gothic and Literary Doubles* (Basingstoke: Palgrave Macmillan, 2003); Elton E. Smith and Robert Haas, eds, *The Haunted Mind: the Supernatural in Victorian Literature* (Lanham: Scarecrow Press, 1989); Masao Miyoshi, *The Divided Self* (New York: New York University Press, 1969).
47. See, for example, Bruce Stewart, ed., *That Other World: the Supernatural and the Fantastic in Irish Literature and its Contexts*, 2 Vols (Gerrards Cross: Colin Smyth, 1988); Neil Cornwell, "Pushkin and Odoevsky: the 'Afro-Finnish' theme in Russian Gothic," in Smith and Hughes, eds, *Empire and the Gothic*, 69–87; Avril Horner, ed., *European Gothic: a Spirited Exchange, 1760–1960, passim.*
48. Andrew Tudor, *Monsters and Mad Scientists: a Cultural History of the Horror Movie* (Cambridge, MA: Basil Blackwell, 1989); Alain Silver, *More Things Than Are Dreamt Of: Masterpieces of Supernatural Horror from Mary Shelley to Stephen King in Literature and Film* (New York: Limelight Editions, 1994).
49. Esther Schor, ed., *The Cambridge Companion to Mary Shelley* (Cambridge: Cambridge University Press, 2003); Victor Sage, *Le Fanu's Gothic: the Rhetoric of Darkness* (Basingstoke: Palgrave Macmillan, 2004); Robert Miles, *Ann Radcliffe: the Great Enchantress* (Manchester: Manchester University Press, 1995).
50. Benjamin F. Fisher, IV, *The Gothic's Gothic: Study Aids to the Tale of Terror* (New York: Garland Press, 1987); Frederick F. Frank, *Gothic Fiction: a Masterlist of Criticism and Research* (Westport CT.: Meckler, 1987); Ann B. Tracy, *The Gothic Novel, 1790–1813: Plot Summaries and Index to Motifs* (Lexington: University Press of Kentucky, 1981).
51. Horace Walpole, *The Castle of Otranto* and *The Mysterious Mother*, ed. Frederick S. Frank (Peterborough: Broadview, [1764 & 1781] 2003); Charlotte Dacre, *Zofloya; or, The Moor: a Romance of the Fifteenth Century*, ed. Adriana Craciun (Peterborough: Broadview, [1806] 1997); L. T. C. Rolt, *Sleep No More: Railway, Canal and Other Stories of the Supernatural*, ed. Susan Hill (Stroud: Alan Sutton, [1948] 1996).

# 2
# Theorizing the Gothic

*Jerrold E. Hogle*

The sustained analytical teaching of "Gothic" fiction (now including film) has developed slowly and relatively recently, to say the least. For most of the twentieth century, despite its continuous production of Gothic tales, plays, and motion pictures, Gothic fiction-making has only rarely been deemed worthy of serious scholarly and student attention. One reason, of course, starting in the late eighteenth century soon after Gothic fiction began, has been the critical consignment of it to the "low culture" of "pulp" literature, which has long bred "an inherent distaste" among most academics "for a genre at once too visceral (*and* [supposedly] too ephemeral) and too popular."[1] This literary class system, too, has only been reinforced by the growing dominance of the so-called "New Criticism" from the 1930s to the mid-1960s. This mode of analysis based on an explicit theory of literary language, though never rigidly unified across its practitioners, commonly values the "organic" text: a tightly woven interaction among dense symbols whose conflicting overtones, while clearly in play, can be worked into a unity built out of the contradictions, a *concordia discours* peculiar to the truly "literary," that establishes the best literature as dense high art within clear genres designed primarily for a coherent aesthetic response. Under this rubric, increasingly basic to the teaching of literature since the 1930s, Gothic works have understandably been set aside as "inferior." After all, since Horace Walpole recommended a "blend" of "the two kinds of romance, the ancient and the modern," as the basis of "a Gothic Story" in his 1765 Preface to *The Castle of Otranto*,[2] the Gothic has frequently displayed generic instability, a visible and unresolved conflict between retrograde and progressive discourses, from aristocratic and middle-class ideologies (as one example) to alchemy and modern science (as another), that prevents its ironies from ever being organically interfused and its monsters and ghosts from reconciling their tensions between death-seeking and life-affirming tendencies. Even the verbal style of most Gothic works, combining the hyperbolic with the "probable" as Walpole urged, has seemed too much of a pastiche to be taught extensively as part of "great literature" at Western universities, at least until the late 1970s.

True, there have been exceptional defences of the "best" Gothic in studies based on some assumptions from the New Criticism,[3] even as those same assumptions are still used on occasion to expose inartistic disunity in the Gothic generally.[4] More common in the early-to-mid twentieth century, however, have been "old historicist" affirmations, occasionally linked to the "history of ideas" best defined by Arthur O. Lovejoy in the 1930s and since. In this view, generally, the rise and survival of the Gothic, with all the conflicts on the surface of its texts, gains its coherence from its reflection of a pervasive deep unity among certain Western beliefs during a given period, or across several periods, of time.[5] For Devendra P. Varma in 1957 and Maurice Levy in 1968, Enlightenment rationalism and revolution have so emptied out the symbols of a supplanted medieval Christianity that the "Gothic" has arisen to provide individual imaginative access to what is left of "the numinous" sense of an underlying Spirit,[6] or at least to a mental "intending" of "deep space" and "sublime terror" that could replace the expansiveness of a divinely-occupied cathedral,[7] while the same "Gothic" also includes symbolic constructs of "beautiful" good and "terrifying" evil to be used in the place of decayed External Absolutes of which only ruined symbols are left in the modern world. Still, faced with persistent depredations of "popular culture" and the dominance of the New Criticism in deciding literary quality, these approaches have remained little more than indicators of a "less essential" branch of literary history. They have had influence on teaching mostly when the Gothic has been brought in momentarily as a highly conflicted and self-undermining eddy on the margins of the "main flow" of Western literature.

The scholarly setting for teaching the Gothic, though, has since become *very* different, opening this mode and its offshoots to much more academic teaching and interpretation. The forces behind that shift are what I here propose to explain, even to the point of showing how they can best be used to teach a Gothic text. While the Gothic has now "morphed" into a panoply of forms, from an ongoing output of Gothic novels and films to *Doom* and *Resident Evil* video games,[8] these exfoliations of an already unstable mode could still have been kept "in their place" by modern attitudes had not several different schemes of cultural and literary theory been either revived in new guises or newly created from the later 1960s through the 1980s and beyond. We can and should teach the Gothic as we do now, I would argue, even to the point of strengthening some insights of the New Criticism *and* old historicism,[9] because analytical perspectives have arisen in academic theory and practice that have *retheorized* what the Gothic is most fundamentally about and so given it a new importance as an object of valuable study. The teaching of the Gothic today is the product of a reactivated psychoanalysis, a post1950s feminism which has expanded into "gender studies," a resurgent Marxism, a genuinely "new historicism" combining cultural anthropology with Derridean "deconstruction," and several forms of "cultural studies" that have come to include "postcolonial" theory and criticism, among other strands. All of these together, challenging the standards set by New Criticism and high/low culture distinctions, have brought the Gothic forward as a major cultural force by the very nature of their assumptions and thereby drawn some Gothic "classics" (*The Mysteries of Udolpho* [1794], *Frankenstein* [1818], *Dr. Jekyll and Mr. Hyde* [1886]) to the centre of what a liberal arts education must encompass if a college student is be truly "literate" about what Western culture includes. I now want to look at how and why all this has happened and to exemplify these developments along the way by sketching several "new English" ways by which we can now teach one Gothic "classic": Bram Stoker's *Dracula* (1897), perhaps the text *most* revived and reinterpreted by the theorizing of the Gothic over the last four decades.

Even when its assumptions are being questioned, it has been *psychoanalysis* in the twentieth century that first rescued the Gothic from mere popularity and made it a means to understand Western thinking and culture more deeply. Sigmund Freud helped begin this process in 1908 by seeing the sublimation and symbolizing of unconscious drives as more readily apparent in popular fiction than in most published writing.[10] He then exemplified his 1919 sense of "the uncanny," the frightening reappearance of what is unconsciously "familiar" in "unfamiliar" figures,[11] by critically interpreting E. T. A. Hoffmann's semi-Gothic tale "The Sandman" (1817), where dim memories from the narrator's childhood, partly real and partly fictive (such as the "Sandman" legend), reappear in his later life to confront him with several drives he has repressed, from his Oedipal sexuality, including his fear of castration, to an utterly prerational compulsion towards death, all of which have driven him since infancy and now arise in disguises outside him to haunt him from his own and his culture's hidden depths. This pointing to Gothic as especially indicative of the relationship between conscious life and the infantile/archaic unconscious has gained additional force since the 1930s, when Andre Breton saw the Walpolean Gothic as a precursor of modern surrealism in its "intense fear of the return of the powers of the past" sequestered in the unconscious[12] and Edmund Wilson solves the mysteries in Henry James' extremely Gothic *The Turn of the Screw* (1898) by claiming that the governess-narrator has projected this tale's adulterous ghosts out of her preconscious need to enact her repressed sexual longings in disguise.[13] Even H. P. Lovecraft ends up supporting this view in general when he questions formulaic Freudianism in "Supernatural Horror in Literature" (1939) but then admits that Gothic horror arouses the most biologically basic "inner instincts" embedded in our "subconscious mind" from the early evolution of the human race.[14] By the late 1950s and early 1960s, when Maurice Richardson and Lowry Nelson, Jr., firmly root the Gothic and ghost stories in "repressed fantasies" from early stages of both the self and civilization,[15] Gothic has become valued as the quintessential literary precursor of Freudian thought, which is therefore a revealing way to read Gothic. After all, Freud's spatial description of the unconscious and its "dream-work" has clearly been developed from the very topography of now-visible surfaces and primeval depths essential to the design of the Gothic itself.

Even so, it was the 1960s that further recast psychoanalysis enough to make it an extremely fertile field for exfoliating and revaluing the Gothic. Leslie Fiedler strikingly joins Freudianism to Marxism in the early 1960s to reveal the Gothic as re-enacting conflicts between different classes and stages of civilization while it also plays out individual traumas born from the struggles between generations. In the process he establishes the Gothic as basic to an Anglo-American literature haunted often by "the fear that in destroying the old ego-ideals of Church and State, [America] has opened the way for the inruption of darkness" in many forms.[16] Meanwhile, with the international circulation of his *Ecrits* in 1966, Jacques Lacan has promulgated a language-based and highly theatrical psychoanalysis, steeped in Nietzschean self-staging, Saussurean linguistics, and Heideggerean existentialism, which aptly reads those aspects of Gothic that emphasize the stagy performance of self cast into a struggle for coherence in the face of many haunting "others." Among these are the familial and symbolic locations of the supposed "Law of the Father" (as in many Gothic patriarchs, mansions, and inquisitions) and the "Other" that is language in all its dimensions, from constructs of sanctioned order to the drift of free association across signifiers "floating" like ghosts as they suggest the absence, hence the death, of the multiple meanings to which they might point. Not surprisingly, therefore, parts of Lacan's own readings of literature[17] have been carried over into real advances in the interpretation of Gothic texts. In the early 1970s, Stoker's *Dracula* is given the first thoroughly Freudian reading of its sexual symbolism by Christopher Bentley, who proudly echoes Ernest Jones's 1931 psychoanalysis of the whole "vampire" tradition.[18] But *Dracula* is opened up even more in later work to expose the Lacanian dynamic among the many rival characters in the novel's stagy world[19] and to explain its contest between the "obsessional" discourse of male science and logic and an unstable, pre-Oedipal "hysterical" counter-language of outlawed associations, drawn forth in women by Dracula's bite.[20]

It is consequently one extension *and* critique of Lacanian psychoanalysis that has brought the Gothic even more to the forefront in the 1980s and 1990s. Julia Kristeva's *Powers of Horror* (1980) argues that the pre-Oedipal level of radical instability felt most by us all as an archaic site of horror (a kind of "fore-language" prior to any discourse close to what for Lacan is the unbearable welter of the senseless "Real") is the betwixt-and-between condition, which can reappear in many different forms, of being half-inside and half-outside the mother and thus halfway between death and life. Human subjects as they develop assert their identity by "abjecting" this, and potentially any such, complex of contradictions—in the sense of "throwing [it] off" into an other or "throwing [it] under" the Law of the Father (*ab-ject*)—and the resulting "abject" can return to haunt the would-be self as the most primally and archaically "uncanny" of externalized monstrosities, each one a mixture of irreconcilables that we both long for and fear to recognize.[21] Via this sense of abjection, which is reconnected to the non-sense of the "Real" in the Lacanian–Marxist work of Slavoj Zizek,[22] archaized Gothic "others" from Frankenstein's creature to Mr Hyde to the Phantom of the Opera[23] can now be read as the distortion-mirror sites of numerous impossible, yet basic, contradictions thrown off onto them by Gothic heroes or heroines, as well as by cultural norms, so that consistency of being can be at least claimed by a cultural majority. Dracula in this extension of psychoanalysis becomes the "abject" of numerous primal anomalies that his onlookers cannot face in themselves, ranging from the "undead" crossing of life with death and the blurring of the human with the bestial (the possibility of *de*volution after Darwin) to the dissolution of constructed gender-norms (since he can feed from his breast as much as he can penetrate women *and* men) and a great deal more.[24]

By the time psychoanalysis has reached this point, meanwhile, it is clear that the Gothic has also been raised to new importance by the stunning effulgence of *feminist* criticism in the late 1960s and 1970s. Though never settling into one fixed scheme of assumptions (appropriate to its questioning of older patriarchal fixities), this revolution in scholarship has both (a) worked to recover denigrated or lost writing by women from being left out of the literary "canon" most taught in schools and universities—which has rightly brought new attention to many female Gothic novelists and playwrights—and (b) reread many long-interpreted, as well as rediscovered, texts to bring out within them the suppression and reassertion of women's condition, thought, and uses of language amid male-dominated social structures designed to make them marginal—which foregrounds the scene in Walpole's *Otranto* most echoed in later Gothic: the entrapment of a terrified woman in an archaic dark passage between a patriarchal castle and a patriarchal abbey.[25] The result in Gothic criticism has been, first, the exposure of how "literary women" have declared their distinctiveness early by the means of a Gothic mode reworked extensively from potentials in Walpole;[26] then the confluence of many feminist approaches, from Anglo-American to French and beyond, to open up the entire history of the Gothic to the struggles and assertions of woman through and within it;[27] and ultimately the writing of thorough feminist studies that connect women in the Gothic to the entire construction of "domestic ideologies"[28] or the positioning of the feminine within the institutions of patriarchy exaggerated by the Gothic that keep threatening to penetrate any boundaries of self-protection or distinction that women construct.[29] Along the way Stoker's *Dracula* has come to be vividly exposed as a site where women unleash their repressed sexuality in ways both desired and forbidden in the 1890s,[30] as a playing out of Victorian fears that women may *be* vampires sucking substance and power out of men,[31] and as a presentation of what acting as a "New Woman" might mean at Stoker's time and since, in reaction to a label proposed by American feminist Sarah Grand in 1894 and cited by Mina Murray Harker in *Dracula* itself.[32]

As feminism has worked through its main assumptions, though, several sympathizers have found the politics and verbal composition of "gender" (always a social schema or code, as opposed to biological "sex") to be far more extensive and complex than the subjugation of just Anglo women. Gender constructs are so many and so mobile, Teresa de Lauretis reminds us in 1987, that they should never be seen as "the property of bodies" in fact but as "the product of various social technologies" that take a blurry array of physically sexual orientations and/or racial appearances or mixtures and turn them into categorized "differences" that allow social power to be exercised by or over those groups so compartmentalized, at least for a time.[33] In this way, differences *within* or *between* women are codified or elided, and the relations between or within *men* as well become organized into groupings of the "proper" or "improper," all as the result of what Michel Foucault since the mid-1970s has called the different "deployments" of "bodies and pleasures" into artificial "discourses" (such as those of supposed "hetero"-sexuality, those of "homo"-sexuality) at different points in Western history.[34] This "gender theory" perspective bursts into Gothic studies around 1985, most extensively with the publication of Eve Kosofsky Sedgwick's *Between Men*.[35] Here, developing concurrent "outings" of the homosexuality in the lives of certain "founding" Gothic authors (Walpole, William Beckford, M. G. "Monk" Lewis),[36] Sedgwick shows how fictionalized placements of women "between men" who really use females to effect each other, especially in the Gothic from *Otranto* to *The Monk* (1796) and after, produce "homosocial" power relations (just "proper" enough) that both play out and conceal "homosexual" desires or potentials (manifestly "improper" within the governing "deployments" of discourse). The Gothic now becomes newly important as a locus of disguised struggles between several constructions of gender and resistances to them, including the tensions surrounding gay and/or lesbian relationships *and* cross- or interracial sexualities, as characters are pulled from conventionally demarcated surfaces "down" towards more dark, fluid, and abjected depths where cultural, as well as conscious, categories fade into each other.

1984–85 thus also marks the entrance of gender criticism into the study of *Dracula* via an epochal essay by Christopher Craft.[37] The wide circulation and reprinting of this piece has opened up the many moments of homoerotic attraction and gender mixing in a novel seemingly committed to strict boundaries of sexual orientation and gender, as when its vampire Count is aroused by the throat of Jonathan Harker and is able to feed Mina blood from his breast as though he were as maternal as he is patriarchal. In the aftermath of this effort, the permeability and enforcements of gender constructions throughout the Gothic have become frequent critical targets; witness work in the 1990s on animalized "masculinity" in the Gothic;[38] the multiplication of "femininities" (including lesbian ones) in Gothic novels and films;[39] the conflicted sublimation of male homosexuality in the later Gothic,[40] especially after the trial of Oscar Wilde, himself an author of Gothic in 1891 with *The Picture of Dorian Gray*;[41] and the problem of distinguishing, as many are still doing, between the Walpolean "male" and the Radcliffean "female" Gothic,[42] even as these schemes invade each other frequently, as gender criticism suggests they must.

Something of an apogee is reached in this approach with the work of Judith Halberstam by 1995, in which she sees Stoker's Dracula as a prime example of a "technological" act of culture whereby one symbolic "all-purpose monster" is made into the site of many different "fears" at the time "about race, class, gender, sexuality, and empire," with all of these "fragments of otherness" projected "into one body" (similar to the Kristevan "abject") so that they collectively seem *over there* rather than the *parts of us* they actually are.[43] Halberstam is especially distinctive when she shows the "aquiline"-faced Count embodying "the Jew of anti-Semitic discourse" among his harbourings of "othered" races and classes. But she finally admits she cannot make this case without her gender theories being inflected by *Marxist* ones, particularly important for emphasizing how much Dracula's quasi-"Jewish" hoarding of gold recalls Marx's own sense in *Grundrisse* (1857–58) of "capital . . . sucking in living labour as its soul, vampire-like."[44] By mining this vein, in fact, she extends a Marxist approach to the Gothic which more broadly goes back to Fiedler but gains its greatest momentum in the late 1970s and early 1980s. In 1978, Franco Moretti published an initial version of what became a longer piece, "Dialectic of Fear," in his 1983 essay collection, *Signs Taken for Wonders*.[45] Here both Mary Shelley's *Frankenstein* and Stoker's *Dracula* are vividly revealed as "displac[ing] the antagonisms and horrors evidenced *within* society *outside* of society itself" (84), especially the antagonisms between classes, class-based belief-systems ("ideologies") pulled between the retrogressive and progressive, and groups positioned differently because of the economic profit for some and the market-driven exploitation of others. Dracula in this view displaces a complex of social threats: capitalism personified in his sucking-up of labour and labour's proceeds *and* maverick economic individualism too far outside of state control *and* a quasi-aristocratic threat to progressive capitalism that tries to monopolize monetary exchange and circulation, including the traffic in women (whom he wants to hoard as much as he sequesters money). In 1980 this Marxist take gains even greater currency with the first edition of David Punter's *The Literature of Terror*, expanded into two volumes in 1996. Punter intensifies and widens Fiedler's combination of psychoanalysis and Marxism—and thereby gives the Gothic a greatly renewed importance—by showing how the returns of repressed "taboos" in such works over the years reflect how the rising Western middle class, the largest readership of Gothic from Walpole's era on, "displaces the violence of present social structures, conjures them up again as past, and falls promptly under their spell,"[46] using the Gothic to both obscure and reveal in disguise the actual foundations (including the ideological conflicts and "otherings") of middle-class life.

Yet Marxism by itself has not lasted long as a dominant voice in the redefinition of the Gothic—unless we see it as continuing in the growing output of "*new historicism*," of which it is certainly a part, in the 1980s, 1990s, and the early 2000s. Developing rapidly out of studies in the English Renaissance by Stephen Greenblatt, Jonathan Dollimore (the more Marxist of the two), and others in the early 1980s, "new" historical interpretation differs from the "old" by *not* assuming a coherent worldview underlying the writing of a particular period or author and instead accepting socioanthropological perspectives about clearly-framed, but multidimensional, historical situations similar to the schema of Victor Turner or Clifford Geertz. Historicized moments now become teeming interactions among coterminous events, multiple events and texts, many different types of texts and public performances, and different discourses (or "voices") within or between classes of people, nearly all of which circulate elements between each other continuously, with each influencing the others, and do so in an arena of *conflicts* among beliefs rather than settled conceptions that only seem to dominate a period.

The extensive "intertextuality" of this view, dissolving the New Critical borders between the "literary" and "nonliterary," draws in the poststructuralism of "deconstruction" as practiced by Jacques Derrida starting in the mid-to-late 1960s. This acceptance of words, paragraphs, and works differing from yet deferring to many others from many locations, as it happens, suits the tendency in Gothic writings from Walpole on, to present themselves as texts of other texts and as the pasting together of different vocabularies (such as those of "old" and "new romance" at once) drawn from several locations outside the present work, all of which are openly regarded in the Gothic as ghost-like signifiers of other signifiers recalling and anticipating still other signifiers that are ghosts of other such ghosts. The consequences in criticism of the Gothic have sometimes been almost purely deconstructive readings,[47] but more often they have incorporated deconstructive intertextuality in historicized readings of Gothic works that present the very "nature" of such works, and thus newly *celebrate* this multigeneric "genre," as a deeply conflicted crisscrossing of already-promulgated discourses (including technologies) of an era that carry ideological "baggage" with them and clash with the baggage in competing frames of reference. A supreme example is Jennifer Wicke's new historical/deconstructive/gender-inflected reading of *Dracula* as fissured and even vampiric (sucking in the many forms of textualized life it ingests) in being explicitly composed out of "media in its many forms" during the 1890s, from newspaper-reporting and secretarial stenography to "automatic writing," criminology, and scientific notation—the ultimate result being primarily "a mass of typewriting," as the novel puts it, ideologically unresolved.[48]

In keeping with its intertextual emphasis, moreover, new historicism has also kept welcoming other earlier critical vocabularies suited to its interweaving of the literary with so much already-textualized history. New historical visions of warring beliefs have been helpfully advanced by pulling in the highly linguistic, but still Marxist, work of Mikhail Bakhtin, through he wrote mainly in the 1920s and 1930s. After all, he advances a sense of popular novels, as opposed to aristocratic epics, as "dialogically" intermixing retextualizations of multiple cultural "voices" (which carry ideologies with them) that dramatically encounter each other in novelistic space rather than one of them subsuming the others. The special aptness of this way of reading to cacophonous *Gothic* novels has been well demonstrated recently by Jacqueline Howard in a sharp refutation of the New Critical disparagement of Gothic.[49] Meanwhile, Foucault's later work on historical "discourses of power" as well as sexuality, most of all in *Discipline and Punish* (1975),[50] has theorized the construction of anatomizing discourses useful for the surveillance of suspects or convicts and how it was gradually turned across the nineteenth century into ways for individual minds to discipline themselves. The applicability of this progression to borrowed languages of self-fashioning *and* self-control in the frequently paranoid Gothic has therefore been articulated in Foucauldian terms by Jose Monleon in a semi-Marxist fashion[51] and Robert Miles in a more Nietzschean mode.[52] The bulk of "new historicist" Gothic criticism, however, has remained mainly intertextual, concerned with the way the Gothic processes the nonliterary discourses and methods of cultural exchange at a particular span of time, whether it be the period when the Gothic was just beginning,[53] the decades when empirical perception was turned into the "spectral" uncanny by way of the late eighteenth-century technologies of phantasmagoria,[54] the Romantic struggle to re-establish "high culture" writing by redefining and "raising" the "low,"[55] the mutations in fiction and drama prompted by the changes in the cultural geography of the Victorian city and countryside,[56] or the late nineteenth-century interfaces between the expansion of literacy and British imperialism[57] and the anxiety-prompting affinities between theories of decadence, the debate over evolution, blurred sexual boundaries, increased criminality, imperial politics, changes in medicine, Freudian psychology, and the inherently anxious Gothic, *Dracula* included, as the nineteenth century turned into the twentieth.[58] Since "new historicism" is also unusually conscious of how the past is changed by the present perception of it, so much so that such criticism often notes the ways the past and present effect the understanding of each other, some recent work on Gothic even explains *that* intertextuality well, as we see in the quite distinctive view of *Dracula* as prepostmodern offered by Nina Auerbach.[59]

The effect of "new historicism" on exfoliating the cultural references and relevance of the Gothic, in fact, has been so extensive as to change the way Gothic texts are now being republished for students and their teachers. The standard of Gothic works edited for study is now being set by the Broadview Press "Literary Texts" series, which has reissued numerous Gothic novels and dramas either in editions where multiple texts interface with each other (such as Walpole's *The Castle of Otranto* with his 1768 play *The Mysterious Mother*[60]) or in volumes where the main text is both internally annotated and followed by extensive intertextual material (including reviews) from its contemporary contexts, a fine example being the Broadview edition of *Dracula*.[61] Similarly prompted by new-historicist intertextual pressures, recent Norton Critical Editions—again, with a *Dracula* among them[62]—are adding adjacent and contemporary texts to the more recent critical essays that have always accompanied the annotated main work; and the newer Case Studies in Contemporary Criticism volumes, designed to train students in using the latest critical theories by following a major text with one essay on it from each of five approaches, have started to include "Contextual Illustrations and Documents" between the work and the critical pieces, as in the extensive compilation under that title in their very recent *Dracula*.[63] Even less prominent Gothic writings are being gathered together and republished within this wave of intertextual recoveries. Once-disregarded Gothic *plays* and *short stories* are now available in well-edited scholarly collections,[64] along with the earliest nonfiction documents on the theory and criticism of the Gothic in the eighteenth and nineteenth centuries.[65] There are consequently unprecedented textbook-aids for the teaching of Gothic writing now, and the primary reason is the demand for these—and for more editions of Gothic texts—prompted by what "new historicism" has done, along with its immediate theoretical predecessors, to rehabilitate Gothic works of several types as key windows into the changing psychology, gender-politics, ideological debates, uses of language, and dynamic tensions of history in the modern world since the eighteenth century.

At the same time, the resurgence of Gothic as worthy of study would not be as complete as it is without the added emphases encouraged by *"cultural studies,"* partly because of how complex and far-reaching, and how intermingled with new historicism and gender studies, it has turned out to be. The reinvigorated Marxism that helped launch this critical movement (though it has long since expanded) out of the Birmingham Centre for Cultural Studies in England in the 1970s, for one thing, has focused attention on the class-struggles and hypocrisies in distinguishing "high" from "low" art and culture, a problem that has defined and plagued the Gothic in and since Walpole's *Castle of Otranto*. Now the Gothic is being studied as a prominent cross-generic site that is *about* the construction of "high vs. low" in particular works,[66] even as the criticism of the Gothic has long been and remains divided over its cultural status. Concurrently, too, the cultural-studies questioning of popular culture as "low" has raised *cinema studies* in scholarly stature, thereby giving rise to work on how popular Gothic films are deeply rooted in myriad cultural contradictions.[67] The same stance has then raised equal interest in "subaltern" voices once kept out of high-cultural sight, from those of enslaved and working-class populations within Western societies to those once in the colonies, now the decolonized spaces, of Anglo-European empires. The recovery of enslaved perspectives has given a new focus to *American* Gothic studies, which now sees the Gothic as drawing forth, even enabling the articulation of, the racial "undersides" of a troubled US history.[68]

The growing "colonial and postcolonial" strand of cultural studies, meanwhile, inspired by Edward Said as well as the Birmingham School, has greatly widened the range of what we now see the Gothic symbolizing in fiction, theatre, *and* film. The deep connections between Gothic, racism, "othering," and empire from the eighteenth century on has now revealed its many articulations from Mary Shelley to Bram Stoker and the virulent prejudices made visible by them.[69] The new attention to the "postcolonial," in turn,[70] has opened up numerous spaces outside Western Europe and America as darkly symbolized by the Gothic, in the past and currently, in ways we have rarely examined before. *Dracula* studies, in particular, are now shedding new light on English phobias about Eastern Europe and its once-colonized "other" races, often seen as "oriental" even in film adaptations,[71] while several quite recent *Dracula* readings are bringing out its roots in, and intertextual echoes of, the British conquest and later decolonization of Ireland, from which Stoker himself originally came. Given the complexity of Anglo-Irish relations over centuries and Stoker's own ambivalence about his conflicted cultural affiliations—along with the ideological irresolution that comes with cultural studies and turns out to be characteristic of the Gothic since Walpole—it is not surprising that these new cultural critics all articulate different versions of the inconsistent attitudes that *Dracula* conveys through its disguised echoes of the Irish controversy as it developed into the 1890s.[72]

What cultural studies, its struggles, and its approaches to the Gothic most emphasize in nearly all their forms, though, is how the disciplinary separations that have led to distinct schools of literary theory, among other academic divisions, are being—and should be—increasingly blurred and straddled, particularly where the cross-generic and status-crossing Gothic is concerned. Cultural studies, in fact, along with "high" and "low" culture, has always critiqued the artificiality, even falsity, of many "field" distinctions in academic research and instruction. It is therefore no surprise that cultural criticism often finds roles in its interpretations for psychoanalysis, "French Freud," feminism, gender-questioning, gay-lesbian-bisexual studies, Marxism (of course), deconstructive intertextualism, and several of the strands that "new historicism" has developed, virtually all of which now appear together at times, as we have seen, to show the value of each and the relationships between all of them in thorough readings of important Western texts and genres. This progression has both suited the Gothic especially well, given its inherent multiplicity of affiliations and conflicted values, and has helped us define and articulate what the Gothic *is* and can be—at last—to the greatest extent in its history and the history of literary study. Now there is no good reason *not* to teach the Gothic as part of an advanced curriculum of cultural understanding and *many* reasons to bring all the recent lenses of interpretation to bear on it—even parts of New Criticism and "old" historicism—since the Gothic's very nature demands, because we now see it includes, multiple angles of approach to its subjects.

Indeed, as advanced education now stands, Gothic can be used to teach several theories and approaches, just as several theoretical modes of reading can be employed to teach the Gothic, and even the same Gothic text, all at once or in a succession of different approaches. The Case Studies edition of *Dracula*, for example, has been influenced by, and thus tries to articulate, all the trends that have been presented here, to the point where it *both* explains and demonstrates each by way of Stoker's texts and its contexts *and* shows each reaching out to parts of the others so that they can all finally be combined for the greater understanding of a major Gothic novel. That volume thus provides one model, though hardly an exclusive one, by which the Gothic or just *Dracula* could be taught, given all I have shown, *or* a means by which influential theories of reading might be discussed, in conjunction with primary texts *of* theory, with one text or type of text available for comparing their different effects on interpretation. Such a confluence of options never would have been possible in the academic "English" of even fifteen years ago. But now it is vibrantly becoming the norm, considering both the recent history of theory and the way that very history has so powerfully resituated the "Gothic" as one of the primary modes by which Western culture articulates its fears, hopes, and underlying conflicts in the modern and postmodern worlds.

## Notes

1. Clive Bloom, "Horror fiction: in search of a definition," in David Punter, ed., *A Companion to the Gothic* (Oxford: Blackwell, 2000) 157.
2. *The Castle of Otranto: a Gothic Story*, ed. W. S. Lewis and E. J. Clery (London: Oxford University Press, 1996) 9.
3. See Coral Ann Howells, *Love, Mystery, and Misery: Feeling in Gothic Fiction* (London: Athlone Press, 1978); Eve Kosofsky Sedgwick, *The Coherence of Gothic Conventions* (1980), rev. edn (New York: Methuen, 1986); and George E. Haggerty, *Gothic Fiction/Gothic Form* (University Park: Pennsylvania State University Press, 1989).
4. As in Elizabeth Napier, *The Failure of Gothic: Politics of Disjunction in an Eighteenth-century Literary Form* (Oxford: Clarendon, 1987).
5. The most influential early examples of this approach include Edith Birkhead, *The Tale of Terror: a Study of Gothic Romance* (London: Constable, 1921); Eino Railo, *The Haunted Castle: a Study of the Elements of English Romanticism* (London: Dutton, 1927); J. M. S. Tompkins, *The Popular Novel in England, 1770–1800* (London: Constable, 1932); and Montague Summers, *The Gothic Quest: a History of the Gothic Novel* (London: Fortune Press, 1938).
6. Devendra P. Varma, *The Gothic Flame: Being a History of the Gothic Novel in England* (London: Arthur Barker, 1957) 206–31.

7. Maurice Levy, *Le Roman "Gothique" Anglais, 1764–1824* (Toulouse: Association des Publications de la Faculte des Lettres et Sciences Humaines, 1968) 601–43.
8. See Fred Botting, "Aftergothic: consumption, machines, and black holes," in Jerrold E. Hogle, ed., *The Cambridge Companion to Gothic Fiction* (Cambridge: Cambridge University Press, 2002) 277–300.
9. As is done with New Criticism in Howells, *Love, Mystery*, and with "old" historicism in Elizabeth MacAndrew, *The Gothic Tradition in Fiction* (New York: Columbia University Press, 1979).
10. See Freud, "Creative writers and day-dreaming," trans. James Strachey, in Hazard Adams, ed., *Critical Theory Since Plato*, rev. edn (New York: Harcourt, 1992) 712–16.
11. See "The uncanny" in Freud, *Collected Papers*, ed. and trans. Joan Riviere (New York: Basic Books, 1959) 4:368–407.
12. See Breton in Victor Sage, ed., *The Gothic Novel: a Casebook* (London: Longman, 1990) 113.
13. Wilson's argument first appeared in "The ambiguity of Henry James," *Hound and Horn* 7 (1934):385–406.
14. H. P. Lovecraft, *Dagon and Other Macabre Tales* (London: Victor Gollancz, 1967) 141–3.
15. See Maurice Richardson, "The psychoanalysis of ghost stories," *The Twentieth Century* 166 (1959):419–31, and Lowry Nelson, Jr., "Night thoughts on the Gothic novel," *Yale Review* 52 (1963):236–57.
16. Leslie Fiedler, *Love and Death in the American Novel* (1960), rev. edn (New York: Dell, 1966) 129.
17. As in the "Seminar on 'The Purloined Letter'," trans. Jeffrey Mehlman, *Yale French Studies* 48 (1972):38–72, and "Desire and the interpretation of desire in *Hamlet*," trans. James Hulbert, *Yale French Studies* 55/56 (1977): 11–52.
18. See Christopher Bentley, "The monster in the bedroom: sexual symbolism in Bram Stoker's *Dracula*" (1972), in Margaret Carter, ed., *Dracula: the Vampire and the Critics* (London: UMI Research Press, 1988) 25–34.
19. See Richard Astle, "Dracula as totemic monster: Lacan, Freud, Oedipus and history," *Sub-stance* 8 (1979):98–105.
20. See Elisabeth Bronfen, *Over Her Dead Body: Death, Femininity and the Aesthetic* (Manchester: Manchester University Press, 1992) 313–22.
21. See Julia Kristeva, *Powers of Horror: an Essay on Abjection*, trans. Leon S. Roudiez (New York: Columbia University Press, 1982) esp. 1–10.
22. Slavoj Zizek's relevance for Gothic studies is well exemplified in *A Plague of Fantasies* (London: Verso, 1997).
23. See Jerrold E. Hogle, "The Gothic ghost of the counterfeit and the progress of abjection," in Punter, ed., *A Companion*, 293–304.
24. All discussed in Hogle, "Stoker's counterfeit Gothic: *Dracula* and theatricality at the dawn of simulation," in William Hughes and Andrew Smith, eds., *Bram Stoker: History, Psychoanalysis and the Gothic* (Basingstoke: Macmillan—now Palgrave Macmillan, 1998) 205–24.

25. See Walpole, *The Castle*, ed. Lewis and Clery, 26–30.
26. See Ellen Moers, *Literary Women* (New York: Doubleday, 1976) 90–110, 122–40, and Diane Long Hoeveler, *Gothic Feminism: the Professionalization of Gender from Charlotte Smith to the Brontës* (University Park: Pennsylvania State University Press, 1988).
27. As in the whole of Julianne E. Fleenor, ed., *The Female Gothic* (Montreal: Eden Press, 1983).
28. See Kate Ferguson Ellis, *The Contested Castle: Gothic Novels and the Subversion of Domestic Ideology* (Urbana: University of Illinois Press, 1989).
29. As in Eugenia C. DeLamotte, *Perils of the Night: a Feminist Study of Nineteenth-Century Gothic* (Oxford: Oxford University Press, 1990), and Michelle Masse, *In the Name of Love: Women, Masochism, and the Gothic* (Ithaca, NY: Cornell University Press, 1992).
30. See Carrol L. Fry, "Fictional conventions and sexuality in *Dracula*" (1972); Phyllis A. Roth, "Suddenly sexual women in Bram Stoker's *Dracula*" (1977); and Gail B. Griffin, " 'Your girls that you all love are mine': *Dracula* and the Victorian male sexual imagination" (1980), all in Carter, ed., *Dracula*, 35–8, 57–67, and 137–48.
31. See Judith Weissman, "Women and vampires: *Dracula* as a Victorian novel" (1977), in Carter, ed., *Dracula*, 69–77.
32. See Carol Senf, "*Dracula*: Stoker's response to the new woman," *Victorian Studies* 26 (1982):33–49, and Sos Eltis, "Corruption of the blood and degeneration of the race: *Dracula* and policing the politics of gender," in Stoker, *Dracula*, ed. Jean Paul Riquelme (Boston: Bedford/St. Martin's Press, 2002) 450–65.
33. Teresa de Lauretis, *Technologies of Gender: Essays on Theory, Film, and Fiction* (Bloomington: Indiana University Press, 1987) 2–3.
34. See Michel Foucault's *The History of Sexuality, Volume I* (1976), trans. Robert Hurley (New York: Pantheon, 1978).
35. Eve Kosofsky Sedgwick, *Between Men: English Literature and Male Homosocial Desire* (New York: Columbia University Press, 1985).
36. See George Haggerty, "Literature and homosexuality in the late eighteenth century: Walpole, Beckford, and Lewis," *Studies in the Novel* 18 (1986):341–52.
37. " 'Kiss me with those red lips': gender and inversion in Bram Stoker's *Dracula*," *Representations* 8 (1984):107–33, rpt. in Carter, ed., *Dracula*, 167–94, and Glennis Byron, ed., *Dracula: Contemporary Critical Essays*, New Casebooks (Basingstoke: Macmillan—now Palgrave Macmillan, 1999) 93–118.
38. Cyndy Hendershot, *The Animal Within: Masculinity and the Gothic* (Ann Arbor: University of Michigan Press, 1998).
39. See Suzanne Becker, *Gothic Forms of Feminine Fictions* (Manchester: Manchester University Press, 1999), and Pauline Palmer, *Lesbian Gothic: Transgressive Fictions* (London: Cassell, 1999).
40. See, for example, Steven Bruhm, "The Gothic in a culture of narcissism," *Reflecting Narcissus: a Queer Aesthetic* (Minneapolis: University of Minnesota Press, 2001) 144–73.

41. See Talia Schaffer, " 'A Wilde desire took me': the homoerotic history of *Dracula*," *ELH* 61 (1994):381–425.
42. See esp. Anne Williams, *Art of Darkness: a Poetics of Gothic* (Chicago: University of Chicago Press, 1995).
43. Judith Halberstam, *Skin Shows: Gothic Horror and the Technology of Monsters* (Durham, NC: Duke University Press, 1995) 86–106.
44. Halberstam, *Skin Shows*, 102.
45. *Signs Taken for Wonders: Essays in the Sociology of Literary Forms*, trans. Franco Moretti, Susan Fischer et al. (London: Verso, 1983) 83–108. All subsequent references are to this edition, and are given in the text.
46. David Punter, *The Literature of Terror: a History of Gothic Fictions from 1765 to the Present Day*, rev. edn (London: Longman, 1996) 2: 218–19.
47. One example is Jean Paul Riquelme, "Doubling and repetition/realism and closure in *Dracula*," in Stoker, *Dracula*, ed. Riquelme, 559–72.
48. See Jennifer Wicke in "Vampiric type-writing: *Dracula* and its media," *ELH* 59 (1992):457–93.
49. See Jacqueline Howard's *Reading Gothic Fiction: a Bahktinian Approach* (Oxford: Clarendon, 1994).
50. Translated by Alan Sheridan as *Discipline and Punish: the Birth of the Prison*, 2nd edn (New York: Vintage, 1995).
51. In Jose Monleon, *A Specter is Haunting Europe: a Sociological Approach to the Fantastic* (Princeton: Princeton University Press, 1990).
52. See Robert Miles in *Gothic Writing, 1750–1820: a Genealogy* (London: Routledge, 1993).
53. See E. J. Clery, *The Rise of Supernatural Fiction, 1762–1800* (Cambridge: Cambridge University Press, 1995).
54. As in Terry Castle, *The Female Thermometer: Eighteenth-Century Culture and the Invention of the Uncanny* (Oxford: Oxford University Press, 1995).
55. See Michael Gamer, *Romanticism and the Gothic: Genre, Reception, and Canon Formation* (Cambridge: Cambridge University Press, 2000).
56. See Robert Mighall, *A Geography of Victorian Gothic Fiction: Mapping History's Nightmare* (Oxford: Oxford University Press, 1999).
57. For example, in Patrick Brantlinger, *The Reading Lesson: the Threat of Mass Literacy in Nineteenth-Century British Fiction* (Bloomington: Indiana University Press, 1998), and Andrew Smith and William Hughes, eds., *Empire and the Gothic: the Politics of Genre* (Basingstoke: Palgrave Macmillan, 2003).
58. See Martin Tropp, *Images of Fear: How Horror Stories Helped Shape Modern American Culture 1818–1919* (Jefferson, NC: McFarland, 1990); Kelly Hurley, *The Gothic Body: Sexuality, Materialism, and Degeneration at the Fin de Siècle* (Cambridge: Cambridge University Press, 1996); and Susan J. Navarette, *The Shape of Fear: Horror and the Fin de Siècle Culture of Decadence* (Lexington: University Press of Kentucky, 1998).
59. Nina Auerbach, *Our Vampires, Ourselves* (Chicago: University of Chicago Press, 1995).
60. *The Castle of Otranto and The Mysterious Mother*, ed. Frederick S. Frank (Peterborough, ONT: Broadview Press, 2003).

61. Bram Stoker, *Dracula*, ed. Glennis Byron (Peterborough, ONT: Broadview Press, 1998).
62. Stoker, *Dracula: a Norton Critical Edition*, ed. Nina Auerbach and David J. Skal (New York: Norton, 1997).
63. See *Dracula*, ed. Riquelme, 370–406.
64. Most notably Jeffrey N. Cox, ed., *Seven Gothic Dramas, 1789–1825* (Columbus: Ohio State University Press, 1992), and Chris Baldick, ed., *The Oxford Book of Gothic Tales* (Oxford: Oxford University Press, 1992).
65. See E. J. Clery and Robert Miles, eds., *Gothic Documents: a Sourcebook, 1700–1820* (Manchester: Manchester University Press, 2000).
66. In addition to Brantlinger and Gamer, noted above, see Hogle, *The Undergrounds of The Phantom of the Opera: Sublimation and the Gothic in Leroux's Novel and its Progeny* (Basingstoke: Palgrave Macmillan, 2002).
67. Such studies are epitomized best by Mark Edmundson, *Nightmare on Main Street: Angels, Sadomasochism, and the Culture of Gothic* (Cambridge, MA: Harvard University Press, 1997), and David J. Skal, *The Monster Show: a Cultural History of Horror* (New York: Norton, 1993).
68. See Kari J. Winter, *Subjects of Slavery, Agents of Change: Woman and Power in Gothic Novels and Slave Narratives, 1790–1865* (Athens: University of Georgia Press, 1992); Teresa Goddu, *Gothic America: Narrative, History, and the Nation* (New York: Columbia University Press, 1997); and Robert K. Martin and Eric Savoy, eds., *American Gothic: New Interventions in a National Narrative* (Iowa City: University of Iowa Press, 1998).
69. Along with Halberstam, *Skin Shows*, see above all H. L. Malchow, *Gothic Images of Race in Nineteenth-Century Britain* (Stanford: Stanford University Press, 1996).
70. As in Brantlinger, *Reading Lesson*, Smith and Hughes, eds., *Empire and the Gothic*, and such recent work as Lisa Paravinisi-Gebert, "Colonial and post-colonial Gothic: the Carribean," in Hogle, ed., *Cambridge Companion*, 229–57.
71. See Stephen J. Arata, "The Occidental tourist: *Dracula* and the anxiety of reverse colonization" (1990), and David Glover, "Travels in Romania—myths of origins, myths of blood" (1996), both in Byron, ed., *Dracula: Contemporary Critical Essays*, 119–46 and 197–217. Note also Glover's wider uses of cultural studies in *Vampires, Mummies, and Liberals: Bram Stoker and the Politics of Popular Fiction* (Durham, NC: Duke University Press, 1996).
72. See William Hughes, *Beyond Dracula: Bram Stoker's Fiction and its Cultural Contexts* (Basingstoke: Macmillan—now Palgrave Macmillan, 2000); Joseph Valente, *Dracula's Crypt: Bram Stoker, Irishness, and the Question of Blood* (Urbana: University of Illinois Press, 2002); and Gregory Castle, "Ambivalence and ascendancy in Bram Stoker's *Dracula*," in Stoker, *Dracula*, ed. Riquelme, 518–37.

3

# Romantic Gothic

*Lauren Fitzgerald*

Gothic literature was at its height of popularity during the late eighteenth and early nineteenth-century period we now refer to as "Romantic." As Michael Gamer has recently shown, the relationship between these two bodies of literature is "one not simply of passive influence but punctuated by simultaneous appropriation and critique."[1] Relationships within these two movements are similarly complex, in part because not every important change in Gothic studies over the last forty years can be attributed to the influence of Romantic studies. More generally, critical and theoretical developments in English studies, including feminist, psychoanalytic, and poststructuralist approaches, have also had an impact.

Romantic and Gothic scholarship have intersected in important ways through the impact of the critical movement variously known as cultural or historical materialism, "new" historicism, or cultural studies. Though this new approach was felt in Gothic studies independently, with David Punter's seminal *The Literature of Terror* (1980),[2] the emphasis on historicism in Romantic studies has had discernible effects upon Gothic scholarship and especially our understanding of the Gothic "canon" and whether the particular period and authors we should properly consider "Gothic" should be included among the recently widened Romantic canon. In his examination of the complicated valuation of canon formation, John Guillory makes clear that developments in scholarship do not impact curricula and classrooms in smoothly direct ways.[3] However, the evidence suggests that what is taught from and about the Romantic period Gothic has undergone change as well. Nowhere are these scholarly and curricular developments more apparent than in the changing reputation of that paradigmatic Romantic Gothic text, *Frankenstein*, particularly the question of whether to teach the 1818 or 1831 edition (or both).

Though published over thirty-five years ago, Robert D. Hume's and Robert L. Platzner's well-known exchange on "Gothic versus Romantic" makes an excellent starting point because it both sums up previous trends and looks forward to subsequent changes in both Gothic and Romantic studies.[4] Hume's initiation of the debate in 1969 confronts a long tradition of denying the relationship of Gothic and Romantic works that began at least with the distinction William Wordsworth made between the *Lyrical Ballads* and "frantic novels, sickly and stupid German tragedies, and deluges of idle and extravagant stories in verse" in his 1800 Preface.[5] Moreover, as Gamer suggests in his student-friendly introduction to the Romantic–Gothic relationship for *The Cambridge Companion to Gothic Fiction*, the exchange reenacts a more famous debate in Romantic studies between A. O. Lovejoy and René Welleck over whether Romanticism should be seen as containing multiple movements (as "Romanticism*s*") or else are focused around a distinct set of authors addressing specific themes.[6] Like Welleck, Hume maintains that "Romantic" should "denote certain characteristics of certain writers"; Platzner, invoking Lovejoy explicitly, holds to "the cultural heterogeneity of the Romantic movement."[7]

In other words, though ostensibly aiming to "revaluate" the Gothic, much of Hume and Platzner's disagreement stems from a disagreement about how Romanticism should be defined. As a result, in Hume's case especially (as Platzner points out), many of the terms by which Gothic is defined are Romantic. To take the seemingly commonsense matters of authors and period as examples, Hume follows a tradition that mirrors the way in which Romanticism had come to be defined by the "Big Six" male poets (Blake, Wordsworth, Coleridge, Keats, Byron, and Percy Shelley), often periodized between 1789 and 1832. Hume offers up five key novelists (Walpole, Radcliffe, Lewis, Mary Shelley, and Maturin) as what he calls the "serious Gothic writing" of the "original" (1764–1820) period. Its start date is marked by the publication of *The Castle of Otranto* (conveniently proclaimed by Walpole himself) and its conclusion by the publication of *Melmoth the Wanderer*.[8] The characteristics of Hume's Gothic canon are more properly Romantic. It is not simply that Gothic novels share with Romantic poetry "a strong psychological concern" and "the paradoxes of human existence" but that the Gothic fails to resolve these paradoxes for Romantic reasons. Using Coleridge's distinction, in the *Biographia Literaria* (1817), between synthesizing, transcendent, "secondary imagination" from mere "fancy," Hume argues that "Romantic writing reconciles the discordant elements it faces, resolving their apparent contradictions imaginatively in the creation of a higher order. Gothic writing [. . .] has no such answers and can only leave the 'opposites' contradictory and paradoxical."[9] Judged by Romantic criteria, the Gothic necessarily comes up short.

Though Hume's taxonomy would prove the more influential to Gothic studies, Platzner's rejoinder is significant for forecasting key developments in Romantic studies. Especially worth noting is Platzner's critique of Hume's use of "a coherent, one might almost say 'ideological,' definition of Romanticism" to measure both the Gothic and the Romantic. As he claims, "the transcendental metaphysics of the *Biographia Literaria* just cannot be imposed upon so complex and turbulent a period of literary history as the Romantic era without distortion."[10] Platzner's complaints hint at those that would be levelled a decade later by another pair of Romantic critics who would become as emblematic as Lovejoy and Welleck, Marilyn Butler, and Jerome McGann. Like Platzner (and Lovejoy), McGann and Butler argue for seeing "discriminations" rather than commonalities among literary works of the period, and they also criticize critics who reiterate or reify Romanticism's own claims about itself; particularly Coleridge's emphasis on unity and synthesis. McGann famously coined the term "Romantic Ideology" to describe this phenomenon.[11]

There are, however, a number of crucial differences in methods and claims between Platzner, McGann, and Butler. Most important, whereas Platzner counters Hume's Coleridgean view with "ontological qualities and structures" of a uniquely "Gothic imagination,"[12] McGann and Butler call for attention to the historical and cultural contexts in which literature of this period was initially produced and read. Such attention, McGann claims, is a crucial means by which to avoid succumbing to the Romantic Ideology, and particularly "the belief that poetical works can transcend historical discussions by virtue of their links with imagination, through which we see into the permanent life of things" (100). Coming as it does at the very moment when cultural materialism and new historicism emerged in English studies, this call contributed substantially to the social or historicist "turn" in scholarship on the Romantic period. Of the key differences between Butler and McGann, most relevant for us is that, as part of her more extensive enactment of Lovejoy's approach, Butler often considers the Gothic. Her methodological preference for "careful discriminations" in her landmark *Romantics, Rebels and Reactionaries* is apparent even in her treatment of the Gothic "period," which she also views as something other than "a single coherent movement." Instead, she charts two movements, one during "the revolutionary era from about 1760 to about 1797" that loses popularity during the War with France; the other, really "a revival," that resumes two decades later.[13] Butler's inclusion of the Gothic in her discussion of Romantic period works, and as part of the larger historical context, presaged important critical changes.

In Gothic studies, the new attention to history had a profound impact; the mid-1990s witnessing a remarkable number of book-length historicist accounts. Though informed by Punter's diachronic examination of several centuries of Gothic literature, examinations by Robert Miles, Steven Bruhm, Jacqueline Howard, E. J. Clery, and Maggie Kilgour focused synchronically on works from the late eighteenth and nineteenth centuries.[14] Their investigations often continued Butler's challenge to the periodization of the Gothic; Miles, for example, questioning Walpole's position as the point of origin and offering 1750 as a possible alternative.[15] James Watt, Anne Williams, and Gamer joined these scholars in challenging the Gothic as "genre" (or "subgenre") of the novel. Miles is worth quoting on this point: "we are dealing, not with the rise of a single genre, but with an area of concern, a broad subject matter, crossing the genres: drama and poetry, as well as novels" (4).[16]

This new position on the Gothic's "ontology" (to borrow Platzner's term) has presented scholars and teachers with a number of important opportunities for reconsidering what Miles calls the "Gothic aesthetic" (4), aided in no small part by the recent publication of a number of out-of-print Gothic texts, including the Gothic dramas collected by Jeffrey Cox, two editions of Charlotte Dacre's *Zofloya* (1806), and the multivolume *Varieties of Female Gothic*, edited by Gary Kelly.[17] Moreover, if the historicist turn has meant that Gothic works are more likely to have been accorded serious attention in Romantic scholarship, it also seems to have resulted in a focus on the Gothic inflections of Romantic poetry, from works long (if begrudgingly) considered in this light (Coleridge's *Christabel* [1798–1801] and Keats's *The Eve of St. Agnes* [1820] ) to the less obviously Gothic (Coleridge's "Frost at Midnight" [1798] and *The Rime of the Ancient Mariner* [1798] ) to the least likely to be considered Gothic (Wordsworth's "Peele Castle" [1805] and many of his contributions to *Lyrical Ballads*).[18] (More recent work, by Adriana Cracian and Jerrold E. Hogle in particular, blur the Gothic-versus-Romantic distinction still further.)[19] Gamer's monograph *Romanticism and the Gothic* is in many ways the culmination of this trajectory, drawing both on Miles's notion of a portable, permeable Gothic aesthetic and on McGann's critique in order to argue that "Romantic Ideology" is heavily invested in maintaining the Gothic-versus-Romantic distinction. The challenge is clear, according to Gamer:

> as the gothic is no longer what it once was, we must stop trying to define it as having a static identity, and instead try to understand the historical changes and generic transformations that led it to embody its various forms.[20]

It would be difficult to draw hard and fast conclusions about the impact of these developments in Romantic and Gothic studies on the teaching of Romantic period Gothic, yet there is evidence to suggest that curricula have registered these shifts as well, particularly in terms of opening up the Romantic teaching canon to include Gothic works. In a 1989 survey of nearly 250 faculty teaching British Romantic period literature at four-year colleges and universities in the US, Harriet Kramer Linkin found that though courses in the Romantic period "center[ed] firmly on the six traditional male poets" about half also included *Frankenstein*, with significantly smaller percentages addressing works by Radcliffe, Lewis, Beckford, Hogg, Maturin, and Walpole.[21] (She notes a not surprising but relevant correlation between the length of the course and the inclusion of these longer works, suggesting what Guillory sees as the "irreducible material constraint that only so much can be read or studied in a given class" which, in part, enables the syllabus to limit the canon rather than the other way around.)[22] One important classroom resource that both signalled these changes and received a great deal of critical scrutiny in the late 1990s was the Romantic period anthology. Though the inclusion of women poets was of special concern (as it was, in fact, for

Linkin), Gothic writing has sometimes made its way into these texts (or at least into supplementary materials).[23]

More recent (though admittedly more sketchy) evidence suggests that teachers of this period are also more inclined to bring Romantic and Gothic works together synthetically (rather than as a Gothic excursion during the Romantic tour). The recently published MLA guide, *Approaches to Teaching Gothic Fiction*, for example, offers two chapters concerned with overlap of Gothic and Romantic. Marshall Brown looks at connections between Romantic period Gothic and Romantic philosophy (such as Dacre, Radcliffe, and Kant). Explicitly countering the tendency to teach "these two types of literature [. . .] as if they have nothing to do with each other," Cannon Schmitt describes taking his students through connections between Wordsworth and Radcliffe, particularly the shared concerns over "scenes of suffering and victimization."[24] The "Online Syllabi" section of the Romantic Circles web site provides overviews of courses that directly address the intersection of Gothic and Romantic (not surprisingly, one of these courses is Gamer's) as well as connections made through themed courses that incorporate Gothic texts. For instance, and tellingly, Jon Klancher's graduate course "1800/2000: Romanticism and Postmodern Historicisms," included Lewis's *The Monk* (1796) and selections from Reeve's *The Progress of Romance* (1785), as well as courses on Romantic period women writers, travel writing, drama, and authorship, and the Byronic hero, the Shelley Circle, and *Frankenstein* itself.[25]

Another important sign of change in teaching Romantic period Gothic has been the development of invaluable resources for students. The number of texts available in reasonably priced editions rivals the original "effulgence," whether published by large presses or more specialized houses (notably Broadview and Zittaw).[26] Miles and Clery, in particular, have also made it much easier to provide students with a grounded sense of the historical contexts of these works. Most important is their coedited collection *Gothic Documents*, which reprints excerpts from difficult-to-find materials ranging from eighteenth-century translations of relevant selections from Tacitus and Horace, musings on Gothic aesthetics by Hurd, Wharton, and Blair, some of the most scathing of the contemporary responses to Lewis's *The Monk*, and Gothic-leaning political commentary on the French Revolution.[27] Similarly historical and useful is Miles's *Ann Radcliffe: the*

*Great Enchantress*, which, together with Rictor Norton's recent biography, revises earlier notions of Radcliffe as a retiring (and usually pro-Burkean and arch conservative) "authoress" living outside of the public sphere to a historically reflective liberal with Dissenting roots.[28] Clery's *Women's Gothic* historicizes the tradition that has, since Ellen Moers's coinage, been known as "Female Gothic" (and that has tended to remove women writers of Gothic fiction from their broader context).[29] In addition, both have contributed useful chapters to the *Cambridge Companion to Gothic Fiction*, and Miles to *A Companion to the Gothic*.[30]

Without doubt, the most widespread changes to the teaching of Romantic period Gothic centre on *Frankenstein*. In 1969, Hume despaired that "serious critical discussion" of Shelley's novel "was rare."[31] Now, however, its reputation having increased remarkably, *Frankenstein* is the only truly canonical work of the Gothic "canon" (one that is, moreover, and in contrast to other Romantic period Gothic texts, collected in a standard edition of its author's works, edited by Nora Crook and Pamela Clemit).[32] There are various ways of accounting for *Frankenstein*'s rise, including its consideration of questions associated with Romantic poetry while at the same time having been composed by a woman writer.[33] Also relevant is the historicist turn in Romantic and Gothic studies; though the novel is extraordinarily inviting to every critical method, approaches to *Frankenstein* have been deeply influenced by new historicism and cultural studies at the very material level of available student texts. For example, a number of recent editions include discursive materials aimed at providing students with a sense of the cultural context in which Shelley wrote and was read.[34] More dramatically, the last fifteen years have seen a widespread republishing of the first, 1818 edition in reasonably priced paperbacks that appear to be quickly displacing the 1831 version as the text of *Frankenstein* to teach. Significantly, it is the 1818 edition of *Frankenstein* that has recently been anthologized.[35] That this shift is a function of the historicist turn is evident from the argument, first made by Anne Mellor, that teachers choose this text because it provides a greater proximity to its true historical context. Butler makes a similar case in her essay "*Frankenstein* and Radical Science" as well as in her edition of the 1818 text for Oxford World's Classics.[36]

The emergence of the 1818 edition of *Frankenstein* as the new standard, both for scholarship and for teaching, is an exciting development, and not simply because it provides us with a new set of materials for classroom use. Rather, as suggested by J. Paul Hunter's Norton Critical edition of the novel, which reprints both Mellor's and Butler's essays, the new focus on the 1818 text can itself be usefully addressed in the classroom, as a means of discussing canon formation and textual choices. Moreover, as Jacqueline Foertsch points out in a discussion of teaching both the 1818 and the 1831 texts in the same course, since several editions of the 1818 text also provide the substantial changes Shelley made in her 1831 revisions, including her introduction and a number of provocative emendations; it is also possible to explore with students the ways that these revisions themselves offer, or substantially evoke, important contexts for the novel.[37] Mellor argues that one such context is Shelley's increasing political conservatism between 1818 and 1831. (For her, this is another crucial reason to choose the 1818 version.) Butler, in her introduction to the Oxford edition, makes a compelling case for reading Shelley's revisions as registering a backlash against the sort of materialist (or "radical") science that the first edition had fully absorbed. Finally, in a heart-felt plea for "parity of esteem" for both versions of the novel, Nora Crook counters Mellor's argument directly (and Butler indirectly), pointing out that the changes to Elizabeth's origins, for example, might well suggest Shelley's support of the Italian liberation rather than a wish to elide the earlier suggestions of "incest."[38]

Along with using Shelley's revisions to present students with these varying (and contested) contexts, I find it useful to focus on what these changes say about the shifting reception of Gothic in the later Romantic period (and, indeed, among recent Romantic scholars). What strikes me most about the 1818 version is that it is perceived by recent Romanticists to be somehow more "Romantic"; and the 1831 version, if only by default, as "Gothic." Mellor, for instance, begins her case for the 1818 version with "the same reasons that students of Romanticism prefer the 1805 edition of Wordsworth's *Prelude* to the final 1850 edition." Butler makes a similar appeal to the earlier versions of *The Prelude*.[39] In this way, then, *Frankenstein* serves as the paradigmatic Romantic Gothic text.

A useful place to begin looking at these "Romantic" and "Gothic" versions of *Frankenstein* is with a comparison of the two strikingly different prefatory pieces for the two editions. The 1818 Preface, by

Shelley's first and most important reader, her husband Percy, is remarkable not least for the force with which it rejects "merely weaving a series of supernatural terrors," "the disadvantages of a mere tale of specters or enchantments," and "the enervating effects of the novels of the present day."[40] This last point sounds remarkably like the passage from the Preface to *Lyrical Ballads* I quote above, as well as Wordsworth's lament over the "degrading thirst after outrageous stimulation" among the turn-of-the-century reading public.[41] Percy Shelley, like Wordsworth before him, seems determined to shield subsequent interpretations of the text at hand from any potential Gothic associations. Reviews of the 1818 version suggest that Percy Shelley's attempts were successful: readers responded to the Godwinian rather than Gothic associations, particularly because of the dedication to Mary Shelley's father in the first edition.

The contrasts offered by Mary Shelley's 1831 "Author's Introduction" are instructive. She claims that her intentions were to achieve precisely the Gothic effects Percy rejects, to "speak to the mysterious fears of our nature and awaken thrilling horror—to make the reader dread to look round, to curdle the blood, and quicken the beatings of the heart" (195). The well-known parallel Shelley draws between herself and Victor Frankenstein, and between his creation and her "hideous progeny" (197), only underscores this apparently Gothic vision of the novel (something her publisher seems to have supported as well since, according to Wolfson, the 1831 edition was published on Hallowe'en and bound with Frederick Schiller's *The Ghost-Seer*).[42] In so doing, Butler holds, "Mary Shelley deflected attention from the historical sources and implications of her text by introducing an exaggerated, sensationalized diversion concerning its psychic origins."[43] As "exaggerated" and "sensationalized," the 1831 version is, in other words, Gothic, all the more so, perhaps, precisely because it is distanced from its historical origins.

Comparing Percy's Preface to Mary's Introduction can lead to other important Romantic Gothic (or Gothic Romantic) moments in the 1831 version of *Frankenstein*. The reference both Shelleys make to the potential "effects" of such texts might well remind students of the scenes of reading elsewhere in the novel, such as Walton's, Victor's, the Creature's, or Henry Clerval's. Of these, Shelley substantially rewrote all but the Creature's scene. The general impression of these changes is to make an even stronger case for the sometimes-dangerous effects of reading. One passage especially worth talking to students about is Walton's much revised comments on his plan to go "to 'the land of mist and snow' " (10). In the 1831 version, Walton both calls attention to and explains the "allusion" to Coleridge's *Ancient Mariner* (perhaps Shelley worried that later readers would not catch the reference). He also discloses "a secret" not explored in the earlier version: "I have often attributed my attachment to, my passionate enthusiasm for, the dangerous mysteries of the ocean, to that production of the most imaginative of modern poets" (201).

Along with providing entrée into another important Gothic Romantic revision (the glossed version of Coleridge's poem appeared the year before the first edition of *Frankenstein* was published), Walton's fuller reflections on the effects of *The Rime of the Ancient Mariner* offers a means of addressing Hume and Platzner's debate about Romantic and Gothic "imagination." The imagination that Walton attributes to Coleridge, ironically enough, conjures up the sort of Gothic influence that Coleridge himself had worried over in his reviews of Gothic texts,[44] whereas Percy Shelley's Preface forwards an "imagination" that could have come straight from *The Defence of Poetry*, "delineating human passions more comprehensive and commanding than any which the ordinary relations of existing events can yield" (3). Of course, no one text can do justice to the question of what Gothic or Romantic ostensibly (or "ontologically") "is" (to return to Platzner). But the revisions Shelley made to the 1831 edition and what they suggest about her changing interpretation of the novel and her audience goes a long way towards presenting to students the ongoing tensions during this period (and later) between Gothic and Romantic.

## Notes

1. Michael Gamer, *Romanticism and the Gothic: Genre, Reception, and Canon Formation* (Cambridge: Cambridge University Press, 2000) 28.
2. David Punter, *The Literature of Terror: a History of Gothic Fictions from 1765 to the Present Day* [1980] 2nd edn (London and New York: Longman, 1996).
3. John Guillory, *Cultural Capital: the Problem of Literary Canon Formation* (Chicago and London: University of Chicago Press, 1993).

4. Robert D. Hume, "Gothic versus Romantic: a revaluation of the Gothic novel," *PMLA* 84 (1969) 282–90; Robert L. Platzner and Robert D. Hume, " 'Gothic versus Romantic': a rejoinder," *PMLA* 86 (1971) 266–74.
5. William Wordsworth, Preface to *Lyrical Ballads*, 2nd edn [1800], Rpt. *Romanticism: an Anthology with CD-ROM*, ed., Duncan Wu, 2nd edn (Oxford and Cambridge: Blackwell, 1998) 357–66, at 359.
6. Michael Gamer, "Gothic fictions and Romantic writing in Britain," *The Cambridge Companion to Gothic Fiction*, ed. Jerrold E Hogle (Cambridge: Cambridge University Press, 2002) 85–104, at 85; A. O Lovejoy, "On the discrimination of Romanticisms," *PMLA* 39 (1924) 229–53; René Welleck, "The concept of Romanticism in literary scholarship," *Comparative Literature* I (1949) 1–23, 147–72.
7. Platzner and Hume, "Gothic versus Romantic," 269, 272.
8. Plaztner and Hume, "Gothic versus Romantic," 268. In establishing this Gothic "canon," Hume follows several earlier twentieth-century critics, including Montague Summers, *The Gothic Quest: a History of the Gothic Novel* [1938] (New York: Russell and Russell, 1964), J. M. S. Tompkins, *The Popular Novel in England 1770–1800* [1932] (Lincoln: University of Nebraska Press, 1961) and Lowry Nelson Jr. "Night thoughts on the Gothic novel," *Yale Review* 52 (1963), 236–57. (Hume's contemporary, Robert Kiely, follows a similar canon, though because of his somewhat broader subject, he expands the list slightly. *The Romantic Novel in England* [Cambridge: Harvard University Press, 1972].) The consolidation of this list of authors seems to begin as early as the 1790s, with contemporary reviews (see Lauren Fitzgerald, "The Gothic properties of Walpole's legacy: Ann Radcliffe's contemporary reception," *Fictions of Unease: the Gothic from Otranto to* The X-Files, eds Andrew Smith, William Hughes, and Diane Mason [Bath: Sulis Press, 2002) 29–42] ).
9. Hume, "Gothic versus Romantic," 288–90.
10. Platzner and Hume, "Gothic versus Romantic," 272, 267.
11. Marilyn Butler, *Romantics, Rebels and Reactionaries: English Literature and its Background, 1760–1830* (Oxford and New York: Oxford University Press, 1981) 6–7, 184–5: Jerome J. McGann, *The Romantic Ideology: a Critical Investigation* (Chicago: University of Chicago Press, 1983) 17–20, 47. All subsequent references are to this edition, and are given in the text.
12. Platzner and Hume, "Gothic versus Romantic," 270, 267.
13. Butler, *Romantics*, 184, 8, 156–8.
14. Robert Miles, *Gothic Writing 1750–1820: a Genealogy*, 2nd edn (Manchester and New York: Manchester University Press, [1993] 2002). All subsequent references are to this edition, and are given in the text; Steven Bruhm, *Gothic Bodies: the Politics of Pain in Romantic Fiction* (Philadelphia: University of Pennsylvania Press, 1994); Jacqueline Howard, *Reading Gothic Fiction: a Bakhtinian Approach* (Oxford: Clarendon, 1994); E. J. Clery, *The Rise of Supernatural Fiction, 1762–1800* (Cambridge: Cambridge University Press, 1995); Maggie Kilgour, *The Rise of the Gothic Novel* (London and New York: Routledge, 1995).
15. Miles, *Gothic Writing*, 1.

16. James Watt, *Contesting the Gothic: Fiction, Genre and Cultural Conflict, 1764–1832* (Cambridge: Cambridge Univerisity Press, 1999); Anne Williams, *Art of Darkness: a Poetics of Gothic* (Chicago and London: University of Chicago Press, 1995); Gamer, *Romanticism*.
17. Jeffrey N. Cox, ed., *Seven Gothic Dramas 1789–1825* (Athens: Ohio University Press, 1992); Charlotte Dacre, *Zofloya; or, The Moor*, ed. Adriana Craciun (Peterborough, ON: Broadview, 1997) and ed. Kim I. Michasiw (Oxford: Oxford University Press, 1997); Gary Kelly, ed. *Varieties of Female Gothic*. 6 vols. (London: Pickering and Chatto, 2002).
18. See Miles, *Gothic Writing*, chapter 9; Williams, *Art of Darkness*, chapters 16 and 17; Gamer, *Romanticism*, chapters 1 and 3.
19. Adriana Craciun, *Fatal Women of Romanticism* (Cambridge and New York: Cambridge University Press, 2003); Jerrold E. Hogle, "The Gothic ghost as counterfeit and its haunting of Romanticism: the case of 'Frost at Midnight'," *European Romantic Review* 9 (1998) 283–92 and "The Gothic–Romantic relationship: underground histories in 'The Eve of St. Agnes'," *European Romantic Review* 14 (2003) 205–23. Hogle also edited a special issue of *Gothic Studies* on "Romanticism and the 'New Gothic'," *Gothic Studies* 3.1 (2001).
20. Gamer, *Romanticism*, 9–10.
21. Harriet Kramer Linkin, "The current canon in British Romantic studies," *College English* 53.5 (1991), 548–70 at 548–9, 554–5.
22. Linkin, "The current canon," 556, Guillory, *Cultural Capital*, 29–30.
23. The CD-ROM of Duncan Wu's *Romanticism: an Anthology with CD-ROM*, which is edited by David Miall and Wu, features summaries of Gothic works, contemporary reviews, and illustrations. The most recent (Seventh) edition of *The Norton Anthology of English Literature*, edited by M. H. Abrams and Stephen Greenblatt (New York and London: W. W. Norton, 2000) includes the full text of *Frankenstein* for the first time in its Romantic Period section. Also new is its online supplement, which surveys "Literary Gothic" and offers paper topics and quizzes. (*Norton Topics Online* (2000) <June 7, 2005> http://www.wwnorton.com/nael/welcome. htm.) For discussion of the controversy over these and other anthologies, see the special issue of *Romanticism on the Net* edited by Laura Mandell: "Romantic anthologies" *Romanticism on the Net* 7 (August 1997) [June 7, 2005] <http://users.ox.ac.uk/~scat0385/guest.html>.
24. Marshall Brown, "Philosophy and the Gothic novel," and Cannon Schmitt, "Suffering through the Gothic: teaching Radcliffe" in Diane Long Hoeveler and Tamar Heller, eds., *Approaches to Teaching Gothic Fiction: the British and American Traditions* (New York: The Modern Language Society of America, 2003) 46–57, 115–21 at 119.
25. Laura Mandell and Vince Willoughby, eds., "Online syllabi," *Romantic Circles*, ed. Neil Fraistat and Steven E. Jones [June 7, 2005] http://www.rc.umd.edu/pedagogies/syllabi/ index.html#menu.
26. Robert Miles, "The 1790s: the effulgence of Gothic," *The Cambridge Companion to Gothic Fiction*, ed. Jerrold E. Hogle (Cambridge: Cambridge University Press, 2002) 41–62.

27. E. J. Clery, and Robert Miles, eds, *Gothic documents: a Sourcebook 1700–1820* (Manchester and New York: Manchester University Press, 2000).
28. Robert Miles, *Ann Radcliffe: the Great Enchantress* (Manchester and New York: Manchester University Press, 1995); Rictor Norton, *Mistress of Udolpho: the Life of Ann Radcliffe* (London and New York: Leicester University Press, 1999).
29. E. J. Clery, *Women's Gothic: from Clara Reeve to Mary Shelley* (Tavistock: Northcote House, 2000).
30. E. J. Clery, "The genesis of 'Gothic' fiction," *The Cambridge Companion to Gothic Fiction*, ed. Jerrold E. Hogle (Cambridge: Cambridge University Press, 2002) 21–40; Robert Miles, "The 1790s," and "Ann Radcliffe and Matthew Lewis," *A Companion to the Gothic*, ed. David Punter (Oxford: Blackwell, 2000) 41–57.
31. Hume, "Gothic versus Romantic," 285.
32. Nora Crook and Pamela Clemit, eds, *The Novels and Selected Works of Mary Shelley*, 8 vols (London: Pickering Masters, 1996).
33. Stephen C. Behrendt, "An overview of the survey," *Approaches to Teaching Shelley's* Frankenstein, ed. Behrendt (New York: The Modern Language Association of America, 1990) 1–6, at 1.
34. Documents suggesting the cultural contexts of the novel are included in *Frankenstein: Complete, Authoritative Text with Biographical, Historical, and Cultural Contexts, Critical History, and Essays from Contemporary Critical Perspectives*, ed. Joanna M. Smith, 2nd edn (Boston and New York: Bedford/St. Martin's, 2000); and in *Frankenstein; or, the Modern Prometheus*, ed. Susan J. Wolfson (New York: Longman, 2002). Reviews and other relevant documents are provided by *Frankenstein, or the Modern Prometheus: the 1818 Text*, ed. Marilyn Butler [1994] (Oxford and New York: Oxford University Press, 1998); *Frankenstein; or the Modern Prometheus: the 1818 Version*, ed. D. L. MacDonald and Kathleen Scherf (Peterborough, ON: Broadview, 1994); and *Frankenstein: the 1818 Text, Contexts, Nineteenth-Century Responses, Modern Criticism*, ed. J. Paul Hunter (New York and London: W. W. Norton, 1996).
35. In 1990, Behrendt reported that the majority of teachers of *Frankenstein* used the 1831 version, "Editions," *Approaches to Teaching Frankenstein*, 9–11 at 10. Less than a decade later, Pamela Clemit claimed that the 1818 text was "fast becoming the standard text for serious students" "Mary Wollstonecraft Shelley," *Literature of the Romantic Period: a Bibliographic Guide*, ed. Michael O'Neill (Oxford: Clarendon, 1998) 284–97, at 285. The 1818 version of the novel is included in the Romantic Period section of the *Norton Anthology*. Wolfson's Longman edition (also the 1818 text) is intended to supplement *The Longman Anthology of British Literature*.
36. Anne Mellor, "Choosing a text of *Frankenstein* to teach" [1990] and Marilyn Butler, "*Frankenstein* and radical science" [1993], in Mary Wollstonecraft Shelley, *Frankenstein*, ed. Hunter, 160–6, 302–13; *Frankenstein*, ed. Butler.
37. Jacqueline Foertsch, "The right, the wrong, and the ugly: teaching Shelley's several *Frankensteins*," *College English* 63.6 (2001) 697–711. Of

the student editions of the 1818 text, Butler's and MacDonald and Scherf's include in appendices the substantive 1831 revisions. (Wolfson's edition has only one of Shelley's substantial revisions.) Maurice Hindle's edition of the 1831 text also includes these revisions in an appendix, *Frankenstein; or, the Modern Prometheus* (Harmondsworth: Penguin, 2003). Foertsch helpfully suggests supplementing 1818 versions that do not include these revisions with one of the many inexpensive 1831 versions, 699.

38. Nora Crook, "In defense of the 1831 *Frankenstein,*" *Mary Shelley's Fictions: from* Frankenstein *to* Falkner, ed. Michael Eberle-Sinatra (Basingstoke: Macmillan—now Palgrave Macmillan, 2000) 1–21 at 3, 5–6.
39. Mellor, "Choosing," 160; Butler, "*Frankenstein,*" 304.
40. Shelley, *Frankenstein*, ed. Butler, 3. All subsequent references are to this edition, and are given in the text.
41. Wordsworth, Preface, 359.
42. Wolfson, ed. *Frankenstein*, xxxv.
43. Butler, ed. *Frankenstein*, xxlii.
44. See Gamer, *Romanticism*, 98–100.

# 4
# Victorian Gothic

*Julian Wolfreys*

## I. Introduction

If one is to teach a subject such as "Victorian Gothic," the initial gesture has to be to question the very grounds on which the subject is built. If we are approaching a particular form, genre, or structure, rather like Jonathan Harker approaching Castle Dracula, or Poe's anonymous narrator who draws near the home of Roderick Usher one Autumn afternoon in *The Fall of the House of Usher* (1839), we would do well to pause before the house we are about to enter. Unlike our Gothic predecessors, we would benefit from pausing in our journey before rushing headlong into what may well prove to be a haunted house. Halting is necessary. For in questioning how the house comes to be built, we actually make it possible to exhibit in the teaching of our subject not only the structures that inform, but also the ghosts that disturb both the form itself and the equally haunted presuppositions by which we would otherwise have proceeded.

In this consideration of how one orients oneself to so vast a subject as "Victorian Gothic" what I propose is only the merest of openings of the subject. In reflecting also on how one approaches teaching a subject the very identity of which is fraught from the beginning, a degree of circumspection is necessary. This essay thus begins by suspending its own development, to ask: what is *Victorian* about "Victorian Gothic"? What is Gothic in the ontology of "Victorianism"? Raising such interrogations, I shall argue through the present essay that it is impossible to speak of such ontologies. The signs that we have come to read as "Gothic" arrive in the nineteenth century so as to disrupt any secure ontological formation and thereby mark the period in question as one of modernity in crisis.

Such procedure might in its prevarications appear an unnecessary annoyance. Yet no pedagogy of the "Victorian Gothic" can take place *as if* the ontology of the genre or subject were already in place. Take the very phrase "Victorian Gothic": whatever provisional, contentious identity there might be to be found, "Victorian" does not simply modify historically the Gothic. Rather, the two terms exist in an agonistic embrace. Theirs is a desirous and destructive strife. They may be perceived as contesting with, and constantly redefining one another, much like Henry Jekyll and Mr Hyde, Frankenstein and his creature, or Dorian Gray and the prosopopoeic manifestation of his "soul" that is his portrait.

Moreover, my caution is not without precedent. In an article the purpose of which is to address the principal features of "The Victorian Gothic," Peter Kitson draws attention to certain problematic issues, without questioning the ontology. He remarks, for instance, that "there are many definitions of 'Gothic'."[1] Such definitions have to do either with the reiterated insistence of form, content, and feature, or else with the "effects these fictions have in raising the anxieties of its audience" (165). Then the structure of Gothic narrative is "fragmented or confusing . . . an overall unity masked by digressions, detours, and prolixity" (165). However, after the 1820s Gothic is translated into a mode rather than being a discernible form (165). In this acknowledgement, while giving some attention to what he calls "the Gothic revival" between the 1820s and 1890s, with reference principally to Dickens, Collins, and Le Fanu as "transitional," Kitson's concentration is on sensational and melodramatic fictions of the *fin de siècle*.[2] In the last two decades of the nineteenth century the Gothic reappears, as if it were some manifestation or the return of the repressed. As Kitson indicates, its features are the attention given to somatic fears, anxieties over Empire and the purity of identity, phobias occasioned by perceived decadance, feminization, homosexuality, the threat of empire's others, and the widespread sense of social and cultural degeneration, given pseudoscientific valorization in the works of eugenicists and anthropologists such as Cesare Lombroso and Max Nordau.

As far as this narrative goes, it is accurate enough. I have no argument with Kitson's faithful and lucid assessment. However, that which is conventionally acknowledged as the period of high Victorianism from the 1840s to 1880s is read implicitly as the time of Gothic's subordination, translation, and marginalization. The translation from genre into modality after the 1820s implicitly bears in it the assumption of a devaluation of "Gothic." Indeed, this is borne out by Kitson's analysis of Collins and Le Fanu, in the details of which he reads the anticipation of *fin de siècle* Gothic.[3] Thus "Victorian Gothic" is an evacuated identity. Not having a "properly" Gothic identity of its own, sensation and melodramatic fiction of the period in question comes to be bracketed on the one hand by the Gothic-proper and, on the other, the return of the Gothic in the *fin de siècle*. As I have already implied and wish to argue further, asking the question of the "Victorian Gothic" will permit access to another view of Gothic's apparent epochal quietus.

## II. A simple story?

Once upon a time, so the story goes, the Gothic as literary genre made its first recognized appearances in the second half of the eighteenth century. A provisional date often assigned to the inauguration of the Gothic is 1764, with the publication of Horace Walpole's *The Castle of Otranto*. The Gothic persisted largely through novels but also made "cameo" appearances in poetry and in plays such as Joanna Baillie's *Orra* (1812) until the first quarter of the nineteenth century. Its "final" formal expression is often acknowledged with reference to one of two or three publications: either Mary Shelley's *Frankenstein* (1818), Charles Maturin's *Melmoth the Wanderer* (1820), or *Vathek* by William Beckford (1823). The Gothic had a life, up till then, of just over half a century. In that time amongst the key publications of the genre were the novels of Ann Radcliffe, perhaps the most memorable being *The Mysteries of Udolpho* (1794), and Matthew Lewis' *The Monk* (1796).

But what of the elements, the narrative conceits or devices, the figures or motifs that are taken as belonging to the Gothic? What makes the Gothic Gothic, and how much of the Gothic remains in nineteenth-century novels as the material and ghostly remnants and traces that persist in Victorian novels? One aspect of the Gothic was its expression of inner fears, of fantasies, of visions, and of hauntings. In this sense, the Gothic provided articulation of the repressed dimensions of the human psyche. Ghosts often figure as the externalized and prosopopoeic manifestations of such psychological disturbances. More generally, Gothic has been read as questioning the boundaries of the self, whether psychoanalytically or nationally. In this latter aspect, Gothic at the end of the eighteenth century has been taken as a form of narrative concerned with the parameters of Englishness, and the threat to those psychic and cultural borders. Hence Gothic fiction returned to common narrative concerns with foreigners, with Catholics, brigands, monks, and those Europeans who embodied for the English reader the irrational, the sensuous, and the excessive. The landscape of the Gothic was frequently wild, rugged, tormented by savage atmospheric conditions and home to decaying castles or ruined manorial houses. It is also a landscape haunted not only by ghosts but also occasionally vampires and other liminal, monstrous figures.

We are all familiar with the tropes, features, and moods of the Gothic. As Eve Kosofsky Sedgwick remarks, "you know the important features of its *mise en scène*: an oppressive ruin, a wild landscape, a Catholic or feudal society. You know about the trembling sensibility of the heroine and the impetuosity of her lover. You know about the tyrannical older man."[4] Further, with regard to the novel's form, "it is likely to be discontinuous and involuted, perhaps incorporating tales within tales, changes of narrators, and such framing devices as found in manuscripts or interpolated histories" (9). There are many other details to which Sedgwick refers in the opening of her study, such as echoes, subterranean locations, the inference of incest, doubles, dreams, the priesthood, themes of guilt and thwarted inheritance, madhouses, and extended nocturnal narrative sequences.[5]

In response to the question, "What is 'Gothic'?" Robert Miles has asked, "what could be less problematic" than the genre's definition?[6] What appears across the Gothic is that repeatedly it addresses a "deeper wound" as David Punter has it, bringing back the psychological dimension of the genre, "a fracture, an imbalance, a 'gap' in the social self which would not go away."[7] However, Miles takes us further, when he remarks that "Gothic writing needs to be regarded as a series of contemporaneously understood forms, devices, codes, figurations, for the expression of the 'fragmented subject'. It should be regarded as literary 'speech' in its own right . . . Gothic formulae are not simply recycled, as if in the service of a neurotic, dimly understood drive; rather, Gothic texts 'revise' one another" (3). The Gothic is not simply *about* something else. It is, itself, a discursive and heterogeneous site, internally riven and without a proper identity, that addresses itself to the "fragmented subject" in history (Miles 1993, 4). To put this another way, "Gothic exists in relation to mainstream culture in the same way as a parasite does to its host . . . Gothic represents, then, a cultural knot."[8]

As Punter and Miles' remarks imply, the Gothic is hardly a genre at all. Nor is Gothic not containable to one period. Given its own internal heterogeneity, Gothic mutates endlessly, coming to take its shapes according to the culture or historical moment, as a *perversion* (to borrow Punter's term) that informs us ineluctably that *this is who we are*. Having no proper form as such, Gothic is a constant phantasmic representation of the meaning of being, in all its historicity.

If there is a "Victorian Gothic" therefore, the outward signs by which it appears to resemble the earlier late-eighteenth-century form are merely coincidental. Such traces are merely the most obvious and available figures for disfiguring the self in its acts of self-reading and self-representation. In overflowing itself, the so-called Gothic affirms that there is no Gothic as such. The implications of this for the idea of a "Victorian Gothic" are numerous and profound. On the one hand particular aspects of nineteenth-century English identity remain haunted by earlier cultural anxieties and perceptions concerning national identity and being. On the other hand, the traversal of Gothic tropes beyond the genre or period of the "Gothic-proper" erase at least in part periodic boundaries and so unsettle the possibility on a broader historical stage of assigning "Victorian" as a cultural and historial adjective. It is as if the phantoms of the Gothic arrive so as to illuminate in encrypted form the Victorians to themselves.

## III. Interrogations

Given all that I have said, and given the conventional wisdom, which imposes an historical frame marked by the 1820s and the 1880s and 1890s, essentially reducing everything in between to the transitional or otherwise to deflect readings of the Gothic onto some obvious stage effects in genre fiction such as detective narratives, sensation novels, or ghost stories, it has to be asked again: was there a "Victorian Gothic"? Without assuming the possibility of a stable ontology, what we are naming "Victorian Gothic" may not amount to much more than a number of occasional, if frequent, effects or tropes, themselves the traces that survive an earlier literary form. That "not much more" is found widely however; like a parasite in its middle-class host's body, the trace of the gothic is everywhere, and cannot be dismissed merely in terms of the transitional or reduced to particular inflections in genre fiction. As one editor of Mary Elizabeth Braddon's sensation novel *Lady Audley's Secret* (1862) has it, "The modernity of . . . setting and characters added to the suspense and horror."[9] Furthermore, the Victorian Gothic reflects "an increasing instability in the concepts of privacy and personal identity in a newly urban and technological society" (29). The marks or signs of Gothic that arrive repeatedly in Victorian fiction complicate and disturb that fiction in its more or less realist presentations of the English to themselves.

On the other hand, there is an understanding that the language of any given literary text and the structures that produce particular effects are always themselves inescapably material, cultural, ideological, epistemological, and historical in the manner of their intercommunications and their communications—or failures thereof—with the reader. Bearing such matters in mind, I will strive to open for the reader the ways in which the Gothic assumes a particular series of singular forms or modes of presentation and representation. Such modalities are themselves the profound signs of the historicity of the texts in question, the apprehension of which allows for recognition of the darker aspects of nineteenth-century culture, and which in being both popular *and* subversive, were embraced by the Victorians as much as they may be said to reveal their anxieties.

To consider briefly a few examples of "Victorian Gothic": *The Strange Case of Dr Jekyll and Mr Hyde* (1886) exhibits in its narrative a staging of existential and psychic crisis for the subject occasioned by the perception of the fragmentation of subjectivity occasioned by a perception of modernity. Novels such as *Wuthering Heights* (1847), *The Moonstone* (1868) or many other Wilkie Collins' novels, or Richard Marsh's *The Beetle* (1897), express fears of the frequently foreign Other. Le Fanu's novels and Bram Stoker's *Dracula* (1897) can also be read for the "Gothicization" of English anxieties over the Irish. In *Dracula* and in other vampire narratives such as Vernon Lee's one may read fears concerning cultural degeneracy, sexual ambivalence or decadence, or even encoded worries about sexually transmitted diseases.

But what of the less immediate, if not less obvious locations of the Gothic remainder? Charles Dickens provides the reader with some interesting sites of hybrid representation and the staging of instances informed by the Gothic impulse. Most if not all Dickens' novels and many of his short stories exhibit particular signs of the Gothic, including malevolent strangers, nocturnal scenes, or swarms of phantoms. His collaborative effort, *The Haunted House* (the latter written in 1859 with Hesba Stretton, George Augustus Sala, Adelaide Procter, Wilkie Collins, and Elizabeth Gaskell) provides singular pedagogical opportunities for its hybridities and tensions.[10] As Peter Ackroyd observes in his Foreword, the opening story written by Dickens, though "somewhat Gothic," is "very much part of its modern period. The railway engine is mentioned in the first paragraph and indeed the concern with ghosts was itself an aspect of the 1860s, when various spirit mediums paraded their skills in front of credulous audiences" (vii). Dickens is quite blatant about the apparently "atypical" context of the story itself: "Under none of the accredited ghostly circumstances, and environed by none of the conventional ghostly surroundings, did I first make acquaintance with the house which is the subject of this Christmas piece" (3). He continues, in a perhaps comic, but certainly ironic manner thus: "There was no wind, no rain, no lightning, no thunder, no awful or unwonted circumstance of any kind . . . More than that, I had come to it [the house of the title] direct from a railway station . . . and, as I stood outside the house, looking back upon the way I had come, I could see the goods train" (3). It is as if the inauguration of a modern ghost story requires the acknowledgement of the absence of the traces of the Gothic, for the story to be both "modern" (i.e., Victorian) *and* Gothic in the new style. Irony announces the very possibility of the Gothic's revenance in the instance that the Gothic appears to be banished and reassurance is at hand in the guise of modern technologies of transport.

At the same time, elsewhere, the Gothic is at work. In the sixth of the eight stories comprising *The Haunted House*, the enigmatic puzzle that torments the subject in conventional Gothic tales is reduced to a mere siglum, the letter *B* appended to a letter signed *B* (71–82). Perhaps in partial parody, but certainly in imitation of Gothic setting, mode, and idiom, Dickens' narrator poses the inquiry concerning the letter: "When I established myself in the triangular garret which had gained so distinguished a reputation, my thoughts about him were uneasy and manifold . . . With profitless meditations I tormented myself much . . . from the first, I was haunted by the letter B" (71). The subject places himself in a somewhat neglected location in the house; his mind is uneasy, he is troubled, and troubles himself. Haunting arrives "from the first" as Dickens has it—that is to say, it returns from the very beginning, doing so in the form of the graphic trace, the letter. This is, we might conjecture, an exemplary moment of Victorian Gothic. In the face of nothing more than the trace, and acknowledging that writing's communication is always a matter of ghostly transport that, in returning, disturbs the subject's perception, haunting, and thus the "modern" manifestation of the Gothic in the nineteenth century, comes down to this revenance.

Inscription accounts for many of the manifestations of haunting and the Gothic effect in Victorian literature, whether in the form of found letters or in the haunting power of the proper name. The stitched letters *d.n.f.* in a watch silk haunt Arthur Clennam, as the trace of his father's voice returning from beyond the grave in *Little Dorrit* (1865). Even names in Dickens are occasionally made ghoulish, grotesque, or else have Gothic implications, as the example of the name of the schoolmaster, Bradley Headstone, from Dickens' last novel, *Our Mutual Friend* (1865) suggests. Whether one considers the flight of Bill Sykes into the countryside, following the murder of Nancy, in *Oliver Twist* (1838), or, again, the dying of Paul Dombey, in which the extended death scene is euphemized as the "old-fashion" in *Dombey and Son* (1848), the signs of Gothic are there.[11]

As Paul dies, the passage of life-to-death is recorded with a distinctly Gothic inflection: "As the reflection [of the sun] died away, and a gloom went creeping up the wall, he watched it deepen, deepen, deepen, into night" (292). Paul is dying; the reader is aware of this, but Dickens intensifies the apprehension of the impending death through the temporal shift registered here and, with that, the arguably Gothic motion of the creeping gloom, with that repetitious, "deepen, deepen, deepen." Perhaps also Gothic here, though less visible than felt one might say, is the sense that, in that repetition, the sentence assumes what speech act theory would describe as a performative effect: repetition "deepens" the reading subject's awareness and reception of the encroaching, consuming darkness, which is simultaneously real and perceptual, phenomenologically apprehended. Later comes a repetition, this time in Paul's perceptions as the day, again, moves on towards night: "he . . . would . . . be troubled with a restless and uneasy sense again—the child could hardly tell whether this were in his sleeping or his waking moments" (293). Here we read the hallucinatory shift in subjective ground, a destabilization of perception that in the Gothic-proper is attributed to external forces, at least initially. Here however, the condition is phenomenological, psychosomatic.

Paul's corporeal-psychological condition changes to the extent that the world of his room is the scene of constant shifting hallucination, so that "the people round him changed . . . unaccountably" (294). Finally, there appears to Paul an unnamed figure "with its head upon its hand" (294), who returns again and again but never speaks. Dickens constructs the passage in such a manner that Paul's uncertainty about the character—is it his father?—becomes that of the reader also. What we therefore read is that representation itself is haunted by the disturbance to Paul's perception. Home, the most familiar location, is written as inescapably haunted, and what I describe as the spectralization of the Gothic is in full force here. For, unlike earlier Gothic novels, the effect is neither local, nor is it maintained diegetically within the narrative frame. The haunting is, we might say, the narrative; concomitantly, simultaneously, narrative is Gothicized. It is in this slippage, and the erasure of perceptual and formal boundaries between form and content, that one dimension of Victorian Gothic is revealed—the irreversible and performative destabilization of the borders of narrative and medium.

One observes then how the Gothic is translated, even as it simultaneously transforms elements of comedy, the grotesque, melancholy, and melodrama. Also noteworthy is the extent to which in the nineteenth century the Gothic is domesticated. While Gothic elements such as foreigners and thunderstorms remain, they are now placed in English landscapes, and on many occasions into the Victorian home itself. There are to be found lurking here and there a mad woman in an attic, as in *Jane Eyre*, or a spectre, as in *Wuthering Heights*. Forced to spend the night at Wuthering Heights, Mr Lockwood encounters a ghost outside the window of his bedroom: "As it spoke, I discerned, obscurely, a child's face, looking through the window—Terror made me cruel; and, finding it useless to attempt shaking the creature off, I pulled its wrist on to the broken pane, and rubbed it to and fro till the blood ran down and soaked the bed-clothes."[12]

Peculiar to this scene, a sign of its historicity, is that haunting takes place in a farmhouse in Yorkshire, not some foreign castle. The narrator being haunted is not a young woman but a middle-aged man, while the ghost is that of a child. And the scene is doubly Gothic, inasmuch as the appearance of the spectre is not so much violent as it causes in the protagonist an act of cruelty more usually associated in the conventions of Gothic with those who persecute the protagonists, narrators, and heroines of Gothic novels. The "Victorian Gothic" is clearly marked by discernible differences from its predecessors. Not least amongst these differences is, whether one considers Paul Dombey or Mr Lockwood, or for that matter the narrator of George Eliot's strange tale of uncanny foresight, *The Lifted Veil* (1859), an internalization of the Gothic as the articulation, and often the self-reflexive division, of Victorian subjectivity.

And, as we see from the Dombey home, from Audley Court in Braddon's novel and Wuthering Heights, another of the chief differences is this—that England and the English home are no longer "safe" or "familiar." If England is still "home," it is also "unhomely," those places supposedly most familiar having now been rendered threatening, uncanny.[13] An Englishman's—and woman's—house, is no longer a castle, but the location where what haunts—death, the ghost of a child—reminds one that the uncanny "is in reality nothing new or alien, but something which is familiar and old-established [hence Dickens' phrase for death, 'the old-fashion'] in the mind and which has become alienated from it" (217). Considering *Wuthering Heights* one last time, it is not, we see, Heathcliff, the outsider, but the ghost of the dead Cathy, who returns to haunt her home. Everything, as Freud has it, that is uncanny, is that which "ought to have remained secret and hidden but has come to light" (200). Moreover, as with the example of *Dombey*'s shift to performative instability, it is the very form of *Wuthering Heights* that is disruptive. As Nicholas Royle has argued, it is "extremely complex, bewilderingly rapid and intense. It is in certain respects . . . like a dream . . . it is . . . the labyrinthine strangeness of this structure which constitutes the force of this narrative."[14] We come to see how that which is most transformed, haunted within itself, is the very form of the English novel itself in the mid-nineteenth century. Far from simply representing the "labyrinthine strangeness" of the Gothic abode, the novel itself becomes informed by—and as—the Gothic force in the disturbances of its narrative manifestations. It is as if, for the Victorians, the novel were a haunted house.

What comes to be assembled in such a narration of the "Victorian Gothic" is therefore the construction of a cultural machinery of representation that stresses both the anxieties or desires of the subject and also, more fundamentally, an intuition of the modernity of his or her subjectivity in those very places where he or she should feel safest being under threat. English subjectivity is in crisis in the nineteenth century. *Crisis* is the condition of its being, it is a constituent element of bourgeois subjectivity, whether from perceived foreign threats or from the transformation of the world around it, a world once thought and still remembered as familiar. The "Victorian Gothic" in its heterogeneity and difference addresses without announcing directly a multiplicity of alterities as the contingent facets of identity's modernity. Those gestures that trace alterity in their responsibility to Victorian otherness affirm and articulate an otherwise inchoate, haunting, and haunted identity in ruins. Again this is not just the articulation of anxiety, doubt, or fear. It is instead, more neutrally one form that self-representation, the self-reading of identity takes. What we come to read is thus better apprehended as a *hauntology* rather than an ontology. In this spectral guise is the encoded expression of the text's historicity. It is that which puts the Victorian in "Victorian Gothic."

## IV. Translated Gothic: Le Fanu

So far, so Gothic; or at least apparently so—for many such features are also to be found in other novels throughout the nineteenth century, which could not be called Gothic. *The Pickwick Papers* (1837) has old castles (well, one), a tyrannical older man, trembling heroines and impetuous young(ish) men. Manuscripts are discovered, there are interpolated histories, grotesques, ghosts (or at least stories about them), insane characters, a prison, and even an extended nocturnal narrative or two. It has an involuted, if not discontinuous or labyrinthine form. It would be an act of critical perversity though to describe *Pickwick* as even a parody of Gothic. Yet, as the brief list suggests, one finds numerous traces of the Gothic. They are in effect pervasive remnants, ruins of older narrative modes that remain to construct, even as they contradict or otherwise trouble the ontology of the modern subject at a given historical moment. Let us take the work of Joseph Sheridan Le Fanu as an example of such translation effects, and in order to trace the force of the Gothic in nineteenth-century fiction.

Le Fanu's critical reception in the twentieth century was restricted largely to "*aficionados* of the Gothic horror story" as Victor Sage remarks in a recent study.[15] However, subsequently, and following various interventions from a number of critical perspectives, "Le Fanu, today, stands at the conjunction of Irish Studies, Gothic Studies and the study of the Victorian Sensation Novel" (1). Thus, Le Fanu is "inscribed in a dialectic of *production*" typical of nineteenth-century literary hybridity.[16]

As Sage shows, from the 1830s to the 1870s Le Fanu's constant devices of bearing witness, attestation, reconciliation, and resurrection or "revenancy" belong to the language of the high-Victorian Gothic. Also addressed are the aesthetics of corruption. All such motifs and formal effects are read in relation to the different levels of textual and material or historical hybridity, which make Le Fanu's novels so complex and entertaining, and which intimate a comparison with Dickens. As Sage comments of *The House by the Churchyard* (1861), hybrid relation announces itself in the intermixing of horror, "comedy, romance, and a theatrical kind of grotesque" (60). Later novels such as *Wylder's Hand* (1863) abandon the hybridity of "the 'Churchyard laugh' ," but retain the hybrid interanimation intrinsic to Le Fanu's modes of narration, as well as those of Dickens and Wilkie Collins (Sage 77). Through the intermixing of genres, writers such as Le Fanu and Dickens estrange the reader from the illusion of authority in interpretation.

*Uncle Silas* can serve here as our principal illustration. The Gothic, with its attendant narrative devices such as superstition, the uncanny, and the grotesque, offers a series of layers and frames through which the text addresses, amongst other things, theological, and therefore ideological, issues in the 1840s and 1850s. The double temporal frame of the novel puts to work a number of doctrinal resonances between the two decades, thereby making possible layers of cultural, religious, and political threat at both historical moments, from the fear of revolutions to the domestic concerns over Methodism and Puseyism. Such broad echoes inform Le Fanu's heroine, Maud's, "sense of the Other" and connect her singular perceptions to "specific doctrinal and behavioural transgressions in Victorian culture" (Sage 105).

In addition, drawing on various visual effects borrowed from magic lantern shows known as *phantasmagoria*, the idea of retinal after-images, and the lighting effects of Dutch painters, Le Fanu creates a world in which "chiaroscuro dominates the twilight world in which his characters live" (118). While Le Fanu's effects are undeniably his own, and his work with such figures and forms of representation are markedly singular, nevertheless such representational manifestations take place in the Victorian Gothic everywhere. This is a world, we might say, in which the analogy "is explicitly between the portrait and the coffin." This is no mere aesthetic scene-setting however: for, with regard to *Uncle Silas*, "chiaroscuro is the mode of Maud's perception of almost everything. She sees through a post-Radcliffean veil of 'superstition' and 'ghostliness', a register which is deeply romantic and 'Gothic', but largely mistaken" (Sage 119).

The codes of Gothic are translated on the one hand by formal and aesthetic modes of representation, which in turn are transformed into a phenomenology of perception that is not wholly trustworthy, and on the other, through the elements of textual hybridity, by contemporary ideological and theological echoes. In this, the authority of perception is undermined, readerly competence questioned, and the frames and codes by which narrative structure, framing, and agency constructed, illuminated. Tracing our way carefully through the labyrinthine folds of a novel such as *Uncle Silas*, we come to see "the mapping between the old eighteenth-century structure and the Gothic anti-Catholic plot of this novel. We can see Le Fanu creating his own new Gothic rhetoric out of a traditional set of moral oppositions between hypocrisy and candour" (Sage 130). And it is precisely this marking of the text by conflicting material, textual, and historical signs that reveal the Victorian Gothic.

## V. Conclusions

Coming to the conclusion of this essay, it might be worthwhile to consider endings as beginnings, or at least as turning points. At the risk of hyperbole *Frankenstein* (1818) might be read as the eschatological text of the Gothic-proper. At the same time, however, it is also available to us as the inaugural text of the "Victorian Gothic," with its multiple narrators, found documents, its suspicious engagement with psychology and medical science. Its structural qualities usher in and invent an alternative model for Gothic, one that abandons for the most part the focus on the past and the foreign Other. While as early as 1798–9, Jane Austen was already writing her parody of the Gothic, *Northanger Abbey* (1818), it is not until nearly twenty years into the nineteenth century that *Frankenstein* arrives, just a year after *Northanger Abbey* was finally, posthumously published, to update the Gothic. Or perhaps, to turn back to a term already employed, translate is a better word. *Frankenstein* transforms narrative conventions, turning them away from a fragmented and repetitive mode towards a fragmentation simultaneously of corporeality and corpus, body and text.

What is a shared feature of a seemingly disparate group of texts such as *Frankenstein* and those that I have discussed in passing? Common to many if not all are instances of haunting, death, and moments of the uncanny, motifs that mediate Victorian cultural self-reflexive concerns. In the Victorian Gothic there is frequently to be read a preoccupation with interpolated narrative and found documents or a reliance for the piecing together of the narrative through the witness of multiple narrators, as if one witness were unequal to the responsibility of testimony, or otherwise not to be trusted. Narratives, in the form of fragments of paper and illustrative tales, arrive to suspend principal narrative motion. That which arrives is also that which returns. It never arrives for a first time, even though in any given novel, the arrival is the first visible appearance, whether for the characters of the novel or for the reader. Having been told before, having been written down prior to the moment of its appearance, every arrival is also a return.

To put this in another, more spectral manner, every apparition is a *revenant*, a ghost the very condition of which is traced in its coming-back, its only being able to appear, becoming visible, through its coming back (*re-venire*). The story, the tale, the letter, the documentary account of the eyewitness—each of these provides the reader with another instance of a fragmentary interruption, which is also a manifestation. These are not simply moments of description, of mentioning or narrating something else, that something else often being an example of a Gothic or horrific incident. Their very appearances enact and therefore use the Gothic, or at least some aspect of it: its elements, its tropes, its images, its rhetoric, its devices, or a combination of those. Thus the traces or texts, the voices or inscriptions, and the interlaced, interweaving of several of these are performative. They disrupt and fragment the narrative and novel in which they figure, and which they disfigure, transforming it into its own grotesque and improper body. The novel becomes a dismembered, and re-membered Gothic body, which, in being stitched together gathers the traces of its heterogeneous memories in an act of narrative revivification. Such material, if not corporeal re-membering is also a mnemotechnic process, that phantasmagoric act by which memory makes the dead, the past, appear *as if* it were alive, projected for our imaginations. And this, we may suggest, is the most Victorian aspect of the Victorian Gothic, as well as being its most Gothic aspect, which it is necessary to read, to teach, to learn. To be modern for the Victorians meant to remember, and to suffer passively the haunting effects of the past, if that past, in having been forgotten, did not return to haunt one's self, one's personal subjectivity or cultural identity all the more violently. In its many Gothic inflections, the Victorian scene of writing is thus one, as Peter Garrett has recently remarked, in which Victorian self-consciousness is "always in tension with the forces of the unconscious" and the narrative past.[17]

## Notes

1. Peter J. Kitson, "The Victorian Gothic," in William Baker and Kenneth Womack, eds., *A Companion to the Victorian Novel* (Westport CT: Greenwood Press, 2002) 163–76, 164. All subsequent references are to this edition, and are given in the text.
2. See Kitson, 165–8.
3. See Kitson, 165–7.
4. Eve Kosofsky Sedgwick, *The Coherence of Gothic Conventions* (London: Methuen, [1980] 1986) 9. All subsequent references are to this edition, and are given in the text.
5. See Sedgwick, 9–10.
6. Robert Miles, *Gothic Writing 1750–1820: a Genealogy* (London: Routledge, 1993) 1. All subsequent references are to this edition, and are given in the text.
7. David Punter, Review of *The Failure of Gothic: Problems of Disjunction in an Eighteenth-Century Literary Form*, by Elizabeth Napier, *The Times Higher Education Supplement*, 20 March 1987.
8. David Punter, "Introduction: of apparitions," in Glennis Byron and David Punter, eds., *Spectral Readings: Towards a Gothic Geography* (Basingstoke: Macmillan—now Palgrave Macmillan, 1999) 1–8, 3.

9. Natalie M. Houston, "Introduction," in Mary Elizabeth Braddon, *Lady Audley's Secret* (1862), ed. Natalie M. Houston (Peterborough, ON: Broadview Press, 2003) 18–19. All subsequent references are to this edition, and are given in the text.
10. Charles Dickens et al., *The Haunted House* (1859), Foreword Peter Ackroyd (London: Hesperus Press, 2003). All subsequent references are to this edition, and are given in the text.
11. Charles Dickens, *Dombey and Son* (1848) ed. Peter Fairclough, Int. Raymond Williams (London: Penguin, 1985). All subsequent references are to this edition, and are given in the text.
12. Emily Brontë, *Wuthering Heights* (1847) ed. Ian Jack, Int. Patsy Stoneman (Oxford: Oxford University Press, 1998) 20–1.
13. As some readers will be aware, I am relying here on a specific notion of the "uncanny," presented by Freud. Sigmund Freud, "The 'Uncanny'," (1919) *Standard Edition* Vol. 17, 219–56; rpt in *Writings on Art and Literature*, Foreword Neil Hertz (Stanford: Stanford University Press, 1997) 193–233. All subsequent references are to this latter edition, and are given in the text.
14. Nicholas Royle, *Telepathy and Literature: Essays on the Reading Mind* (Oxford: Basil Blackwell, 1991) 36.
15. Victor Sage, *Le Fanu's Gothic: the Rhetoric of Darkness* (Basingstoke: Palgrave Macmillan, 2004) 1–2. All subsequent references are to this edition, and are given in the text.
16. Margaret Russett, *De Quincey's Romanticism: Canonical Minority and the Forms of Transmission* (Cambridge: Cambridge University Press, 1997) 6.
17. Peter K. Garrett, *Gothic Reflections: Narrative Force in Nineteenth-Century Fiction* (Ithaca, NY: Cornell University Press, 2003) 9.

# 5
# Postmodern Gothic

*Lucie Armitt*[1]

> Freud's essay [on "The 'Uncanny' "] is, perhaps above all, a teaching. It teaches us about . . . the uncanny and ourselves. It teaches us about teaching.[2]

When Nicholas Royle makes this observation about Freud's essay, he is partly drawing attention to the lacunae within it. Freud's essay is written, it seems to me, in the style of a "final say"—why, otherwise, such compulsive recourse to dictionary definitions? Like a lot of Freud's work, "The 'Uncanny' " reads as an attempt to cancel out all previous debates (in this case of a supernatural or superstitious nature) in the name of that single, resolving Ur-narrative, psychoanalysis. Yet what really makes Freud's essay uncanny, is that "The 'Uncanny' " unravels itself even in the act of being written/read and, in the process, appears to take on a life of its own. So it becomes a great text with which to argue and work, hence Royle's allusion to the teaching scenario for, in his view, Freud's essay becomes "an extraordinary text for what it does not say, as well as for what it does. It constantly says more or less or other than what it says" (7).

Teaching and researching within a literary framework is an exercise in active contradiction: for when we teach we look to open up debate, using literary methodologies to assure our students that there are as many readings as there are readers. However, once we come to write our research, we close our ears to our own pedagogical codes: now we buy into an illusory conceit that we have the right (not to mention the ability) to some kind of "final say." Therefore, when we come to research into how we teach something called "the Postmodern Gothic" the contradictions start to multiply. When discussing the postmodern one opens up to irresolution, but when discussing the Gothic one starts to close in: beginning with the brooding canvas of the sublime, one gradually narrows the focus, ultimately exchanges agoraphobia for the claustrophobic.

## The Gothic world of the teaching academy

From a university teacher's point of view, one may feel that the Quality Assurance Agency (QAA)-speak of Learning Outcomes and Benchmarking criteria have, in themselves, brought a broodingly Gothic feel to the late twentieth-/early twenty-first-century teaching academy. Certainly the inference of its metadiscourse seems to have been spawned by the uncanny, for in one of Freud's linguistic explorations of the term we find what we suspect to underlie the rhetoric of Quality-speak, namely that it will bring to light certain sinister pedagogical shortcomings that would otherwise be "[c]oncealed, kept from sight, so that others do not get to know of or about [them]".[3] Of course, few of us believe the new Quality rhetoric to be capable of such revelations: a poor university teacher will not be improved by the production of paperwork, whereas a good university teacher may well find his/her real pedagogic quality obscured by that same paperwork. However, overlooking these reservations, more follow. As I reflect upon the particular Learning Outcomes attached to my own undergraduate special option, "The Nineteenth- and Twentieth-Century Gothic Narrative," I ponder whether any of the predicated learning outcomes upon which I base this teaching are actually particularly *meaningful* when situated within a specifically Gothic frame.

As Alan Sinfield, in his own critique of the foundational bases for the QAA's Benchmark Statement for English observes, "The problem with the statement . . . is that it is organized as core and periphery," hence "That 'English' and 'literature' might exert some ideological pressure is not contemplated," so it fails to adequately grasp the importance of the reader's (here, specifically, the student's) role in the *construction* of alternative reading positions and therefore, presumably, the interrogation of easy assumptions foundational to a belief in "authorizing" literature. Instead, Sinfield claims, benchmarking returns us to the implicit assumption "that there is a right way to read . . . Our fitness [as university teachers of English] is confirmed by the reading; the reading is guaranteed by our fitness."[4] This is certainly bad news for the Gothic, where "fitness" always bows to the pre-eminence of chronic disease.

## Teaching reading in a Gothic frame

Certainly, Gothic is centrally founded upon the principle that it belongs to periphery rather than core. Indeed, its very origins place it as such. So, at its inception, where theories of the Enlightenment situate themselves as "core" values of the Eighteenth century, the Gothic becomes a narrative reaction against this civilizing centrality. At the same time, there is a kind of folding back upon itself. As Fred Botting puts it, although Gothic appears as a reaction against the age of the Enlightenment, it also operates as a form of homage to it:

> Gothic functions as the mirror of eighteenth-century mores and values . . . its darkness allows the reason and virtue of the present a brighter reflection . . . [Therefore] Gothic history . . . not only delivers a sense of discontinuity through inversion and distancing, but also allows for a perfected reflection . . . [5]

Indeed, there is another sense in which the Gothic complicates questions surrounding periphery and core, and this is because it is one of those areas of the English University curriculum that is especially dependent upon an interdisciplinary focus and hence fractures any clear distinction between (core) English literature and (peripheral) popular fiction, film, and television. One can no more understand or teach the Gothic without considering the role of film and film theory within the development of textual understanding, than one can teach contemporary women's fiction without recourse to Women's Studies. And, where some may like to assume that any resultant contamination of the core is due to this flirtation with the periphery, I have found that it is through an understanding of those theories of spectatorship that seem to belong to the periphery that I have come to understand better precisely what makes that core central. To put it more transparently, the emphasis upon the visibility of the screen and its boundaries in cinema has prompted a more physical awareness of the spectator's relation to that screen than we have conventionally had in relation to reading narratives—and Gothic, with its emphasis upon physical response (chills in the stomach, raised hairs on the back of one's head) is particularly well suited to this type of approach.

## Narrative worlds and their limitations

Where Gothic literature and cinema meet, however, we find increasing preoccupation with the boundary-negotiations between worlds. For instance, according to Dennis Giles, cinematic texts:

> Lure the viewer to the movies by offering "dangerous" visions of potentially traumatic material . . . from which outside the theatre, we are expected to turn away in shame, guilt or emotional turmoil. Yet at the same time that it threatens to transgress prohibitions, the industry promises a vision which the viewer knows will be psychologically and ideologically safe. By the terms of the viewing contract, desire will be engaged, then domesticated by the textual strategies; fear will be aroused, then controlled.[6]

This clarity of definition is also characteristic of the literary Gothic for, as I have said elsewhere, "it is conventional to read space in terms of the enclosures that define it and the world beyond those enclosures in terms of the inside from which it differs. Gothic narratives are particularly preoccupied by such considerations."[7] From this point of view there are distinctions to be drawn between what some might see as the atavism of the traditional Gothic and the kind of pedagogical atavism that underlies the impulse to benchmark. In the act of looking backwards, the Gothic assaults, rather than affirms the centre against which it struggles. Though its worlds (if not its films) remain largely black and white, the unsuspecting protagonist nevertheless enters that dark, inner world only in order to learn a lesson about the "real" world of daylight, even if it is one s/he may well wish s/he had not learnt. The Gothic, then, teaches us hard lessons and its methodology for doing so relies on narrative encounters with the page. This realization reveals an internalized and internalizing pedagogy innate to the Gothic, which in itself operates as a metonymy for the broader study of university English. It is a very old notion that the reading of literature is intrinsically "improving" of the mind, not just intellectually but morally. Still, if it retains any credibility, surely we will expect it to be most true when reading the Gothic, for it must be here, in our respective encounters with monstrosity that we stand to gain most from the errors of others and perhaps be less likely, therefore, to err ourselves.

## The compulsions of the Gothic reader

And yet, of course, if this supine posture were characteristic of how we read books, they would have lost not only their appeal, but also their ability to teach us anything. More recently, Scott Brewster has made active reading his model for the Gothic encounter, opening his essay with the insistent warning, "[r]eading Gothic *makes* us see things." Gothic is our tutor on some level, then, and its pedagogical impulse is intrinsically punitive: we learn, whether we like it or not (and, of course, as Giles's observations remind us, there is complex response to liking and not liking in any Gothic narrative, where what we like about the reading is what we decidedly would not like elsewhere). Moreover, Brewster continues, "Gothic's inexhaustible capacity to generate readings resembles an intoxicating excess of meaning."[8] Despite the apparently nonstudent-friendly vocabulary of an "inexhaustible capacity to generate reading" and the need to deal with "an . . . excess of meaning" in 3,500 words (or whatever), we find that students will and do rise to the challenge if one places it within a Gothic frame.

Hence, this excessive textual dimension actively makes Gothic a model teaching tool worthy of "core" status, not least because for all the talk of Learning Outcomes, no teacher worth her salt wants to use literature (Gothic or otherwise) simply to teach students to write essays. Instead, we look to induce in all students of the Humanities precisely what the Gothic deals in best: an insatiable and monstrous appetite (in this case for reading) that will provoke a radical metamorphosis within the reading subject. And what, more specifically, do we choose to communicate? Precisely the type of complex intellectual debates one can only have with difficulty in other, perhaps more canonical, areas of the curriculum: the importance of an understanding of differing theoretical approaches to texts (via psychoanalysis, feminism, Queer theory), precisely because the material of the Gothic is always about the interrogation of authority and its powerful discourses. In this Gothic encounter with a range of identity politics, then, Sinfield's vision of the various countercultural positions from which one might choose to read "differently," returns.

## Confronting the postmodern

And yet, at that uncanny return to Sinfield's critique, we find him hitting the problem of the postmodern head on: "As soon as identity politics emerged as a way of raising suppressed voices, postmodern theorists started dismantling the concept of identity" (439). How, then, can one teach something called the Postmodern Gothic, when what the Gothic does best appears to be dismantled by postmodernity? Nor is it simply the unity of the subject that is dismantled: in the challenge posed by a loss of faith in metanarratives, how does one go about articulating a Gothic vision without God, History, or Reason to counter? This puzzle seems, at least in part, to underlie many of the concerns voiced by academics at the apparent demise of the Gothic. In his student-oriented book, *Gothic*, Botting implicitly concludes by blaming postmodernism for what he deems to be the Gothic's redundancy, in this case through a reading of Francis Ford Coppola's *Bram Stoker's Dracula* (1992):

> Coppola's film mourns an object that is too diffuse and uncertain to be recuperated . . . Drained of life, a life that in Gothic fiction was always sustained in an ambivalent and textual relation of horror and laughter, sacrificial violence and diabolical play, the romanticism of Coppola's *Dracula* presents its figures of humanity in attenuated and resigned anticipation of an already pervasive absence, undead, perhaps, but not returning . . . With Coppola's *Dracula*, then, Gothic dies . . . Dying, of course, might just be the prelude to other spectral returns.[9]

The apparent weakness in the final sentence, here, is also the source of its potency; Gothic does, indeed, refuse to die, even if/when (?) it should. Here, I am reminded of an unanticipated Learning Outcome arising from a recent Masters level module of my own, "Theorizing the Gothic," in which students explore a number of differing theoretical approaches towards defining the Gothic. As the course progressed, we found the Gothic being variously defined as "a repetition . . . of that which one did not know could be repeated," a "recounterfeiting of the already counterfeit," and "a reconstruction of the past as the inverted, mirror image of the present."[10] In other words, and as the opening to this essay has already implied, intellectual paradox looms large in the Gothic, even—perhaps especially—in the hands of its finest critics. No wonder that what my students learned (inadvertently, as it first seemed) was how to make and play games with the Gothic.

The first, Gothicopoly, is based on the well-known London board game and perhaps needs no further explanation except to mark, here, its rehearsal of the core/periphery interface; the second, "Gothic Spotting," is a performative travel game. Journeying East–West/West–East along the North Wales coastal railway line, players are challenged to construct a Gothic narrative out of the places, situations, sights, and people encountered or seen en route. Satirical in flavour, the game emerges out of the students' shared euphoria that, in the right hands, "all can be Gothic," while simultaneously signalling their shared realization of the dangers inherent in flirting too closely with intellectual contradiction: if Gothic can be "Anything," it is actually "Nothing."

To return to the capital focus of Gothicopoly, in an article titled "The Contemporary London Gothic," Roger Luckhurst takes issue with the amorphous contagion that leads us to find the Gothic everywhere, and in everything. Luckhurst's countercritique of this tendency focuses on contemporary urban culture, or what he calls "the notable revival over the past twenty years of a newly Gothicized apprehension of London."[11] Perhaps it is inevitable that, in our shared sense of the threat posed to society by postmodernity, Gothic metaphors will surface unawares, but Luckhurst challenges us to question the true value of this preoccupation to the Gothic itself. Citing, as an example, Martin McQuillan interviewing Peggy Kamuf, Luckhurst fastens on the playfulness inherent in McQuillan's approach: "Are you a scholar who deals in ghosts?" McQuillan asks Kamuf, to which she replies, "Yes . . . although I'm not sure I would have said so with as much conviction before *Specters of Marx*" (527).

Luckhurst goes on to ground his resistance in the lack of materiality projected by Deconstruction:

> the critical language of spectral or haunted modernity that has become a cultural-critical shorthand in the wake of *Specters of Marx* can go only so far in elaborating the contexts for that specific topography . . . indeed, the generative structure of haunting is symptomatically blind to its generative loci. (528)

Without a social context (however complex its focus upon that context), the Gothic is impotent; for all its fascination with the body (blood letting, animated corpses, walking spectres), it is the body politic upon which it really comments. From Franco Moretti to Ellen Moers, what critics pick up on again and again are both the material ideologies encoded in these texts and the corresponding Gothic monsters enabled by their revolts.[12] Luckhurst's geographical focus is particularly helpful, here, as he employs the topography of the "real" city as the foundation upon which to base his literary analysis. Focusing on texts that interweave fictional gothic narratives with "real" historical excavations of London sites, he grounds the Gothic within both a contemporary cultural reading and an awareness of a pre-existing, foundational, literary Gothic heritage in relation to which Gothic books are written and will be read. Gothicism, he reminds us, cannot float, wraith-like, free of all anchors, for to do so is simply to turn it in upon itself:

> Unable to discriminate between instances and largely uninterested in historicity . . . the discourse of spectralized modernity . . . can only replicate tropes from textual sources, punning spiritedly around the central terms of the Gothic to produce a curious form of meta-Gothic that elides object and instrument. (535)

Luckhurst's essay is also helpful in considering the *teaching* of the Gothic, for it is certainly the case that teaching is both innately material and geographical: by which I mean it takes place in a specified location, at a specific time, and involves real people participating in a "grounded" debate. Unlike reading it is inescapably performative and, as such, marked out by physical boundaries (this room not that one, this seating structure, not that). If one teaches the Gothic on a sunny spring afternoon, is the student experience the same as if one is teaching the same text to an evening class on a stormy November night? What might be the geographical impact on the teaching scenario of the role played by "place" in Gothic? Writing, as I am, on the edge of the Snowdonia National Park in North-West Wales, Luckhurst's references to the Isle of Dogs, the Greenwich Observatory, Canary Wharf, or the East End have no more grounding in "my" reality than Stevenson's London, with its "chocolate-coloured pall," its "gin-palace[s]," or its "shop fronts . . . like rows of smiling saleswomen."[13] It is not, of course, that I do not "know" contemporary London, in the usual sense of the term, but that London is, nevertheless, not only an entirely metropolitan space (and hence culturally distinct from North Wales's predominantly rural economy), but also a city located in a foreign country which I am, nevertheless, assumed to call "home."

This reference to the foreignness of urban spaces returns us to Freud's "The 'Uncanny' " in which, we recall, he tells a story about his travels to Italy. Walking "through the deserted streets of a provincial town," he finds that no matter how hard he tries to avoid doing so, he simply cannot help returning to:

> a quarter of whose character I could not long remain in doubt . . . I hastened to leave . . . But after having wandered about for a time . . . suddenly found myself back . . . I hurried away once more, only to arrive by another detour at the same place yet a third time. (359)

Is Freud's problem, here, the literal "foreignness" of his experience, or is it true that the metropolitan landscape(s) that are assumed to be such fitting signifiers for postmodern experience are, in some sense simultaneously "foreign" even when "known"? Peter Brooker puts it thus:

> As I stood . . . waiting for a late train on London Bridge station . . . I realised that . . . maps and surveys, a long shelf of social, economic and cultural histories meant I "knew" New York better than I "knew" London where I have lived for over twenty years.[14]

Perhaps, in the midst of empirical knowledge lurks not only the unknown, but also the unknowable. In former times this "unknowableness" would have taken on a spiritual dimension; for Freud it would have been a testimony to the unconscious; under postmodernity it becomes an internalized and internalizing question about the self in relation to environmental existence. We might argue that we not only literally but philosophically construct the environment in which we live, for representations of the city/place/country we know are no more "real" than representations of the city/place/country we do not. Brooker's essay does not set out to explore the Gothic, but as he traces the landscape of postmodernity uncanny moments rise unbidden. So, in another scene of uncanny pedestrianism, Brooker walks home contemplating the urban darkness as "No place for a woman to walk alone" and, before this, looking out across the railway tracks, notices "the blackened brick wall of an office building. Amazingly there were lights on inside the building, though no sign of office workers" (3). The structure becomes, in that moment, a kind of haunted house, an emptiness in which lack of habitation becomes substituted with autosuggestion. As Freud might put it, the office block, in this moment of incongruous illumination, takes on definition as one of those "things, persons impressions, events and situations which are able to arouse in us a feeling of the uncanny in a particularly forcible and definite form" (347). Inevitably, one would find oneself wondering if the lights had suddenly come on of their own accord, or if, in this strangely lighted space framed by darkness, one might become subjected to a nocturnal inversion of Hitchcock's *Rear Window* (1954).[15] An alternative inversion also suggests itself, in the uncomfortable feeling one experiences when sitting by an illuminated, curtain-less window at night: what monster will suddenly rise up from beneath the window frame and press its grisly face to the pane?

What begins to emanate from Brooker's essay is the realization that he need not give voice to the Gothic, for its haunting effect is laid bare in his surrounds. Contemplating the nature of urban existence, Brooker observes:

> On one side of our minimal coexistence in city crowds and public places there is the full but circumscribed familiarity of immediate relationships in households and demarcated neighbourhoods . . . But on the other side of stark coexistence there is estrangement: the look of the unknown, and the risk and threat this brings. (5)

Even when Brooker summarizes his view of "writing in relation to the city" as "tracking the forms of a 'changing same'," (17) what strikes me in the phrase is its similarity to a Freudian interpretation of the Uncanny. Freud, having taken up the best part of four pages of his essay with a long list of semantic variants on the term "Heimlich" and its compounds, "especially the negative 'un-': eerie, weird, arousing gruesome fear," famously continues: "What interests us most in this long extract is to find that among its different shades of meaning the word 'heimlich' exhibits one which is identical with its opposite, 'unheimlich'," (344–5). In summary, the uncanny takes root at that moment at which formerly reassuring, homely familiarity shifts, albeit slightly, and becomes foreign. Under the terms of psychoanalysis, of course, that foreignness lies within the psyche and is therefore at the root of all being. Pondering the easy symmetry between urban postmodernity and the uncanny, the inverse question almost begins to shape itself: "Is it, then, possible to consider the postmodern Gothic *beyond* a metropolitan frame?" Iain Banks would seem to say, "Yes."

## Teaching *The Crow Road*

That Iain Banks's *The Crow Road* (1992) is a book about teaching and learning should be clear the moment we find the central protagonist and primary narrator is called [ap]Prentice McHoan. Moreover, Prentice is a university student (studying History, in Glasgow) and, as the "real" student's representative in the text, his core narrative function is to learn how to read. Prentice begins the text as a slow learner, not just because he "admit[s] defeat on the subject of the links between agricultural and industrial revolution and British Imperialism," but because he is also behind with the "core" reading he needs to do for us, namely the deciphering of his (missing, presumed dead) Uncle Rory's creative writing notebooks, written in a particularly torturous form of shorthand:

> *(CR: !B kills H!!? (save)*
> *(jlsy? Stil drwnd)*[16]

As his outraged pseudo-Aunt/ex-lover/former partner of Rory, Janice Rae, utters (tutor-like) "You mean you haven't read them all?" (260).

Rory's notebooks are, in fact, a perfect test case for how to read any Gothic narrative. The signifiers on the surface are, like Freud's essay, compulsive reading purely because there is enough of fear and desire in them to tantalize while the narrative spaces and gaps force us to exhume a protracted and incomplete comprehension. Prentice senses (and so on some level "knows") that the "real" story lies elsewhere and that what he is searching for requires a missing palimpsestic layer. Cataclysmically, halfway through trying to decipher the folder of material Janice gives him he leaves it behind on the train. Haunted by the removal of this compelling text, he becomes increasingly preoccupied by its absence, in response to which his appetite for a Gothic climax transforms him into Brewster's pathologically driven "model" Gothic reader: "Reading Gothic, we compulsively interpret random signs, haunted by the possibility that we may be deluded, that we have not seen enough or have seen too much" (291). Where Freud's own compulsions lead him to read dreams, Prentice's lead to a compulsion to "dream-read": "Even now, months later, I had dreams about reading a book that ended half-way through, or watching a film which ended abruptly, screen whiting-out . . . Usually I woke breathless . . . " (262). In fact, even after Prentice has pieced together the secret (it turns out there is an old set of eight-inch flexible computer disks tucked away at the back of his father's desk which, after a protracted exhumation involving computer analysts on both sides of the Atlantic, turns out to contain the missing files), he (and others) remain more swayed by the likelihood of his insanity than his clarity of thought: "Prentice; you read a couple of things your uncle wrote and suddenly you're accusing people of murder? Come on" (413).

However, if Banks's novel is a perfect text to employ in a course designed to teach undergraduate students to read Gothic, is it as easily placed to teach the specifically Postmodern Gothic? Like Luckhurst's London Gothic, Banks's Gothic vision is geographically grounded, though in this case in central Scotland. Despite frequent sojourns into Glasgow, the orientation of the novel as a whole is rural and, in fact, deals at least in part with a landscape more at home in the works of Radcliffe or Shelley. And yet, unlike in the work of those writers, the Romantic Sublime is evoked by Banks in part as self-parody. Take, for instance, the following extract from chapter three:

> Fortingall is a modest hamlet in the hills north of Loch Tay, and it was there in the winter of 1969 that my Aunt Charlotte was determined to consummate her marriage. Specifically, she wanted to be impregnated beneath the ancient yew tree that lies in an enclosure within the graveyard of the small church there; she was convinced that the tree—two thousand years old, according to reliable estimates—must be suffused with a magical Life Force.
>
> It was a dark and stormy night (no; really), the grass under the ancient straggling, gnarled yew was sodden, and so she and her husband, Steve, had to settle for a knee-trembler while Charlotte held onto one of the overhanging boughs, but it was there and then—despite the effects of gravity—that the gracile and quiveringly prepossessing Verity was conceived, one loud night under an

> ink black sky obscuring a white full moon, at an hour when all decent folk were in their beds and even the indecent ones were in somebody's, in a quaint little Perthshire village, back in the fag end of the dear old daft old hippy days.
>
> So my aunt says, and frankly I believe her; anybody wacko enough ever to have bought the idea there was some sort of weird cosmic energy beaming out of a geriatric shrub in a back-end-of-nowhere Scottish graveyard on a wet Monday night probably hasn't the wit to lie about it. (60)

Here we again encounter a place simultaneously "homely" and "foreign." Spoken in the language of colloquial familiarity, the legendary nature of this family plot renders it simultaneously "strange." In fact, Banks's use of truth in this text is characteristically postmodern, in that while the geographical details of the passage are "true," they are conveyed as false. So, this Scottish graveyard is not in the "back-end-of-nowhere," but the "back-end-of-*somewhere,*" for Fortingall, the graveyard and the Ancient Yew in question all "really" exist—as much as London Bridge or Canary Wharf. In fact (and as his naming of that elusive, idealized "Other" Verity also implies), *The Crow Road* is in many ways a book about the allure of competing truths; the narrative proves polyphonic at times, the many narrators including, in three italicized passages, a disembodied voice. Later we learn these are extracts from Rory's notebooks related, as it were, in advance of its discovery by Prentice and, therefore, effectively in and through the voice of a dead man. In this uncanny evocation of the presence of the one who does not exist, we might argue Banks's novel to be an old-fashioned ghost story put through a postmodern filter: all we have upon which to stabilize the text's "truth" is the word of a man for whom death becomes a speech act.

In teaching *The Crow Road*, then, I also teach my students to question easy assumptions about contemporary existence. As Prentice stares out across the Atlantic Ocean he tells us that "The sun had dipped behind North Jura, and abandoned the sky to a skeined mass of glowing clouds, sinking through the spectrum from gold towards blood-red, all against a wash of deepening blue" (300). The setting is idyllic, pastoral and almost timeless, until we realize that what he is sitting on is a piece of postmodern art—a "giant, corroded lump of concrete and steel" (300) sculpted by his dead friend, Darren Watt.

Immediately, "timelessness" is shattered by both chronology and death. The Gothic element builds in the supernatural effect of the discordant clash between sea and steel: "when the tide was at the right level, it produced noises like a ghost trapped in badly tuned organ-pipes, sonorous slammings as waves opened and slammed shut heavy doors like hinged manhole covers . . ." (301).

Quite simply, there are no "purely" rural environments any more, hence Banks's wry, knowing use of a kind of self-parodic environmental humour. Nevertheless, if the unknowable can lurk within the predominantly built environment of the city, how much less can it be fathomed when used to confront the dark paradox of rural postmodernity? As that deadening student question "But aren't we reading too much into this?" resonates in my head, I pause to contemplate the pedagogical illogicality of even *trying* to inspire in others a desire to learn using the Postmodern Gothic, a form of literature which is so determined to provoke a resistance to the belief that anything can ever be "really" known. Now, how do I turn *that* into a Learning Outcome . . . ?

## Notes

1. This essay is dedicated to Fran Harvey, Chiara Luis, Sarah McCaffery, and Beth Spillman, with thanks.
2. Nicholas Royle, *The Uncanny* (Manchester: Manchester University Press, 2003) 7. All subsequent references are to the edition, and are given in the text.
3. Sigmund Freud, "The 'Uncanny'," in *The Penguin Freud Library, Vol. 14, Art and Literature*, ed. Albert Dickson (Harmondsworth: Penguin, 1990) 335–81, 344. All subsequent references are to the edition, and are given in the text.
4. Alan Sinfield, " 'Below sea-level, the mark is inverted': benchmarking and the reader," *Textual Practice* 16, 3 (2002), 435–41, 436–8 passim. All subsequent references are to this article, and are given in the text.
5. Fred Botting, "In Gothic darkly: heterotopia, history, culture," in David Punter (ed.) *A Companion to the Gothic* (Oxford: Basil Blackwell, 2000) 3–14, 5. All subsequent references are to the edition, and are given in the text.
6. Dennis Giles, "Conditions of pleasure in horror cinema," in Barry Keith Grant (ed.) *Planks of Reason: Essays on the Horror Film* (Metuchen, NJ: Scarecrow Press, 1984) 38–52, 39.
7. Lucie Armitt, "The fragile frames of the bloody chamber," in Joseph Bristow and Trev Lynn Broughton (eds) *The Infernal Desires of Angela Carter: Fiction, Femininity, Feminism* (London: Longman, 1997) 88–99, 90.

8. Scott Brewster, "Seeing things: Gothic and the madness of interpretation," in Punter (ed.) *A Companion to the Gothic*, 281–92, 281 (my emphasis). All subsequent references are to the edition, and are given in the text.
9. Fred Botting, *Gothic* (London: Routledge, 1996) 180.
10. David Punter, "Shape and shadow: on poetry and the uncanny," in Punter (ed.) *A Companion to the Gothic*, 193–205, 194; Jerrold E. Hogle, "The Gothic ghost of the counterfeit and the progress of abjection," in Punter (ed.) *A Companion to the Gothic*, 293–304, 295; and Botting, "In Gothic darkly," 5, respectively.
11. Roger Luckhurst, "The contemporary London Gothic and the limits of the 'spectral turn'," in *Textual Practice* 16, 3 (2002) 527–46, 527–8. All subsequent references are to this article, and are given in the text.
12. Franco Moretti, *Signs Taken for Wonders*, trans. Susan Fischer, David Forgacs and David Miller (London: Verso, 1983); Ellen Moers, *Literary Women* (London: The Women's Press, 1986).
13. Robert Louis Stevenson, *The Strange Case of Dr Jekyll and Mr Hyde and Other Stories* (Harmondsworth: Penguin, 1979) 48 and 30 respectively.
14. Peter Brooker, *New York Fictions: Modernity, Postmodernism, the New Modern* (London: Longman, 1996) 3. All subsequent references are to the edition, and are given in the text.
15. In *Rear Window* (dir. Hitchcock, 1954), an injured convalescent witnesses a murder in a neighbouring apartment. In Hitchcock's film the murder takes place in broad daylight.
16. Iain Banks, *The Crow Road* (London: Abacus, 1992) 261 and 349. All subsequent references are to the edition, and are given in the text.

# 6
# Gothic Sexualities

*Steven Bruhm*

After fifteen years of teaching Gothic literature and queer theory, I have come to regard the phrase "Gothic sexualities" as self-evident, even somewhat redundant. All Gothic appears in some way to register sexual anxieties and tensions, as Eve Kosofsky Sedgwick's important *Between Men: English Literature and Male Homosocial Desire* made clear.[1] Sexuality, as it comes to us through a history of Freudian, post-Freudian and queer thought, is nothing short of Gothic in its ability to rupture, fragment, and destroy both the coherence of the individual subject and of the culture in which that subject appears. As an analytical tool for both scholarship and classroom teaching, the kind of work Sedgwick inaugurated has allowed us to ask new questions of the Gothic in its representation of sexuality, power, and pleasure. In much criticism on the Gothic, sexuality has been the purview of a feminist criticism that reads—correctly—issues of gender in the Gothic as explorations of power inequities. A critic like Michelle Massé, for example, sees the Gothic's preoccupation with masochism as a schooling of its women readers into submission, an acceptance of compulsory femininity; while Anne Williams locates the Gothic within the fall of the patriarchal family and considers the ways in which women might fashion their own poetics within that fall.[2] This long and rich history of feminist criticism has opened crucial avenues for addressing problems of gender in the Gothic, but I find that many of my students, 85% of whom are female, find these analyses no longer as exploratory or surprising as they once were, precisely because they presuppose the ubiquity of women's oppression that they then seek to confirm.

Queer theory, conversely, allows for a new purchase on sexuality by focusing on the vicissitudes of male as well as female sexuality. It has opened up discussions of sexual pleasure that were eclipsed by feminist considerations of power inequities, and indeed allows for the very idea of "power" in sexuality to be rethought. Given this new terrain of sexual inquiry, the Gothic has become a perfect mode for the interrogation of sexual power and sexual pleasure. Like the queer episteme itself, the Gothic disrespects the borderlines of the appropriate, the healthy, or the politically desirable. It resists the authority of the traditional or received and insists, with more or less gleeful energy, on making visible the violence underpinning the sexual norms that our culture (including a culture imagined by feminism) holds most sacred.

In her early work on the Gothic and the queer, Sedgwick established possible lines of inquiry only some of which she would take up later on. In particular, her development of a rubric of homophobia within the psychoanalytic context of paranoia draws liberally on a Freud she later leaves behind. "Particularly relevant for the Gothic novel," she wrote, "is the perception Freud arrived at in the case of Dr. Schreber: that paranoia is the psychosis that makes graphic the mechanisms of homophobia" (91).[3] She finds in a significant body of classic Gothic novels (she names *Caleb Williams* [1794], *Frankenstein* [1818], *Confessions of a Justified Sinner* [1824], *Melmoth the Wanderer* [1820], and *The Italian* [1797] as obvious candidates) a recognizable and structurally coherent plot in which "one or more males [. . .] not only is persecuted by, but considers himself transparent to and often under the compulsion of another male" (91). From here Sedgwick quickly locates her thematics within a history of homophobic and antiaristocratic persecution, deftly crafting an analysis that owes as much to Michel Foucault as it does to Freud, to argue that "[t]he Gothic novel crystallized for English audiences the terms of a dialectic between male homosexuality and homophobia, in which homophobia appeared thematically in paranoid plots" (92).[4]

In her next two major books, *Epistemology of the Closet* and *Tendencies*, Sedgwick returned to the mechanisms of that homophobia to articulate fully an epistemic problem for straight-identified masculinity in a straight-identified culture.[5] The Gothic novel, she argued, arose at a time (the mid-eighteenth century in England) when male sodomitic behaviour became much more visible and a cause of *judicial* (rather than only religious) concern. This visibility resulted in the random persecution of homosexual men, a "pogrom-like" violence that,[6] for Sedgwick, also coloured the way nonhomosexual men saw their relationships with one other (*Between Men*, 83–96). The result was, in her analysis, a double movement policing the way men interact: "Not only must homosexual men be unable to ascertain whether they are to be the objects of 'random' homophobic violence, but no man must be able to ascertain that he is not (that his bonds are not) homosexual" (*Between Men*, 88–9). After Sedgwick, we can no longer read or teach the Gothic undertones of Oscar Wilde's *The Picture of Dorian Gray* (1891) (*Epistemology*, 131–76), Henry James's "The Beast in the Jungle" (1903) (*Epistemology*, 182–212), or even Jane Austen's *Sense and Sensibility* (1811) (*Tendencies*, 109–29) without deploying a queer lens that situates these texts within mechanisms of homophobic paranoia and epistemologies of closeted desire.

To the degree that Sedgwick uses Freud's discussion of Dr Schreber to illustrate intersections of homoerotic identification and homophobic paranoia, she draws on an old-school version of psychoanalysis that foregrounds structures of psychopathology within everyday life. While Sedgwick herself is not a psychoanalytic critic, her strategies mesh with a typical psychoanalytic reading of the Gothic, particularly Freud's "The Uncanny," where what is frighteningly foreign and alien to us is, paradoxically, that which is most familiar and quotidian; the "uncanny" or "*unheimlich*" is most often produced by an encounter with something local, endemic to the self's structures of desire, something that "ought to have remained secret and hidden but has come to light."[7] Sedgwick sees the mandatory affiliation of men within the symbiotic structures of capitalism and the sentimental bourgeois family as an always already eroticized scene but one that must deny its own *eros*. That *eros*, significantly, is necessary in order to make bourgeois culture work, for men to promote their own interests and the interests of other men, and for more primitive structures of exogamy to pass as heterosexual romance. In so arguing, she offers us a brilliant take on the anxieties of "straight" masculinity and what she calls the "treacherous middle stretch of the modern homosocial continuum" (*Epistemology*, 188), a middle stretch that is thoroughly Gothicized because it circles around secrets that constantly risk coming to light. In her reading of straight masculinity and its repressions, heterosexuality takes on the air of the uncanny in that it projects onto the monstrous other (the homosexual) the image it must passionately yet tacitly embody. In some senses, modern heterosexual masculinity is ineluctably Gothic.

While Sedgwick's work on Schreber and paranoia touches upon the possible psychogenesis of queer desire, it does not linger there. Sedgwick is not interested in—indeed, she is quite suspicious of—depth psychology models for "explaining" gay or lesbian desire, as if gay or lesbian desire per se were in need of explanation. The problem for her is in psychoanalysis's supposed definitions of the normal, and in particular, the hetero-normal. Like the broader culture itself, psychoanalysis, Sedgwick argues, sees the family as biologically based and therefore somehow "normal." Inevitably, then

> the paths of desire/identification for a given child are essentially reduced to two: identification ("Oedipal"), through the same-sex parent, with a desire for the other-sex parent; or identification ("negative Oedipal"), through the other-sex parent, with a desire for the same-sex parent. If the so far undiminished reliance of psychoanalytic thought on the inversion topos were not enough to insure its heterosexist bias, its heterosexist circumscription would nonetheless be guaranteed, if it is not already caused, by the fact that the closed system of "the family," within which all formative identification and desire are seen to take place, is limited by tendentious prior definition to parents—to adults already defined as procreative within a heterosexual bond. (*Tendencies*, 63–4)[8]

I will return momentarily to the question of identification and desire as generating queer critique, but here it suffices to say that for Sedgwick, the delimitation of gender and sexual roles within psychoanalytically sanctioned, family-style heterosexuality can only produce a Gothic prison to which one can capitulate or against which one can rage. What poses as normal is a violent circumscription of possibility.

The Gothic prison that Sedgwick imagines the family to be—a prison built on the foundation of psychoanalysis—becomes an unacknowledged laboratory for Judith Butler, arguably queer theory's most influential and subtle psychoanalytic critic. In a chapter of her 1993 book *Bodies that Matter* significantly entitled "Phantasmatic Identification and the Assumption of Sex," Butler nuances the heterosexist guarantee that Sedgwick locates in psychoanalysis's family romance and, for my teaching practice, opens up a field of diverse and provocative representations of sexuality. Like Sedgwick, Butler is interested in "the symbolic demand to assume a sexed position."[9]

In the Oedipal family scenario, this sexuality takes on a particularly Gothic flavour in that it is most often assumed through the spectre of punishment: the boy will be castrated if he does not identify with heterosexual manhood, and the girl will be punished for not accepting her castration if she does not identify with a disempowered heterosexual womanhood. In this scheme, Butler would agree with Sedgwick that the femme man and butch dyke are mere "inarticulate figures of abject homosexuality" (96), failures to operate within the normal developmental paradigms of heterosexuality, ghosts that roam the fields beyond—or perhaps enclose—the culturally and fictionally normal. However, while Sedgwick seeks to avoid the Gothic proscriptions of this model by offering a more spacious terrain of familial identifications (in the essay I cited above, she proposes the queer uncle as one possibility), Butler wants to remain within the normative field and ask what kinds of spaciousness can be imagined there. Taking literally Freud's contention that what is repressed and kept from consciousness is often that which most forcefully constitutes the parameters of consciousness, Butler asks:

> what happens if the law that deploys the spectral figure of abject homosexuality as a threat becomes itself the inadvertent site of eroticization? If the taboo becomes eroticized precisely for the transgressive sites that it produces, what happens to oedipus [*sic*], to sexed positionality, to the fast distinction between an imaginary or fantasized identification and those social and linguistic positions of intelligible "sex" mandated by the symbolic law? ( 97)

Thus, for Butler, "Sexuality is as much motivated by the fantasy of retrieving prohibited objects as by the desire to remain protected from the threat of punishment that such a retrieval might bring on" (100). The fascination with retrieving the prohibited is both psychoanalytic and Gothic: Caleb Williams opens Falkland's private trunk to discover the aristocrat's dirty secret of murder and cover-up; an unsupervised Jonathan Harker heads straight for the wing of the castle that Dracula has expressly forbidden him to enter; and physician Louis Creed rejects everything he knows about medical science to disinter his dead son Gage, rebury him in the Pet Sematary, and thus re-establish his own potency as a father/doctor.[10] In classroom practice, then, a reading of the Gothic through Sedgwick and Butler not only anatomizes the sexual fantasies and transgressions of otherwise respectable citizens, but it offers a rubric by which those transgressions can be read as queer interventions in straight culture. The Gothic in this way bespeaks desire in a complex and often contestatory way, as it continually veers from the proper paths of its story into the labyrinths of the unlawful.

Like Sedgwick, Butler is taking up a simple distinction proposed by Freud in 1923 between identification and desire, one that for him establishes the foundation of "normal" sexual development. Using the Oedipal father as the object of desire (although the mother will work just as well), Freud writes:

> It is easy to state in a formula the distinction between an identification with the father and the choice of the father as an object. In the first case one's father is what one would like to be, and in the second he is what one would like to have. The distinction, that is, depends upon whether the tie attaches to the subject or the object of the ego. The former kind is therefore already made possible before any sexual object-choice has been made.[11]

For Butler, the simplicity of this model is belied by its contradictions, ones that subtend and complicate the paranoid Gothic as Sedgwick described it above. Butler points out that, according to Freud, normative heterosexual desire requires identification with a same-sexed body (the son for the father, the daughter for the mother) and is produced by a deflection of desire across this body and onto the other sex. That the same-sexed body should be invested with this kind of desire for otherness means that there can be no clear division between what we identify with and what we desire, for any identification achieved through desire makes both the identification and the desire multiple, polyvalent. In the Freudian scheme, gendered subjectivity can only be achieved—precariously—by denying the desirous attraction *to* or *for* the body that one is paradoxically required to desire an identification *with*. Any singular subject position, according to this logic, involves a repudiation, and any repudiation, as the Gothic knows, risks eroticizing the thing repudiated; it makes it more attractive as a central phantasm. Butler rewrites Freud's ratio of desire with the following:

> To identify is not to oppose desire. Identification is a phantasmatic trajectory and resolution of desire; an assumption of place; a

> territorializing of an object which enables identity through the temporary resolution of desire, but which remains desire, if only in its repudiated form. (99)

This is the kind of psychic terrorism Sedgwick found to be endemic to the Gothic: the strength of the repression is proportionate to the strength of the desire for the thing being repressed, and in a male-privileged, bourgeois culture, that repression or repudiation produces the crucial remainder of desire for the thing loathed/loved: Victor Frankenstein for his Creature; Jonathan Harker for Dracula's brides and for Dracula himself;[12] Dorian Gray for the vile *döppelganger* of his own portrait; even Eleanor, the heroine of Shirley Jackson's *The Haunting of Hill House* (1959), whose tortured relationship to her dead-yet-still-tyrannical mother is readable through her lesbian attraction to her housemate Theo.[13] If the Gothic makes visible the mandatory nature of heterosexual identities/identifications, it makes equally clear the erotic allure of the homoerotic as a forbidden, repudiated, yet magnetic underside of the hetero identity.

Queer theory's emphasis on the complex dynamics of sexual desire, then, has opened paths of inquiry for both teaching and research that feminist preoccupations with gender did not take up and that could not be adequately theorized by a strictly "gay studies" approach to literary criticism—that is, seeking out homosexuals in literature to celebrate them or to bemoan their demise.[14] In particular, queer theory has insisted on a riskier and less validating approach to questions of sexual identity, questions that the Gothic has always made inescapable in their profound ambivalence. To explore these questions in a more focused way, I want now to turn to a novel that makes them its very subject matter, Anne Rice's 1976 *Interview with the Vampire*. Rice's novel is a meditation on the dynamics of the Oedipal family and the sea changes the family has undergone thanks to the parameters of a homosexual discourse modelled after Freud. Rice's Catholic use of perversion allows students to consider the otherwise buried dynamics of family life, here rendered with Gothic clarity. Moreover, she offers a perfect test case for the teaching of queer psychoanalysis as she charts with precision the imprecisions of the "phantasmatic trajectories and resolutions of desire" that Butler outlined above.

At its simplest level, *Interview with the Vampire* reads like a Freudian case study. The novel is a single-session confession of a queer vampire before an interested interviewer, a confession that tracks the vampire's childhood—both as a human and as a bloodsucker—his erotic relationships, and his life as a "parent," all with an eye to explaining what psychological dynamics *made* him, what intersections of desire and identification formed his personality. And as Freud would have it, everything begins in childhood. Early in his life, Louis was catapulted from the status of son to that of father in the Oedipal family: "My father was dead then," he tells the interviewer, "and I was the head of the family."[15] This position, predictably, brings immediate conflict. His brother Paul preferred fanatical religious devotion to the kind of social life his mother expected him to lead, so Louis as brother/father found that he "had to defend [the brother] constantly from my mother and sister" (6). This role of paternal surrogate (the Oedipal father battling the mother for the affections of the son) begins a chain of displacements that carry throughout the novel, for while the father figure is supposed to provide a model with which the son can identify, Louis-as-father sees in his brother an erotically desirable figure as well as a religious saint: "He had the smoothest skin and the largest blue eyes. He was robust, not thin as I am now and was then [. . .] but his eyes [. . .] it was as if when I looked into his eyes I was standing alone at the edge of the world [. . .] on a windswept ocean beach" (7). Following Paul's suicide, the primary erotic figures in Louis's life bear the phantasmatic traces of this man for whom he was once brother and father. In one particularly rich scene, Louis has returned to the church where his brother's funeral had taken place. Once inside, he has a highly ornate vision of Lestat's funeral, but the corpse is not Lestat's:

> I stood there staring down not at the remains of Lestat, but at the body of my mortal brother [. . .] There was my brother, blond and young and sweet as he had been in life [. . .] His blond hair brushed back from his forehead, his eyes closed as if he slept, his smooth fingers around the crucifix on his breast, his lips so pink and silken I could hardly bear to see them and not touch them. (148)

Straight psychoanalysis can take us some distance toward understanding this vision: Lestat is the same-sex replacement for a brother Louis loved, and who killed himself after a quarrel with Louis over religion; that Lestat should arrive to vampirize Louis during a particularly intense moment of guilt over Paul's death suggests that Lestat (and vampirism) are merely replacements for the now fetishized dead brother. What makes the relationships more difficult here is the overdetermination of each figure in the erotic scheme. Not only did Paul figure as Louis's brother and son, but Lestat himself comes to Louis as a father (he makes Louis into a vampire); a mother (as Louis recounts drinking from Lestat's wrist, he "experience[es] for the first time since infancy the special pleasure of sucking nourishment, the body focused with the mind upon one vital source" (20); and *son*: Lestat takes up the position of the dead brother whom Louis had fathered, but more importantly Lestat needs Louis to kill his (Lestat's) father, which he is unable to do himself. This need is ironic, moreover, given that Lestat is already the Oedipal son who has killed the vampire who made him (and who will be killed, repeatedly, for this crime). Lestat's position with Louis seems, then, to replicate Louis's with Paul: in both Lestat and Louis, another man is the central erotic figure at the same time that he is metonymic, a displacement or substitute for that figure, and this metonymic displacement more often than not casts the male in a number of (often conflicting) gendered and sexualized positions. If psychoanalysis is fond of charting a line of engagement back to some singular originary source, it finds itself both satisfied and frustratingly queered in *Interview with the Vampire*, satisfied in that Rice is fixated on tracing straight lines of infection and identification, yet queered because these lines continually bifurcate, shoot off in many directions at once, and so destroy any ratio of gendered identification to sexualized desire that a heteronormative psychoanalysis might want to detect.

Questions of originary desire arise most clearly in the character of Claudia, the five-year old child whom Lestat and Louis have made into a vampire. As an object of Louis's desire, Claudia seems to function both as a simple source of nourishment and as a replacement for some lost maternal presence in the vampire's life. But beyond a displacement for Louis's own absent mother, Claudia functions in the novel as the impossible Oedipal child, she who demands an identification with the parent but whose desires seem to be completely independent of parents. At the moment of her creation, we see a Claudia who defies the Freudian scheme of drawing identity from the parent: still a mortal child, who has been all but drained of blood, she nearly kills Lestat as she drinks from his wrist, a thirst that suggests vampirism well before she dies and actually becomes a vampire. She does have moments of almost Dickensian vulnerability—she demands to know which of her "parents" is her *real* parent (108), which one has made her a vampire, and she spends much of the novel seeking a mother to replace the one she lost to the plague—but ultimately Claudia is terrifying because she refuses to occupy the category of "child."

She is marked by a knowingness that both fascinates and terrifies Lestat and Louis: her body is that of a child, but "[h]er eyes were a woman's eyes" (94); "Claudia was mystery. It was not possible to know what she knew and what she did not know" (100). For all of her physical weakness, "She knows! . . . She's known for years what to do," Lestat claims (106). She then punctuates her Oedipal quest for origins by killing her fathers' mother–daughter pair of servants and placing their corpses in a sentimental tableau ("the arm of the mother fastened around the waist of the daughter, the daughter's head bent against the mother's breast" [106]) and covering them with shit. What Lestat knows about what Claudia knows in this scene is really that she can undo the logic of parental identification by end-running the parents' powers. While physically Claudia may be in a state of arrested development, epistemologically she is already well beyond learning vampirism from the grown-ups. Little wonder, then, that Claudia quickly takes over from Lestat in teaching Louis how to kill humans (121–22), and that she is instrumental in the multiple murders of Lestat and others of her ancestral tribe (192). The child becomes the mother of the man in a way that not only skews the psychoanalytic formula of cross-parental identifications, but *queers* it, positing the female child as father to the son who fathered (and mothered, and lovered) her.

The novel's climax comes with the introduction of the vampire Armand into Louis and Claudia's domestic dyad. In many ways, Armand continues the chain of erotic and identificatory displacements that has constituted all relationships in *Interview with the Vampire*. He stands in as an ostensibly kinder and gentler version of Lestat, becoming Louis's homoerotic focus, and in so doing is an object of competitive hatred for the "daughter" Claudia. Indeed, like any attentive Oedipal child, Claudia assumes that this new parent wants her dead—and she's not wrong; Armand will be responsible for the murder of Claudia and her "mother" at the end of the novel. But while Armand fits the typical scheme of lover for the preferred parent and threat to the cathected child, his presence suggests that he could be a lover to this hating child as well: Claudia relates to Louis "the trance [Armand] put me in so my eyes could only look at him, so that he pulled me as if my heart were on a string. [. . .] He rendered me powerless!" (249). This morass of desires and fears, of *queer* desires bounded by Oedipal fears, has by now become totally legible in *Interview*, as Rice makes them as commonplace as soap-opera plots. What happens next, though, is most intriguing.

Into this queerly Oedipal arrangement immediately comes a figure of sexual desire and parental identification for Claudia: the replacement mother Madeleine. As if conjured out of a psychoanalytic dream-text, Madeleine is the wish fulfillment for Claudia, serving her need both for a doting mother and a same-sex lover (since, in this novel, all lovers are both spouses and parents, or spouses and children, depending on the line of infection). Claudia's desire for a lesbian lover/mother easily assuages her fear of the new gay/Oedipal father, at least momentarily, but Rice, having read her Freud (she's too early to have read her Butler), allows for no easy fit. Just as Armand had provided a kind of "gay heterosexuality" to the family—replacing the old father Lestat as the new father—so does Madeleine provide a lesbian heterosexuality to this new Oedipal configuration. At the same time that she is becoming Claudia's lover/mother, she is Louis's lover as well (Louis is conscripted as surrogate biter because the child Claudia is not powerful enough to create a vampire). Rice makes clear the heterosexual desire here " 'If you were a mortal man,' says Madeleine to Louis, 'If I could only show you my power [. . .] I could make you want me, desire me!' " (268)—but it is a heterosexual desire that refuses to remain in one place. Madeleine has both a "straight" desire for Louis (whose power she wants) and a queer desire for Claudia, for whom she wants to be mother, daughter, and lover. Put another way, the surrogate-parental Madeleine wants *to be* and *to have* Claudia at the same time. As a child who cannot die, Claudia can replace the endlessly replicated dolls that Madeline has manufactured to replace her daughter who did die, as if the chain from same-sex daughter to lesbian lover were seamless.[16] In this final configuration of domesticity, Rice fictionally demonstrates what Butler wants us to know philosophically, that the desire for one parent in no way regulates or delimits sexual identification or desire elsewhere, because the desire for a parent is itself an amalgam of same-sex and cross-sex desires. If psychoanalytically modelled culture depends upon the repudiation of the homoerotic to constitute its normative structures, *Interview with the Vampire* repudiates the repudiation and makes visible the instabilities of the Freudian formula.

If I find myself drawn to post-Stonewall, queerly resonant novels like *Interview with the Vampire*, then, it is because of their ability to infuse some life-blood into bodies of concern that risk degenerating, like the European vampire Louis and Claudia kill, into mindless animated corpses (191). One of these bodies is that of the "student" as imagined by current theories of pedagogy and political progressiveness. It is currently the vogue in North America that students' classroom experiences must be rendered "safe" and "nurturing" above all else, their subjectivity (provided it is not one of historical privilege) affirmed at every turn. This "safety first" model of teaching is one that second-wave feminism and early gay studies have been all too willing to enable. When it comes to gender and sexuality, Eng Lit syllabi are meant to offer positive models with which we can identify. Novels like Rice's, conversely, demolish the comfort of claiming identity not because the identities claimed are those of monsters (this identification can itself be fun) but because she overdetermines the very process of identification itself, shooting it through with forbidden, repudiated, and paranoidly suppressed desires. *Interview with the Vampire* eroticizes the very things we repudiate (homosexuality, heterosexuality, pedophilia, incest, whatever) in order to claim our identities as gay, straight, liberal, politically responsible, and so on. Rice may not, in the end, champion the gay cause or promote the kind of same-sex domesticity that homos now seek as they run to the altar to exchange vows before the State, and for this I am truly grateful. As a self-identified gay professor who wants to trouble the significations of "gay," I bring the psychoanalytic Gothic to students precisely to resist the ubiquity of normalizing programmes like "identity" and its bridesmaids. The queer Gothic may be discomforting, but it is perhaps the most effective and popular tool available for understanding the many repudiations that are needed to constitute normalcy.

## Notes

1. Eve Kosofsky Sedgwick, *Between Men: English Literature and Male Homosocial Desire* (New York: Columbia University Press, 1985). All subsequent references are to this edition, and are given in the text.
2. See Michelle Massé, *In the Name of Love: Women, Masochism, and the Gothic* (Ithaca: Cornell University Press, 1992); and Anne Williams, *Art of Darkness: a Poetics of Gothic* (Chicago: University of Chicago Press, 1995).
3. Sigmund Freud, "Psychoanalytic notes on an autobiographical account of a case of paranoia (*Dementia Paranoides*)," in *The Standard Edition of the Complete Works of Sigmund Freud, Vol. 12*. Trans. James Strachey. (London: The Hogarth Press and The Institute for Psychoanalysis, 1958).
4. Michel Foucault's most famous discussion of nineteenth-century networks of power discourse regarding homosexuality can be found in *The History of Sexuality: Volume I: An Introduction*. Trans. Robert Hurley (New York: Pantheon, 1978).
5. Eve Kosofsky Sedgwick, *Epistemology of the Closet* (Berkeley: University of California Press, 1990) and *Tendencies* (Durham: Duke University Press, 1993). All subsequent references are to these editions, and are given in the text.
6. Here Sedgwick is drawing on the work of Alan Bray in *Homosexuality in Renaissance England* (London: Gay Men's Press, 1982).
7. Sigmund Freud, "The Uncanny," in *The Standard Edition of the Complete Works of Sigmund Freud, Vol. 17*, Trans. James Strachey. (London: The Hogarth Press and The Institute for Psychoanalysis, 1955) 225.
8. The inversion topos, popular in theories of sexology at the turn of the twentieth century, claimed that the "homosexual" was really a gendered soul trapped in the opposite-sexed body, so that the homosexual male was really a woman in a man's body and the lesbian a man in a woman's body. We need only watch *Silence of the Lambs* (Director Jonathon Demme, 1991) to realize what a long shelf life this notion has, especially for Gothic representation.
9. Judith Butler, *Bodies That Matter: On the Discursive Limits of "Sex"* (New York: Routledge, 1993) 96. All subsequent references are to this edition, and are given in the text.
10. Bram Stoker, *Dracula* (Oxford: Oxford University Press, 1983); Stephen King, *Pet Sematary* (New York: Penguin, 1983).
11. Sigmund Freud, "Identification," in *The Standard Edition of the Complete Works of Sigmund Freud, Vol. 18*. Trans. James Strachey. (London: The Hogarth Press and The Institute for Psychoanalysis, 1955) 106.
12. For a full discussion of the homoeroticism underlying *Dracula*, see Christopher Craft, " 'Kiss me with those red lips': gender and inversion in Bram Stoker's *Dracula*," *Representations* 8: 107–33.
13. Mary Shelley, *Frankenstein, or the Modern Prometheus* (Oxford: Oxford University Press, 1980); Shirley Jackson, *The Haunting of Hill House* (New York: Viking, 1959).

14. One such gay reading is George Haggerty's on *Interview With the Vampire*, the novel I am about to discuss. See "Anne Rice and the queering of *Culture*" in *Novel: a Forum on Fiction 32*: 5–8. I find Haggerty's analysis perceptive and important but I find disappointing his ultimate criticism of Rice that she fails to "give credence to alternative sexualities" (17). I ask my classes to be less concerned about what is "good for gays" than about what queerly disruptive interventions we can detect in a novel's effects.
15. Anne Rice, *Interview with the Vampire* (New York: Random House, 1976) 6. All subsequent references are to this edition, and are given in the text.
16. For a rich (and ghostly) discussion of the homoerotics of playing with dolls, see Kathryn Bond Stockton, "Growing sideways, or versions of the queer child," in *Curiouser: On the Queerness of Children*, ed. Steven Bruhm and Natasha Hurley (Minneapolis: University of Minnesota Press, 2004) 277–315.

# 7
# Female Gothic

*Avril Horner and Sue Zlosnik*

Together and apart, in one way or another, we have been teaching "Female Gothic" for twenty years. When we began, we thought we knew what we meant by the term; now we are not so sure. Over the years, our students have raised difficult questions that have challenged the category for us. More generally, developments in both Gothic studies and gender theory have made the term "Female Gothic" contested and contentious. Recently, a conference at the University of Glamorgan and a double issue of the journal *Gothic Studies* devoted to the topic have borne witness to the historical, conceptual, and semantic range covered by the title "Female Gothic."[1]

At the beginning of the 1980s we were both teaching conventional canonical courses in institutions that had yet to experience the "crisis in English studies" which was to stamp its imprint on English departments in the UK during the following decade and beyond. Occasional work for the extramural department of another university gave us the opportunity to offer the kind of courses in women's writing that we could not at that time incorporate into the day job. Stimulated by the burgeoning of feminist theory and criticism, first from Britain and the USA and then from France, we enthusiastically introduced our eager amateur students to texts and ideas that were considered, in the words of one of our former (male) colleagues, as "marginal to the history of ideas." Thus we made our own contribution to that branch of literary studies which Elaine Showalter had dubbed "gynocritics": the retrieval, re-evaluation and valorization of the voices and writing of women.[2] With our students we soon encountered a problem that had been helpfully articulated by Patricia Stubbs, writing in 1979:

> I think the failure to break away from . . . subjectivism indicates that one of the problems encountered by explicitly feminist novelists at the end of the last century is being encountered by the current generation of women writers. This is a difficulty peculiar to realist fiction—that of how to incorporate into a form whose essential characteristic is the exploration of existing realities, experiences and aspirations which go well beyond the possibilities afforded by that reality. This explains . . . the increasing importance of non-realist narrative forms in contemporary women's writing.[3]

Our early foray into teaching "Female Gothic" began with the unlikely figure of Jane Austen. We had taught a successful summer school on Austen, approaching her work through the feminist perspectives opened up by Sandra M. Gilbert and Susan Gubar and others in the late 1970s and early 1980s.[4] Challenging the received notion that Austen's early novel, *Northanger Abbey* (published posthumously in 1818), is merely a burlesque of the Gothic, Gilbert and Gubar claim that it is "a Gothic story as frightening as any told by Mrs. Radcliffe."[5] Indeed, they argue that Austen's narrative is itself Gothic, in fact an example of Female Gothic, in the way it lays bare the severe limits on self-determination suffered by young women in the late eighteenth century. Catherine "cannot make sense of the signs of her culture"; she is "a character trapped inside an uncongenial plot" (142). The novel's happy ending seems to be almost parodic, serving to recuperate Catherine into the realist plot of domestic fiction. At the same time the power of Female Gothic is glimpsed and although such texts as Ann Radcliffe's *The Mysteries of Udolpho* (1794) appear to be held up to ridicule as "horrid" novels, Catherine's reading of them opens up a space within the narrative that allows the apprehension of the dark features of an oppressive patriarchy.[6]

Alongside Gilbert and Gubar's *The Madwoman in the Attic* (1979), two other critical texts proved key in our exploration of Female Gothic at that time: Ellen Moers' *Literary Women* (1976) and Juliann Fleenor's edited collection, *The Female Gothic* (1983). The influence of Moers' book is clear in Gilbert and Gubar's tome. Both focus on the lives and strategies of women writers under patriarchy; Moers is generally credited with having invented the term "Female Gothic," which she makes the title of her chapter on Mary Shelley's *Frankenstein*, Emily Brontë's *Wuthering Heights* (1847) and Christina Rossetti's "Goblin Market" (1862). In our first course on "Female Gothic," taught in the autumn following our Austen summer school, these were the texts that followed *Northanger Abbey*. The opening statement of Moers' chapter appears certain and definitive: "What I mean by 'Female Gothic' is easily defined: the work that women writers have done in the literary mode that, since the eighteenth century, we have called the Gothic." She immediately proceeds to problematize it by going on to say: "But what I mean—or anyone else means—by 'the Gothic' is not so easily stated except that it has to do with fear."[7]

*Literary Women* influenced a generation of feminist critics, turning them more towards women as writers and moving them on from the earlier wave of challenging images of women in male-authored texts. In a parallel development, there was an awakening of critical interest in Gothic writing. David Punter's historically informed *The Literature of Terror* in 1980 was a landmark publication that traced a trajectory of Gothic fiction from its eighteenth-century inception into the present day, challenging the categorization of Gothic as a fictional genre confined to the late eighteenth century and recognizing its ambiguous status as "popular" literature. Fleenor, in her introduction to *The Female Gothic*, identifies the negative critical reception of Gothic as being associated with a perception of it, from the first, as "a feminine form."[8] Already, in the Fleenor collection, there is ample evidence that critics were beginning to find the category "women" highly problematic. A later text on our first "Female Gothic" course threw this question into sharp relief. Our students found an apparently inexhaustible subject for debate in Daphne du Maurier's *Rebecca* (1938); their unwillingness to accept the demonization of the first Mrs de Winter, as the plot of the novel seems to demand, opened up questions to which critics are still attempting to offer answers. Our inclusion of Carter's *The Magic Toyshop* (1967) prompted heated discussions concerning the nature of female desire; women and economic dependency; the home as a place of entrapment—all in tune, of course, with work being done in the 1980s by feminist theorists both in the UK and North America concerning the positioning of women in a Western capitalist patriarchal culture.[9] Such lively debates provided an alternative perspective not only on literature but also on gender relations and structures of power, for us as well as for our students. Analysis of literary texts was often validated by reference to personal experience—in tune again, perhaps, with the contemporary privileging of confessional writing as somehow "authentic," a critical drift which itself deliberately challenged Enlightenment values—including the claim to "objectivity"—seen as dominant in academia. It was a heady moment which released a lot of laughter as well as anger. There is no doubt, as Lauren Fitgerald notes, that "Feminism . . . was instrumental in institutionalizing Gothic studies."[10]

By the early 1990s one of us had set up an undergraduate module entitled "Female Gothic" at a university in the north of England. The module was popular, especially with women students and it ran for about ten years.[11] The syllabus, like that of many Gothic modules, was Anglo-American-Canadian in its emphasis and ran from Radcliffe to Atwood.[12] The syllabus shifted slightly from year to year but texts taught frequently included: Ann Radcliffe's *The Italian* (1797); Charlotte Brontë's *Villette* (1853); Christina Rossetti's "Goblin Market" (1862); Charlotte Perkins Gilman's *The Yellow Wallpaper* (1892); Daphne du Maurier's *Rebecca* (1938); Carson McCuller's *The Member of the Wedding* (1946); Sylvia Plath's *The Bell Jar* (1963); Jean Rhys's *Wide Sargasso Sea* (1966); Angela Carter's *The Magic Toyshop* (1967) and "The Bloody Chamber" (1979); Fay Weldon's *The Life and Loves of a She Devil* (1983); Toni Morrison's *Beloved* (1987); Margaret Atwood's *The Robber Bride* (1993). The appearance of similar modules in the UK and North America during the 1990s confirmed that Female Gothic as a specific subgenre was well established and that Gothic writing by women had become the focus of a number of critical projects. Some of these continued with the work of re-evaluating or retrieving the work of lost women authors; others sought to position such work more closely in its historical and cultural context; some adopted particular theoretical approaches in order to explore Gothic writing by women—Anne Williams used Kristevan theory in her *Art of Darkness: a Poetics of Gothic*, for example, and Robert Miles used Foucault's work in his *Ann Radcliffe: the Great Enchantress* (both published in 1995).[13] Many academics who concentrated on Gothic writing by women critiqued the feminist literary approaches of the 1980s, in particular the tendency to represent female characters as passive and as victims. From the standpoint of the 1990s, such readings were seen as negatively reinforcing both conventional gender stereotypes and the idea that the plot of many women's lives was inevitably one of constraint and incarceration. It had by this time become important to see women and female characters in Gothic texts as autonomous, powerful, and transgressive; hence perhaps the critical emphasis on the "nay-saying" of Radcliffe's heroines and the enormous popularity of Angela Carter's work on Female Gothic courses during that decade. That word "transgressive," carrying a then glamorous resonance of the work of Lacan, gave Female Gothic a new currency in the 1990s: Female Gothic, according to Elaine Showalter in 1991, could be seen as a mode of writing which corresponded to "the feminine, the romantic, the transgressive, and the revolutionary."[14] This call to arms was accompanied by a problematization of earlier feminist perspectives on women's writing generally and on Female Gothic writing in particular. Not surprisingly, then, work began to appear that claimed the Female Gothic for male writers: as Donna Heiland notes, Tamar Heller, in her book *Dead Secrets: Wilkie Collins and the Female Gothic* (1992) showed how Collins used the tropes of Female Gothic "to write narratives about forms of power and authority—literary, familial, political—in Victorian culture."[15] In the same year, Alison Milbank's *Daughters of the House: Modes of the Gothic in Victorian Fiction* examined male authors' appropriation of Female Gothic. Conversely, in a special issue of the journal *Women's Writing*, entitled "Female Gothic Writing" and published in 1994, Milbank defines Gilbert and Gubar's *The Madwoman in the Attic* itself as an example of "male" Gothic in that it:

> orchestrates narrative tropes of penetration into a secluded and privileged interior—here Western literary history—by a deliberately transgressive protagonist—itself, or the woman writer—who in turn seeks release from the limits to her identity fashioned by society, history and morality.[16]

Gender studies and queer theory had arrived and, with them, a more nuanced critical perspective on writing and sexual identity—and a much sharper sense of the complex nature of sexual identity in relation to performance, national identity, class, and race. During the same decade, poststructuralism combined with gender studies and queer theory to produce a rejection of essentialism and a vigorous scepticism towards the terms, definitions, and narratives that had accrued around the words "Female Gothic."

In such a climate, students began to question the meaning of the term and academics began to interrogate its validity. In the mid 1990s we were working on our study of Daphne du Maurier as a Gothic writer.[17] We had been influenced both by Anne Williams's book and Eugenia DeLamotte's work on boundaries in Gothic texts and, in particular, by her insistence that "the problem of the boundaries of the self was a crucial issue for women in some special ways—ways that sometimes manifest themselves even in a woman's portrayal of a male protagonist."[18] These works and many others provided paradigms of Female Gothic writing against which to test our readings of du Maurier's novels and short stories. Inevitably, we found ourselves questioning some of the assertions made in such studies. For example, both DeLamotte and Williams agreed that the Female Gothic resists unhappy or ambiguous closure—a formula which works when applied to many (but not all) eighteenth-century Gothic novels by women and most modern airport or "drugstore" Gothic texts—but which did not work when applied to Charlotte Brontë's *Villette* or Jean Rhys's *Wide Sargasso Sea*. It certainly did not seem to fit du Maurier's *Rebecca*. And although Brontë follows the Radcliffean agenda of explaining away the supernatural (another previous litmus test for Female Gothic), many women writers of the Gothic—such as Charlotte Dacre and Angela Carter—do not. Nor was it possible to divide Male and Female Gothic writing respectively into texts of horror and terror. None of these criteria seemed to work when we looked closely at Daphne du Maurier's fiction. Indeed this tendency to polarize critically the supposedly characteristic features of Gothic writing by men and women seemed to reveal more about the social/political agenda of Anglo-American feminism than it did about du Maurier's writing. For although du Maurier clearly used what, by the 1990s, was recognized as the standard Female Gothic plot in novels such as *Jamaica Inn* (1936) and *Rebecca* (the heroine confined to a mysterious or sinister building and dominated by an older, powerful man), her fiction deviates from the template of Female Gothic writing in many ways. Indeed, du Maurier's tendency to move between male and female narrators (and therefore between "masculine" and "feminine" subject positions) suggested to us that her work defied categorization according to the formulae established by critics such as Eugenia C. DeLamotte, Anne Williams, and Jacqueline Howard.[19] Inevitably we found ourselves concluding that perhaps such formulae were too restrictive if they seemed to exclude work by the woman who wrote *Rebecca*. We decided that du Maurier's own sense of identity involved a negotiation between what she perceived as the male and female aspects of herself in a continually self-conscious performative process of gender identification. Our book argues that her Gothic writing is a way of inscribing this process; hence it seems to resist identifying itself as characteristically Female or Male. Indeed, it is likely that Gothic writing appealed to her because of the very fact that it destabilizes all kinds of boundaries, including those of gender. In the process, however, her work developed so as to offer a critique of "masculinity" and "femininity." Such an agenda is not limited to work by women writers, however, as Heller and Milbank had already argued.

By the time we came to write an essay on the novels of Barbara Comyns in 2002, the term "postfeminism" had been born and both feminist literary criticism and the category of Female Gothic had come under attack. Indeed, for many young female academics, feminist literary criticism seemed so *passé* as to be hardly worth considering; we have both witnessed young women shift uncomfortably in their seats at conferences here and abroad at the very mention of the phrase—as if a mother with embarrassing social habits had entered the room.[20] By 2002 the categorization of Female Gothic was being seen in some quarters as reductive in its tendency (or so the argument went) to psychologically universalize female experience or oversimplify the cultural function of Gothic as a mode of writing. Chris Baldick and Robert Mighall, for example, argued that the impact of feminist literary studies upon readings of the Gothic had been "mixed" and that indiscriminate readings of texts conspired to dehistoricize Gothic writing by women. While acknowledging the value of studies such as Kate Ferguson Ellis' *The Contested Castle* (1989) and Jacqueline Howard's *Reading Gothic Fiction* (1994), they suggested that:

> On the other hand, the construction since the 1970s of the predominately universalising category of the "female Gothic," as an embodiment of some invariable female "experience" or of the archetypal "female principle," leads straight out of history into the timeless melodrama in which (wicked) "male Gothic" texts always express terror of the eternal "(M)other" while (good) female gothic

> texts are revealed to be—as Anne Williams claims—not just "empowering" but "revolutionary."[21]

This robust challenge to the concept of Female Gothic writing and the feminist practice which had reified it as a separate category provoked us to look closely at our own assumptions again. In our essay on Comyns, a neglected British author, whose novels combine literary realism with Gothic interludes and moments of magic realism, we set out once more to test the work of a gifted woman writer against the various definitions of Female Gothic.[22] Once again, the exercise proved problematic. Cruelty in Comyns' novels does not recognize stereotypes; like Charlotte Dacre in *Zoyfloya, or The Moor* (1806), she presents women as being as capable of cruelty and exploitation as men. In her fictional world, there are few happy endings and men are just as likely to as women to become victims. However, all her novels seem to portray a woman's ability to hold on to economic independence, her own space, and her own identity as in constant tension with the need to love and be loved. Those women who do not manage to keep these elements in balance find themselves psychologically obliterated by others. Perhaps this threat of obliteration of the female self—whether through psychological abuse, physical incarceration, or actual murder—is something which informs all works we might describe as Female Gothic and is a particular dimension of the fear we recognize as Gothic in its origins. However, such a definition would arguably allow the inclusion of works such as Iain Banks' *The Wasp Factory* (1984) within Female Gothic—despite its relative absence of female characters and its apparent zestful celebration of body horror and masculine aggression—on the grounds that Frank Cauldhame's "real" biological self as female has been almost obliterated by his Frankenstein-like father through a mixture of hormone treatment and dysfunctional family narrative. This should give us pause for thought, perhaps. Conversely, would one include Poppy Z. Brite's *Lost Souls* (1992) on a Female Gothic module simply because its author is female?

We have outlined here the way our interrogation of the term Female Gothic has inflected some of our research projects because, of course, our research directly influences what and how we teach. We no longer teach Gothic fiction by women separately, but present it as in dialogue with other texts and genres, including Gothic fiction by men, just as one might present Mary Shelley's *Frankenstein* as a text in dialogue with Rousseau's *Émile* (1762). We do, however, ask students to consider the significance of constantly recurring tropes, motifs, and plots in Gothic fiction by women—for example, the constant reworking of the folk-tale "Bluebeard" by women authors.[23] This inevitably leads them to consider issues of power and control within the family and the relation of these to particular ideological and social formations. In our teaching of Gothic writing by women we now offer various definitions of Female Gothic but we also situate those definitions (as we have tried to do in this essay) within their historical and cultural moments. We thus seek to make students aware of academic knowledge as something always in process and as inevitably informed by contemporary ideas and prejudices. We encourage students to test the categories of Male and Female Gothic writing against their own readings of specific texts and to relate such readings to current ideas about canonicity and gender identity.

Other women critics have tackled the issue in their own ways. In order to avoid falling into the trap of essentialism or specious generalization, some have refined and redefined the term by focusing on a particular genre or a particular period, or indeed, challenging its currency. E. J. Clery, in her *Women's Gothic: From Clara Reeve to Mary Shelley* (2000), for example, claims that not only the energetic portrayal of passion by writers such Clara Reeve, Sophia Lee, Ann Radcliffe, Joanna Baillie, Charlotte Dacre, and Mary Shelley but also the fact of their professional status as writers have been neglected because they do not fit neatly into conventional definitions of Female Gothic.[24] Angela Wright, who also concentrates on early women writers of the Gothic, argues strongly for the inclusion of Clara Reeve's *The Old English Baron* (1777) and Sophia Lee's *The Recess* (1783–85) on any Gothic Fiction course, since their textual hybridity "forces students to think about the generic categorizations historical novel, Gothic novel, and the more recent critical term 'female Gothic'."[25] Diane Long Hoeveler redefines Female Gothic as "Gothic feminism"—"born when women realized that they had a formidable external enemy—the ravening, lustful, greedy patriarch—in addition to their own worst internal enemy: their perception of their sexual difference as a weakness."[26] She teaches texts by Mary Wollstonecraft, Ann Radcliffe, Jane Austen, Charlotte Dacre, and Mary Shelley in relation to both history (the rise of the middle class in England) and theory (Bakhtin and Foucault) in order to show how women used their supposed sexual "weakness" in order to manipulate matters to their advantage. Susanne Becker concentrates on writing by twentieth-century English and Canadian women in her *Gothic Forms of Feminine Fictions* (1999).[27] Diana Wallace has chosen to focus on women's Gothic historical fictions, a project which informs both her teaching at Master's level and her own research.[28] Paulina Palmer celebrates lesbians as transgressive in her *Lesbian Gothic: Transgressive Fictions* (1999). Helene Meyers tackles head on, in *Femicical Fears: Narratives of the Female Gothic Experience* (2001), the problematic nature of Female Gothic by arguing that:

> contemporary female-authored plots—plots in which women are killed or fear for their lives—constitute possibilities for understanding and intervening in the vexed and sometimes acrimonious feminist debates about victimology, essentialism, female agency, and the female body that have proliferated in recent years.[29]

As Donna Heiland notes, the terms Male and Female Gothic remain pliable: "what we have seen are robust considerations of gothic that coalesce around specific issues and methodologies, making overarching arguments that often include consideration of the relationship between gender and genre" and which "have in common the recognition that identity is discursively constructed."[30]

Given the conceptual problems of trying to define "Female Gothic" as a critical term and its chequered history as an aspect of feminist teaching practice, what are the justifications for continuing to discuss Gothic writing by women in this way? Perhaps we should remind ourselves what teaching Gothic fiction in this manner allows us to emphasize. Such a focus legitimately allows us to pay close attention to the representation of women's experience, particularly in relation to the family dynamic and female roles within it; economic dependency or independence; the relationship between law, property, and gender. It allows us to explore fears associated with the body, including those associated with puberty, childbirth, the menopause, and ageing. It enables us to consider the changing significance that the social class system and social rites of passage (such as marriage) have had for women at particular historical moments. It lets us dwell on the nature of female desire and its relation to the idea of transgression. It goes without saying that all these issues can be found portrayed in non-Gothic fiction—but arguably Gothic fiction, in its traffic with fear, sharpens our sense of how women might be more vulnerable—physically, politically, socially, and emotionally—in certain situations than men. Teaching Female Gothic writing also invariably leads to discussion of the social construction of gender (particularly in relation to class and national identity) and to debates concerning the making of the literary canon. It is obvious that all these issues need to be historically situated and that they can be inflected—and perhaps enriched—by some consideration of Male Gothic writing. These emphases presuppose a poststructuralist feminist agenda rather than a postfeminist one. We applaud that as a teaching strategy; it is still needed in an age when women, in general, earn and own less than men throughout the world. So long as women do not have complete equality with men, there is a case for the sort of special focus that teaching Female Gothic allows; if we refuse to "think back through our mothers" we shall create ghosts of our own.[31]

## Notes

1. The Female Gothic Conference at the University of Glamorgan took place on 22 July 2004. The double issue of *Gothic Studies* devoted to "Female Gothic" (6, 1), published in May 2004, was edited by Andrew Smith and Diana Wallace.
2. Elaine Showalter, "Feminist criticism in the wilderness," in Elaine Showalter (ed.), *The New Feminist Criticism* (New York: Pantheon, 1985).
3. Patricia Stubbs, *Women and Fiction: Feminism and the Novel 1880–1920* (1979; London: Methuen, 1981) 234.
4. See for example, Sandra M. Gilbert and Sandra Gilbert, *The Madwoman in the Attic* (New Haven and London: Yale University Press, 1979) 107–83; Margaret Kirkham, *Jane Austen, Feminism and Fiction* (London: Athlone, 1983); Mary Poovey, *The Proper Lady and the Woman Writer: Ideology as Style in the Works of Mary Wollstonecraft, Mary Shelley and Jane Austen* (London; Chicago; University of Chicago Press 1984).
5. Sandra M. Gilbert and Sandra Gilbert, *The Madwoman in the Attic*, 143. All subsequent references are to this edition, and are given in the text.
6. About a decade or so later, Claudia Johnson developed this reading of Austen's work in her *Jane Austen: Women, Politics and the Novel* (Chicago: University of Chicago Press, 1988).

7. Ellen Moers, *Literary Women* (1976; London: The Women's Press, 1978) 90.
8. Juliann E. Fleenor (ed.), *The Female Gothic* (Montreal and London: Eden Press, 1983) 8.
9. For example: Cora Kaplan, *Sea Changes: Culture and Feminism* (London: Verso, 1986); Juliet Mitchell, *Women: the Longest Revolution: Essays on Feminism, Literature and Psychoanalysis* (London: Virago, 1984); Andrea Dworkin, *Pornography: Men Possessing Women* (New York: Perigee, 1981); Catharine MacKinnon, *Feminism Unmodified: Discourses in Life and Law* (Cambridge, MA: Harvard University Press, 1987).
10. Lauren Fitzgerald, "Female Gothic and the institutionalization of Gothic studies" in Andrew Smith and Diana Wallace (eds) *Gothic Studies* 6:1 (2004), 8–18, 9. This essay provides an excellent overview of the area.
11. Avril Horner set up this module at Salford University; since her move to another university it has been taught by Janice Allan.
12. Despite the gradual emergence of work on European Gothic texts (some of which are available in translation), most Female Gothic modules are still resolutely Anglo-American; some also include work by male Gothic authors. A module running at the University of Virginia in the States, for example, lists on its syllabus Ann Radcliffe's *The Mysteries of Udolpho* and *The Italian*, Matthew Lewis's *The Monk* and Mary Shelley's *Frankenstein* (all taught by excerpts). Diane Long Hoeveler's module "The Female Gothic" at Marquette University lists as required texts Ann Radcliffe's *A Sicilian Romance*, Mary Elizabeth Braddon's *Lady Audley's Secret*, Daphne du Maurier's *Jamaica Inn*, Margaret Atwood's *Alias Grace* and Joyce Carol Oates's *Haunted* (plus a selection of ghost stories by women). The "Female Gothic" module taught at Salford University in the UK includes Ann Radcliffe's *The Italian*, Jane Austen's *Northanger Abbey*, Charlotte Brontë's *Villette*, Charlotte Perkins Gilman's *The Yellow Wallpaper*, Daphne du Maurier's *Rebecca* and Angela Carter's *The Bloody Chamber* (plus a session on Gothic film).
13. Anne Williams, *Art of Darkness: a Poetics of Gothic* (Chicago and London: Chicago University Press, 1995) and Robert Miles, *Ann Radcliffe: the Great Enchantress* (Manchester: Manchester University Press, 1995). The chapter entitled "Night*mère*'s milk: the male and female formulas" focuses on the difference between Male and Female Gothic writing.
14. Elaine Showalter, *Sisters' Choice: Tradition and Change in American Women's Writing* (Oxford: Clarendon, 1991) 129.
15. Donna Heiland, *Gothic & Gender: an Introduction* (Oxford: Blackwell, 2004) 183.
16. Alison Milbank, "Milton, melancholy and the Sublime in the 'female' Gothic from Radcliffe to Le Fanu," *Women's Writing* 2:1 (1994) (Special Number: "Female Gothic Writing" edited Robert Miles) 143.
17. This was published as *Daphne du Maurier: Writing, Identity and the Gothic Imagination* (Basingstoke: Macmillan—now Palgrave Macmillan, 1998).
18. Eugenia C. DeLamotte, *Perils of the Night: a Feminist Study of Nineteenth-Century Gothic* (New York and Oxford: Oxford University Press, 1990) 25.

19. See Jacqueline Howard, *Reading Gothic Fiction: a Bakhtinian Approach* (Oxford: Clarendon, 1994).
20. This is perhaps indicative of the current zeitgeist in academia which seems at times to mimic market economy vocabulary in its peremptory dismissal of modes of thought that were, in fact, profoundly influential in the second part of the twentieth century. We frequently hear young colleagues describe New Historicism as "old hat now" and Foucault's work as "old fashioned." There are, of course, exceptions: Helene Meyers, for example, laments the fact that " 'the race for theory', as well as the shift to gender studies, has further eroded academic support for the study of women writers qua women writers—especially those not already canonized" (*Femicidal Fears: Narratives of the Female Gothic Experience* [New York: State University of New York Press, 2001]) x. Perhaps there is a paper to be written, via Claire Kahane's work in the 1970s on Gothic, as a confrontation with the mothering and the problems of femininity, on the Female Gothic and embarrassment . . .
21. Chris Baldick and Robert Mighall, "Gothic criticism" in David Punter (ed.), *a Companion to the Gothic* (Oxford: Blackwell, 2000) 227.
22. Six of Barbara Comyns' novels are still available from Virago. They are: *The Vet's Daughter* (1959); *A Touch of Mistletoe* (1967); *Our Spoons Came from Woolworths* (1950); *Sisters by a River* (1947); *Who was changed and Who was Dead* (1954) and *The Skin Chairs* (1962). *The Juniper Tree* (1985), one of her best novels, is now out of print. Our essay was published as "Skin chairs and other domestic horrors" in Andrew Smith and Diana Wallace (eds), *Gothic Studies* 6:1, 2004, 90–102.
23. Examples include Charlotte Brontë's *Jane Eyre*, Daphne du Maurier's *Rebecca*, Angela Carter's *The Magic Toyshop* and "The Bloody Chamber" and Margaret Atwood's "Bluebeard's Egg."
24. E. J. Clery, *Women's Gothic: From Clara Reeve to Mary Shelley* (Tavistock: Northcote House in association with the British Council, 2000) 14.
25. Angela Wright, "Early women's Gothic writing: historicity and canonicity in Clara Reeve's *The Old English Baron* and Sophia Lee's *The Recess*" in Diane Long Hoeveler and Tamar Heller, *Approaches to Teaching Gothic Fiction* (New York: Modern Language Association of America, 2003) 101.
26. See Diane Long Hoeveler, "Teaching the early female canon: Gothic feminism in Wollstonecraft, Radcliffe, Austen, Dacre, and Shelley" in Hoeveler and Heller (eds), *Approaches to Teaching Gothic Fiction*, 109. See also her *Gothic Feminism: the Professionalization of Gender from Charlotte Smith to the Brontës* (University Park: Penn State Press, 1998) and "The construction of the female Gothic posture: Wollstonecraft's Mary and Gothic feminism" in Andrew Smith and Diana Wallace (eds), *Gothic Studies*, 30–44.
27. Susanne Becker, *Gothic Forms of Feminine Fictions* (Manchester: Manchester University Press, 1999).
28. Diana Wallace runs a module offered on the MA in Gothic Studies at the University of Glamorgan entitled "Gothic histories: women's Gothic

historical fictions"; her book is entitled *The Woman's Historical Novel: British Women Writers, 1900–2000* (Basingstoke: Palgrave Macmillan, 2005).

29. Helene Meyers, *Femicidal Fears: Narratives of the Female Gothic Experience* (New York: State University of New York Press, 2001) xi–xii.
30. Donna Heiland, *Gothic & Gender: an Introduction*, 183.
31. Virginia Woolf, *A Room of One's Own* (1929; Harmondsworth: Penguin Books, 1972) 76.

# 8

# Adapting Gothic from Print to Screen

*Anna Powell*

> . . . most people would "know" about Dracula from films rather than from Stoker's novel.
>
> (Ken Gelder)[1]

Gothic is an intertextual mode that crosses media boundaries. Its widest channel is film, of which there are thousands. As teachers of Gothic in the current cultural climate, we should acknowledge that our students come to us having viewed more Gothic films (increasingly on DVD rather than at the cinema) than have read Gothic novels. English Studies now includes both the adaptation process and film itself as a distinct field with commonality to literary study. Cross-referencing the two modes is mutually enhancing. Films with Gothic themes and styles offer us a rich resource for curriculum development and pedagogical practice.

My chapter addresses the implications of this Gothic cross-pollination for our teaching within an expanding English curriculum impacted by Film and Cultural Studies. I will explore the aesthetic and theoretical place of Gothic Film in a broad-based English Studies. My own approach has moved from print to screen over twelve years of teaching Gothic and remains in process as the subject area develops. I will be arguing that teachers of Gothic adaptation benefit from supplementing their literary expertise with concepts and practices from Film Studies. A preliminary grounding in this will significantly augment classroom practice.

In our department, the free-standing study of Gothic film has been augmented by the recent development of a Joint Honours degree in English and Film. My unit is also open to other English and

Humanities students with a nonformal knowledge of film. Gothic films may, of course, circulate outside the English subject field altogether. At Manchester Metropolitan University, for example, they are subsumed into units on the history of horror film run by the Art History Department. Some institutions might be amenable to interdepartmental or cross faculty initiatives in curriculum development and the sharing of staff expertise in teaching or dissertation supervision.

Like Creative Writing within the English syllabus, Gothic Film offers scope for practical creative input and project work. The making of short videos enables an original interpretation of Gothic themes. Clearly there are resource implications here, as many English departments lack specialist staff and equipment. Interdepartmental initiatives might possibly repay investigation. In my department, fortunately, two English lecturers run a discrete video-making unit; a potentially supportive resource for Gothic film projects and dissertations. Practical projects are advisably only undertaken by self-motivated students prepared to develop their own practical skills in directing, shooting, and editing. Such projects need to generate agreed marking criteria (such as those of Creative Writing) by including a critical rationale to theorize their Gothic components.

Gothic film might function as a supplementary stimulus to a written text given primary precedence on the syllabus. Thus, films are addressed chiefly in terms of their commonality with novels; rather than their medium-specific properties. They could, however, be fruitfully analysed in their own right. Methods of developing a more film-specific approach involve intertextual "close-reading" or the inclusion of film analysis without literary precedent. To facilitate this, cinema-specific concepts are helpful (with handout materials for reference).[2] Film clips illustrate Gothic formal techniques such as the animated shadows and vertiginous camerawork in the "old dark house" of Robert Wise's *The Haunting* (1963). My indicative case-study will focus on film adaptations of Bram Stoker's *Dracula* (1897).

## Adapting the Gothic

The staple role of film in English Studies is its adaptation (however loose) of literary texts.[3] Standard definitions of Gothic, such as Fred Botting's, introduce thematic and cultural issues common to both media. Students will benefit from a foundational awareness of differences and similarities between novels and films. Pivotal issues here are narrative structure, mode of address, characterization, reading and viewing. Sociohistorical approaches might expose factors of production and distribution, with their foundational economic determinants. The complexities of screenplay writing, casting, cinematography, *mise-en-scène,* and sound effects enable substantial comparative work with texts. This avoids an imbalance that might imply the aesthetic superiority of literary forms over cinematic expression.

Beginners to adaptation appreciate a comparative table in columns as an initial stimulus to discussion. The distinction between a literary author and a film *auteur* considers the authorial "voice" of the director as extratextual "star" with a distinctive "signature." The underrated role of the screenwriter could also be studied. The private processes of novel reading differ sharply from the public viewing experience of an audience. A film's running time is typically two hours viewed at one sitting. This limits the developmental detail and gradual readerly engagement over several days of sporadic novel consumption.

The novel's psychological interiority can be contrasted to the movie "action hero" defined by physical presence and performance. Psychoanalytical film theory, however, posits the viewer's own psychological engagement in reading the text. Casting, which operates intertextually, is crucial. Type-cast Gothic actors like Vincent Price, Peter Cushing, and Ingrid Pitt are interpreted via their repertoire of roles across films. Novels can analyse complex social and philosophical issues, but films *show* them. Although their stimulus to thought appears to be simpler here, the viewer's own response, though initially sensory, might operate comparable levels of conceptualization during or after the film.

The structural and temporal determinants of narrativity merit close comparison. Complex narrative structures may be pared down or removed in the "classic realist" mainstream movie; yet art-house cinema utilizes its own complex forms of "parametric" narration.[4] Vladimir Propp's narrative functions and Tsvetan Todorov's structuralist Fantastic are applicable to both film and novel. In both cases, their work challenges student readings based on character psychology.[5] Propp's work is particularly relevant to the nonrealist characterization of the Gothic. The language of the novel may, of course, be compared to the "language" of film, but over-schematic equations like that of shot with sentence, editing with punctuation, or iconography with imagery are problematic.

Close-reading workshops on questions of adaptation make productive seminars. Small groups compare literary extracts with corresponding clips. Despite the increase of DVDs in classrooms, my own preference is for clips on video. These can be cued in at precisely the right shot in a sequence rather than searching within chapters. I schedule regular screenings of set texts (on Wednesday afternoons) and expect student familiarity with both film and novel prior to sessions. Although there is plenty of scholarly material treating literature and on film separately, there is surprisingly little that offers equal consideration to literary and cinematic techniques in adaptation. It is more usual to find literary work that makes passing comparison; or treats Gothic films and novels in distinct chapters. Fortunately, new work is being published that redresses the imbalance. Until this gains wider circulation, students can work with separate critical material on each version to make their own intertextual connections.

A contentious slant on adaptation is raised by Wheeler Winston Dixon, who asserts "two essential caveats" to the pedagogic use of Gothic film: an aesthetic disapproval of "inferior" films and the censorship of "graphic violence" as unsuitable for use in class.[6] He rejects Kenneth Branagh's *Mary Shelley's Frankenstein* (1994), for example, both for its "overly violent" images and its "flashy tracking shots," although these are the very elements my students find appealing. Dixon's preference for the literary "original" is questionable from the perspective of Film Studies. Many adaptations could be regarded as aesthetically "superior" to their source novels. Films of Stephen King novels such as Brian De Palma's *Carrie* (1976) with its rich colours and textures or Stanley Kubrick's cerebral elegance in *The Shining* (1968) immediately spring to mind. Both, of course, feature familial brutality and graphic murders. Dixon's second caveat may be governed by censorship in the USA, but his taste-based criteria invokes the still-unquiet ghosts of *Scrutiny*.

Dixon warns against using "loose" adaptations in class, instead of making that very looseness an important question for discussion. Ironically, the very strengths of the 1930s horror films he valorizes lie in their deviations from the "original." The addition of the split-screen love triangle in Rouben Mamoulian's *Dr Jekyll and Mr Hyde* (1932), for instance, raises intriguing issues in its denial of Robert Louis Stevenson's homoerotic world. Film adaptations of Gothic novels are reduced to being "merely a springboard for the screenwriter's imagination" and Dixon relegates their value to "a useful adjunct to the detailed examination of the writers" (251).

David Punter, on the other hand, is a firm advocate of cinematic adaptation. Punter validates the stylistic and thematic commonality between horror films and early Gothic fiction. Each popular form demonstrates "a surprisingly high level of erudition, actual on the part of its makers and also imputed to its audience, and also a very high level of textual virtuosity."[7] Both rework melodramatic conventions within "a complex and contemporary psychological argument" (99). Comparing Mary Shelley's *Frankenstein* and James Whale's film adaptation (1931), Punter notes their common responses to technological change.[8] As Shelley's novel reflects the rise of the printing press and bourgeois readership, so Whale's film incorporates sound technology to intensify the viewer's emotional responses. Such technological determinants make valuable study. Punter's work offers a psychoanalytic approach to the mode and its readers. He indicates that the development of the horror film is "closely interlocked" with the belated spread of Freudian theory (97). The contemporaneity of the birth of psychoanalysis and late Gothic is well worth exploring. Michel Foucault's history of sexual practices in which the psychoanalytic term "produces" the psychosexual symptom is apposite here.[9]

Punter values the "self-ironising" Gothic films of the 1960s by Roger Corman in the USA and the British Hammer Horror director Terence Fisher (108). These low-budget films revisit literary tales from a contemporary perspective. Their thematic and narrative additions offered psychosexual and cultural relevance to their own predominantly youthful audiences. In Corman's "Poe Cycle," such as *The Tomb of Ligeia* (1964) the screenwriter mixed elements from Poe's brief tales and supplemented them by elements from mainstream narrative film. Nevertheless, Corman has produced a "self-consistent" set of horror films in which elements of Poe are "imbedded" in their expressionistic *mise-en-scène* (104). Punter's balanced approach evaluates each medium by its own formal and ideological criteria as well as by its adaptive strategies.

Heidi Kaye offers useful pointers for comparative class work. She indicates how different characteristics of literature and film produce different meanings as contextual determinants like war, sexuality, science, and politics shift.[10] She also asserts that visualization lessens the ambiguity and sympathetic aspects of those novelistic monsters which "virtually escape definition." Student debate on this can be augmented by reference to what Peter Hutchings calls "horror's new monsters" such as Hannibal Lecter or Freddy Krueger with their neo-Gothic aspects.[11]

Lisa Hopkins offers a distinctive perspective on screen versions of Gothic novels, which suggests a disparity between their interpretations of the mode. Her thesis argues that Gothic is "most present only when most conspicuously absent" in most Jane Austen novels, for example, but that the films based on them foreground their occluded Gothic aspects.[12] This works vice versa, in her claim that the most Gothic novels produce the least Gothic films. Hopkins also contentiously includes some pre-Gothic literary texts into the "haunted and contradictory" Gothic canon such as *Hamlet* and Richardson's *Clarissa* (150). Her readings, as well as being useful within Gothic units, could extend the mode's criteria to the study of other texts on the English curriculum.

The dynamics of gender are prominent in Gothic theory, yet far less criticism exists on gender in cinema than in literature, despite film's overt social referentiality. My unit "Gender and the Gothic" considers adaptations via feminist literary theory students may have encountered elsewhere on their course. We compare the female Gothic in Shirley Jackson's *The Haunting of Hill House* (1957) and Wise's *The Haunting*; lesbian Gothic in Sheridan Le Fanu's novelette *Carmilla* (1872) and Roy Ward Baker's *The Vampire Lovers* (1970); and Neil Jordan's version of Anne Rice's *Interview with the Vampire* (1994) with Rice's screenplay for their takes on male homoeroticism.[13] Recommended background reading includes "classics" of cinematic gender studies such as the work of Barbara Creed, Carol Clover, Bonnie Zimmerman, and Richard Dyer.[14] My own psychoanalytically-informed study of vampire fictions includes close textual comparisons of *Carmilla/The Vampire Lovers* and novel and film versions of *Interview with the Vampire*.[15]

Kim Wheatley's article on gender politics in novel and film versions of *Rebecca* (1940) is relevant here.[16] Wheatley indicates a "contagion" between characters and sets operant via Hitchcock's "preternatural" presentation of *mise-en-scène*. She shows how cinematography extends this as the camera "follows an invisible Rebecca around the boathouse" (135). Wheatley usefully distinguishes between forms of character doubling in each medium. A movie "insistently presents us with the illusion of autonomous human beings," so it is less effective than a novel at the structural use of doubled characters (136). Despite this issue, Wheatley's study does validate the Gothic qualities of both forms.

## Gothic film as film

The terms "Gothic" and "horror" involve a complex overlap of characteristics. Films not based on literary originals often include enough material of Gothic significance to merit study in their own right. Scholarly work on Gothic films is often subsumed under of Horror Film's substantial aegis. Peter Hutchings cautions against the negative evaluation that regards horror as a "vulgar, exploitative version of Gothic" (89). Gothic, he argues, is "a distinctive mode which influences a wide range of cultural forms while horror, and especially the horror film, is best seen as a genre, a more narrowly circumscribed area of cultural activity" (104). His distinction of the terms is open to further debate.

In UK film studies, culturalist and sociohistorical work on horror can be sifted for its relevance to Gothic. Ian Conrich suggests that the existence of Gothic Film Studies per se is problematized by the sheer "omniformity" of Gothic cinema; which leads scholars to focus on specific subdivisions such as the "dystopian visions of tech noir" or "psycho-thrillers such as *Seven*."[17] Furthermore, films like the *Alien* series (1979–97) and *Event Horizon* (1997) straddle the Gothic/Science-fiction divide and can be read from both perspectives. It is worth inviting students familiar with both genres to identify cross-generic Gothic features by debating whether, for instance, *Alien* is Gothic horror or sci-fi.

Some horror subgenres, such as the slasher movie, do not deploy period settings. For Hutchings, their use of the past "as a barbaric force which interrupts and threatens a more mundane, everyday world" locates them within the Gothic paradigm (94). Teachers familiar with the horror film tradition might have fewer qualms with its "exploitation" of graphic sex or violence than those who avoid these elements. Suburban Gothic fantasies like Wes Craven's *A Nightmare on Elm St* (1984) deserve more than a passing mention, asserts Punter, if we want to explore the "social significance of the forms of terror" (97). The Gothicization of ethnicity is also much more overt in horror films such as *White Zombie* (1932), *The Night of the Living Dead* (1968) and *Candyman* (1992) than in earlier Gothic literature where it may be concealed or marginalized. Such films offer plenty of scope to explore this vital issue. I use *Candyman*, with its vengeful slave revenant, to address racist themes in Gothic via Julia Kristeva's concept of abjection.

My final section considers the role of film in Gothic teaching via a case-study of three film versions of *Dracula*. As much literary criticism already focuses on Stoker's novel, I will here foreground the film-specific properties and pedagogic possibilities of the adaptations. The number of teaching sessions spent on this material, adaptable to different abilities, depends on particular objectives. It can work for either a one-off exercise in close-reading or be developed as several interlinked sessions analysing textual and contextual implications in greater depth.

## Case-study: *Dracula* from print to screen

Cinematic Draculas are, argues Hopkins, "analogous to the ways in which perceptions of the novel have changed over time" (110). They might draw on other literary vampires or reference other films in the subgenre. Filmic renderings of Stoker's novel transpose it into colour, light, and sound. Some versions, like *Bram Stoker's Dracula*, deliberately seek to validate their literary antecedents whilst adding elements of plot and character.[18] My focal texts are F. W. Murnau's *Nosferatu* (1922), Werner Herzog' *Nosferatu* (1979) and Coppola's film, with their very distinct historical contexts. Arriving in the vampire's domain, Jonathan Harker is transported to the castle by a mysterious coachman, who may be the count himself.[19] This climactic sequence transmutes Stoker's densely descriptive prose into images and music (played by accompaniment in the case of Murnau) and a minimal use of language.

Rather than expecting students familiar with the slick GCI of Hollywood horror to automatically share my enthusiasm for *Nosferatu* as a silent film, I start by identifying aspects that may initially alienate them. Expressionist acting style seems melodramatic to students familiar with contemporary variants on method acting. The actors here deploy an unnatural body language that mimics the diagonal composition of shots and acts out inner states. The *mise-en-scène* draws on folk tradition and early nineteenth-century German romanticism, both with their plethora of Gothic relevance. In Murnau's film, Gothic and Expressionist elements combine. Innovative *mise-en-scène* and cinematography mix Gothic motifs with the sensory distortions of experimental cinema.

The early circulation of Murnau's *Nosferatu*, literally determined by its literary model, can be used to discuss creative "originality." Stoker's widow, Florence, had attempted to place copyright injunctions on the film, without success.[20] Henrik Galeen's script changed character names and removed the Crew of Light, focusing on the destruction of the vampire by Ellen/Nina (Mina) through self-sacrifice. Comparison with other Expressionist films such as Robert Wiene's *The Cabinet of Dr Caligari* (1926) help to delineate its specifically cinematic status.

Unlike Stoker's sparse description of Dracula's "very red lips and sharp-looking teeth" (10) and reddish-hued eyes, the "look" of Murnau's Count Orlock (Dracula) is central to the cinematic version in several senses.[21] Orlock's opaque black eyes hypnotize Ellen/Nina as he locks his baleful stare onto her fearful gaze from the warehouse window. His grotesque appearance combines animal and plant: bat-ears, rat-teeth and root-like fingers. Orlock is also rendered uncanny by superimposition and extreme camera angles. His large, hooked nose and pointed cap overtly recall racist caricature.[22] Despite its period setting, the film clearly reflects attitudes in Weimar Germany in the 1920s. Anti-Semitic paranoia informs the theme of a vampire who comes from the East, accompanied by plague rats, to undermine prosperous German society. The film can indeed be read as a "national allegory" in which a woman's "purity" is sacrificed for the "pure" German folk.[23]

The sequence begins with Hutter (Harker) set down by his coachman who will "go no further." Hutter crosses the bridge to Orlock's domain, the intertitled "land of the phantoms." The sequence displays powerfully affective *mise-en-scène* and cinematography. The vampire's geography is expressed in high contrast arrangements of light and dark. This visual conflict is the shifting foundation of Orlock's shadow-realm with its physical, psychological, and metaphysical dimensions. The serpentine motion of Orlock's carriage follows its own jagged trajectory. Moving with unnatural velocity, it scuttles down, beetle-like, with the jerkiness of stop motion. Dark pines at top left of frame dominate the long-shot composition. Their spiky, fang-like shadows form a diagonal split with Hutter's patch of sunlight at bottom right.

Swallowing Hutter, the coach shudders back uphill between light and darkness, shaking its passenger's body and mind. By crossing the bridge and accepting the ride, Hutter seals his contract with the vampire. His moral and metaphysical inversion is expressed by Murnau's celebrated negative footage. The reversal of light and dark blackens the sunlight and turns shadow into a white fog, which reduces the coach to a phantom imprint. The director's antirealist abstraction renders the vampire driver as a composition of triangles as he drops Hutter outside the castle. The turret forms a visual rhyme with his pointed hat and his nose. As well as signalling his thematic imperiousness, Orlock's forward gesture with his whip cuts across the frame in a diagonal line. It points beyond the frame's confines to another level of reality.

The gate swings open to engulf Hutter. In the next shot, Orlock appears from within a cavernous archway to greet his guest. Temporal ellipses stress the unnatural speed of the vampire's transformations. Between shots, he has impossibly changed in both appearance and demeanour. He moves stiffly, with hunched back and incurved arms, in a visual rhyme with the shape of the archway. His rigid body, tight black garb and angular shoulders suggest that he is always, already in his coffin. In this undead state, Orlock is freed from human laws of time, space, and motion to control living creatures and inanimate objects by the force of his unnatural will.

Orlock's domination of Hutter is stressed by the vampire's foregrounding in mid-frame as the camera renders his over-the-shoulder viewpoint. A creature of enclosed spaces, the Count is often framed by dark arches, which provide claustrophobic frames within the frame. As Hutter and Orlock enter the castle's cavernous interior, the vampire's funereal black is absorbed by his native element of darkness. Hutter, in his pale greatcoat, stays visible for longer, before he, too, is swallowed up by darkness.

My second choice is Herzog's remake of *Nosferatu* for its intertextual relation to both the novel and the earlier film. The stylistic and thematic implications of this 1979 remake of its Weimar predecessor are politically suggestive. For Gelder, Herzog reused his vampire " 'positively' to critique the bourgeois characteristics of the German people" (98). The film also revisits the history of German romanticism. Although the setting is ostensibly the early nineteenth century, its use of folk culture (with gypsy encampment), and of Wagner's music, refers to more recent political perversions of the romantic tradition. The film could be read as a critique of Nazi appropriation of the Sublime and of Gothic/Teutonic revivalism.

The visual motifs of the earlier film haunt Herzog's *Nosferatu*. Both use the warped silhouette of a ruined castle to foreshadow the advent of the Count. This visualizes Stoker's "vast ruined castle" whose "broken battlements showed a jagged line against the moonlit sky" (14). Where Murnau made the vampire's realm of shadow and light, Herzog mixes uncanny blue light with darkness. Herzog minimizes dialogue to echo the earlier film's intertitles. In preference to Murnau's disjointed, jerky editing, Herzog favours long, slow takes which elongate time and produce a drowsy, hypnotic effect on the audience independently of the vampire's presence. His theme here is the individual ego engulfed by the forces of nature. The early Romantic paintings of Caspar David Freidrich with their solitary figures surveying rugged landscapes are formative here, locating Herzog's Gothic within the Sublime aesthetic.

Lacking transport, Harker is compelled to journey on foot. As he walks away from a static foreground, he is subsumed into a long shot of the hazy mountainous landscape. His figure is replaced by slow shots of rocks blurred by mist as the landscape's nonhuman force implies the vampire's anomalous meld of natural and unnatural. Traced downwards by a vertiginous camera, waterfalls end in a dwarfed and depersonalized human observer. The camera appears to following Harker's own downward gaze, but then disorients our expectations when it rediscovers him looking up, being not above, but below the waterfall.

Harker's angst-ridden facial expression signals the overwhelming otherness of this landscape. He is aurally overwhelmed by choral music that repeats the vampire's "theme" of a reverberating, wordless cadence. Natural features seem to spy on the intruder from their own perspective. Hutter is followed from behind by a shaky, hand-held camera and "observed" from a set-up within a cave. A series of shots replace him by blurred, amorphous images of the sky obscured by swirling mists. The silhouette of Harker from behind against a dusk-blue sky tracks away without giving us his anticipated reaction-shot, then he disappears from view as Wagnerian horns and a fluid camera lead the viewer into the clouds.

Harker's entrancement corresponds to Stoker's description of him "sleeping" before entering the castle. Darkness is pierced by bright blue light that heralds a floating, silent coach. This whiskered driver is clearly not the Count himself like he was in Stoker or Murnau. Herzog's interpretation here intensifies the mystery of the vampire and the atmosphere of suspense. The coach floats Harker into the castle courtyard. Bewildered and bareheaded, his vulnerability prepares us for his vampire host's potency. Double doors glide apart to reveal a shadowy, robed figure in a conical hat. Hesitant, low-key greetings break the film's long silence as the Count's beautiful, sad eyes fix on his guest. Students generally find the melancholic intensity of Klaus Kinski's Dracula the most "human" and sympathetic portrayal (and its predecessor, Max Shreck's inhuman vampire, the most fearsome) The vampire leads Harker into the castle's candle-lit interior and the closing of doors behind them provides a natural cut before the next sequence.

Coppola's film is overtly distinct from his sources, yet it quotes Herzog's version and other vampire films as well as Stoker's novel. For Hopkins, Coppola's "wildly camp" adaptation is "ironic, complexly referential" in its intertextuality (111). Gelder notes how a novel titled *Bram Stoker's "Dracula"* by vampire novelist Fred Saberhagen appeared *after* the screenplay by James V. Hart and "works over" Stoker's novel, cribbing passages wholesale (90). These intertextual borrowings (and Stoker's own wide use of sources) repay further study.

*Bram Stoker's Dracula* shifts the historical context to Stoker's own *fin-de-siècle* with its technological advancements of the railway and the cinematograph. Hopkins contrasts these visual technologies to those of the novel, which are "primarily auditory or text-based: Dr Seward's phonograph, Mina's typewriter, and the telegraph service" (111). In a move authenticating the film's literary credentials, however, Harker's journal entry for 25 May appears physically in close-up as his voice-over reads it. Dracula's eyes are superimposed over a blood-red sunset suggesting that Jonathan is under his surveillance, as in Herzog's film, and can read his mind. Despite the map of Transylvania superimposed over Harker's face on the train, the film's locales are overtly artificial; unlike the geographical specificity of location shooting in the other two films.

Like Herzog, Coppola depicts the black silhouette of the coach with bare-branched trees against an indigo sky. A thunderclap rends our ears and a jag of lightening splits the screen as we are bombarded by a condensed version of Stoker's storm. As Harker alights, a fellow-traveller gives him a crucifix and a warning "for the dead travel fast" in (subtitled) local dialogue. A long shot reveals Harker left alone in a misty and initially featureless place. Its Gothic nature is signalled as the camera swoops up to a wayside crucifix on which a wolf's skeletal face is splayed in grimacing close-up. As though the bones were reanimated, a lightening flash illumines a living wolf. All three films depict the vampire's carriage as anomalous in its movements. Here, it floats in slow-motion out of the mist. Its armoured driver recalls "medieval" knights like those of Ken Russell's *Gothic* (1986). An arm covered in plated scales is stretched unnaturally by computer-generated imagery (CGI) and shoves Harker into the coach. They travel in speeded-up motion, reminiscent of Murnau's staccato shots, as a lightening flash reveals pack of wolves trailing them.

Horace Walpole's *The Castle of Otranto* (1764) is invoked by the castle's resemblance to a giant seated figure in armour; perhaps based on Stoker's reference to a Carpathian mountain called "God's Seat" (7). Blue rings of fire are borrowed from the novel but also echo the creation of the robot Maria in Fritz Lang's Expressionist *Metropolis* (1927). The gate's huge, spiked bars visually imprison the impassive Harker by superimposition. Wielding his "arabesque" lamp, Dracula greets Harker with Stoker's familiar words, "Welcome to my house" (16). His blood-red, gold-embroidered robe replaces the other versions' black by its Technicolor excess. The multicoloured lamp highlights the Count's waxy, mask-like face with its deep-set eyes and sardonic smile. As the portcullis creaks, shadows adopt a life of their own, expressionist-style, and glide across the entrance-hall independent from their source. Following Stoker's description, Harker crosses the threshold and into the vampire's lair. A close-up of Vlad Drakul's portrait recalls the most substantial liberty Coppola takes with Stoker's novel: his added prologue of Vlad's tragic human life.

As cineliteracy increases, the significance of film in Gothic Studies becomes even more significant. Students are initially attracted to the Gothic via its wider cultural manifestations as well as still-popular literary forms. They enjoy the prospect of studying material in college that they already consume for pleasure outside. Recruitment for Gothic classes rises steadily each year. My current second year unit attracts approximately fifty students and several third years opt for Gothic dissertations with a film component. To support this burgeoning field, further scholarship on Gothic adaptation would be welcome. Tracing the transmutation from print to screen offers a fascinating challenge for an English curriculum expanding its scope to include newer media for the Gothic imagination.

## Notes

1. Ken Gelder, *Reading the Vampire* (London: Routledge, 1994) 86. All subsequent references are to this edition, and are given in the text.
2. Standard introductory books on cinematic concepts are James Monaco, *How to Read a Film* (Oxford: Oxford University Press, 1981); Susan Hayward, *Key Concepts in Cinema Studies* (London and New York, Routledge, 1996).
3. Introductory textbooks on adaptation include Deborah Cartmell and Imelda Whelehan, *Adaptation: From Text To Screen* (London and New York: Routledge, 1999); Robert Giddings and Erica Sheen, eds, *From Page to Screen: Adaptations of the Classic Novel* (Manchester: Manchester University Press, 1999); Brian Mcfarlane, *An Introduction to the Theory of Adaptation* (Oxford: Clarendon Press, 1996).
4. David Bordwell, *Narration in the Fiction Film* (New York and London: Routledge, 1986).
5. Tzvetan Todorov, *The Fantastic: a structural approach to a literary genre,* trans. Richard Howards, 2nd edn, Louis A. Wagner, ed. (London and Cleveland: Case Western University, 1973). Vladimir Propp, *The Morphology of the Folktale,* trans. Laurence Scott (Austin and London: University of Texas, [1928] 1968).
6. Wheeler Winston Dixon, "Teaching Gothic literature through filmic adaptation," in Diane Long Hoeveler and Tamar Heller, eds, *Approaches to Teaching Gothic Fiction: the British and American Traditions* (New York: Modern language Association of America, 2003) 244–51.
7. David Punter, *The Literature of Terror: a History of Gothic Fictions from 1765 to the Present Day: Vol 2, The Modern Gothic* (London and New York: Longman, 1996) 97. All subsequent references are to this edition, and are given in the text.
8. Punter, 99.

9. Michel Foucault, *The History of Sexuality, Vol 1: An Introduction*, trans. Robert Hurley (New York: Vintage Press, 1980).
10. Heidi Kaye, "Gothic film" in David Punter, ed., *A Companion to the Gothic* (Oxford: Blackwell, 2000) 180–92, 190.
11. Peter Hutchings, "Tearing your soul apart: horror's new monsters" in Victor Sage and Allan Lloyd Smith, eds, *Modern Gothic: a Reader* (Manchester: Manchester University Press, 1996) 89–103, 94. All subsequent references are to this edition, and are given in the text.
12. Lisa Hopkins, *Screening the Gothic* (Austin: University of Texas Press, 2005) 150. All subsequent references are to this edition, and are given in the text.
13. Shirley Jackson, *The Haunting of Hill House* (London: Robinson, [1959] 1999). Sheridan Le Fanu, *Carmilla* [1872], in Alan Ryan, ed., *The Penguin Book of Vampire Stories* (Harmondsworth: Penguin, 1988) 71–137. Anne Rice, *Interview with the Vampire* (London: Futura, [1976] 1987). For a *mise-en-scène* analysis of *The Haunting*, see Anna Powell, *Deleuze and Horror Film* (Edinburgh: Edinburgh University Press, 2005) 166–74.
14. Barbara Creed, *The Monstrous Feminine: Film, gender and psychoanalysis* (London and Hew York: Routledge, 1993); Carol J. Clover, *Men, Women and Chainsaws: Gender in the Modern Horror Film* (London: BFI, 1992); Richard Dyer, " 'Children of the night': vampirism as homosexuality: homosexuality as vampirism," in Susannah Radstone, ed., *Sweet Dreams: Sexuality, gender and popular fiction* (London: Lawrence and Wishart, 1988) 47–72; Bonnie Zimmermann, "Daughters of darkness: the lesbian vampire on film," in Barry K. Grant, ed., *Planks of Reason* (Metuchen, New Jersey, Scarecrow Press, 1984) 153–63.
15. Anna Powell, *Psychoanalysis and Sovereignty in Popular Vampire Fictions* (Lewiston, New York; Queenston, Ontario; and Lampeter, Wales: Edward Mellen Press, 2003).
16. Kim Wheatley, "Gender politics and the Gothic in Alfred Hitchcock's *Rebecca*," in *Gothic Studies*, 4, 2 (November 2002), 133–44. All subsequent references are to this edition, and are given in the text.
17. Ian Conrich, "Gothic film" in Marie Mulvey Roberts, ed., *A Handbook to Gothic Literature* (Basingstoke: Macmillan now Palgrave Macmillan, 1998) 76–81, 76.
18. As well as claiming to be an "authentic" adaptation of Stoker's novel in the title, the tie-in documentary *The Making of Bram Stoker's Dracula* reveals the cast studying the novel in preparation for their roles.
19. Bram Stoker, *Dracula* (Oxford and New York: Oxford University Press, [1897] 1983) 10–16. All subsequent references are to this edition, and are given in the text.
20. Gelder, 94.
21. Gelder, 94.
22. See Lotte Eisener, *The Haunted Screen* (London: Secker and Warburg, [1952] 1973), and Sigfried Kracauer, *From Caligari to Hitler: a Psychological History of German Film* (Princeton: Princeton University Press, 1947)
23. Gelder, 97.

# 9
# American Gothic

*Allan Lloyd-Smith*

As Leslie Fiedler exuberantly claimed, American fiction has been "bewilderingly and embarrassingly, a gothic fiction, nonrealistic and negative, sadist and melodramatic—a literature of darkness and the grotesque in a land of light and affirmation."[1] That makes the American Gothic what Poe might have called a "legitimate" means for exploring at least one significant thread in a no longer defensive or embarrassed literature. The pitfalls are immediately obvious, those nonrealistic and negative, even sadist and melodramatic features are hard to find in Emerson or Thoreau, not to mention Howells, and to teach American literature through a glass darkly is to distort as much as to sharpen the outlines of what may have been previously suppressed. For that reason, among others, I teach the Gothic as an upper level course, for final year students who at UEA have four years of earlier acquaintance with American writing. Even so, the effects of a Gothic point of view as powerful attractant can cause a warping in judgement such that the Gothic seems to turn up everywhere, even in the most apparently innocent of texts.

The Gothic does however manifest itself in quite surprising places, if one takes it to be not simply a matter of form or genre, but sees it as an inflexion signalled by such a small detail as the unremarked manacles of the domino in Herman Melville's "The Bell-Tower" (1855).[2] This resonates with an apparently off-hand epigraph: "Like negroes, these powers own man sullenly; mindful of their higher master; while serving, plot revenge" (121). The manacles swerve this story from its ostensible critique of technological hubris towards another reading concerning the interplay between arrogance and race in American society, subterraneanly linking these together through the notion of the fatally cracked (Liberty) Bell. Is this truly Gothic? The American version of Gothic tropes can be more sudden, less a matter of genre and more of an irruption of profound historical and social anxieties, requiring an understanding of context for recognition. Again, this means that a relatively sophisticated student group is better placed to pick up and evaluate the sometimes subtle pointers to a full reading of oblique texts.

But even a sophisticated student of American literature may have neither the background in English and European Gothic evident in American writers such as Charles Brockden Brown, Edgar Allan Poe, or Herman Melville, nor enough time in the pressure of study for three academic units at once to engage in such reading. Few will have read Ann Radcliffe, and their knowledge of Mary Shelley or Bram Stoker is more probably gleaned from film than fiction. Even more disturbingly, many of them will not even have read *Moby-Dick* (1851) in entirety, and so it is not unusual to find reference in student essays to Melville as a primarily Gothic writer. Charles Maturin, or James Hogg do not figure in their literary world at all, although some may have read Robert Louis Stevenson's *The Strange Case of Dr. Jekyll and Mr. Hyde* (1886) Much of this material has to be supplied by the seminar leader, and it frequently re-emerges in garbled versions when the students are brave enough to answer an examination question on the European Gothic in relation to American development of the form. Fred Botting's book *The Gothic* is helpful here as a brief and readable outline of essential knowledge.[3]

The first session of any unit has to negotiate a paucity of preliminary reading whilst avoiding the pitfall of establishing a pattern of lecturing by the seminar leader that may result in the atrophy of individual student responsibility for the discourse of the class. A brainstorming session works well here, in which suggestions from the group of the major elements in Gothic are written up on the board and then linked according to examples given by the students and the tutor. This model allows for mini lectures as appropriate and the introduction of relevant texts that are not on the course but need to be mapped as possible resources in individual work. Rather than simply noting an ignorance of Radcliffe, say, her work may be mentioned in terms of landscapes of the Gothic; the picturesque and the sublime, tropes of pursuit and incarceration, architectural settings, the role of the female protagonist. Some may go on to read her; others will at least know what they do not know. It is usually possible also to at least suggest the significance of the French Revolution, the implications of its American predecessor, the situation of women, the implications of slavery, and so on. That session usually concludes with a mini lecture on the development of American Gothic over the nineteenth century, and brief discussion of some contemporary Gothic texts.

Conveniently, perhaps, the first powerful American novelist, Brockden Brown, was an enthusiastic Gothicist for much of his career, and certainly in the novels for which he is best remembered, *Wieland, Arthur Mervyn, Edgar Huntly*, and *Ormond*, all written within a period of two years between 1798 and 1799.[4] Much influenced by William Godwin (and in turn an influence *on* both Godwin and Mary Shelley), Brockden Brown introduced horror within the domestic milieu and, more significantly, within the disturbed minds of his narrators and protagonists. Theodore Wieland, for example, is responsible for the gruesome murder of his wife and children when inspired by voices he attributes to God; the story is written by his agitated sister Clara, who is his next target for sacrifice. Brockden Brown's prose is fairly indigestible for present day students: clumsy, latinate, verbose, and repetitious, it is distinctly an acquired taste. For that reason class discussion focuses on a brief story—almost a sketch—to be found in Charles Crow's anthology *American Gothic*, which serves as a very useful unit text, to be complemented by additional readings as required. Brockden Brown's story "Somnambulism" (1805) is (quite typically) inspired by a gazette account which by quotation at the beginning sets up an insistent explicatory framework for the following first-person account of a man who may have sleepwalked and perhaps, while in that state, have murdered the girl with whom he is obsessed.[5] In *Wieland* (1798) Brockden Brown wrote prefatorily:

> the incidents related are extraordinary and rare. Some of them, perhaps, approach as nearly to the nature of miracles as can be done by that which is not truly miraculous. It is hoped that intelligent readers will not disapprove of the manner in which appearances are solved, but that the solution will be found to correspond with the known principles of human nature. (*Wieland*, "Advertisement" 23)

He further defended his bizarre material by appeal to "physicians, and to men conversant with the latent springs and occasional perversions of the human mind" (23), thus setting an agenda that was to be followed by most of the subsequent American Gothicists, and particularly by Poe and Hawthorne. Brockden Brown's insistence on the realistic origins of his stories (*Wieland* was also inspired by a newspaper account) provides an occasion for the introduction of Scottish Common Sense philosophy which dominated American intellectual life at this time and a discussion of the relation between the Gothic and enlightenment thought.[6] But "Somnambulism" is also rewarding as a text for seminar work because it peculiarly instances a coming into being of Gothic tropes in the act of creation. In particular, the anxious narrator in wishing to prevent the departure of his object of unrequited affection dwells on the perils of her proposed night time journey, and fears that the carriage may smash into a tree. This hypothetical tree grows into a notorious large oak astraddle the road, and the carriage duly runs into it; this becoming the spot where the girl is murdered, her father and servant having gone for help. The extent to which the giant tree suggests an unwanted paternal and patriarchal power produces useful class discussion, as does the terrifying appearance of a double in the tale, the supposedly harmless wilderness idiot Handyside (also previously forgotten by the narrator in looking for reasons to avert the journey) who apparently flits around the carriage before its catastrophe, uttering manic cries and laughter. That wilderness figure with its maniacal laughter recurs in later American Gothic and gives an opportunity to begin discussion of the wilderness and frontier aspects of this literature.[7]

Subsequent sessions are student-led in that each includes two or more class presentations, introducing a topic/author and suggesting possible lines for exploration. These are not graded, given the difficulty of objective assessment of in-class performance, but the students are encouraged to produce a page or two of photocopied notes for the group and some feedback is usually given from the tutor. But the principal feedback system here is from the peer group itself: each member of the seminar fills in a response form evaluating presentation performance in both practical and academic areas. The form asks whether the presenter addressed the whole group, or just the seminar leader, and invites observation of factors that may have affected the presentation, such as speaking inaudibly, reading from notes exclusively and not looking up, nervous tics or other features that should be addressed. It also scores the length of the presentation, the adequacy of research work, and whether the respondent learned new material from this presentation. The point of this is to address a range of areas. Suggestions as to appropriate Gothic topics are given for these presentations, which may be as specific as a discussion of Brockden Brown in relation to contemporary political and cultural issues such as the Federalists and Republicans and the sensationalist psychology of his contemporary Dr Benjamin Rush; or of more general issues, including the the role of Poe in the development of horror and psychology in the gothic genre, Gilman, Wharton, and Spofford in relation to recent critical work on the "Female Gothic," or Pynchon and Gibson concerning postmodernism and the Gothic, and the "cybergothic." This procedure enables a more widely interactive class situation, avoiding intellectual ping-pong with the tutor to the exclusion of others. It draws attention to pitfalls and goals for presentations, and helps students to evaluate and change their public presentation skills. The anonymous forms are collected and read by the tutor before being delivered to the presenter for feedback. This increases the stakes in that peer pressure is remarkably powerful. Since introducing this technique student commitment in presentation work has greatly increased. The form itself reminds students who are not yet presenters of what will be expected of them, and finally it empowers the student group and moves them away from the notion that their only role is to achieve a seminar leader's positive assessment. Of course this strategy is not itself without some pitfalls; notably that blind loyalty appears quite frequently. But even then, other members of the group will make helpful critical comments. I have sometimes found that a startlingly original presentation may not be registered as such by the group, and on occasion conversely, sloppy work can be judged to be thorough and impressive. But on balance this has proved a very useful way to improve the quality of oral presentations, and very few try to evade it, even though it is ungraded. Sometimes a good deal of tutor led discussion is required to sort out the most useful Gothic issues from accounts that have strayed away from the principal aim, but it is surprising how often even biographical snippets can contribute a productive angle for discussion. Of course the students also fill in a feedback form on the unit itself in the penultimate session, in effect assessing the tutor and the unit as a whole; most of these suggest that the student feedback mechanism is appreciated. Another resource used in this unit is *Blackboard*, the online teaching aid that facilitates access to appropriate Gothic study materials, and the students are also encouraged to make use of web sites such as *The Sickly Taper* and the *Online MLA Bibliography* in approaching their essay.

Washington Irving—not generally seen as a Gothicist—provides an opportunity to open up the theme of Gothic humour by considering "Rip Van Winkle" "Sleepy Hollow" and "The Adventure of the German Student."[8] By the time Irving wrote his tales in the 1820s the Gothic had fallen from its dominant position and become the object of satires such as Peacock's *Nightmare Abbey* (1818) and Austen's *Northanger Abbey* (1818) By relating Irving's appropriation of European folk tales to the nationalism of such collectors as Sir Walter Scott it is possible to introduce themes of early American national identity formation and to reread "Van Winkle" in terms of New York State legacies from the American Revolution, specifically the loyalist residue suggested by the retention of George III's face on the sign of the new hotel that replaces the old tavern by the time of Rip's reawakening. The face is now signifying George Washington, an outrageous economy hinting at the loyalist sympathies of these tucked-away American Dutch villages. Such close readings for implicit historical and political significance are also applied to "The German Student," a story that might be seen as an urban legend of Paris during the French Revolution's Terror.[9] This tale is of a bookish youth, lost in neoplatonic exhumations of the likes of Paracelsus, who becomes an enthusiast of the new theories of equality, freedom, and free love. Enamoured by a beautiful woman in his dreams, he encounters her one night, weeping at the base of the scaffold. Wolfgang takes her home and consummates their new love after swearing himself hers forever and dispensing with the old forms of marriage. In the morning, while he is out, the police arrive and find her body draped over his bed; on their removing the black neckband she wears her head rolls to the floor: " 'Do you know anything about her?' said Wolfgang eagerly. 'Do I?' exclaimed the officer: 'she was guillotined yesterday'."[10] Irving's narrator concludes the story by swearing that it is true, having heard it himself from the student at a madhouse in Paris. On the face of it simply an absurd tall tale, this story works well as a means to discuss the political anxieties raised in America by the French Revolution, the conservative response to new European ideas, including romanticism, and, of course, the issues of gender and sexual instabilities encountered in the Gothic. Above all, as with Irving's other (and numerous) mockingly Gothic pieces, it reminds the students of the importance of the comic in this literature, especially in its American manifestations, and thus prepares for a sophisticated reading of, say, Edgar Allan Poe's tales of terror.

One of the problems with Poe is that for literary historical reasons his work has been taken very seriously, and it can be a struggle to overcome the students' previously solemn encounters with this instigator of a new, abrupt, and immensely influential, mock-Gothic tradition. The problem is to take laughter seriously, that is, to point out the seriousness of Poe's underlying themes while appreciating (somewhat against the critical consensus) that after all, this is comic writing. The opening of "The Fall of the House of Usher" (1839) provides a starting point for such investigations, when Poe's narrator describes his feeling of insufferable gloom at the setting of the house as "unrelieved by any of that half-pleasurable, because poetic, sentiment with which the mind usually receives even the sternest images of the desolate or terrible." Instead it is like the "hideous dropping off of the veil" experienced after revelling in opium, "an iciness, a sinking, a sickening of the heart—an unredeemed dreariness of thought which no goading of the imagination could torture into aught of the sublime."[11] Not Burke's sublime then, it is worse, much worse! This gives occasion for some examination of the concept of the sublime and its relation to Gothic writing of the period, while acknowledging Poe's subversive appropriation of the current fashion and its potential for the description of ontological crisis. It is an apocalyptic revision of the psychological traumas of Brockden Brown's protagonists; no longer describing the deranged person in a sane world, Poe offers ontological derangements in an insane universe. His narrators insist that they are not mad, and in a way they are not; it is the world that is mad. And as for any presumed world beyond, Valdemar reports back from his postdecease hypnotic trance "For God's sake!—quick!—quick!—put me to sleep or, quick! Waken me!—quick! *I say to you that I am dead*!"[12] The pun on the quick and the dead may or may not be intended; the impossibility of the speech act "I am dead" certainly is.[13] After the mesmeric passes are performed, Valdemar initiates a long tradition of horror endings by rotting away at once into a putrescent mess upon the bed. There is nothing beyond, except the impossibility of existence, and a long line of horror films in the future.

But if Poe responds well to philosophical and literary scrutiny, as the developer of the concise horror tale, the short story, and the detective genre, he also enables discussion of a puritan-horror lineage pointing towards Emily Dickinson and perhaps to Lovecraft, and Poe's specific situation as Southern gentleman manqué invites attention to his representation of racial issues in *The Narrative of Arthur Gordon Pym* (1838), "The Black Cat" (1843) and "Hop-Frog" (1850); introducing a theme that runs throughout this unit, the pressures and inflexions of slavery and its legacies in the United States.[14] Poe's work encourages an appreciation of Toni Morrison's thesis in *Playing in the Dark* on the role of blackness in the white literary imagination, and leads the students to begin to see American Gothic as less a subordinate genre, more an appropriate vehicle for the displaced representation of real horrors in the American past.[15] His example also enables students to move past feelings of dismay at realizing the racism of some cherished writers towards a more precise appraisal of how such themes are buried within the literary structures and even the language of this literature. Similarly, what might be called Poe's sentimental sadism towards women prompts appraisal of the situation of American women in the early nineteenth century as well as his own biography, and this in turn feeds into a revisionary view of his Gothic detection in "The Murders in the Rue Morgue" (1841) (why are the victims mother and daughter, and their fate so horrific; for what human aberrations might the Ourang-Outang stand in?), "The Mystery of Marie Roget" (1850) and "The Purloined Letter" (1845).[16] As this moves more towards a psychoanalytical focus it develops aspects of the Freudian reading, specifically in "The Uncanny" (1919), exploring the themes of the doll, and the double (in "William Wilson") and echoing some of the discussions of Brockden Brown's work.[17]

Clearly Poe provides enough material for a whole unit on his American Gothic, which might indeed be a proposal for MA-level work, where one could engage with the arguments of Jacques Lacan, Jacques Derrida, and Barbara Johnson on "The Purloined Letter" and Roland Barthes on "The Facts in the Case of M. Valdemar" (1845).[18] But in view of the goals of this unit, which include a reorientation of understandings that students will already have, through the sharpened focus of a particularly directed rereading, it is rewarding to consider writers who have not been seen as predominantly Gothicists, such as Nathaniel Hawthorne. Most of the students will already have read

*The Scarlet Letter* (1850), Some have encountered a few of Hawthorne's tales, but *The House of the Seven Gables* (1851), *The Blithedale Romance* (1852), and above all, *The Marble Faun* (1860) are, and for most of them remain, uncharted territory.[19] Focus stays on the tales—for practical pedagogical reasons—but much encouragement is given towards extending perspectives by reading the lesser-known novels. One or two do, although my visions of intelligent and informed responses to the Gothic through scrupulous interrogation of *The Marble Faun* have not been realized yet. It is too long, too demanding, and too idiosyncratic for these groups. "Alice Doane's Appeal" (1835), "The Birthmark" (1843), "Young Goodman Brown" (1835) and "Rappaccini's Daughter" (1844) are, however, most effective texts for classroom use and, together with "The Minister's Black Veil" (1836), enable most of the pertinent issues to be raised.[20] With Hawthorne, efforts have to be made to encourage a focus on the specifically Gothic aspects of his writing. Here, for example, a student writes in the end-of-semester examination about the importance of religion:

> [Besides gender] the other major issue that is implemented in *The Scarlet Letter* is the role of religion. At the time of publication there had been many anti-Catholic riots in America. This was not only because of Puritanism being so dominant in the nation, but also because of Catholic immigrants taking jobs [. . .] Hester has committed the sin of adultery and is given the scarlet letter. This is the Puritan way of dealing with this issue. However, the Catholic way could have been through confession and the church absolving the sin. Many Puritans saw this as "cheating" and that Catholics could buy their way into heaven. They felt that you have to be punished properly and physically [. . .] it is ambiguous whether Hester is punished effectively for her sin. [Hawthorne] lets the reader make up their own mind.[21]

Where discussion might have productively moved on to Dimmesdale's self-mortification and the stigmata on his breast, or Chillingworth's demonic thrust for his confession, or more broadly to the question of anti-Catholicism as a motif and drive in Gothic literature the essay runs aground on the familiar sandbar of Hawthorne's ambiguity. Hawthorne's fascination with Puritan religion does however give an opportunity for the seminar to explore how the hell-fired apocalypticism and remorseless self-scrutiny of American Puritanism plays into a psychologized nineteenth-century inwardness in his and other Gothic writers' constructions of disorientated lost souls. "Rappaccini's Daughter" encourages discussion of the Gnostic heresy (of which Hawthorne certainly knew, after his rummaging in religious tracts in the attic of the Old Manse he rented from Ralph Waldo Emerson) in respect of the story's inverted version of Eden and switching of the roles of the creator and the tempter (not to mention the gender reversal between Adam and Eve).[22] As with Maturin and Hogg, the more students can be persuaded to learn of theological issues from the period, the more they understand the roots of this particular version of Gothic.

Hawthorne said of Herman Melville after their meeting in Southport, England: "He can neither believe nor be comfortable in his unbelief; and he is too honest and courageous not to try to do one or the other."[23] That devastating uncertainty lies at the root of his "hell-fired" book, *Moby-Dick*, after writing which Melville claimed he felt spotless as the lamb. It is an intensely religious quest, a pursuit of the transcendental power behind nature, but one in which—unlike Emerson's, Thoreau's, or even, finally, Hawthorne's—that power is conceived of as malign. The Melville session refers to the Gothicism of *Moby-Dick*, its horrifying old ship and the scampering demons of the "Try-Works," its "Whiteness of the Whale" chapter on the horrors of whiteness and absence in nature, its mysterious Parsee, Fedalla; but again for pedagogical reasons the seminar focuses on Melville's short stories from *The Piazza Tales* (1856), chiefly "Benito Cereno" and "The Bell-Tower."[24] In "Benito Cereno" the whiteness is racial, contrasted with the blackness of the figures of the ship, the San Dominick, which appear first like cowled Dominican monks in a crumbling monastery or ancient villa of the sea, then come into focus as the ship's slave cargo, and finally as its demonic masters.[25] Melville addresses the issues of American slavery and the involvement of complacent northerners in that trade, but his deeper reach is into an investigation of the nature of evil. Babo, the ringleader of the slave revolt, is more than simply a figure of justified retribution, he, like Claggart in *Billy Budd Foretopman* (published 1924), seems to be a representation of some deeper malignity, "a depravity according to nature" as it is put in that novella.[26] Here also is an opportunity to address the American response to the excesses of the Haitian

Rebellion,[27] and the consequent fears of black insurrection that gripped the pre-Civil War South, as well as Melville's depiction of the intricate codependency of slaves and masters, figured in a Hegelian motif on the stern of the ship (and refigured in two entwined human figures at the denouement) which shows "a dark satyr in a mask, holding his foot on the prostrate neck of a writhing figure, likewise masked" (66–8). By the climax of the story the dark satyr in a mask has morphed into the naive northern American captain, Delano, whose foolish benevolence and trust has thus far saved his life and his ship (the amusingly named Bachelor's Delight). The students have some problems with the overt racism of the story; especially the Conradian anticipation of the scene in which Delano says to the rescued but mentally crippled Captain Cereno, " 'You are saved: what has cast such a shadow upon you?' 'The Negro,' Cereno replies" (90). This thread of race imprinted within American Gothic is further developed in discussion of the appearance of Gothic tropes in the slave narratives and, drawing upon students' earlier acquired information about American literature, the Gothic elements of *Uncle Tom's Cabin* (1852). The theme is picked up again in later seminars, specifically in close reading of Kate Chopin's story "Désirée's Baby" (1893), where the issue of racial inheritance becomes a division within the self, allowing a consideration of what may be called the racial uncanny.[28] The adopted Désirée, married to a white slaveholder, discovers that her child is clearly of mixed race. She kills herself and the baby after her husband Armand's vicious rejection, leaving the story to unveil his family secret; that to avoid the American prejudice against their mixed marriage, his mother being black, his parents had emigrated to France. It is not clear whether Armand (who seems to have had relations and probably a child, with at least one black woman on his estate) was aware of his inheritance. But the story signals early enough that racial trauma suffuses the narrative when it describes Armand Auvigny's house, L'Abri: "The roof came down steep and black like a cowl, reaching out behind the wide galleries that encircled the yellow stuccoed house" (340). By this point in the unit the students are able to read such clues very competently.[29] As the racial issues have become no longer black and white, no longer outside but rather within, this provides occasion for investigation of Abraham and Torok's ideas on the "family secret" and the effects of what they call the "phantom."[30]

But to return to Melville and "The Bell-Tower"; while this story contains a racial theme, as I suggested at the beginning of this piece, it is more explicitly concerned with technological hubris, being an early instance of what may be called techno-Gothic, as we explore more thoroughly in a later seminar on Thomas Pynchon's *The Crying of Lot 49* (1965) and William Gibson's *Neuromancer* (1984).[31] Melville responded to the new industrial might of the States, so massively demonstrated in the Civil War, with a despairing poem "The Conflict of Convictions" that shows the direction of his prescience:

> I know a wind in purpose strong—
> It spins *against* the way it drives
> Power unanointed may come—
> Dominion (unsought by the free)
> And the Iron Dome,
> Stronger for stress and strain,
> Fling her huge shadow athwart the main;
> But the Founders' dream shall flee.
> (1860–1861)[32]

From Melville's to Ambrose Bierce's tales is a movement that crosses the gulf of the Civil War and opens a new more overtly cynical and knowing strain of Gothic in "The Death of Halpin Frayser" (1893) and "The Moonlit Road" (1893).[33] In these stories rather than offering the realistic despair of his war fables Bierce undermines the foundations of domestic life. The startling cynicism of his tales gives a useful introduction to later nineteenth-century negations and the modernist world of realism and naturalism. These two stories in particular open up discussion of the great period of the ghost story, and its psychological dimensions (seen here in the deranged Oedipality that seems to underlie both). That leads on to Charlotte Perkins Gilman's "The Yellow Wallpaper" (1899), "The Giant Wisteria" (1891), and Harriet Prescott Spofford's "The Amber Gods" (1863), developing the relations between the ghost story and sexual politics, an ongoing theme related here to other work from Emily Dickinson's poetry to Edith Wharton's "The Eyes" (1910), Henry James' "The Jolly Corner" (1909) and "The Turn of the Screw" (1898).[34] These are discussed in a framework suggested by such critics as Elaine Showalter and Eve Kosofsky Sedgewick (specifically concerning homosexual panic), along with my own piece in *Victorian Studies* on implicit suppressions of child abuse in *The Turn of the Screw*.[35] In the twentieth century, Southern Gothic is introduced by discussion of William Faulkner's "A Rose for Emily" (1930) and *Sanctuary* (1931), along with Chopin.[36]

Further seminars include later twentieth-century modulations of Gothic motifs, pastiche, and new versions of social trauma seen in technology and cyberspace, Aids, and revisions of the vampire in, for example, the novels of Anne Rice and the stories of Poppy Z. Brite. In the final session the students are invited to report back on the unit, and to offer an example of recent American Gothic in the form of a short story or movie clip of interest to the group. Feedback is generally enthusiastic and often includes recognition of the range of topics this unit has encouraged, frequently together with some astonishment that the Gothic has so much to offer in comparison with the students' expectations at the beginning of the course.

Essay questions (2,500–3,000 words) for this unit include comparative issues, such as the ways in which American Gothic writing differs from European models in its uses of landscape and nature. Other topics include the internalizing of the Gothic as psychology, the significance of race, or differing attitudes to gender. Such concerns as the politics of revolution, America's specific racial legacies, the rise of feminism, ideas of atavism and degeneration in the late nineteenth century, or the importance of Protestantism in the Gothic tradition are all effective themes for sustained investigation. In more formalist terms we can ask whether it is useful to make the distinction, as Ann Radcliffe did, between horror and terror, and how would this work in considering American Gothic writing (for example, of Poe, Bierce, Lovecraft, Anne Rice, Poppy Z. Brite). Similarly, when Poe claimed that *his* terror was "of the soul" rather than of Germany it is productive to ask what he meant, and how this might be applied to other works such as *The Turn of the Screw* using perhaps such concepts as the "return of the repressed" or "domestic terror." Another possible subject is the notion of the fetishistic "Gothic object" in American fictions, in for example, the scarlet letter itself, or Little Eva's curl in *Uncle Tom's Cabin*. For those interested in psychoanalytical interpretation there might be an invitation to discuss Gothic writing in terms of its recourse to the uncanny, using Freud's 1919 essay on "The Uncanny," and more recent commentaries. Alternatively, we can observe that the Gothic is sometimes considered to be particularly concerned with sadistic and masochistic impulses and consider how these texts situate the reader in relation to such elements. A popular choice for many students is to note that the "double" often appears in Gothic writing, and to ask if this is also true of the American variety? More social/historical issues can be addressed through the concept of Transgression in Gothic fiction, or in asking whether the Gothic is especially concerned with the past, or with family genealogy. Discussions of representation of the vulnerable, or monstrous body, or the concept of the fantastic in American Gothic have also proved productive, and enquiries into representations of the house and architecture, or landscape spaces work well across a range of Gothic texts.

Beyond the intrinsic interest of Gothic's flamboyance in style and substance, the fascination of excess and the flaunting of taboo, a close focus on American Gothic helps to achieve other aims. In looking at the changes within a genre over time the students are introduced to a map of literary history and gain a sense of dominant literary movements without being asked to accept that knowledge as an end in itself. Poe's relation to enlightenment ideas and the development of American romanticism, for example, can emerge when and as relevant to an understanding of his Gothicism, which can expand to include discussion of the American transcendentalists and even the French Symbolists. Psychoanalytical literary theory from early American psychology through Freud to Lacan or Abraham and Torok is received as exciting and useful rather than obscurantist. A sharpened sense of formal narrative structures follows from examination of how Gothic texts are shaped to produce particular effects. Above all, perhaps, the students gain a revived interest in historical issues concerning race, gender, Darwinism, the frontier, industrialism, urbanism, and technology, and the markers of social trauma often hidden within popular fictions.

## Notes

1. Leslie Fiedler, *Love and Death in the American Novel* [1960] (New York: Delta, 1966) 29.
2. Herman Melville, "The Bell-Tower" in Charles Crow, ed. *American Gothic: an Anthology 1787-1916* (Malden, MA, and Oxford: Blackwell, 1999) 129. All subsequent references are to this edition, and are given in the text.

3. Fred Botting, ed. *The Gothic* (Cambridge: Cambridge University Press, 2001).
4. Charles Brockden Brown, *Arthur Mervyn Charles Brockden Brown's Novels*, ([1887], McKay; facsimile reprint, New York: Kennikat Press, 1963) v. II; Charles Brockden Brown, *Edgar Huntly; or, Memoirs of a Sleepwalker* [1799] (Kent, OH: State University Press, Bicentennial Edition, 1984); Charles Brockden Brown, *Ormond: Charles Brockden Brown's Novels*, ([1887], McKay; facsimile reprint, New York: Kennikat Press, 1963), v.VI; Charles Brockden Brown, *Wieland, or, The Transformation* [1798] (New York: Harcourt Brace and World, undated facsimile of 1926 edition). All subsequent references are to this edition, and are given in the text.
5. Charles Brockden Brown, "The Bell-Tower" in Charles Crow, ed. *American Gothic: an Anthology 1787–1916* (Malden, MA, and Oxford: Blackwell, 1999) 7–18.
6. See Terence Martin, *The Instructed Vision: Scottish Common Sense Philosophy and the Origins of American Fiction* (Bloomington: IN: Indiana University Press, 1961).
7. As explored, for example, in David Mogen, Scott P. Sanders, and Joanne B. Karpinski, eds, *Frontier Gothic: Terror and Wonder at the Frontier in American Literature* (London and Toronto: Associated University Presses, 1993).
8. Charles Neider, ed. *The Complete Tales of Washington Irving* (New York: Doubleday, 1975). "Rip Van Winkle" is in the Crow anthology.
9. Previously difficult to obtain for student use, this story is now readily available via the internet at: www.shortstories.computed.net/irvinggerman10. html and other sites.
10. www.shortstories.computed.net/irvinggermanstudent.html.
11. Edgar Allan Poe, "The Fall of the House of Usher" in Charles Crow, ed. *American Gothic: an Anthology 1787–1916* (Malden, MA, and Oxford: Blackwell, 1999), 86–97, 86.
12. Edgar Allan Poe, "The Facts in the Case of M. Valdemar" in Charles Crow, ed. *American Gothic: an Anthology 1787–1916* (Malden, MA, and Oxford: Blackwell, 1999) 81–6, 86.
13. See also Roland Barthes's famous essay on this impossibility "Textual Analysis of Poe's 'Valdemar' " in *Untying the Text: a Post-Structuralist Reader*, Robert Young, ed. (London: Routledge, 1987) 133–61.
14. Edgar Allan Poe, *Arthur Gordon Pym* (Harmondsworth: Penguin Books, 1975). "Hop-Frog" is in the Crow anthology; for "The Black Cat" see *Selected Writings of Edgar Allan Poe*, Edward H. Davidson, ed. (Boston: Houghton Mifflin, 1956).
15. Toni Morrison, *Playing in the Dark: Whiteness and the Literary Imagination* (Cambridge, MA: Harvard University Press, 1992).
16. "The Murders in the Rue Morgue," "William Wilson" and "The Purloined Letter" are available in such collections as G. R. Thompson, ed., *The Selected Writings of Edgar Allan Poe* (New York and London: Norton, 2004). "The Mystery of Marie Roget," www.esever.org/books/poe/mystery_of_marie_roget.html.

17. Sigmund Freud, "Das Unheimliche" 1919, *Standard Edition of the Complete Psychological Works*, ed. and trans. James Strachey (London: Hogarth Press, 1953). Also available in the *Pelican Freud Library, vol 14* (Harmondsworth: Penguin, 1985).
18. "The Murders in the Rue Morgue," "William Wilson" and "The Purloined Letter" are available in G. R. Thompson, ed., *The Selected Writings of Edgar Allan Poe* (New York and London: Norton, 2004). "The Mystery of Marie Roget," www.esever.org/books/poe/mystery_of_marie_roget.html.
19. Nathaniel Hawthorne, *The Scarlet Letter; The House of the Seven Gables;The Blithedale Romance; The Marble Faun*, in *The Centenary Edition* (Columbus, OH: Ohio University Press, 1974).
20. "Alice Doane's Appeal," and "Young Goodman Brown" are available in the Crow anthology; "The Birthmark," "Rappaccini's Daughter" and "The Minister's Black Veil" are easily found in such collections as Brian Harding, ed., *Nathaniel Hawthorne, Young Goodman Brown and Other Tales* (Oxford: Oxford University Press, 1987).
21. End-of-semester examination paper, anon.
22. Contributions from born-again Christians, although rare, can be very stimulating in this class, although one sometimes wonders whether a number may be suffering in silence at such heresies.
23. Randall Stewart, ed., *The English Notebooks of Nathaniel Hawthorne* (New York: Russell and Russell, 1962).
24. "The Bell-Tower" is in the Crow anthology; "Benito Cereno" is available in such collections as Richard Chase, ed., *Herman Melville: Selected Tales and Poems* (New York: Holt Rinehart and Winston, 1950).
25. The Dominicans, of course, were responsible for the Inquisition. This also provides an opportunity to discuss how Melville plays with his readers' assumed anti-Catholicism, and the Protestantism of the Gothic genre, as explored by Vic Sage. The ship's name may also mean "without master."
26. In Chase, ed., *Herman Melville: Selected Tales and Poems*, 322.
27. See Eric Sundquist, *To Wake the Nations: Race in the Making of American Literature* (Cambridge, MA, and London: Harvard University Press, 1993) 27–199.
28. "Désirée's Baby" is available in Crow, *American Gothic*, 339–43. All subsequent references are to this edition, and are given in the text.
29. They are, of course, working on the essay assignments at this time, and the level of discourse becomes in consequence, more sophisticated.
30. Nicolas Abraham "Notes on the phantom: a complement to Freud's metapsychology," *Critical Inquiry* 13(2): (1987) 287–92. Nicolas Abraham and Maria Torok, *The Wolf Man's Magic Word: a Cryptonymy*, translated by Nicholas Rand (Minneapolis: University of Minnesota Press, 1986 [1976] ). On Nicolas Abraham and Maria Torok see, for example, Esther Rashkin, "Tools for a new psychoanalytic literary criticism," *Diacritics* 18:4 (1988) 31–52.
31. Thomas Pynchon, *The Crying of Lot 49* [1966] (London: Picador, 1982); William Gibson, *Neuromancer* [1984] (London: Harper Collins, 1995).

32. In Chase, ed., *Herman Melville: Selected Tales and Poems*, 382.
33. "The Death of Halpin Frayser" is in the Crow anthology, and "The Moonlit Road" is from Ambrose Bierce, *Can Such Things Be?* [1893] (London: Jonathan Cape, 1926).
34. Charlotte Perkins Gilman's "The Yellow Wallpaper" is available in *The Norton Anthology of American Literature* (New York: Norton and Co., 1998) as is Edith Wharton's "The Eyes," and Henry James' "The Jolly Corner." Gilman's "The Giant Wisteria," and Harriet Prescott Spofford's "The Amber Gods" are included in the Crow anthology, as are some relevant Emily Dickinson poems and James' "The Turn of the Screw."
35. Allan Lloyd-Smith, "A word kept back in 'The Turn of the Screw,' " *Victorian Literature and Culture* Vol. 24, 1998; Elaine Showalter, *Sexual Anarchy* (London: Virago, 1992), Eve Kosofsky Sedgwick, *Epistemology of the Closet* (New York and London: Harvester Wheatsheaf, 1990).
36. "A Rose for Emily," xroads.virginia.edu/~drbr/wf_rose.html.

# 10
# Imperial Gothic

*Patrick Brantlinger*

In *Gothic*, Fred Botting writes that at "the end of the nineteenth century familiar Gothic figures—the double and the vampire—reemerged in new shapes, with a different intensity and anxious investment as objects of terror."[1] They reemerged in conjunction with Victorian excitement about geographical exploration; controversies and conflicts generated by "the new imperialism"; renewed interest in the occult and supernatural; the rise of social Darwinism and the eugenics movement and anxieties about cultural and racial degeneration. The double and the vampire, as well as other key figures and conventions of Gothic literature, changed accordingly, often appearing in the subgenre of "imperial Gothic" fiction. They frequently also showed up in new guises in the closely related subgenre of science fiction, as in many of H. G. Wells's novels and short stories.

In early Gothic romances, the monstrous, the supernatural, and the terrifying are typically linked to the foreign—the sublime, far reaches of the Italian Alps in Ann Radcliffe's *Mysteries of Udolpho* (1794), for example; or Geneva, Germany, and the Arctic in Mary Shelley's *Frankenstein* (1818). So perhaps it was inevitable that, as interest in and writing about the British Empire increased during the 1800s, Gothic romances and works of fiction utilizing Gothic elements would increasingly have for their settings such locales as India, the South Pacific, and central Africa. "Imperial Gothic" narratives typically follow a quest romance pattern that takes European characters to exotic, mysterious, faraway places and that also often mirrors the last, great geographical explorations and mappings of the globe and especially of central Africa. Imperial Gothic is related to, and in part an offshoot of, the explosion of imperialist adventure fiction, much of it written for boys, in the second half of the nineteenth century. Indeed, many stories and novels written with boy-readers in mind are also examples, or partial examples, of imperial Gothic fiction, including such bestsellers as Robert Ballantyne's *The Coral Island* (1858), Robert Louis Stevenson's *Treasure Island* (1883), and H. Rider Haggard's *King Solomon's Mines* (1885). Of the three, *The Coral Island* is the least self-consciously Gothic; yet it brings its trio of plucky boy-heroes into imminent peril of death, through storms, shipwreck, and encounters with both pirates and cannibals, while occasionally also hinting at the sublime and the supernatural.

Following my chapter on "Imperial Gothic" in *Rule of Darkness*, a number of studies have dealt with the topic, sometimes in relation to classroom teaching. Besides Botting's brief account of the 1890s, these include a chapter in David Punter and Glennis Byron's *The Gothic*, two of the essays in Andrew Smith and William Hughes's *Empire and the Gothic* including Smith's on Haggard, and in Diane Long Hoeveler and Tamar Heller's *Approaches to Teaching Gothic Fiction: the British and American Traditions* there is Heller's "Heart of Darkness: teaching race, gender, and imperialism in Victorian Gothic Literature."[2] Especially if works of imperial Gothic are taught together with one or more of the three major monster stories of the nineteenth century *Frankenstein, Dr Jekyll and Mr Hyde* (1886), and *Dracula* (1897) issues of imperial expansion, race, geographical exploration, gender and sexuality, science and religion, and realism versus romance can all be raised, thus enriching students' knowledge of Victorian culture, the history of the British Empire, and Gothic fantasy more generally—down to the present and such obvious "spin-offs" as the Indiana Jones and Star Wars movies.

In courses that feature imperial Gothic fiction, I find it useful to begin with *Frankenstein* for several reasons. First, it provides a link back to the early versions of Gothic romance, through which students can gain some understanding of the conventions of the genre. Second, more clearly than other early examples of Gothic fiction, *Frankenstein* foregrounds two related aspects of the Enlightenment that were of central importance in the emergence of imperial Gothic: scientific experimentation and geographical exploration. The parallel that Mary Shelley draws between Captain Walton's overreaching voyage to the Arctic and Victor Frankenstein's overreaching scientific experimentation helps to illustrate for students how Gothic writing challenges easy notions of progress through reason, science, and the exploration of the unknown. The demonically possessed or insane scientist, whether Faust or Frankenstein, is always a figure expressing anxiety about Enlightenment rationality breaking loose from religion and tradition, and he is often matched by the mad (or at any rate, rash) or else "gone native" explorer in imperial Gothic fiction. Painting Enlightenment rationality in sable hues, Gothic romances ask, with John Milton and the Bible, if knowledge is evil or destructive instead of a source of goodness and progress? One of Goya's etchings is entitled, "The dream of reason produces monsters" and this is one of the main themes of *Frankenstein*, which of all the early Gothic romances is also most directly related to science fiction. The connections between early Gothic, imperial Gothic, and science fiction become especially vivid for students if they read *Frankenstein* in tandem with Wells's *The Time Machine* (1895) or *The Island of Dr Moreau* (1896).

It also helps to have students read novels and stories that combine realist and imperial Gothic elements, such as Charlotte Brontë's *Jane Eyre* (1847), Wilkie Collins's *The Moonstone* (1868) or Charles Dickens's *Great Expectations* (1861). Critics have often noted that traces or "ghosts" of the Gothic show up even in narratives usually deemed realistic. In *Great Expectations*, for instance, Pip compares himself to Frankenstein, and one of his monsters is the convict Magwitch, whom Pip first encounters in the cemetery where his father is buried, and who returns from his Australian exile as, metaphorically, a terrifying revenant. Pip is, moreover, "haunted" throughout the novel: by convicts, crime, and prisons; by his guilty memories of Joe, Biddy, and home; by Mrs Joe's murder; by wraithlike Miss Havisham and by the image of Estella. While the Australia of *Great Expectations* is a blank slate, a place where Magwitch can make a fortune and then, from long distance, try to make a "gentleman" out of Pip, Collins' "sensation novel" *The Moonstone* treats India as a Gothic sphere of historical violence, guilt, and mystery. The sensation fiction of the 1860s, a subgenre to which *Great Expectations* perhaps also belongs and which typically blends realistic with Gothic ingredients, foregrounds those "most mysterious of mysteries, the mysteries which are at our own doors," as Henry James put it.[3] But they also often make use of imperial and foreign settings as places of exile and sources of mystery.

In late Victorian culture, the imperial Gothic trend reflected both a new interest in occultism—séances, magic, Spiritualism, Theosophy, even Buddhism—and an increasing emphasis on and anxiety about the British Empire. These tendencies paralleled, and in part expressed, a growing awareness among novelists and critics alike that the hegemony of fictional realism was waning, just as its cultural double, science, was being challenged anew. Stevenson, Haggard, Wells, Andrew Lang, and W. E. Henley all affirmed "romance" to be a genre superior to or at least more fundamental than the realist novel, and all but the last of these authors wrote versions of imperial Gothic fiction (Henley was primarily a poet and critic). For his part, Joseph Conrad edged away from realism of the George Gissing or Émile Zola variety by calling his approach to fiction impressionism. His novels and short stories—*Heart of Darkness* (1902), *Lord Jim* (1900), "An Outpost of Progress," (1896) and others—utilize Gothic romance conventions in partly parodic fashion; like traditional works of realist fiction, they are antiromances.

Once students have identified formal and thematic Gothic elements in *Frankenstein, Dr Jekyll and Mr Hyde* or *Dracula*, they can look for similar elements in imperial Gothic romances such as Haggard's *She* and Wells's *The Island of Dr Moreau*. Formalist analysis should connect readily to issues of content and effect. For instance, do the monsters—Frankenstein's creature, Mr Hyde, and the bloodthirsty Count—fit any obvious racial stereotypes? How do the psychological processes of racial othering or stereotyping operate, and are they at work in *Frankenstein* or *Dracula*? Even though they claim to know the story whether they have read it before or not, students are always surprised to learn that the original Frankenstein's monster does not come equipped with a square head and bolts, like a robot or cyborg; he is instead of a drab olive complexion, with straight black hair—perhaps a hint of racial darkness or Orientalism—a discovery they often resist. In *Gothic Images of Race in Nineteenth-Century Britain*, however, Howard Malchow connects Mary Shelley's nightmare story to slavery and abolitionist discourse.[4] It is also connected to a version of Orientalism through the story of the Turkish exiles. As Tamar Heller points out, "what one could call the Gothicization of the racial other in nineteenth-century fiction is a sign of anxiety about the hybridization of white and black, colonizer and colonized" (159). If ever there was a hybridized creature, it is Frankenstein's monster, made out of various persons' body parts.

Captain Walton's arctic voyage can also help to illustrate the tradition of the imaginary voyage in English literature that goes back to Shakespeare's *The Tempest* (1611) and beyond, a tradition that has many connections to actual geographical exploration and to the expansion of the British Empire. This is evident, for example, in Daniel Defoe's *Robinson Crusoe* (1719) and Jonathan Swift's *Gulliver's Travels* (1726). Crusoe's dread of the cannibals is a proto-Gothic aspect of that classically realist text and Gulliver's fantastic voyaging has some claim to being an ancestor of science fiction. It is always worth stressing, moreover, the Gothic and imperial continuities from early (say, *Gulliver's Travels*) to contemporary (*Star Wars*, for instance). Voyaging into outer space—or through time, as does Wells' Time-Traveller—are humans more likely to encounter monsters or creatures similar to ourselves? Are we ourselves monstrous to those we perceive as monsters? Whether monsters or not, are those terrestrial or extra-terrestrial others likely to be pacific or violent, welcoming or exterminating, like colonizers and natives throughout the history of empires?

In the 1870s and 1880s, a number of works with Gothic overtones utilized exploration motifs or took the form of imaginary voyages. They include Edward Bulwer Lytton's *The Coming Race* (1871) and Samuel Butler's *Erewhon* (1872). Like Wells's *The Time Machine* and most other versions of imperial Gothic, both of these stories combine exploration with fantasies about Darwinian evolution. The underground world of Bulwer Lytton's Vril-ya, a race of monsters who seem to be simultaneously angelic and demonic, and who one day may surface to dominate or destroy the human species is in part a techno-utopia, something like Edward Bellamy's future America in *Looking Backward* (1888). Both *The Coming Race* and *Erewhon* raise the issue of the utopian versus dystopian aspects of Gothic romances, as well as imperial Gothic fictions such as *She* (1887) and *Heart of Darkness*, science fiction, and imaginary voyages in general. In several ways, *The Coming Race* more obviously combines elements of Gothic romance and science fiction than does Butler's *Erewhon*, although that imaginary voyage also has its Gothic moments.

Reading selections from some of the journals of explorers, especially those that themselves make use of Gothic tropes such as Richard Burton's *To the Lake Regions of Central Africa* (1860) and Henry Morton Stanley's *Through the Dark Continent* (1878), can provide helpful comparisons with such imperial Gothic fictions as Haggard's *King Solomon's Mines* (1885) and *She* as well as with Conrad's *Heart of Darkness*. Fictional explorers, such as Haggard's Allan Quatermain, Horace Holly, and Leo Vincy, Wells' Time-Traveller, or Sir Arthur Conan Doyle's Professor Challenger, are next-of-kin to scientists and also detectives, including the most famous detective of all, Sherlock Holmes. Though Holmes usually does not travel far from London, he does not have to: his Gothic—extreme, quasi-demonic—rationality can reach out from the metropolis to nab even long-distance criminals in such examples of imperial Gothic as *The Sign of Four* (1890) and "The Speckled Band" (1883). Furthermore, explorations of the supernatural were often likened to geographical exploration, as in Doyle's spiritualist Gothic fantasy, *The Land of Mist*, which appeared in the same year as William Butler Yeats's *A Vision* (1925). Professor Challenger, Lord John Roxton, and the other British heroes are "seeking fresh worlds to conquer. Having exhausted the sporting adventures of this terrestrial globe," they are "now turning to those of the dim, dark and dubious regions of psychic research."[5] That both *The Land of Mist* and *A Vision* were published in the 1920s suggests some of the continuities between late-Victorian and modernist British literature, including the continuation of Gothic themes and conventions into the twentieth century and beyond. Getting students to think about why imperial Gothic fiction and its cultural corollary, interest in the occult, arose just as both major geographical exploration of Africa and the hegemony of fictional realism were winding down may not be easy, but it can generate intriguing close readings and paper topics.

Appealing mainly to young male readers, writers of imperial Gothic romances and imperial adventure fiction produced stories that are relentlessly masculine in orientation and often overtly misogynistic. In *She*, Horace Holly is explicitly, comically misogynistic. As he is falling in love with Ayesha, Holly thinks of himself as a single, ugly, sensible "fellow of my college, noted for what my acquaintances are pleased to call my misogyny."[6] What does Haggard's mocking of Holly's misogyny tell us about Haggard's own misogyny? Is misogyny also at work in *Treasure Island, The Time Machine*, or *Heart of Darkness*? Cannon Schmitt notes that Haggard's *She*, Stoker's *Dracula*, and Richard Marsh's *The Beetle* (1897) all "exploit the fear of an invasion of Britain by a monstrous femininity originating beyond the pale of an occidental Europe understood as normative."[7] This is true as well of Queen Tera, the revivified mummy in Stoker's *Jewel of the Seven Stars* (1903, revised 1912). All of these Gothic texts displace the threats of the independent New Woman and of female suffrage onto the "dark" regions of the world, beyond the boundaries of the official Empire. Like the encounters with Circe and the Sirens in *The Odyssey*, stories of male adventures in which fearsome or demonic females threaten to dominate or destroy the male characters are easy to analyse in terms of sexual fetishism and the figure of the *femme fatale*. Is it the case, therefore, that imperial Gothic is, at least in terms of gender politics, the antithesis of what Ellen Moers famously called the "Female Gothic"?[8] Why is it that there are no major examples of imperial Gothic fiction written by women? In my experience, raising these questions usually generates lively discussions.

According to all of its late-Victorian champions, romance stresses action instead of characterization or psychological complexity. Rather than tracing the maturation of its protagonists as in realistic *Bildungsromans*, in Peter Pan fashion imperial Gothic romance stays within or regresses back to the daydreams and psychic energies of childhood. This is not simply because so much imperial Gothic fiction was like *Treasure Island* and *King Solomon's Mines*, written with boy-readers in mind, but also because many authors understood the romance genre to be regressive in a positive sense, back to the mythic, the primitive, and the natural as well as the childlike. When Haggard's Allan Quatermain returns to South Africa in the novel which bears his name, civilization is seen as tame and unexciting. Repeatedly, the jungle, the ocean, the wilderness, the far reaches of empire are viewed not just as exotic, but as places of mystery, adventure, and excitement, and also of reconnection with the primal energies of childhood and nature. As Andrew Lang put it, the purpose of Imperial Gothic romances like Haggard's and Stevenson's was to appeal to "the Eternal Boy" in their readers.[9]

If in earlier Gothic romances a primary threat and source of terror was demonic possession or, what amounts to the same, selling one's soul to the devil, in imperial Gothic narratives a primary, often terrifying threat is "going native" or reverting to savagery. But this threat can also be a main source of pleasure and excitement for boy-heroes like Stevenson's Jim Hawkins or Ballantyne's trio of plucky English lads in *The Coral Island* who must fight and, of course, defeat the pirates and the cannibals with the weapons of the pirates and the cannibals. And after their adventures, the boy heroes are able to return to civilization, all the better for the dangers they've encountered and overcome. In any event, the late-Victorian writers of imperial Gothic romances typically see their chosen genre as entailing a healthy and even necessary form of regression, as in Lang's assertion that "not for nothing did Nature leave us all savages under our white skins; she has wrought thus that we might have many delights, among others 'the joy of adventurous living' and of reading about adventurous living."[10] Arthur Machen, author of many tales of Gothic horror in the 1890s and after, defined literature itself as "the endeavour of every age to return to the first age, to an age, if you like, of savages."[11]

If some versions of "going native" were exciting, putting heroes and readers once again in touch with the primal energy of life or nature or "buried self," to use Matthew Arnold's Gothic phrase (the title of one of his poems), others, as in the case of Kurtz in *Heart of Darkness*, were both terrifying and destructive. Kurtz's dying words, "The horror! The horror!" are quintessentially Gothic, nightmarish. Students may wonder about versions of "going native" today, and whether these are constructive or destructive, pleasurable or terrifying? They are likely to mention "reality television" shows like *Survivor*; I tend to counter with missionaries, Peace Corps volunteers, CIA agents, and anthropologists doing fieldwork. And if adventures in the far reaches of empire often had their positive effects, the threat of civilization being overrun by the barbarians or of degenerating into the subhuman, as in *The Time Machine* and *Dracula*, was the *fin de siècle*'s nightmare par excellence. "Within the broad category of imperial gothic," writes Lynn Pykett, can be found:

> atavistic fantasies about the reversion of whole civilizations to barbarism, as, for example, in Richard Jefferies's apocalyptic fantasy *After London* (1885); invasion narratives—such as *Dracula* and *She*—in which London is threatened with invasion by other-worldly representatives of ancient civilizations who wish to colonize the heart of empire; and narratives of reincarnation and spiritual [demonic] possession.[12]

Although imperial Gothic fiction typically displaces domestic social, political, and psychological anxieties onto the far reaches of the

Empire or the world, just as typically the Empire "strikes back," through what Stephen Arata calls fantasies of "reverse colonization."[13]

In regard to the relationship of imperial Gothic to science fiction, of major significance to the shaping of both subgenres was Darwin's theory of evolution. One finds its traces everywhere in late-Victorian and Edwardian literature; in examples of imperial Gothic fiction, a standard Darwinian motif is that of atavism or degeneration—the regression to some earlier, more primitive, more monstrous evolutionary stage, as in *Dr Jekyll and Mr Hyde* and *Dracula*. Two good short stories to include on an imperial Gothic reading list are Sheridan Le Fanu's "Green Tea" (1872), in which the protagonist is terrorized by a fiendish, hallucinatory monkey, and Sir Arthur Conan Doyle's "The Adventure of The Creeping Man" (1903), in which the title character, using a primate hormone something like Viagra, becomes increasingly apelike. These can serve as temporal place-markers for, roughly, the beginning and end of the heyday of imperial Gothic fiction; both stories, moreover, foreground the fear of evolutionary degeneration or atavism. Short readings or illustrations from Thomas Henry Huxley's 1863 *Man's Place in Nature* and about the first sightings of gorillas in central Africa in the 1860s by French explorer Paul de Chaillu can contextualize the emergence of primates as figures of monstrous degeneration. And then there is the "apelike" Mr Hyde, the dwarfish, violent monster hiding within the civilized Dr Jekyll; Hyde is also, of course, a stereotypic, nightmare version of the Irish hooligan. Students are always familiar, moreover, with Tarzan of the Apes and later cinematic fantasies about our nearest relatives, including *King Kong* (1933, remade 1976 and 2005) and *Planet of the Apes* (1968, remade 2001).

The figure of the vampire, as in *Dracula*, is also one of atavism and degeneration. A related instance of atavism is evident in Rudyard Kipling's short story, "The Mark of the Beast," (1890) in which an Englishman who has desecrated a Hindu temple becomes a werewolf. Although Kipling's masterpiece *Kim* (1901) is not an example of imperial Gothic—it is too brightly lit and relentlessly upbeat—it is a variant of the imperial adventure story featuring a boy-hero. And many of his other stories are, like "The Mark of the Beast," versions of imperial Gothic that express his interest in the occult. These range from the early, rather whimsical ghost story "The Phantom Rickshaw" (1888) to such late tales of the supernatural as "The Madonna of the

Trenches" (1926). Haggard and Kipling had many conversations about ghosts and other spiritual and psychic matters, and Haggard even claimed that he converted his famous Anglo-Indian friend to belief in reincarnation.[14] But it seems more likely that Kipling maintained a sort of sckeptical ambivalence toward the occult: he could wax satirical about it in a story like "The Sending of Dana Da" (1888) while also fantasizing quite sentimentally about life after death in "Wireless" (1902) and "They" (1904).

Just as the first Gothic romances were in part reactions to Enlightenment rationality, the late Victorian rejection of fictional realism in favour of romance and the interest in the occult were both in some measure responses to the growing dominance of the sciences and of scientific rationality. By the 1880s and 1890s, corresponding to the closing down of the western frontier in North America, there was the completion or near-completion of the geographical exploration and mapping of the rest of the planet. After the 1884 Berlin Conference came "the scramble for Africa" and the carving up of the so-called "dark continent" into colonies by the European powers.[15] In *The Lost World*, Sir Arthur Conan Doyle's 1911 example of imperial Gothic, science fiction, and imaginary voyage, a newspaper editor says: "the big blank spaces in the map are all being filled in, and there's no room for romance anywhere."[16] But the intrepid heroes find such a space anyway in the Amazon basin, where time has stopped and dinosaurs still roam, the original of *Jurassic Park* (1993).

Nevertheless, by 1911 not only had almost all of the "blank spaces" of the world been explored and mapped by geography and cartography, but the other sciences—biology, physics, chemistry, astronomy, psychology—all seemed to be rapidly vanquishing regions of darkness and mystery. For that very reason, writers such as Doyle, Stevenson, Haggard, Wells, and Kipling felt it imperative to make room for romance and mystery anyway. They found they could do so often by claiming science as an ally. So Doyle's greatest invention was his master detective Sherlock Holmes, who himself vanquishes mystery by exercising his almost supernatural powers of scientific observation and deduction. So did Wells, through utilizing the hybrid genre that he called "scientific romances," but which soon came to be called "science fiction." In *The Time Machine, The Island of Dr Moreau*, and *The Invisible Man* (1897), Wells offers anew the Gothic figure of the scientific over-reacher and the first two stories are also examples of the imaginary voyage. Wells's tropical island fantasy in particular deals with the interconnected themes of empire, race, and evolution. "In Moreau's hands the 'other' is reduced to the status of an object, to be formed or reshaped at will," write David Punter and Glennis Byron:

> we can see here a metaphor for the ways in which the violence of empire has so frequently been translocated, reterritorialized onto an "empty" island; this again accords with a certain imperial discourse, in which the land that falls under the rule of empire is perceived as "empty" because its previous inhabitants—native American, Australian aboriginal—are denied the status of the human. (46)

In short, Dr Moreau's cruel reshapings of the Beast People by the scalpel allegorizes the colonizing process, with its supposed "civilizing mission" which was often little more than a cover for exterminating first peoples.

In commenting on his "scientific romances" in general, Wells wrote: "I simply brought the fetish stuff up to date, and made it as near actual theory as possible."[17] One way to think about both imperial Gothic and science fiction is to consider just exactly what Wells meant by "the fetish stuff." The origin of the word "fetish," from Portuguese and the early days of the slave trade along the west coast of Africa, has its obvious imperialist and racist aspects. In many Victorian exploration narratives, fetishism continues to be the main sort of "superstition" attributed to the cultures of "the dark continent." But Wells is applying the term to his own stories, and to western magic or, perhaps, pseudoscience—whatever it is that scientific over-reachers such as Dr Moreau and the Time Traveller practice. Marx on commodity fetishism and Freud on sexual fetishism are also applying the concept to Western, not to African, culture. Exploring their theories of fetishism can help to illuminate aspects both of late-Victorian occultism (itself invariably fetishistic) and of early anthropology, another scientific discourse that contributed much to imperial Gothic fiction. A key text in that regard is Edward Burnett Tylor's *Primitive Culture* (1871), with its theories of cultural "survivals" and of "animism" as the earliest form of religion. Tylor considered modern occultism a "survival" of sorts, recreating aspects of "savage philosophy and peasant folk-lore." But he also seemed to agree with the champions of romance when he declared that "the mental condition of the lower races is the key to poetry, nor is it a small portion of the poetic realm" which that thesis covers.[18]

Racial stereotypes themselves—of course, a main mode of characterization in imperial Gothic fiction—are fetishistic, at once loathed and desired, repellant and erotically charged. Here, the figure of the vampire, as most notably in Bram Stoker's *Dracula*, is a compelling one: those fangs, those fingernails, the oversexed monster.

*Dracula* is, of course, very different from most boys' adventure novels such as *Treasure Island*, but it is the most vivid example of a late-Victorian "reverse colonization" narrative, and it combines Gothic, science fiction, and imperialist–racist ingredients in complex ways. As many critics have argued, the Count is a monstrous version of decadent aristocrat and imperialist exploiter, whose family history, as he tells it to Jonathan Harker, reads like an indictment of all empires in general as versions of political vampirism:

> We Szekelys have a right to be proud, for in our veins flows the blood of many brave races who fought as the lion fights, for lordship. Here, in the whirlpool of European races [. . .] they found the Huns, whose warlike fury had swept the earth like a living flame, till the dying peoples held that in their veins ran the blood of those old witches, who, expelled from Scythia, had mated with the devils in the desert. Fools, fools! What devil or what witch was ever so great as Attila, whose blood is in these veins? [. . .] Is it a wonder that we were a conquering race?[19]

In *The Literature of Terror,* David Punter calls Dracula "the final aristocrat."[20] Perhaps so; but he was not the final imperialist. Nor was Conrad's Mr Kurtz. Hannah Arendt's *The Origins of Totalitarianism* (1951) is a major and accessible analysis of the interconnections between imperialism, racism, and fascism–Nazism than can help to explain how Stoker is identifying, in Gothic, nightmare fashion, vampirism with imperialism.[21] And taken together, Le Fanu and Stoker are examples of a specifically "Anglo-Irish Gothic tradition," as David Glover puts it. "Paradoxically it is *Dracula,*" writes Glover, "at first glance among the least Irish of all Stoker's texts, that goes furthest in establishing his pedigree as a distinctively Irish writer."[22] Exploring why this should be the case, and indeed why there should be an Anglo-Irish Gothic tradition that is also at least covertly anti-imperialist, may help students to understand much about the history of Victorian and modern British fiction, culture, and politics.

Of all the works of fiction produced in nineteenth-century Britain, *Frankenstein, Dr Jekyll and Mr Hyde,* and *Dracula* are the three that have been most often filmed and they are also among the most frequently taught in undergraduate literature classes. Even if one does not include them in a course on imperial Gothic fiction, students will have vivid notions about them. A major question to raise in any course on the Gothic, then, is why they have been so immensely popular? Why are tales of terror and monstrosity at once riveting and pleasurable? Is terror, at least in fictional form, pleasurable, and therefore in some way or other related to desire? One finds these questions posed in the aesthetic writings of the late eighteenth century, concurrently with the rise of the Gothic "tale of terror"; in Edmund Burke's *Enquiry* into the sublime, for example, which reads like a recipe book for the Gothic romance:

> Whatever is fitted in any sort to excite the ideas of pain, and danger, that is to say, whatever is in any sort terrible, or is conversant about terrible objects, or operates in a manner analogous to terror, is a source of the *sublime,* and therefore, so long as it is not directly threatening or destructive, a source of aesthetic pleasure.[23]

Darkness, immensity, the supernatural, thoughts of death, and also "the ruin of monarchs, and the revolution of kingdoms" (106) can all be evocative of feelings of sublimity. And so, too, may be the superstitions of barbarians, a topic that suggests a connection to empire:

> Almost all the heathen temples were dark. Even in the barbarous temples of the [native] Americans at this day, they keep their idol in a dark part of the hut, which is consecrated to his worship [. . .] For this purpose too the druids performed all their ceremonies in the bosom of the darkest woods. (100)

For "the darkest woods," imperial Gothic romances substitute versions of "the heart of darkness"—King Leopold's Congo, cannibal islands, Transylvanian castle—and then also bring idolatry or "the fetish stuff up to date" by making it an integral aspect of what Ursula Le Guin has called "the language of the night," the language of dreams, myths, archetypes, and fantasy. She is referring specifically to her own chosen genre of science fiction, but what she says applies equally well to imperial Gothic and, indeed, to all Gothic romances:

> Those who refuse to listen to dragons are probably doomed to spend their lives acting out the nightmares of politicians. We like to think we live in daylight, but half the world is always dark; and fantasy, like poetry, speaks the language of the night.[24]

Enabling students to interpret that language as it appears in imperial Gothic or Gothic romances more generally is an excellent way of helping them to understand aspects both of their own "buried selves" and of literary, cultural, and political history.

## Notes

1. Fred Botting, *Gothic* (New York: Routledge, 1996) 135.
2. Patrick Brantlinger, *Rule of Darkness: British Literature and Imperialism, 1830–1914* (Ithaca: Cornell University Press, 1988) 227–53; David Punter and Glennis Byron, *The Gothic* (Oxford: Basil Blackwell, 2004). All subsequent references are to this edition, and are given in the text; Andrew Smith and William Hughes, eds, *Empire and the Gothic: the Politics of Genre* (London: Palgrave—now Palgrave Macmillan, 2003); Tamar Heller, "Heart of Darkness: teaching race, gender, and imperialism in Victorian Gothic literature," *Approaches to Teaching Gothic Fiction: the British and American Traditions*, Diane Long Hoeveler and Tamar Heller, eds (New York: Modern Language Association, 2003) 159–67. All subsequent references are to this edition, and are given in the text.
3. Henry James, "Miss Braddon" *The Nation* 1, 9 November 1865:593–94, quotation at 593.
4. Providing students with selections from Howard Malchow's *Gothic Images of Race in Nineteenth-Century Britain* (Stanford: Stanford University Press, 1996) may be useful in dealing with this question.
5. Sir Arthur Conan Doyle, *The Land of Mist* (New York: Doran, 1926) 132.
6. H. Rider Haggard, *She: a History of Adventure* (New York: Penguin Books, 2001) 163.
7. Canon Schmitt, *Alien Nation: Nineteenth-Century Gothic Fictions and English Nationality* (Philadelphia: University of Pennsylvania Press, 1997) 19.
8. Ellen Moers, *Literary Women: the Great Writers* (New York: Doubleday, 1977) 19.
9. Lang quoted in H. Rider Haggard, *The Days of My Life* (London: Longmans, Green, 1926) 2 vols, 2: 206.

10. Quoted in Joseph Bristow, *Empire Boys: Adventures in a Man's World* (London: HarperCollins, 1991) 116.
11. Brantlinger, *Rule of Darkness*, 232.
12. Lyn Pykett, "Sensation fiction and the fantastic in the Victorian novel," *The Cambridge Companion to the Victorian Novel*, Deirdre David, ed. (Cambridge: Cambridge University Press, 2001) 209.
13. Stephen Arata, *Fictions of Loss in the Victorian Fin de Siècle* (Cambridge: Cambridge University Press, 1996) 107–32, 107.
14. See Brantlinger, *Rule of Darkness*, 244.
15. The racist phrase, "the dark continent," itself suggests a gothicization of Africa. See my analysis of that phrase in *Rule of Darkness*, 173–97.
16. Sir Arthur Conan Doyle, *The Lost World* (New York: Review of Reviews, 1912) 13.
17. Wells quoted in Brian Aldiss, *Billion Year Spree: the True History of Science Fiction* (New York: Schocken, 1974) 9.
18. See Brantlinger, *Rule of Darkness*, 232.
19. Bram Stoker, *Dracula* (Oxford: The World's Classics; Oxford University Press, 1983) 28–9.
20. David Punter, *The Literature of Terror: a History of Gothic Fictions from 1765 to the Present Day* (London: Longman, 1980) 257.
21. See Brantlinger, *Rule of Darkness*, 268.
22. David Glover, *Vampires, Mummies, and Liberals: Bram Stoker and the Politics of Popular Fiction* (Durham: Duke University Press, 1996) 25.
23. Edmund Burke, *A Philosophical Enquiry into the Origin of Our Ideas of the Sublime and the Beautiful* (Menston, England: Scolar, [1757] 1970) 58. All subsequent references are to this edition, and are given in the text.
24. Ursula K. Le Guin, *The Language of the Night: Essays on Fantasy and Science Fiction*, Susan Wood, ed. (New York: G. Putnam, 1979) 11.

# 11
# Postcolonial Gothic

*Gina Wisker*

Teaching the postcolonial Gothic provides us and our students with a rich set of issues, theories, and potential problems as well as delights. The Gothic itself, ambiguous, a mix of the realistic and the imaginary, asks us to step back from any straightforward historical realism and read at the very core of what literature and the arts are about, i.e. representation and interpretation, the symbolic, and the use of strategies of estrangement and engagement to explore and challenge cultural, social, psychological, and personal issues. Reading the Gothic demands a certain kind of estrangement; defamiliarization on the one hand and imaginative leaps of faith on the other. Students engaged with the Gothic are likely to have to become adept at deconstruction, reading between the lines of the seemingly bourgeois hegemonic text to seek the meanings and challenges of the Gothic's strange, fantastic disturbances and disruptions. Reading postcolonial writing is another potentially fraught experience. They are presented with cultural difference and the demand that such a gap of knowledge be at least a little bridged with necessary contextual information, and some understanding of different worldviews beyond the facts of the everyday reality of the differences posed by geography, climate, or history. Postcolonial texts are strange sometimes even to those whose cultures have produced them. Because of their postcolonial nature they query, undercut, question, and problematize the imposed, internalized values and interpretations of history and of the colonizers' worldviews.

Introducing theory is essential quite early on but in my teaching I first try to engage students with their personal and critical responses and in so doing home in on confusions and excitements, then build in the theory which will allow critical interpretation. One area of danger in reading and studying the postcolonial Gothic is the possible tendency to view these strange works from strange places as naïve, folk tale, the fantasy ways in which a maybe simpler (because foreign) or merely different people try to explain events they cannot fully comprehend. Those attitudes come dangerously close to some of the statements made by colonizers, imperialists, and settlers who saw both an empty space before them, and very "primitive" cultures, so set about reinterpreting both space and culture within their own frameworks of interpretation, affected as those were by their own histories, locations, perspectives, and worldviews. Students approaching the postcolonial can also be somewhat dismayed by the vast array of critical approaches and terminology—hybridity, cosmopolitan theory, whether there is a hyphen in postcolonial or not (and what it actually defines) and the very minefield of linguistic and value-related articulations which it uses (is hybridity OK to use, or is it insulting? What about Black?). It is an uncharted territory navigated by clever folk who like to impress and exclude. Like strange lands, postcolonial theorizing emphasizes the exclusion of those who do not fit in to a scheme and set of interpretations, a linguistic register and critical worldview whose arcane rules and regulations seem frequently there to obfuscate and confuse rather than lead towards enlightened attempts at making some kind of sense of what is being read and discussed.

For me in teaching the postcolonial Gothic the two absolutely key elements are the theory they share—that of Otherizing, excluding, and destroying or recognizing the rich differences of an Other we construct in order to somehow feel clearer and more secure about our own stable identities, however individual or national. Kristeva is central to this in my own theorizing and teaching. One strategy I use for introducing her themes is to construct a rather straightforward reading, and by making it accessible, encourage students to return to the original and move into further complexity. We look at the ways in which, in her *Powers of Horror*, Kristeva identifies abjection of that which is Other than ourselves and therefore both fascinating and disgusting, and in need of exclusion from us so that we might recognize ourselves as whole.[1] Here and later in *Strangers to Ourselves* she shows that the Other is a monster of our own making.[2]

We might find ourselves teaching postcolonial Gothic texts in a course specifically focused on the postcolonial or on the Gothic, in which case, there is some general background information, critical assumptions, and approaches as well as contexts which might well be introduced in the normal way as part of the class. We might as soon teach some of these texts or extracts of them on courses and in sessions which are not specifically geared either to the postcolonial or the Gothic. Let us look at dealing with postcolonial Gothic texts in each of these instances on the assumption that to a greater or lesser extent students will need some cultural, historical background in which to place their texts, and some introductory work on the critical ideological bases of the postcolonial and of the Gothic.

## Ensuring knowledge of context

In the context of undergraduate classes in the UK, many students are unaware of colonial discourses and somewhat silenced in the face of the unknown. They might find it difficult to articulate an engagement with the texts of writers whose experiences of life in no way seems to match their own.

In the UK, although most of us have not suffered the physical and psychological abuse as have those suffering denial and silencing at the hands of slave traders or white settlers over time, still an apartheid of the intellect has been imposed on us. We might well have been starved of the reading, the insights, the cultural awareness, of experience and articulation of that experience by colonial and postcolonial writers. This is not the polite inquisitiveness of the complacent: we need to know, we need to share, but not to appropriate. Oddly, perhaps, like Betty Govinden the South African critic, we too have been "subjected to colonial discourse and simultaneously prevented from criticising empire 'textuality' " with those protected absences, that already "too full" curriculum replete with the old and the new canonical texts.[3] Textual choices, forms, and treatments are vehicles for shaping, guidance, control, and limitation. As Elleke Boehmer has pointed out, colonizers use a variety of textual representations in order to render recognizable the unfamiliar and new. Treaties and declarations, records, logs, and the couching of descriptions of the new and strange in familiar forms, myths, endowing them with familiar names paralleling them with those from back home are all ways in which colonizers have sought to feel comfortable in new worlds, familiarize and then to own through redescription.[4]

In teaching postcolonial Gothic texts from different contexts, it is a difficult negotiation to both establish some familiarity and pattern, making the different accessible, and to facilitate a situation where its differences define themselves, speak for themselves.

## Strategies for teaching the postcolonial Gothic

As a teacher I want to both challenge my students and to ease them into reading postcolonial Gothic, aware of the difficulties of reading texts which disrupt meanings and question the real, which defamiliarize the conventional representations and interpretations as well as providing a challenge to cultural security. Picking out some key moments from familiar texts such as E. M. Forster's *A Passage to India* (1924), opening up discussions about the ways of reading the first few confusing pages of *Beloved* (1987) can all start the debates going, moving from the familiar into less familiar space. We will need at some point to move into the more uncharted territory of other examples of the postcolonial Gothic produced by contemporary postcolonial writers.

### Strategies used in teaching

1. Cultural identification: I ask students to say where they or their families come from and where they have visited. This highlights and celebrates cultural diversity and makes it comfortable to speak from a culturally inflected subject position whether that might be Essex, or the Cameroons.
2. Offering opportunities to identify with the experiences of Otherizing and subaltern silencing, speaking our anger at marginalization—the ways in which colonized people are erased, silenced, denied, refused.
3. Recognizing the unfamiliar and identifying the familiar within the unfamiliar. This is an important step that involves and encourages students to feel sufficiently discomforted to question values and sufficiently comfortable with theories and similarities or experience to develop a freedom of expression and so to be able to identify that they do have something to say, rather than being overwhelmed.
4. Providing cultural, historical, and political context for the reading of the works. This helps encourage reflection on personal experience, the voicing of any insecurities and a gradual move towards engagement and expression.

5. Moving forward from rather conventional contextual analysis and response with a space to recognize that operating within familiar strategies of analysis of expression and technique might well be reproducing the denials and refusals of which these texts speak. This enables us to acknowledge then that we might not easily be able to recognize the validity of different forms of expression and so should try and work out where they come from and why, and how they express what they express—using critical values and testimony from both postcolonial critics and the writers or speakers themselves.

In working with each postcolonial Gothic text, we need to consider students' initial preconceptions and experiences, their knowledge and their interests of the broad subject area and the specific issues dealt with in the texts. So we look at issues and questions which arise from the postcolonial context—cultural, historical, social, economic, gendered, religious—the specific colonial and imperial practices with which this text engages and how it engages with them—language, forms, imagery, issues and questions which arise from the Gothic—the specific social/psychological personal issues with which the text engages using the Gothic, Gothic tropes, imagery, and formulae operated in the text and how and why, and to what effect, noticing any particular (1) difficulties/blockages (2) ways in (3) surprises/delights/insights/new perspectives affirmed by either the postcolonial aspects or the Gothic aspects of the text. I ask a range of questions with small groups working on passages and these questions prompt a recognition of difference, the unfamiliar, Otherness; I then split this down into both the Gothic and the postcolonial.

### Key concepts

Developed as an imaginative response to the reason and rigour of the Enlightenment, the *Literary Gothic* is not only a set of formulae and characteristics, but a product of the imaginative lives of the particular people, times, and locations from which it springs, and whose complacent certainties, whose legitimated and sanctioned versions of history, the present, the future, and values, it disturbs. As such then, the general characteristics and tales might recur throughout a variety of literary Gothic examples, from the origins in late eighteenth century, with Anne Radcliffe's *Mysteries of Uldopho* (1794) and

Horace Walpole's *Castle of Otranto* (1764). These characteristics include split selves, confined spaces, deception and duplicity, invasion, engulfment, and implosion. Different preoccupations, different fantasies and terrors are produced in different contexts, themselves expressed in different settings and scenarios. Fears about identity, inheritance, and purity as well as the locations of distant Italian and other foreign castles and monasteries are specific to the times of Radcliffe and Walpole, albeit reproduced in and reshaped in different times and places, as those of the threatened purity of women (more inheritance and a sense of the need to defend Victorian ideal womanhood) and foreign property acquisition, hence intrusion into the sanctity of both home and homeland which infuse *Dracula* (1897), are specific to its time and places. Contemporary Gothic, for example by John Hawkes, Michelle Roberts, and Ian McEwan is likely to home in on contemporary insecurities such as urban invasion, theft of identity, and domestic unease.

## Postcolonial Gothic

A much contested term, postcolonial is used by critics to suggest both or either the period literary, and other work produced historically after the end of colonization, colonial, or imperial rule and sometimes work which is in dispute with that rule and produced while the rule is still in place.[5] Other critics argue that the legacy of economic dependence, cultural appropriation, and covert rule such as the economic influences of multinationals, effectively prevents people from moving beyond colonial influence. The most straightforward use of "postcolonial" suggests after the end of colonial rule and also critiques the effects of that colonial or imperial rule.

We might expect in the postcolonial Gothic that fantasies, fears, and desires will mirror those of the times and of the people. David Punter's *Postcolonial Imaginings: Fictions of a New World Order* (2000)[6] is a good place to start with criticism of the postcolonial Gothic. Punter asserts that postcolonial experience is inevitably haunted by a colonial past; the repressed return (like ghosts) and traces of the legacy of silence, pain, humiliation, and dispossession reappear in spectral figures. Ideologically it is important not to start to categorize the explorations of the unconscious and the supernatural in the postcolonial literary Gothic as sites for frissons of difference and pleasure, a problem faced by postcolonial critics, but to try and appreciate the achievements of the texts in their own right. As another critic, Jean Franco has pointed out, the danger is a response to our celebration of difference rather than our insistence on hierarchy, but it is a danger nonetheless:

> . . . the discourse of recognition becomes possible when heterogeneity is valorised by the increasingly routinised metropolis. At this moment, the Third world becomes the place of the unconscious, the rich source of fantasy and legend recycled by the intelligentsia, for which heterogeneity is no longer a ghostly, dragging chain but material that can be loosened from any territorial context and juxtaposed in ways that provide a constant frisson of pleasure.[7]

African-American/Afro-Caribbean history is a common feature. Morrison's *Beloved* rewrites both the guilt-ridden period of slavery, and its aftermath, its poisoned legacy.

## A postcolonial Gothic text: teaching and ways in *Beloved*

*Beloved* is a popular way into the postcolonial Gothic and a widely "set" text. It is also a key example of African-American and Afro-Caribbean women's horror or the ghost story. Toni Morrison recognizes the importance, the difficulty of writing using strategies of the fantastic, in this case the Gothic combined with the political edge of the postcolonial:

> . . . the tone in which I could blend acceptance of the supernatural and a profound rootedness in the real time at the same time with neither taking precedence over the other. It is indicative of the cosmology, the way in which Black people looked at the world, we are a very practical people, very down to earth, even shrewd people. But within that practicality we also accepted what I suppose could be called superstition and magic, which is another way of knowing things. But to blend these two works together at the same time was enhancing not limiting. And some of those things were "discredited" only because Black people were "discredited"

> therefore what they knew was "discredited." And also because the press upward towards social mobility would mean to get as far away from that kind of knowledge as possible. That kind of knowledge has a very strong place in my world.[8]

I would probably give students this quotation to focus their reading on the use of magic and history, the Gothic and the postcolonial. My first choice in teaching any text is to invite students to open the first page and read—responding with their sense of enjoyment, with any questions, contradictions, and need for information. We then work to layer in information and to explore issues.

Let us consider this discursive. analytical, and reflective way into *Beloved*. The novel opens with some rather confusing statements: "124 was spiteful, full of a baby's venom."[9] This surprises the reader because there has been no scene setting, no introduction to character, period, or theme as you would find in a traditional nineteenth-century novel. Some historical detail does follow, however, and we are told that Cincinnati Ohio is where the tale is set and at one point in history (the period of the establishment of the community, when the Northern American States started to let ex-slaves live as free people) there had been no street numbers.

Returning to the beginning sentence, "full of a baby's venom" is surprising as babies are not usually considered venomous. This one, however, is a revengeful ghostly presence, who orchestrates strange supernatural events rather like a poltergeist might in a haunted house, 124 is exactly that, a haunted house. The baby ghost leaves handprints in the food, shapes in the mirror, causes spillages and alarm among the whole family in the house. She is a very real presence and this presence has, we are told, frightened away her young brothers, Howard and Buglar. Toni Morrison here creates a historical reality—the dates, places, the event of a real death of a real child at her own mother's protective hands (reported in the newspapers—Margaret Garner's infanticide) and presents the reader with the lived reality of a ghost, using the same tones with the supernatural as she does to record the historical. In this way, she mixes the magical and the historical, the Gothic and the postcolonial to emphasize how our lives are a mixture of the factual and our feelings, myths, and imaginative realities. By setting the tale in several moments in the history of slavery and involving the reader in interpreting the mixture of historical fact, and revived memory, she suggests that the memory of slavery is part of all our heritage. It has to be faced up to, managed, and lived through. People must not forget its horrors, and they must live with them daily (as Sethe does the lived presence of her dead baby, a full-grown ghostly presence, felt as real) but they need to move on, also.

Reading it as a ghost story, I explore the return of the repressed—in this case a dead baby ghost, the sacrificed child victim of the horrifying everyday reality of slavery in its effects on ordinary people's lives. Although the incidents of the tale are set in the mid to late nineteenth century, the process of rememorying and of exorcizing the ghosts of slavery speak to us in the twenty-first century. Morrison's literary Gothic, her ghost story, is no mere entertaining dream, it has designs upon us, it teaches us versions of history which have been erased; it enables African-Americans to reclaim moments of their own past and all of us to weave that past into the growing face of the reclaimed alongside the formally agreed past.

The novel provides such vivid insights into the lived experience of slavery and its legacy that it has had a very powerful effect on readers and, as a film, on audiences. Its combination of history and magic or the supernatural enables readers to engage with both the real, historical moments, the actual events, and the imaginative lived experiences; the ways in which people felt, the ways in which their minds at the times of slavery and ever since can be haunted by the horrors of slavery, haunted as if by a lived presence of a ghost returning, repressed, difficult to live with, difficult to speak about and difficult to ignore.

We read this in relation to its critical reception as well as our own reading practices. I would ask students to consider critical responses which undermined or underestimate the Gothic elements and ask them to explore what is achieved by a Gothic edge, metaphors, and settings—or whether they agree with the critics. In so doing I provide quotations and information about the Gothic and then discuss. Extracts help engage students in academic debate.

Morrison was actually lambasted by some early critics for moving away from the stereotype of being a Black writer concerned with testimony and social realism. Sara Blackburn (*New York Times Review*, 1973) suggested that reporting Black experience would be something she would grow out of, while the *Guardian* critical response to her receiving the Nobel Prize for *Beloved* berated her for the construction of blatantly nonrealistic characters, Pilate the aunt with no navel, Beloved the returned baby ghost and succubus.[10] Of course, this was partly a generalized arrogance on the part of critics who assumed that the speculative fantastic, the literary Gothic, are lesser forms than the socially realistic. Of course also, this is a product of a colonial patronizing response which allows Black women some space to speak but only if they say what is expected and accepted, in a form which is legitimized. Testimony is a necessary response to centuries of silencing and a social habit of ignoring and denying experience. But even testimony is not confined to the factual, historical decision of events. Feelings, hopes, desires, fears are a part of lived experience, and the fantastic imaginative lives of people explored, are voiced and dramatized in the speculative, the mythic, the Gothic. Misunderstanding, silencing, downgrading, and denying this poetic, metaphoric form of expression is every bit as much an oppressive critical constraint as is refusing alternative versions of history defined through testimony. Fantasy and the Gothic are represented as class literary citizens. This is of course not so now; in the early twenty-first century we have suddenly become aware that historically even the nineteenth-century classical realists George Eliot, Mrs Gaskell, Dickens, Henry James, and even the high modernists, Woolf and Forster wrote speculative Gothic fictions. It is an undercurrent now in plain view and culturally and politically this silenced sister, the Gothic, is speaking out in postcolonial writing. Absurd that any critic might have thought that cultures infused with the supernatural and the spiritual, maintained by oral storytelling and song, coded myths and tales, across centuries and continents, might not be expressing themselves in the Gothic, the speculative, the fantastic, the magical, and like all good Gothic, providing spellbinding insights into people's ways of constructing and imagining their lives, coping with and moving beyond constraints and denials, and enabling even against attempts to shackle the imagination.

Students can be invited to engage in a critical discussion about what we expect from the literary Gothic and postcolonial writing; how the two can be fused, and appreciated through study. To do this they will also need some background on the literary Gothic, in a specifically postcolonial context.

### Background and context

A little critical and historical background is woven in to help students' reading. This could include extracts from critical texts on slavery and its history, and on Toni Morrison, including essays and interviews. In my teaching sessions generally, I try to balance informational input—such as introductory arguments, a sense of dialogue with the critics, key terms, historical and cultural context, with student engagement, exploratory talk in small groups discussing the texts and their own reading experiences, and a chance to debate critical reception. What follows is something *I* just happen to have written about *Beloved*, and it includes a synthesis of others' arguments and quotations from Morrison herself. In another context, I would extract from others' comments for student discussion.

As readers, teachers, and students of this novel, we need to contextualize its events. To do this we need to discover the context of the history of slavery; the torture, murder, economic forces. The testimonies of slaves provide inside knowledge of the slave experience. Other secondary sources such as bell hooks' *Ain't I a Woman: Black Women and Feminism* (1981) provide descriptions of the institution, and the treatment of slave women used by slave owners.[11] These women were denied family lives yet forced to be breeders of future slaves, a dehumanizing experience underlying Sethe's own abuse when the men beat her and take her milk. The specific location in time is also important so we need to know about the historical changes which the period of the novel focuses on (1855), when the free States gave homes to freed slaves, but the slaves were unprotected from slave-catchers crossing to recapture those who had escaped. Margaret Garner, who had escaped with her family, saw the slave-catchers coming and tried to kill her four children. The baby girl died, the boys lived. She was convicted of escaping (a property issue) rather than murder.

*Beloved* is essentially a novel about the vitality and intrusiveness of memory, the memory of racial oppression under slavery. Memory or "re-memory" is acknowledged as present, solid, vital. "If a house burns down, it's gone, but the place—the picture of it—stays: and just in my rememory, but out there in the world . . . it's when you bump into the re-memory of someone else" (36). History is portrayed as all around us as a tangible, visible existent that a community can experience, bump into. In this novel, the insanity and absurdity upon which a capitalist society dependent on slavery is founded, translates itself into the lived madness, the haunting of the past within no. 124, the house where first Baby Suggs, the grandmother, then Sethe, the mother, and Denver, her daughter, live. It is over the issue of this tangible history that readers face a problem. *Beloved* is an historically situated, politically focused novel, but it is equally a novel essentially based on an acceptance of the supernatural and magic. We suspend our disbelief when we are told that the baby whose throat Sethe cut to save her from the slave-catchers haunts the house on Bluestone, no. 124, whose red aura provides a presence, however, occasionally malevolent and spiteful, and whose presence effectively isolates Baby Suggs from the community. Previously the centre of community root-working, herbal medicine and mystical powers, as a lay preacher Baby Suggs represented the socially acceptable face of the supernatural's place in a shared society. Like the community around her, however, we have problems as readers, when Beloved actually appears, right at the moment of a new family harmony and sexual unity for Denver, Sethe, and Paul D., one of the last of the "Sweet Home" men who has come to stay in Sethe's life. Footsore and weary from a long journey, confused in her memories about who gave her clothes, taught her ways, Beloved intrudes on family harmony, upsets Sethe's sexual relationship with Paul D. by sleeping with him and forcing him to recognize her. Sexuality, here as elsewhere in Toni Morrison's works, is used, as Susan Willis points out, as a register for the experience of change: "sexuality converges with history and functions as a register for the experience of change, i.e. historical transition."[12]

Beloved is a succubus. She drains the house of love and vitality both spiritual and physical, then forms a strong bond of dependency with Denver, finally turning to Sethe when her mother recognizes her as the daughter she sacrificed. She grows fast as Sethe shrinks and shrivels, and she causes the whole house to be united in a crazy bond. Too much recognition drives Paul D. away, drains Sethe of life as she both serves and battles with the ghost-made-flesh. Beloved is manifest history, the guilt and pain of slavery as it enters personal lives causing brutal, dehumanized actions in self-defence from those denied human rights. For the community this is too much to face, jealous of the celebrations, they failed to warn Sethe of the slave-catcher's arrival. They feel culpable. Here as elsewhere in Morrison's work there is a focus on the relationship of the individual to the community which is explored using the postcolonial Gothic. Some areas students might explore include the community, silence, and breaking silence. "They stopped praying and took a step back to the beginning. In the beginning there were no words. In the beginning was the sound, and they all knew what that sounded like" (259). The noise unlocks Sethe's mind, reunites her with the community; "This is not a story to pass on" ends the novel (275). But it is crucial to pass on the tale in the shape of the novel, not let its horror undermine the ability to confront, live with and move on from memories of slavery and everyday racism This acknowledgement is ultimately empowering for African-Americans, whites, and for Sethe herself. She learns, as Paul points out, "You your best thing, Sethe" (273).

## Conclusion

My own practice in teaching the postcolonial Gothic involves engaging students in terms of their own experience and knowledge, of colonial and imperial histories, issues, and practices and adding to these through discussion using critics, history, context, and textual excerpts led by powerpoint headings and class questions. It also involves engaging and extending students' reflections and arguments in terms of their own explorations of the imaginative critical expression. The postcolonial Gothic offers rich opportunities for engagement with the debates of history and the imaginary and in our work we approach its richness using a mix of the personal and the critical, exploratory talk, close reading, and the problematizing focus enabled by both postcolonial and Gothic criticism and reading practices.

## Notes

1. Julia Kristeva, *Powers of Horror: an Essay on Abjection* (Columbia: Columbia University Press, 1982).
2. Julia Kristeva, *Strangers to Ourselves* (London: Harvester Wheatsheaf, 1991).
3. Betty Govinden, "Learning myself anew," in *Alternation* 2, 2 (1995), 170–83, 175.
4. Elleke Boehmer, *Colonial and Postcolonial Literature: Migrant Metaphors* (Oxford: Oxford University Press, 1995) 14.
5. See Bill Ashcroft, G. Griffiths, and H. Tiffin, eds, *The Empire Writes Back* (London: Routledge, 1989).

6. David Punter, *Postcolonial Imaginings: Fictions of a New World Order* (Edinburgh: Edinburgh University Press, 2000).
7. Jean Franco, "Beyond ethnocentrism: gender, power and the third-world intelligentsia" in *Marxism and the Interpretation of Culture*, Cary Nelson, and Lawrence Grossberg, eds (Basingstoke: Macmillan—now Palgrave Macmillan, 1988) 503–15, 508.
8. Toni Morrison, "Rootedness: the ancestor as foundation" in Mari Evans, ed., *Black Women Writers* (London and Sydney: Pluto Press, 1985) 339–45, 342.
9. Toni Morrison, *Beloved* (London: Chatto and Windus, 1987) 1. All subsequent references are to this edition, and are given in the text.
10. Sara Blackburn, "You still can't go home again" in *New York Times Book Review*, 30 December 1973.
11. bell hooks, *Ain't I a Woman: Black Women and Feminism* (South End Press: Boston, Massachusetts, 1981).
12. Susan Willis, "Eruptions of funk: historicizing Toni Morrison" in *Black Literature and Literary Theory*, Henry Louis Gates, ed. (New York: Routledge, 1984) 263–83, 263.

# 12
# Postgraduate Developments

*Andrew Smith*

This chapter will explore three areas: the developments within humanities postgraduate recruitment in both the UK and North America, the growth in postgraduate recruitment specifically relating to Gothic studies at masters and Ph.D. level over the past ten years and finally, details of particular masters awards either on Gothic studies or which include substantial material on Gothic studies. The exploration of such awards will focus on their typical structure and modes of delivery in order to guide scholars who might be considering similar course design. Throughout, the emphasis is on the comparative experiences of institutions in the UK and North America.

## The humanities context

Doug Steward's article "The Master's Degree in the modern languages since 1966" which was printed in both the *Ade Bulletin* (2004) and the Modern Language Association of America's *Profession 2004*, provides an extremely useful analysis of changes in student recruitment patterns in the US during the period. The analysis also outlines the national context, which in turn explains many of the national differences in the availability of Gothic courses and awards. It is worth noting at this point that whilst there are four awards in the UK and Eire which are focused on the Gothic or which contain considerable Gothic material: the M.Litt. in The Gothic Imagination at the University of Stirling, the MA in Gothic Studies at the University of Glamorgan, the M.Phil. in Popular Literature at Trinity College Dublin, and the MA in English: Popular Literatures at Kingston University, there are no such comparable awards in North America, nor, so the findings from my questionnaire suggest, any immediate intention to offer such awards. However, it should be noted that very popular courses on the Gothic are typically available on a number of MA awards in North America. Such courses are usually attached to certain literary areas such as Romanticism, the Victorians, and American literature. What follows is not a qualitative evaluation of specific Gothic courses but an attempt to explain why the different national contexts make subject-specific awards more viable in the UK and Eire than in North America.

Steward notes that there is statistical evidence on recruitment patterns to MA humanities awards in the US which suggests that during periods of economic depression (as in the 1970s) there was a decline in the number of students seeking to take humanities awards. As Steward comments "Doubts about the economic future appear to have led many toward more vocational programs," meaning that humanities MAs have also become more vocational in order to attract students.[1] Steward notes that debates about the vocational aspects of humanities MA have led to a variety of, not always compatible, conclusions. One view is that an MA in English functions as a step towards taking a Ph.D., so that the MA becomes perceived as vocational as it enables progression to a Ph.D. (a requirement for entering the profession). The MA is therefore in danger of becoming devalued and this is particularly true at the more prestigious research universities: neither Harvard nor Virginia, for example, offers English MAs as terminal degrees. This suggests that MAs from such institutions are awarded when insufficient progress is made towards the Ph.D. Such a view is in keeping with a more instrumental approach to studying humanities subjects and explains why recent statistics indicate that more doctoral students in English are graduating than masters students. Steward notes that there has been much recent debate about revitalizing the humanities MA so that it will appeal to students interested in exploring the attractively interdisciplinary subject-matter and approaches of the humanities combined with some vocational skills acquisitions. In this way the MA could become what Alison Schneider has referred to as "the cure for what has been ailing higher academy for too long: too many Ph.D.s, too few jobs" so that potentially with the MA "Academe's ugly duckling has become its newest darling," and could attract interest from librarians and secondary school teachers looking for promotion.[2]

It is clear from this that the US postgraduate market is largely vocationally orientated. This has implications for the delivery of subjects such as the Gothic; particularly if such courses were to dominate within a particular award. The fact that there is no masters degree on Gothic studies available in the US reflects the perception that such an award would be nonvocational, unless it were a step towards Ph.D. research. This is not withstanding the popularity of specific courses on the Gothic within such MAs. At a time when it seems as though the MA is becoming revitalized and marketed as a potentially vocationally adapted award aimed at librarians and teachers, this has potential consequences for the growth of awards predominately focused on Gothic studies.

The statistical evidence in the UK is largely drawn from data gathered by the Higher Education Statistics Agency (HESA), which has been collecting some relevant information concerning graduation statistics in the humanities from 1994/5. This data was subject to an in-depth analysis by the British Academy in their report entitled "Review of graduate studies in the Humanities and Social Sciences" which was produced in 2001.[3] The HESA statistics, which are specific to English, do not differentiate between MA and Ph.D. enrolments.[4] They do however indicate that over half of such students are registered as part-time and that from 1996/7 to 2001/02 (when the means of calculating these statistics was radically changed) there was an upward trend in recruitment onto postgraduate English degrees, of 20% for full-time students and 10% for part-time students. A report produced in 2001 by The Council of University Deans of Arts & Humanities (CUDAH) entitled "Doctoral futures: career destinations of Arts and Humanities research students" indicated that there was a 20% increase in English Ph.D. graduates between 1996 and 2001.[5] HESA statistics, which go back to 1989, show an even more dramatic increase in the number of postgraduate qualifications awarded in the humanities with an increase between 1989 and 1998 of 113%. This was also a period which coincided with the rapid expansion in the higher education sector in the UK, and during this period there was an increase of 115% in the number of all degrees awarded. Statistics also indicate that there has been a dramatic increase in the number of MAs taken in the pre1992 university sector between 1989 and 1998 of 80%, and an increase of 25% in the number of Ph.D.s. It is clear that the expansion of the higher education sector and the

Research Assessment Exercise (RAE) have had an effect on increasing postgraduate recruitment.

The expansion in higher education has meant that more graduates have entered a competitive job market, and to that end an additional masters degree would appear to be an attractive option for those seeking either further advancement in their careers or to enhance such possibilities at the start of their working career. The expansion in part-time numbers can be partially explained by this pursuit of higher qualifications by those already in work. To this extent there is some similarity with the US context which has also seen an increase in teachers and lecturers taking further qualifications to help career development. The single biggest difference relates to the presence of the RAE, an exercise held every five or six years since 1996, which rates the quality of a department's research output and which influences the levels of funding that departments receive from public monies. Research ratings, although largely determined by the quality of research within a department are also dependent upon other factors including evidence of Ph.D. recruitment and graduation. Although the pre1992 universities have generally been more successful in pursuit of this money than the post1992 universities (the formerly more vocationally orientated polytechnics), there is still evidence that this new sector has made attempts to gain access to RAE funds and this is clear from the growth in postgraduate awards offered in that sector. There is also some evidence, predominately anecdotal, which suggests that English MAs although terminal degrees in themselves, help to recruit future Ph.D. students (and indeed AHRB funding mechanisms often favour an MA completion before supporting Ph.D. research).[6] This seems to suggest that the MA sector in the UK is as vocational as the US market, even though it allows for the presence of awards which would seem to have little direct application to a vocationally orientated market, except as a route into future Ph.D. study. However, the 2001 CUDAH report revealed that 84% of Ph.D. students in Arts and Humanities in the UK indicated that they had undertaken research because of a fundamental interest in the research topic, which was clearly the primary motivation for such study even though 77% also believed that a Ph.D. would help to improve their professional skills.

In relation to MAs, the conclusion is that the MA market in the UK more readily accommodates subject specific awards (possible feeders into specific Ph.D. research) as they advertise the presence of staff expertise and bolster research degree recruitment, both issues which are important in a competitive culture in higher education which has become increasingly dominated by the RAE. However, the students themselves do not necessarily see postgraduate study as essentially vocational, and such considerations do not dominate their choices in the way that they appear to do in North America. A questionnaire (discussed below) designed in part to gauge the level of interest in establishing such awards, revealed that in North America there were no immediate plans to offer awards like this because the postgraduate culture did not support such subject specificity at award level (even though specific courses on the Gothic were popular with students). Indeed the interdisciplinary nature of such awards tended to create more choice for students but lacked the often tightly structured approach characteristically adopted on subject specific MA awards in the UK, where even the broadest of such awards often include core requirements such as the completion of a research methods course and the production of a dissertation.

## The questionnaire

The questionnaire (see Appendix) was sent to either Chairs of English and/or prominent Gothic scholars in fifty-seven departments in the US, Canada, and the UK. There were twenty-six responses. Questions concerned: the growth in Ph.D. recruitment on Gothic topics over the past five and ten years, the topics most popularly followed, the comparative popularity of courses on the Gothic on masters awards, an assessment of whether there exists sufficient postgraduate resources (such as monographs, readers, collections of source materials) to help support postgraduate study, and whether there was a proactive approach towards recruiting international students.

Whilst responses indicated that there were signs of growth in the area of Ph.D. research on the Gothic, it was clear that most institutions had very small numbers of such students ten years ago and indeed five years ago. Of the seventeen institutions that offered Ph.D.s there was growth in numbers in nine such institutions. Typically most of these departments saw growth from one student ten years ago to two five years ago to three currently being supervised. The greatest number of Ph.D. students working on Gothic topics in any department was in the UK, where one department recorded seven doctoral students. In North America the most was five. Indeed the picture looked very similar in both contexts. Of the remaining eight institutions with Ph.D. awarding powers that responded only two had less students than ten and five years ago, although again the numbers were very small. Of the other institutions, they had either stayed the same or had more than they had ten years ago, but less than they did five years ago. In some instances records had not been kept of cases from five or ten years ago, or a respondent was new to the post and had no access to such records, as a consequence the numbers are somewhat skewed suggesting that ten years ago these departments had eleven students, five years ago sixteen, and today thirty-four. This final figure can be adjusted, and if new members of staff, who were often unable to comment on the situation at their institution five or ten years ago are omitted from this census then the numbers for today are twenty-one. This indicates that the area has almost doubled in size over the past ten years and although the figures are selective and small it does represent some considerable progress. On average both the North American departments and UK departments now have two Ph.D. students. However it is also clear that this often represents the loading for one specialist member of staff (certainly in the UK).

Respondents indicated that a diverse range of topics were being pursued from the eighteenth century to the present day. Often such topics were closely associated with Romanticism or the *fin de siècle.* Other popular topics, which often crossed such historical periods included Women's Gothic, Science and the Gothic (which seemed more popular in the UK) Film, and Race and Gender (which seemed more popular in North America).

Of the thirteen institutions which offered masters modules on the Gothic in the past year (at some North American institutions such modules had been "rested" for a year), ten respondents indicated that these modules were the most popular on the award (with one respondent indicating that figures were double those on other masters modules). Again, there is parity here between the North American and UK experiences. Two respondents (one from North America, the other from the UK) indicated that such modules were as popular as other modules, and one North American respondent indicated that they were slightly less popular. Although such modules referred to a wide range of topics, in the UK such topics tended to be historically focused, i.e. forming elements within awards that were predominantly Romantic or Victorian in emphasis, whereas in North America such modules appeared to be largely offered within nonhistorically specific awards, even though the courses themselves were often historical in emphasis. Most awards in both the UK and North America were offering one or two modules on Gothic topics which typically constituted around 15–20% of the modules available to students.

A further question related to the resourcing of postgraduate courses, with respondents asked whether they felt that there existed adequate materials such as readers, and collections of source materials. Of the twenty-one responses to this question eight indicated that they felt that the current provision was about right. One respondent felt that there was too much. The other twelve respondents made a variety of suggestions for developing resources. These included gaining access to often difficult to find texts and authors. There was a feeling that wider access to online or microfiche materials of relatively obscure Gothic sources would help to broaden a research base from which Ph.D. research could be developed, and that it would also help to add depth to the content of masters courses. Such material has become increasingly available in recent years, such as the Sadlier-Black collection at the University of Virginia, a comprehensive selection of which is now available on microfilm from Adam Matthew Publications. However, there are cost implications for such acquisitions and these would require some institutional support. There was a widespread feeling that masters courses in particular would benefit from the publication of more source materials (for example, such as Emma Clery and Robert Miles' *Gothic Documents*).[7] It was also felt desirable to have more readers, or selections of critical essays, although there was some concern that this could lead to simplification and deter postgraduate students from engaging in properly focused research. There were some specific suggestions for readers, which it was felt could support new and emerging areas of interests in the Gothic. These included arguments for readers on Science and the Gothic, on Victorian Gothic, and on the Gothic and its place in the development of English, and American Studies. On a national note it was also felt that the current provision is predominantly British or North American and that there was a lack of material on the Gothic written in other languages than English. One repeated concern was affordability. A number of respondents emphasized the necessity for such texts to be produced cheaply so that students will buy them, rather than them being largely purchased by academic libraries due to prohibitive costs.

Another question related to any plans departments or institutions may have to attempt to recruit students from an international market. It was clear that there was no such strategy in place in North America. Whilst many masters degrees in North America attracted overseas students, principally because of the reputation of the institution, it was not felt that any specific strategy for such recruitment was necessary. In the UK the position was similar, but there was some acknowledgement that this situation is liable to change given the differential fees paid by students from the UK and European Union countries, and fees paid by students coming from non-European Union countries in Europe, and from other parts of the world. Given that this is potentially a very lucrative market, it is likely that UK institutions will want to develop international links, and there was some feeling that courses on the Gothic could provide an "exotic" element within masters awards which might make them more marketable in North America. Any such developments are clearly at a very early stage, but given that it takes longer to gain an MA in North America and that it would be cheaper to study in the UK (even on non EU-rates), this is an area of potential growth.

One of the striking aspects of responses to this question concerning internationalization is the seeming absence of any sustained collaborative links between institutions over the delivery of Gothic courses. The presence of the International Gothic Association (formed in 1991) bears testimony to the international presence of research into the Gothic. Members have worked collaboratively on research projects and on organizing panels at the association's biannual conference. This collection of essays, and the earlier MLA's *Approaches to Teaching Gothic Fiction* edited by Diana Long Hoeveler and Tamar Heller, illustrates the presence of a shared reflective practice on pedagogy and yet there are no shared pedagogic processes in place.[8] It would not be unthinkable, for example, to design an award which is part taught in North America and the UK, and this would help to consolidate and enhance the very strong research links that already exist between North America and UK institutions, a point which I will return to in my concluding comments.

It should also be noted that postgraduates themselves have in recent years played an increasingly prominent role in the development of Gothic studies. Such students have had articles and reviews published in the International Gothic Association's peer-reviewed journal *Gothic Studies* (published by Manchester University Press). They have also been very actively involved in conference organization, and at the International Gothic Association's biannual conference in Liverpool, UK in 2003, two postgraduate members were for the first time elected to sit on the association's Advisory Board. Such activity is a very encouraging sign of the likely continuing vitality of Gothic studies in years to come.

In summary, responses to the questionnaires indicate that there has been clear growth in Ph.D. research into the Gothic over the past ten years, even if the overall numbers are not large. It is also the case that some new areas of research have developed on the Gothic, including interest in how conjunctions of race and gender are represented, interest in national identities, and an interest in science and the Gothic. It is also clear that masters courses on the Gothic are very popular with students. However, what is also clear is that masters awards in North America are not so specifically focused as those in the UK. North American awards encourage a sampling of courses in English and across generic forms and periods. In the UK the emphasis is on awards that have a particular focus to them (on certain periods, or modes of literature), although such awards do run alongside other portmanteau awards which are familiar from the North American model. This is to acknowledge that in the UK postgraduate students generally specialize earlier than in North America. This is not to say that this is preferable to the American model where course diversity is clearly an important and attractive element of masters awards.

The remainder of this chapter will outline some existing awards available in the UK and Eire that are relevant to Gothic studies. Some respondents from North America, whilst acknowledging that such awards are not part of the general model for masters degrees in their country, did nevertheless evidence some frustration with this and expressed an interest in developing such awards if it became viable to do so. The following should help stimulate discussion about this as well to give some practical examples of the kinds of issues and problems which are typically addressed in designing and running such awards.

## Masters of Gothic

The most longstanding award in this area is the pioneering M.Litt. in The Gothic Imagination which has been offered at the University of Stirling, Scotland, since the academic year 1996/7 when the programme was initiated by Professor David Punter. The course runs for one year and is only available on a full-time basis. The award is the most comprehensive of its kind and offers courses from the eighteenth century to the present day. Students attend a weekly core course on the Gothic which runs throughout the two semesters (typically thereafter the summer is spent completing a 20,000 word dissertation). The core course is designed to give students a sense of the historical breadth of the Gothic and consists of discussion of the late eighteenth- and nineteenth-century Gothic in the first semester and twentieth-century Gothic in the second semester. The core is examined by two coursework essays. In addition to this students complete an optional module each semester that consist of guided independent studies which are designed to encourage independent research with tutorial support. Such strands are available in a very wide range of periods and on specific authors (from Mary Shelley to Stephen King); they are also cross generic and include strands on theory, the novel, the graphic novel, and film, with the emphasis predominantly on Anglo-American writings. Students also complete a year-long Research Methods course. The department has particular strengths in the Gothic and currently six members of staff are involved in teaching elements of the award.

Correspondence with Dr Glennis Byron, the course convener for the M.Litt., has revealed that on average the award typically recruits six students. The highest number of students following it at any one time has been eleven, which was felt to be too many for a taught postgraduate award of this kind, and the lowest number has been three. Around 25%–33% of its students are graduates of the University of Stirling, who would typically have been introduced to the Gothic during their undergraduate studies. Candidates for the award usually hold an undergraduate degree in Literature (rather than degrees from other disciplines within humanities), and are drawn from a broad social and racial spectrum, which suggests that there are no particular gender, class, or racial issues involved in the recruitment of students (a feature of all the subject-specific awards discussed here). Indeed the award has been successful in recruiting internationally for its students from Europe, South America, America, and Canada, although there is no proactive strategy to seek such students, the majority of whom find information about the award on the department's web site.

In the past the Gothic strands that students follow have been made available to students taking other Literature masters courses in the department. However, in recent years that has been resisted because such students are often unfamiliar with the historical and theoretical approaches which the Gothic students explore on the core module, and consequently are potentially disadvantaged.

It is clear that an award of this kind provides students with a very thorough grounding in the history, theory, and understanding of scholarship on the Gothic, and the award has also been a good means of recruiting future Ph.D. students. It is also clear that because of the way in which the award is delivered, with an emphasis on independent research backed-up with tutorial support, that recruitment is necessarily limited because of the demands placed on staff time. However, this is not to identify a problem, as small group work is an obvious strength of the award, but that it is worth keeping in mind that this would be an issue to address if the ambitions of designing an award were to attract large groups of students.

The experience of Stirling is instructive on how to construct a stand-alone award that is specifically intended for a particular group of students. The MA in Gothic Studies offered from 2004/5 at the University of Glamorgan, Wales, and designed by myself, is offered in a rather different way. The award can be studied full-time and part-time (i.e. over twelve or twenty-four months). The award consists of a core module which is specifically focused on research methods. This core lasts for one year and is designed to introduce students to the research skills they need to acquire in pursuit of their parallel study of specific topics in the optional modules. The core includes some formal elements relating to the production of bibliographical materials and less formal elements consisting of analyses of various critical theories and how they can be methodologically applied to primary texts. This research core as well as providing the grounding for their other researches, is of particular help in the production of the 15,000–20,000 word dissertation. The core course is common to other students who would be following the MA in Literature, Culture, and Society, which means that a group of around ten students are taking this module at any one time. In addition, new M.Phil./Ph.D. students who have not taken a masters award are encouraged to follow the research methods module. Students select four modules from options that include courses on eighteenth- and nineteenth-century Gothic, *fin de siècle* Gothic, contemporary Gothic, women's writing and the Gothic, and science and the Gothic. Optional courses on the award run for one term and are also offered to students pursuing the MA in Literature, Culture, and Society, although students taking that award are limited to the number of modules that they can follow on Gothic themes. The result is that classes are larger than they would otherwise be if they were only offered to students following the MA in Gothic Studies (in practice numbers of students in seminar groups on optional modules range between one and six). The award was validated late in 2004 which had a consequent affect on recruitment so that figures for the award are currently unreliable. The department offers extremely popular undergraduate modules on the Gothic and as in keeping with other masters degrees offered by the University, such students are likely to constitute the main source for recruitment.

This award is therefore somewhat different to the M.Litt. in The Gothic Imagination offered by Stirling. In many respects it is an award that is embedded within a popular Literature MA, and in terms of the available options constitutes a pathway through that award. It has been designed in such a way that larger numbers would be welcome, perhaps larger than those thought to be desirable on the award at Stirling.

An M.Phil. in Popular Literature available only on a full-time basis has been offered at Trinity College, Dublin since 2004/5 and is codirected by Dr Nicholas Daly and Dr Darryl Jones. The award explores popular forms such as the Gothic as well as Science Fiction and Detective Fiction. The course includes a core that runs throughout the two terms. On the core students are introduced to theories of popular culture and material on the emergence, and characteristics, of certain popular modes of literature, including Romantic Gothic, and Horror. Students also take a term-long research methods course and complete two options from a list of four, two of which "Lost Worlds: Victorian and Edwardian Fantasy Literature" and "Irish Gothic and Fantasy Literature" include significant Gothic content.

Students also complete a 15,000 word dissertation. Correspondence with Nicholas Daly indicates that courses on the Gothic are joint most popular on the award. During the planning stages of the award it was felt that there should be a strong theoretical and historical element which would be reflected in the core. It is intended that the options will be changed on a regular basis and, as with the M.Litt. at Stirling, there is an emphasis given to individual research (although on this award there is more class contact time). As with the MA in Gothic Studies at Glamorgan, this is the first time that the award has been offered and consequently there are no comparative recruitment figures available for analysis. However, it is noteworthy that it currently has eleven students on the award, equalling the maximum achieved at Stirling. Whilst at Stirling such large numbers would constitute a problem, that is not the case with this award where some courses are also offered to students taking the M.Phil. in Anglo-Irish Literature, and where the research methods course is taken by all postgraduates. However, unlike the MA in Gothic Studies offered at Glamorgan, the award is not embedded within a wider modular award, even though some modules are available to other masters students. Around 30% of the students are graduates of Trinity, although Trinity have actively sought overseas recruitment and four of the students have come from outside of Eire (including one from England, one from Poland, and two from North America). The award perhaps does not have the same kind of depth of historical coverage as the awards at Stirling and Glamorgan, but this is inevitable given the different aspects of popular literature that it explores.

An award, which is similar to the Trinity award, is the MA in English: Popular Literatures, offered by Kingston University from 2005/6. The award is available on a part-time and full-time basis. It is comprised of a series of compulsory modules that include, as does Trinity's award, modules on the historical contexts of popular literature, and on the theoretical considerations involved in studying such texts. The award, like those at Stirling, Trinity, and Glamorgan, also includes a research methods module. As with the other awards a dissertation (of 15,000 words) is a central requirement. There is also an additional module which addresses current debates within English Literature. Such a lack of optionality might appear to limit choice, but it is intended that discussions concerning genre on the two historical and theoretical modules will reflect students' interests and small group work on certain topics will be encouraged. This flexible approach allows for student choice within a framework which guides discussion. It is intended that these optional elements within the modules will provide an opportunity for intensive scholarly work on specific texts and authors (in a way which is similar to how the Gothic strands are taught at Stirling).

It is clear that in the UK and Eire there is a sense that subject-specific awards on the Gothic, or which include substantial Gothic elements, are viable. Three of these awards will be offered within a year of each other. In some respects such awards are capitalizing on the popularity of the Gothic at an undergraduate level. The different approaches taken reflect available staffing for such awards, and perhaps certain financial considerations in their delivery (such as Glamorgan's offering of such modules to students on another masters degree, meaning that classes are larger, and therefore more cost-effective to teach). However, the sudden proliferation of such awards is also a consequence of the growth in scholarship on the Gothic. All of the institutions mentioned here have very strong research bases in the Gothic and these awards reflect that. In North America where there is very clear evidence of research expertise, the culture has not typically supported the delivery of such subject specific awards.

In summary, both North America and the UK have seen considerable growth in the areas of postgraduate recruitment in English in general and in courses on the Gothic in particular. Over the past ten years the growth in scholarship on the Gothic has been matched by a corresponding growth in postgraduate students pursuing Gothic courses at masters and Ph.D. level. The fundamental differences between the North American and UK markets is that the latter has traditionally supported the idea of subject specific masters degrees and this has made the development of such Gothic studies awards, or awards which contain considerable material on the Gothic, possible. Many of the respondents in North America evidenced some frustration about not being able to offer similar awards. However, one way ahead would be to develop some genuinely international programmes of study whereby scholars drawn from this community could teach students. An international masters in Gothic studies might sound far-fetched (and may run up against institutional concerns about cost implications and curriculum design), but with a little thought it might just be possible and could be one way of strengthening and coordinating the international community's considerable expertise.

## Notes

1. Doug Steward, "The Master's Degree in the Modern Languages since 1966" in *Ade Bulletin* 136 (Winter 2004), 50–68, 50. Also published in *Profession 2004*, 154–77.
2. Alison Schneider, "Master's Degrees, once scorned, attract students and generate revenue" in *The Chronicle of Higher Education* 21 May 1999 A12., cited in Steward, 61.
3. "Review of graduate studies in the Humanities and Social Sciences" The British Academy 2001. The report can be found at: www.britac.ac.uk/news/reports/gsr/supp2.html
4. The report can be found at: www.hesa.ac.uk/holisdocs/pubinfo/stud.htm
5. "Doctoral futures: career destinations of Arts & Humanities research students" report produced by The Council of University Deans of Arts & Humanities (Leicester: De Montfort University: December 2001), 7.
6. On 1 April 2005 the Arts and Humanities Research Board was replaced by the Arts and Humanities Research Council. The Council emphasizes that it will provide selective financial support to students following masters degrees, either full or part-time, which are specifically intended to prepare students for doctoral study. The Council also provides selective funding for either full or part-time students taking more vocationally-orientated terminal masters programmes. The Council will also provide selective funds for students following a doctorial programme on either a full or part-time basis. See website details at: http://www.ahrb.ac.uk/
7. E. J. Clery and Robert Miles, *Gothic Documents: a Sourcebook 1700–1820* (Manchester: Manchester University Press, 2000).
8. Diane Long Hoeveler and Tamar Heller, *Approaches to Teaching: Gothic Fiction: the British and American Traditions* (New York: Modern Language Association of America, 2003).

# Appendix Questionnaire: Postgraduate Developments in Gothic Studies

## Research

1. How many M.Phil./Ph.D. students working on Gothic topics are there in your department?
2. How does this figure compare with numbers five years ago?
3. How does this figure (from Q 1) compare with numbers ten years ago?
4. Are there any particular topics/authors/periods, which seem to be noticeably popular? If so, could you please list them.

## Taught MAs

5. On your MA awards, are there modules/courses offered on Gothic topics?
6. How popular are these modules in comparison to modules on non-Gothic topics?
7. How many years have these modules/courses been offered?
8. Do you use questionnaires in order to evaluate student feedback on your courses?

## Specific awards

I am aware of three awards which are substantially, if not solely, focused on Gothic topics. These are the M.Litt. in the Gothic Imagination (Stirling), M.Phil. in Popular Literature (Trinity College, Dublin), and MA in Gothic Studies (Glamorgan).

9. Are there any plans to develop similar awards at your institution?

NB: I am conscious that this is perhaps a delicate question and, just to reiterate, any replies will be dealt with in the strictest confidence and will only be referred to in general terms so as to give an indication of potential growth in this area.

## Resourcing

10. Do you feel that the growth in postgraduate numbers is adequately supported by scholarship in the area? If not, what kinds of support material would you like to see? More "Readers," "Source Material" collections?

## Internationalization

In the UK there is some emphasis given to the international dimension of student recruitment (a financially lucrative initiative that many institutions are keen to support).

11. How are you responding to these issues? Through e-learning initiatives? Direct attempts to encourage overseas students to your institution to take up M.Phil./Ph.D.s on Gothic topics?
12. Are there any particular marketing strategies that your university has used in order to encourage such applications?
13. If you are following such initiatives what specific strains does it impose in terms of contact time and resources (e-learning)?

# Further Reading

## General


Aguirre, Manuel. *The Closed Space: Horror Literature and Western Symbolism*. Manchester: Manchester University Press, 1990.

Birkhead, Edith. *The Tale of Terror: A Study of the Gothic Romance*. London: Constable: 1921.

Botting, Fred. *Gothic*. London: Routledge, 1996.

———. ed. *The Gothic*. Cambridge: D. S. Brewer, 2001.

Byron, Glennis and David Punter, eds. *Spectral Readings: Towards a Gothic Geography*. Basingstoke: Macmillan—now Palgrave Macmillan, 1999.

Cavallaro, Dani. *The Gothic Vision: Three Centuries of Horror, Terror and Fear*. New York and London: Continuum, 2002.

Clemens, Valdine. *The Return of the Repressed: Gothic Horror from the Castle of Otranto to Alien*. Albany: Albany State University Press, 1999.

Ellis, Markham. *The History of Gothic Fiction*. Edinburgh: Edinburgh University Press, 2000.

Grixti, Joseph. *Terrors of Uncertainty: The Cultural Contexts of Horror Fiction*. New York: Routledge, 1989.

Hoeveler, Diane Long and Tamar Heller, eds. *Approaches to Teaching Gothic Fiction: The British and American Traditions*. New York: Modern Language Association of America, 2003.

Hogle, Jerrold E., ed. *The Cambridge Companion to Gothic Fiction*. Cambridge: Cambridge University Press, 2002.

Horner, Avril, ed. *European Gothic: A Spirited Exchange 1760–1960*. Manchester: Manchester University Press, 2002.

Howells, Coral Ann. *Love, Mystery and Misery: Feeling in Gothic Fiction*. London: Athlone, 1978.

Jackson, Rosemary. *Fantasy: The Literature of Subversion*. London: Methuen, 1981.

Kilgour, Maggie. *The Rise of the Gothic Novel*. London: Methuen, 1995.

Lovecraft, H. P. *The Supernatural in Horror Literature*. New York: Dover, 1973.

MacAndrew, Elizabeth. *The Gothic Tradition in Fiction*. New York: Columbia University Press, 1979.

Moretti, Franco. *Signs Taken for Wonders*. London: Verso, 1983.

Mulvey-Roberts, Marie, ed. *The Handbook to Gothic Literature*. Basingstoke: Macmillan—now Palgrave Macmillan, 1998.

Punter, David. *The Literature of Terror: A History of Gothic Fictions from 1765 to the Present Day*. London: Longman, 1980. Second Edition, 2 vols, London: Longman, 1996.

———. ed. *A Companion to the Gothic*. Oxford: Blackwell, 2000.

———. and Glennis, Byron. *The Gothic*. Oxford: Blackwell, 2004.

Sage, Victor. *Horror Fiction in the Protestant Tradition*. Basingstoke: Macmillan—now Palgrave Macmillan, 1988.

———. ed. *The Gothick Novel: A Casebook*. Basingstoke: Macmillan—now Palgrave Macmillan, 1990.

Scarborough, Dorothy. *The Supernatural in Modern English Fiction*. New York: Putnam, 1917.

Sedgwick, Eve Kosofsky. *The Coherence of Gothic Conventions*. London: Methuen, [1980] 1986.

Smith, Andrew and Jeff Wallace, eds. *Gothic Modernisms*. Basingstoke: Palgrave—now Palgrave Macmillan, 2001.

———. William Hughes, and Diane Mason, eds. *Fictions of Unease: The Gothic from Otranto to the X-Files*. Bath: Sulis Press, 2002.

Summers, Montague. *The Gothic Quest: A History of the Gothic Novel*. New York: Russell and Russell [1938] 1964.

Varma, Devandra P. *The Gothic Flame: Being a History of the Gothic Novel in England: Its Origins, Efflorescence, Disintegration, and Residuary Influence*. New York: Russell and Russell [1957] 1966.

Wilt, Judith. *Ghosts of the Gothic: Austen, Eliot, and Lawrence*. Princeton: Princeton University Press, 1980.

## Bibliographical guides

Barron, Neil, ed. *Horror Literature: A Reader's Guide*. New York: Garland, 1990.

———. *Fantasy and Horror: A Critical and Historical Guide to Literature, Illustration, Film, TV, Radio and the Internet*. Lanham: Scarecrow, 1999.

Fisher, Benjamin F. *The Gothic's Gothic: Study Aids to the Tradition of the Tale of Terror*. New York: Garland, 1988.

Frank, Frederick, S. *The First Gothics: A Critical Guide to the English Gothic Novel*. New York: Garland, 1987.

———. ed. *Gothic Fiction: A Master List of Twentieth Century Criticism and Research*. Westport: Meckler, 1988.

———. ed. *The Guide to the Gothic II: An Annotated Bibliography of Criticism 1983–1993*. Lanham: Scarecrow, 1995.

Frankl, Paul. *The Gothic: Literary Sources and Interpretations through Eight Centuries*. Princeton: Princeton University Press, 1960.

McNutt, Dan. *The Eighteenth-Century Gothic Novel: An Annotated Bibliography of Criticism and Selected Texts*. New York: Garland, 1974.

Mussell, Kay. *Women's Gothic and Romantic Fiction: A Reference Guide*. Westport: Greenwood, 1981.

Spector, Robert Donald. *The English Gothic: A Bibliographical Guide to Writers from Horace Walpole to Mary Shelley*. Westport: Greenwood, 1984.

Tracy, Ann B. *The Gothic Novel, 1790–1813: Plot Summaries and Index to Motifs*. Lexington: University Press of Kentucky, 1981.

Thomson, Douglass H., Jack G. Voller, and Frederick S. Frank, eds. *Gothic Writers: A Critical and Bibliographical Guide*. Westport: Greenwood, 2002.

Tinkler-Villani, Valeria, Peter Davidson, and Jane Stevenson, eds. *Exhibited by Candlelight: Sources and Developments in the Gothic Tradition*. Amsterdam: Rodopi, 1995.

## Theory

Armitt, Lucie. *Theorising the Fantastic*. London: Arnold, 1996.

Bronfen, Elisabeth. *Over Her Dead Body: Death, Femininity and the Aesthetic*. Manchester: Manchester University Press, 1992.

Carroll, Noel. *The Philosophy of Horror; or, Paradoxes of the Heart*. New York: Routledge, 1990.

Castricano, Jodey. *Cryptomimesis: The Gothic and Jacques Derrida's Ghost Writing*. Montreal: McGill-Queen's University Press, 2001.

Creed, Barbara. *The Monstrous Feminine: Film, Feminism, Psychoanalysis*. London: Routledge, 1993.

Howard, Jacqueline. *Reading Gothic Fiction: A Bakhtinian Approach*. Oxford: Clarendon, 1994.

Kristeva, Julia. *Powers of Horror: An Essay on Abjection*. Columbia: Columbia University Press, 1982.

Powell, Anna. *Psychoanalysis and Sovereignty in Popular Vampire Fictions*. Lewiston, New York, Queenston, Ontario and Lampeter, Wales: Edward Mellen Press, 2003.

Propp, Vladimir. *The Morphology of the Folktale*. Trans. Laurence Scott. Austin and London: University of Texas [1928] 1968.

Punter, David. *Gothic Pathologies: The Text, the Body and the Law*. Basingstoke: Macmillan—now Palgrave Macmillan, 1998.

Todorov, Tzvetan. *The Fantastic: A Structural Approach to a Literary Genre*. Trans. Richard Howards, 2nd edition. Louis A. Wagner, Wagner, ed. London and Cleveland: Case Western University, 1973.

## Romantic

Baldick, Chris. *In Frankenstein's Shadow: Myth, Monstrosity and Nineteenth-Century Writing*. Oxford: Clarendon, 1987.

Behrendt, Stephen C., ed. *Approaches to Teaching Shelley Frankenstein*. New York: MLA, 1990.

Bruhm, Steven. *Gothic Bodies: The Politics of Pain in Romantic Fiction*. Philadelphia: University of Philadelphia Press, 1994.

Clery, E. J., *The Rise of Supernatural Fiction 1762–1800*. Cambridge: Cambridge University Press, 1995.

———. and Robert Miles, eds. *Gothic Documents: A Sourcebook 1700–1820*. Manchester: Manchester University Press, 2000.

Cottam, Daniel. *The Civilised Imagination: A Study of Ann Radcliffe, Jane Austen, and Sir Walter Scott*. Cambridge: Cambridge University Press, 1985.

Gamer, Michael. *Romanticism and the Gothic: Genre, Reception, and Canon Formation*. Cambridge: Cambridge University Press, 2000.

Ketterer, David. *Frankenstein's Creation: The Book, the Monster, and the Human Reality*. Victoria, British Columbia: University of Victoria Press, 1979.

Kiely, Robert. *The Romantic Novel in England*. Cambridge, MA: Harvard University Press, 1972.

Levine, George and U. C. Knoepflmacher, eds. *The Endurance of Frankenstein: Essays on Mary Shelley's Novel*. Berkeley: University of California Press, 1979.

Mellor, Anne K. *Mary Shelley: Her Life, Her Fiction, Her Monsters*. New York: Methuen, 1988.

Miles, Robert. *Gothic Writing 1750–1820: A Genealogy*. London: Routledge, 1993.

———. *Ann Radcliffe: The Great Enchantress*. Manchester: Manchester University Press, 1996.

Mishra, Vijay. *The Gothic Sublime*. New York: State University of New York Press, 1994.

Napier, Elizabeth R. *The Failure of Gothic: Problems of Disjunction in an Eighteenth-Century Form*. Oxford: Clarendon, 1987.

Norton, Rictor, ed. *Gothic Readings: The First Wave, 1764–1840*. New York and London: Continuum, 2000.

Railo, Eino. *The Haunted Castle: A Study of the Elements of English Romanticism*. New York: Humanities Press [1927] 1964.

Smith, Andrew. *Gothic Radicalism: Literature, Philosophy, and Psychoanalysis in the Nineteenth Century*. Basingstoke: Macmillan—now Palgrave Macmillan, 2000.

Thomkins, J. M. S. *The Popular Novel in England, 1770–1800*. Lincoln: University of Nebraska Press, 1961.

Thompson, G. R., ed. *The Gothic Imagination: Essays in Dark Romanticism*. Pullman: Washington State University Press, 1974.

Voller, Jack G. *The Supernatural Sublime: The Metaphysics of Terror in Anglo-American Romanticism*. DeKalb: Northern Illinois University Press, 1994.

Watt, James. *Contesting the Gothic: Fiction, Genre, and Cultural Conflict*. Cambridge: Cambridge University Press, 1999.

## Victorian

Bloom, Clive, ed. *Nineteenth Century Suspense*. Basingstoke: Macmillan—now Palgrave Macmillan, 1990.

Briggs, Julia. *Night Visitors: The Rise and Fall of the English Ghost Story*. London: Faber, 1977.

Brennan, Matthew C. *The Gothic Psyche: Disintegration and Growth in Nineteenth-Century English Literature*. Columbia, SC: Camden House, 1997.

Carter, Margaret L. *The Vampire and the Critics*. London: UMI Research Press, 1988.

Cvetcovich, Ann. *Mixed Feelings: Feminism, Mass Culture, and Victorian Sensationalism*. New Brunswick: Rutgers University Press, 1992.

Daly, Nicholas. *Modernism, Romance and the fin de siècle*. Cambridge: Cambridge University Press, 1999.

Day, William Patrick. *In the Circles of Fear and Desire: A Study of Gothic Fantasy*. Chicago: University of Chicago Press, 1985.

DeLamotte, Eugenia C. *Perils of the Night: A Feminist Study of Nineteenth-Century Gothic*. Oxford: Oxford University Press, 1990.

Dickerson, Vanessa R. *Victorian Ghosts in the Noontide: Women Writers and the Supernatural*. Columbia: University of Missouri Press, 1996.

Dijkstra, Bram. *Idols of Perversity: Fantasies of Feminine Evil in Fin-de-Siècle Culture*. Oxford: Oxford University Press, 1986.

Dryden, Linda. *The Modern Gothic and Literary Doubles: Stevenson, Wilde and Wells*. Basingstoke: Palgrave—now Palgrave Macmillan, 2003.

Garrett, Peter K. *Gothic Reflections: Narrative Force in Nineteenth-Century Fiction*. Ithaca, NY: Cornell University Press, 2003.

Glover, David. *Vampires, Mummies, and Liberals: Bram Stoker and the Politics of Popular Fiction*. Durham: Duke University Press, 1996.

Hughes, Winifred. *The Maniac in the Cellar: Sensation Novels of the 1860s*. Princeton: Princeton University Press, 1980.

Hughes, William. *Beyond Dracula: Bram Stoker's Fiction and its Cultural Context*. Basingstoke: Macmillan, 2000.

———. and Andrew Smith, eds. *Bram Stoker: History, Psychoanalysis and the Gothic*. Basingtoke: Macmilan—now Palgrave Macmillan, 1998.

Melada, Ivan. *Sheridan Le Fanu*. Boston: Twayne, 1987.

Mighall, Robert. *A Geography of Victorian Gothic Fiction: Mapping History's Nightmares*. Oxford: Oxford University Press, 1999.

Miyoshi, Masao. *The Divided Self: A Perspective on the Literature of the Victorians*. New York: New York University Press, 1969.

Pick, Daniel. *Faces of Degeneration: A European Disorder, c. 1848–c. 1918*. Cambridge: Cambridge University Press, 1989.

Pykett, Lyn. *The "Improper" Feminine: The Woman's Sensation Novel and the New Woman Writing*. London: Routledge, 1992.

Robbins, Ruth and Julian Wolfreys, eds. *Victorian Gothic: Literary and Cultural Manifestations in the Nineteenth Century*. Basingstoke: Palgrave—now Palgrave Macmillan, 2000.

Sage, Victor. *Le Fanu's Gothic: The Rhetoric of Darkness*. Basingstoke: Palgrave Macmillan, 2004.

Senf, Carol A. *The Vampire in Nineteenth-Century English Literature*. Bowling, Green: Bowling Green State University Popular Press, 1988.

Showalter, Elaine. *Sexual Anarchy: Gender and Culture at the Fin de Siècle*. New York: Viking, 1990.

Smith, Andrew. *Victorian Demons: Medicine, Masculinity and the Gothic at the fin de siècle*. Manchester: Manchester University Press, 2004.

Smith, Elton E. and Robert Haas, eds. *The Haunted Mind: The Supernatural in Victorian Literature*. Lanham: Scarecrow Press, 1989.

Wolfreys, Julian. *Victorian Hauntings: Spectrality, Gothic, the Uncanny and Literature*. Basingstoke: Macmillan—now Palgrave Macmillan, 2002.

## Female Gothic

Becker, Susanne. *Gothic Forms of Feminine Fictions*. Manchester: Manchester University Press, 1999.
Clery, E. J. *Women's Gothic: From Clara Reeve to Mary Shelley*. Tavistock: Northcote House, 2000.
Ellis, Kate Ferguson. *The Contested Castle: Gothic Novels and the Subversion of Domestic Ideology*. Urbana: University of Illinois Press, 1989.
Fleenor, Juliann E., ed. *The Female Gothic*. Montreal: Eden, 1983.
Gilbert, Sandra M. and Susan Gubar. *The Madwomen in the Attic: The Woman Writer and the Nineteenth-Century Literary Imagination*. New Haven: Yale University Press, 1979.
Heller, Tamar. *Dead Secrets: Wilkie Collins and the Female Gothic*. New Haven: Yale University Press, 1992.
Hoeveler, Diane Long. *Gothic Feminism: The Professionalisation of Gender from Charlotte Smith to the Brontës*. Pennsylvania State University Press; Liverpool; Liverpool University Press, 1998.
Kelly, Gary, ed. *Varieties of Female Gothic*, 6 vols. London: Chatto, 2001.
Massé, Michelle A. *In the Name of Love: Women, Masochism and the Gothic*. Ithaca: Cornell University Press, 1992.
Meyers, Helene. *Femicidal Fears: Narratives of the Female Gothic Experience*. New York: SUNY, 2001.
Milbank, Alison. *Daughters of the House: Modes of the Gothic in Victorian Fiction*. Basinstoke: Macmillan—now Palgrave Macmillan, 1992.
Miles, Robert, ed. *Women's Writing: The Elizabethan to Victorian Period*, Special Number; Female Gothic Writing, 1:2 (Triangle 1994).
Moers, Ellen. *Literary Women*. London: The Women's Press [1976] 1978.
Smith, Andrew and Diana Wallace, eds. *Gothic Studies*, 6/1 Special Issue on "Female Gothic" (May 2004).
Williams, Anne. *Art of Darkness: A Poetics of Gothic*. Chicago: University of Chicago Press, 1995.

## Imperial

Backus, Margot. *The Gothic Family Romance: Heterosexuality, Child Sacrifice, and the Anglo-Irish Colonial Order*. Durham: Duke University Press, 1999.
Brantlinger, Patrick. *Rule of Darkness: British Literature and Imperialism 1830–1914*. Ithaca: Cornell University Press, 1988.
Davison, Carol Margaret. *Anti-Semitism and British Gothic Literature*. Basingstoke: Palgrave Macmillan, 2004.
Malchow, Howard. *Gothic Images of Race in Nineteenth-Century Britain*. Stanford: Stanford University Press, 1996.
McClintock, Anne. *Imperial Leather: Race, Gender, and Sexuality in the Colonial Contest*. New York: Routledge, 1995.
Schmitt, Cannon. *Alien Nation: Nineteenth-Century Gothic Fictions and English Nationality*. Philadelphia: University of Pennsylvania Press, 1997.

Spivak, Gavatry Chakravorty. "Three women's texts and a critique of imperialism," *Critical Inquiry* 12, 1, 243–61.
Stewart, Bruce, ed. *That Other World: The Supernatural and the Fantastic in Irish Literature and its Contexts*, 2 vols. Gerrards Cross: Colin Smyth, 1988.
Valente, Joseph. *Dracula's Crypt: Bram Stoker, Irishness, and the Question of Blood*. Champaign: University of Illinois Press, 2002.

## Postcolonial

Bhabha, Homi K. *The Location of Culture*. London: Routledge, 1994.
Castricano, Jodey. "If a building is a sentence, so is a body: Kathy Acker's *Empire of the Senseless* and postcolonial Gothic." In *American Gothic*, Robert Martin, ed. Iowa: University of Iowa Press, 1998. 202–14.
Newman, Judie. "Postcolonial Gothic: Ruth Prawer Jhabvala and the Sobhraj case." *Modern Fiction Studies* 40 (1994):85–100.
Punter, David. *Postcolonial Imaginings: Fictions of a New World Order*. Edinburgh: Edinburgh University Press, 2000.
Smith, Andrew and William Hughes, eds. *Empire and the Gothic: The Politics of Genre*. Basingstoke: Palgrave—now Palgrave Macmillan, 2003.

## Postmodern

Armitt, Lucie. *Contemporary Women's Fiction and the Fantastic*. Basingstoke: Macmillan—now Palgrave Macmillan, 2000.
Bruhm, Steven. "On Stephen King's phallus, or the postmodern Gothic." *Narrative* 4 (1996):55–73.
Cornwell, Neil. *The Literary Fantastic: From Gothic to Postmodernism*. Brighton: Harvester, 1990.
Haraway, Donna. "The promises of monsters: a regenerative politics for inappropriate/d others" in Lawrence Grossberg, Cary Nelson, and Paula A. Treichler, eds. *Cultural Studies*. New York; Routledge, 1992. 295–337.
Milner, Andrew. "Postmodern Gothic: Buffy, the X-Files and the Clinton presidency." *Journal of Media & Culture*, Continuum (March 2005), 19, 1, 103–16 (14).
Nash, Jesse W. "Postmodern Gothic: Stephen King's *Pet Sematary*." *Journal of Popular Culture* 30, 4 (Spring 1997), 151–60.
Neumeier, Beate. "Postmodern Gothic: desire and reality in Angela Carter's writing." *anglistik & englischunterricht* 48 (1992) 89–98.
Sage, Victor and Allan Lloyd Smith, eds. *Modern Gothic: A Reader*. Manchester: Manchester University Press, 1996.
Zizek, Slavoj. *The Art of the Ridiculous Sublime: On David Lynch's "Lost Highway*." Washington: University of Washington Press, 2000.

## Sexuality

Andiano, Joseph. *Our Ladies of Darkness: Feminine Daemonology in Male Gothic Fiction*. University Park: Penn State University Press, 1993.
Castle, Terry. *The Female Thermometer: Eighteenth-Century Culture and the Invention of the Uncanny*. Oxford: Oxford University Press, 1995.
Halberstam, Judith. *Skin Shows: Gothic Horror and the Technology of Monsters*. Durham: Duke University Press, 1995.
Hendershot, Cyndy. *The Animal Within: Masculinity and the Gothic*. Ann Arbour: University of Michigan Press, 1998.
Hurley, Kelly. *The Gothic Body: Sexuality, Materialism and Degeneration at the Fin de Siècle*. Cambridge: Cambridge University Press, 1996.
Palmer, Paulina. *Lesbian Gothic: Transgressive Fictions*. London: Cassell, 1999.
Sedgwick, Eve Kosofsky. *Between Men: English Literature and Male Homosocial Desire*. New York: Columbia University Press, 1985.
———. *Epistemology of the Closet*. London: Harvester Wheatsheaf, 1991.

## American

Bailey, Dale. *American Nightmares: The Haunted House Formula in American Popular Culture*. Bowling Green: Bowling Green State University Press, Popular Press, 1999.
Bloom, Clive, ed. *Gothic horror: A Reader's Guide from Poe to King and Beyond*. (Basingstoke: Macmillan—now Palgrave Macmillan, 1998).
Bloom, Harold, ed. *Stephen King: Modern Critical Views*. Philadelphia: Chelsea, 1998.
Brogan, Kathleen. *Cultural Haunting: Ghosts and Ethnicity in Recent American Literature*. Charlottesville: University Press of Virginia, 1998.
Carpenter, Lynette and Wendy Kolmar, eds. *Haunting the House of Fiction: Feminist Perspectives on Ghost Stories by American Women*. Knoxville: University of Tennessee Press, 1994.
Cassuto, Leonard. *The Inhuman Race: The Racial Grotesque in American Literature and Culture*. New York: Columbia University Press, 1997.
Christophersen, Bill. *The Apparition in the Glass: Charles Brockden Brown's American Gothic*. Athens: University of Georgia Press, 1993.
Crow, Charles, ed. *American Gothic: An Anthology, 1787–1916*. Oxford: Blackwell, 1999.
Docherty, Brian, ed. *American Horror Fiction: From Brockden Brown to Stephen King*. Basingstoke: Macmillan—now Palgrave Macmillan, 1990.
Edwards, Justin D. *Gothic Passages: Racial Ambiguity and the American Gothic*. Iowa City: University of Iowa Press, 2003.
Fiedler, Leslie. *Love and Death in the American Novel*. Cleveland: World, 1962.
Frank, Frederick S. *Through the Pale Door: A Guide to and Through the American Gothic*. New York: Greenwood, 1990.
Goddu, Teresa A. *Gothic America: Narrative, History, and Nation*. New York: Columbia University Press, 1999.

Gross, Lewis S. *Redefining the American Gothic: From Wieland to Day of the Dead.* Ann Arbour: UMI Research, 1989.

Halttunen, Karen. *Murder Most Foul: The Killer and the American Gothic.* Cambridge: Harvard University Press, 1998.

Hattenhauer, Darryl. *Shirley Jackson's American Gothic.* Albany: State University of New York, 2003.

Kerr, Howard and John William Crowley, and Charles Crow, eds. *The Haunted Dusk: American Supernatural Fiction 1820–1920.* Athens: University of Georgia Press, 1983.

Lloyd-Smith, Allan. *Uncanny American Fiction.* London: Macmillan—now Palgrave Macmillan, 1989.

———. *American Gothic Fiction: An Introduction.* London and New York: Continuum, 2004.

Magistrale, Tony. *Landscape of Fear: Stephen King's American Gothic.* Bowling Green: OH: Popular, 1988.

———. and Michael Morrison. *A Dark Night's Dreaming: Contemporary American Horror Fiction.* Columbia: University of South Carolina Press, 1996.

Malin, Irving. *New American Gothic.* Carbondale: Southern Illinois University Press, 1962.

Martin, Robert K. and Eric Savoy, eds. *The American Gothic: New Interventions in a National Narrative.* Iowa City: University of Iowa Press, 1998.

Meindl, Dieter. *American Fiction and the Metaphysics of the Grotesque.* Columbia: University of Missouri Press, 1996.

Mogen, David, Scott Patrick Sanders, and Joanne B. Karpinski, eds. *Frontier Gothic: Terror and Wonder at the Frontier in American Literature.* Rutherford: Fairleigh Dickinson University Press, 1993.

Ringe, Donald A. *American Gothic: Imagination and Reason in Nineteenth-Century Fiction.* Lexington: University Press of Kentucky, 1982.

Wardrop, Daneen. *Emily Dickinson's Gothic: Goblin with a Gauge.* Iowa City: University of Iowa Press, 1996.

Weinstock, Jeffrey Andrew, ed. *Spectral America: Phantoms and the National Imagination.* Madison: University of Wisconsin Press, 2004.

Wilczynski, Marek. *The Phantom and the Abyss: The Gothic Fiction in America and Aesthetics of the Sublime 1798–1856.* Frankfurt and New York: Peter Lang, 1999.

Winter, Kari J. *Subjects of Slavery, Agents of Change: Women and Power in Gothic Novels and Slave Narratives, 1790–1865.* Athens: University of Georgia Press, 1992.

## Film

Berenstein, Rhona J. *Attack of the Leading Ladies: Gender, Sexuality, and Spectatorship in Classic Horror Cinema.* New York: Columbia University Press, 1996.

Chibnail, Steve and Julian Petley, eds. *British Horror Cinema.* Routledge: London, 2002.

Clover, Carol J. *Men, Women, and Chain Saws: Gender in the Modern Horror Film*. London: BFI, 1993.
Crane, Jonathan Lake. *Terror and Everyday Life: Singular Moments in the History of the Horror Film*. Thousand Oaks: Sage, 1994.
Eisener, Lotte. *The Haunted Screen*. London: Secker and Warburg [1952] 1973.
Grant, Barry K., ed. *Planks of Reason: Essays on the Horror Film*. London: Scarecrow Press, 1984.
———. *The Dread of Difference: Gender and the Horror Film*. Austin: University of Texas Press, 1996.
Hopkins, Lisa. *Screening the Gothic*. Austin: University of Texas Press, 2005.
Hutchings, Peter. *Hammer and Beyond: The British Horror Film*. Manchester: Manchester University Press, 1993.
———. *The Horror Film*. Longman: London, 2004.
Jancovich, Mark, ed. *Horror: The Film Reader*. London: Routledge, 2002.
Kracauer, Sigfried. *From Caligari to Hitler: A Psychological History of German Film*. Princeton: Princeton University Press, 1947.
Newman, Kim, ed. *The BFI Companion to Horror*. London: BFI, 1996.
Pirie, David. *A Heritage of Horror: The English Gothic Cinema, 1946–1972*. New York: Equinox, 1974.
Powell, Anna. *Deleuze and Horror Film*. Edinburgh: Edinburgh University Press, 2005.
Prawer, S. S. *Caligari's Children: The Film as Tale of Terror*. New York: Da Capo, 1980.
Silver, Alain. *More Things Than Are Dreamt Of: Masterpieces of Supernatural Horror from Mary Shelley to Stephen King in Literature and Film*. New York: Limelight Editions, 1994.
Skal, David J. *The Monster Show: A Cultural History of Horror*. Harmondsworth: Penguin, 1994.
Tudor, Andrew. *Monsters and Mad Scientists: A Cultural History of the Horror Movie*. Cambridge, MA: Basil Blackwell, 1989.
Twitchell, James B. *Dreadful Pleasures: An Anatomy of Modern Horror*. Oxford: Oxford University Press, 1985.
Waller, Gregory A., ed. *American Horrors: Essays on the Modern American Horror Film*. Urbana and Chicago: University of Illinois Press, 1987.
Wright, Bruce Lanier. *Nightwalkers: Gothic Horror Movies: The Modern Era*. Dallas: Taylor, 1995.
Wood, Robin. *Hollywood from Vietnam to Regan*. New York: Columbia University Press, 1986.

For more information/resources on teaching English (both print and web-based) please go to the following link on the English Subject Centre web site: http://www.english.heacademy.ac.uk/explore/resources/teachlib/index.php

# Index